Masks and the Mirror

Wizards of Wes Tyree, Volume 1

Larence Lee

Published by Deep Woods Publishing, 2020.

MASKS AND THE MIRROR

First edition. December 31, 2020.

Copyright © 2020 Larence Lee.

ISBN: 978-1954359000

Written by Larence Lee.

To my editors: Kassy, Jean, and Gay. For whom without this book would have never seen the light of day.

To my fellow members of the East Texas Writers Assocation that have inspired and tolerated me.

To my muse, Linda

CHAPTER ONE

"WOAH, WOOOAH," Garsel pulled on the reins.

Bershome jerked his attention away from the landscape of the woods. The rear carriage wheels squealed against the locked breaks, and the coach skidded. It hit a bump and threw him forward to land on his knees, and he almost hit the back of the empty front seat with his head. He shoved himself up, bounced on the front seat, and opened the window behind the driver's legs. "What's going on, Garsel?"

"A dead tree blocks the road, sir."

The seventeen-year-old raked back his shoulder-length brown hair and faced his companion. "Shall we help, Uncle Zarlaam?"

The older man smiled, lowered his foot from against the front seat, "I'll leave that for you to handle while I enjoy the calm of sitting still." He stroked his long beard into semi-civilized order form being windblown.

With a wide grin, Bershome grabbed his staff off the seat, leaped from the carriage to head forward. "Heroct," he spoke to the guardsman who sat in the footman's seat on the back and was looking about with his hand on his bow. "I suppose we could unhitch one of the horses to move it, or I could – "

"Yieeee!"

Bershome spun around to face three screaming men running with swords drawn. He heard the scene repeat itself behind him on the opposite side of the coach.

1

He pointed his staff's head at the men as he muttered, "Sciath." Crackling sparks leaped from the staff. The bandits struck and stuck to an invisible barrier like they had been glued to a wall of glass, blue electrical sparks shimmering all around them. He raised the staff, the barrier disappeared, and the men collapsed to the ground, unconscious or badly dazed.

"Are you all right, Uncle Zarlaam?"

"Fine, Bershome, I'm fine." The coach shook as the older man stepped down.

The guardsman leaped down from the back of the coach, where he had been searching the woods for more bandits, his bow at the ready. The driver had a bow up and watched the woods to the front and other side as well.

"That's the lot of them, Master Zarlaam." The guardsman announced and joined Bershome.

"Heroct, take their weapons, and cast them away."

"Master Zarlaam has three more on the other side," he said.

"Let's drag these around to join their cohorts in crime, sir."

They dragged them to lay all in a row. Heroct pulled a rope from the box on the back of the coach and bound their hands together.

"Bershome, you still have a log to move."

"Yes, Uncle."

Bershome went around front and pointed his staff at the log as he spoke, "Ardu ompal." It rose upright, balanced on the bottom end, and toppled over into the brush. His task completed, he rejoined the others.

One of the bandits stirred, groaned, and looked about. He fought his bonds a moment but stopped when Garsel kicked his leg and shook a finger at him.

"Look at those two," Zarlaam said, pointing at a pair. "They must be twins and hardly fourteen years of age."

"From the resemblance of their faces, I'd say that man is their father, Uncle." Bershome nudged one's boot with his foot.

"I'm inclined to agree. What a pity for a man to be teaching his sons such a thing."

"What will we do with them?" Bershome asked.

"In light of things, I find that a hard decision to make." He sighed.

Two lads stared wide-eyed at Master Zarlaam and then their father.

"I see that all of you are awake now. You, sir," He stepped close to a man in his thirties. "are dressed as a gentleman and was perhaps a noble though your clothes are soiled and a bit worn. Am I correct to assume you are the leader of this rabble?"

The man did not respond to Zarlaam's questions.

"I care not what brought you to this point in life. You know better and have earned your fate. You, on the other hand," he pointed his staff at the man beside the lads, "should be ashamed of yourself for bringing your sons into the life of an outlaw. If we take you to a magistrate, your sons would surely hang at your side on the morrow."

"Please, your Lordship, I beg you to release my sons. A rainstorm destroyed our crops. The baron threw us off our land because we could not pay the taxes. He dared to suggest favors with one of my daughters for them. My wife and three daughters are starving as we all are."

"Bershome, bring out the basket."

He did as instructed. Zarlaam took bread rolls out and tossed one to each man.

The leader looked at Zarlaam. "You choose to give charity to condemned men?" He threw the roll at Zarlaam.

"Actually, I choose to feed hungry men. The charity I offer is your life." Zarlaam pointed his staff at the man and muttered a word. Green sparks of light leaped from the staff and struck the man.

He screeched as he shrank in his clothes.

"Bershome, catch him."

Bershome put his hands on the shirt and pinned down something thrashing about in the clothing. He reached down the collar opening and drew out a squirming screeching rat. He held it for them all to see.

"That man is truly a rat. Toss him out in the woods, lad. He transformed the two bandits into rabbits.

Bershome helped them get free of their clothing, and one disappeared into the bushes while the other scampered off down their back road. He gathered their clothes and pulled a coin pouch from one. "Master, the ringleader had this." He held up the pouch.

Zarlaam turned to address the father and sons. "In a day or so, you will return to normal. Your clothes will be in a pile over that way. We will put that pouch in your pocket." He pointed past them. "I recommend you spend your time rethinking your choices in life. About five miles northwest of here is the property of a Baron Kerlof. He might hire you to work his fields. When you go to see him, tell him the truth. You tried to be robbers and failed. Then give him my name, Zarlaam. I am giving your family a second chance. Do not take for granted the soft heart of an old man. If he does not hire you, continue northwest to the Paxtirea estates. They will hire you if you use my name. I will turn you into rabbits. I recommend you find a patch of brambles to hide in for protection. See that wide-leafed plant?" He pointed to a plant near their heads. "It puts out an odor that will help hide your smell from predators."

He used his staff and turned them into rabbits also. Once released, the three rabbits headed for the plant and rubbed against it. The bigger rabbit pulled a leaf off the bush and rubbed it against a smaller rabbit. Heroct put the pouch into a pants pocket and threw their clothing into a pile hidden from the road.

"Shall we continue our trip to Galley's Cove, gents?" Zarlaam returned to his seat in the coach.

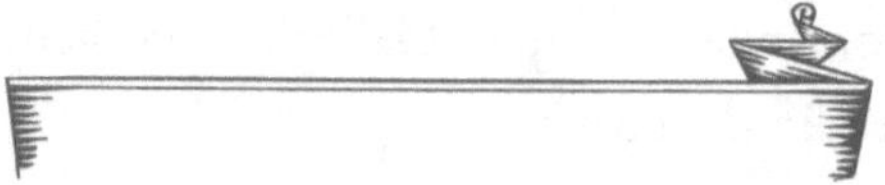

CHAPTER TWO

Bershome poked his head out the window for a better look at the town. Pedestrians, horsemen, wagons, and handcarts choked the avenues as Garsel tried to navigate. Men unloaded trade goods from ships docked in the bay.

"It is not noble to stick your head out like a child and ogle at the passersby."

"Yes, Uncle Zarlaam." He felt the flush of his cheeks as he sat back in his seat.

"Would you rather ride up top with Heroct?"

"No, Uncle Zarlaam."

Shortly, the coach stopped. Garsel opened the door and lent Zarlaam a supportive hand. The master stopped and turned to face the wind from the bay as it teased his hair, and he stood still a moment.

"Bershome, I'm going to take a stroll. Take our list inside to Mister Houson, give him my regards, and get what he has. I'll be back in a bit." He handed him a pack of folded papers and strolled away down the street toward the bay.

"I will go with him," Heroct said.

"From the look on his face, I believe he is seeking, sir. Your presence could interfere."

Heroct and Garsel smiled at Bershome.

Zarlaam's feet carried him onto the wharf. He paused and stood with his eyes closed before a table covered with fish. When he opened his eyes again, he saw a fisherman approaching. He squinted as the man held up a fair size tuna.

"We caught these just this morning, Your Lordship," a man spoke as he held up the large fish.

"Excellent specimen, but I was merely admiring the colors, sir." He stepped around the man and walked farther along the wharf to where nets were strung up to be repaired, and small boats were docked. He stopped. His eyes widened as he stepped close to a particular net to look it over. He raised his hand and ran it across the webbing. He smiled softly and nodded as if he was agreeing with an unspoken statement and looked about. A young lad of about fourteen sat on a crate near a boat threading string on a net mending needle.

"Excuse me, young man."

The boy looked up at him. He raked back his long black hair and tucked it behind his ear. His darkly tanned face bore a darker two-inch jagged scar on his left cheek. His well-developed upper-body bespoke of a great deal of physical labor for a good part of his young life. His deep brown eyes held Zarlaam's gaze without wavering.

"Yes, sir." His response was flat and unconcerned.

"Could you tell me who that net belongs to?"

The boy did not look to where Zarlaam pointed. "It belongs to the boat, Scallywag."

"Who made the net?"

"Her crew."

"Are they about today?"

"The Captain has gone down to the market house to collect for his haul and buy a bottle or two."

"I see. Are there any other crew members about? I'm particularly interested in the one that works on repairing the net the most."

"What for?"

"I'd like to discuss his skills in repairing the net."

"Aren't nothing special about repairing a net." He returned his attention to his needle threading.

"That depends on how you look at it. What is the name of the Scallywag's captain?"

"Gerak Beakler Kalathazar."

"And her first mate?"

"Aren't no first mate on the Scallywag. Just Captain and deck-hand."

"I see. What would the deckhand's names be?"

"I said hand, not hands."

"I beg your pardon for mishearing. Must be old ears acting up with me."

"He answers to any foul name the captain spits out at him. So, take your pick."

Zarlaam stood erect and looked the boy over. He appeared to think for a long moment. He stepped close to the lad and spoke in a low voice. "Fathers give their names to their firstborn for many reasons, Gerak. One is in the hope to carry on the family legacy to fame and fortune."

The boy looked up at him wide-eyed. Zarlaam continued. "Some men don't know how to be a father. They may only know how to be a hard-working fisherman. Ironically, some men develop a taste for the bottle while mourning the loss of their wife to sickness because they loved them so much."

The boy stood and stepped over to the ship's gangplank. "The captain will be back sometime before the tide goes out." He turned and walked aboard the boat.

"Did your father not teach you manners? It is rude to walk off when being addressed by an adult and particularly by nobility."

"I don't like what you are saying. The captain taught me not to use my knife just because of such. So, I chose to walk away."

"I wish to speak with you about your net mending." Zarlaam stepped close to him again.

"Like I said..."

"Hold out your hand."

The lad did not move.

"Come, come. Hold out your hand."

The lad raised his hand palm up, and Zarlaam grasped his wrist. He looked down at it and detected several scars from old cuts and a couple of fresh fin punctures. He also saw calluses from years of hard work aboard the fishing boat. He tucked his staff under his arm against his chest and lay his free hand on the boy's and closed his eyes for a moment.

"You have a strong potential that you know nothing of, Gerak." He looked deeply into the lad's eye. "You can stay here and pursue the life of a fisherman, or you can pursue the potential I speak of."

Gerak eased his hand away from Zarlaam.

"That is something you will have to discuss with the Captain," the lad said and walked across the plank onto the boat.

"Then I'll go look for him at The Crow's Nest."

Gerak's eye widened as Zarlaam turned away.

CHAPTER THREE

Zarlaam turned and walked deeper into the town. Merchants who spotted him tried to show him their wares and sell him something. He smiled and shook his head or waved them off. He strolled along, ignoring all else about him. His staff would make a resounding thump on the ground every few paces as he moved with brisk steps. He made turns left and right at street intersections as if he had lived in the town for ages and knew his destination. He stopped outside a tavern.

A mast pole about ten feet tall stood in the ground just in front of the place. A yardarm and crow's nest were all the mast had on it. This was their signpost for all to be able to locate the establishment by its name "Crow's Nest." For people that could read, a nearby, faded, weather-worn, sign painted on the front of the tavern declared its name.

Zarlaam stepped inside and stood away from the opening a moment to let his eyes adjust to the dimness of the room. The place was filled with sailors, fishermen, and dock workers; some of the roughest looking men in the country. Some men stood at the bar or sat at a table with one hand on their drink and the other resting on or near the handle of their knife or grip of a sword. He eased his way around the tables until he reached the bar. He placed a coin on the counter.

The fat-bellied bartender sauntered toward him. "What's your poison, sir?"

"I believe I would like to try a draft of ale, please."

The bartender grabbed a tin mug and filled it with a dark brew from the barrel spigot behind him. He put the drink on the bar with a clunk, took the silver coin, and walked to the other end of the bar where he had been conversing with a burly-looking man.

Seeing that he was getting no change, Zarlaam picked up his drink and sipped the tepid ale. He looked about the tavern and spied an older version of the boy from the dock. The man leaned back in his chair as he savored his drink. When the glass was empty, he set it on the table and refilled it from the bottle.

Zarlaam walked over to his table. "Hello, Captain. May I join you, sir?"

The sailor did not look up. "Bring your own bottle."

Zarlaam sat across from him and sipped his ale as the seaman examined him over his glass, then set the empty glass down, and grasped his bottle.

Zarlaam lay his hand flat on the table, and the men exchanged stares. "You don't want to drink any more tonight, sir." Zarlaam spoke so that no one else heard him.

The seaman eye giggled back and forth a moment. He paused with the bottle just over his glass. He eased it back down on the table. "What can I do for you, sir?"

"I would like to have a word with you about your son."

"What has he done? I ain't paying for no damages. He done 'em, he can work to pay 'em off. A man must be responsible for himself and the consequences of his actions."

"Excellent perspective, sir, but he has done nothing wrong. Could we retire to a place more private for a discussion, Captain?"

"Why?"

"I was wondering how old your son is. Also, I would like to discuss his education."

"He turned thirteen last spring. He can read. His mother saw to that."

"Wonderful."

"He can cipher too. I taught him the importance of knowing math, so he doesn't get cheated at the scales."

"A proper fatherly thing to do. I am sure you have done your best to raise him after the loss of your lovely wife."

"I'm teaching him the fisherman's trade. We have been fairly prosperous the past two years."

"That's good to hear."

"Kalthazar!" A short, heavy-set man came waddling over to the table, followed by two lean and taller versions of himself. The man sported a gaff hook on a five-foot pole in his hand. Kalthazar did not look up as he lifted the bottle to pour a drink but stopped and set it back down.

"Whatcha want, Molean?"

"Baxter told me you brought in a hefty weight with your catch today. How is it that you can catch a bumper haul of fish in a single morning when the rest of us spend two or three days to catch half that many?"

"Well," Kalthazar said as he looked at Zarlaam with a crooked grin, "some people own a fishing boat, while others are fishermen."

"I've fished these waters twenty-five years. That is longer than you. I know where to fish and when. What is your secret? It can't be luck. It happens too often."

Kalthazar stood. He was a head taller than Molean as he looked down with a frown, wrinkled nose, and squinted eyes at the man. "Two years longer don't count for spit. Mess with me, and you will be wearing that gaff hook for a nose ring."

"It ain't natural for you to be bringing in all those fish."

"Actually, Captain Molean," Zarlaam said with his ale half raised to his mouth, "he rescued a mermaid and nursed her broken arm. She charmed his nets in her gratitude." He watched the man over his mug as he drank.

Molean looked at Zarlaam then back at Kalthazar as if looking for a hint of betrayal to the gentleman's outrageous statement in the fisherman's eyes. The more Molean thought about the idea, the wider his own eyes grew. His outburst of laughter was as if in defense of his common sense.

"The interesting thing about a mermaid's charm," continued Zarlaam, "is that it will not work except for him, with his nets, and only on his boat."

They all looked at him in disbelief as he took another sip of his ale. "Captain Kalthazar, may we have that conversation I asked about?"

"Aye, on the Scallywag. Bring a bottle." He grabbed his half-empty bottle from the table and left without a word.

Molean looked at Zarlaam. "Did you mean what you said about his nets being charmed?"

"Many things are possible, Captain, but first, you must truly believe in mermaids."

"I don't believe you."

"Your prerogative, Captain. But I ask; why would a mermaid lie to me?" Zarlaam said as he stood up. "Excuse me, please."

Zarlaam walked to the bar. "Bartender, I'll have one of your finest bottles of whiskey that Captain Kalthazar prefers, please." He placed a silver coin on the bar. The bartender clunked a down a bottle. He looked at the coin and then at Zarlaam with a slight smile but did not release the bottle. Zarlaam added a couple of copper coins.

"This should make us even for the ale and bottle all told, sir."

The man's eyes danced in their sockets. He scratched his head and took the coins. Zarlaam claimed the bottle and left the tavern. He let out a great sigh of relief once he was out the door. "You shouldn't overcharge a man for a mug of ale just for being a well-dressed stranger." He half muttered to himself as he strolled through the town back to the boat docks. He found Captain Kalthazar sitting by the tiller and leaning back with his feet propped up on a tackle box.

"Permission to come aboard, sir?" Zarlaam paused at the plank.

"Aye."

He stepped aboard the boat and worked his way around a pile of nets to sit on the rail facing the captain.

"Here is you a gift, I believe this will be to your liking, in appreciation for indulging me with your time, sir. If I may say something, it is best if you only drink one glass in an evening," he said, surrendering the bottle to the captain.

"Thank you. That was quite a yarn you gave ole' Molean back there," he chuckled.

"I'm certain it left him wondering."

"I'm tired of having to leave in the middle of the night to keep him and his crew from following me out to sea. Maybe he will leave me be now."

"Perhaps. Captain, my name is Zarlaam Paxtare. I wish to offer your son a furtherance of his education of sorts."

"What do you mean, of sorts?"

"Excellent observation of my words, sir. First, I would like to ask you if your fishing luck was as good before your son joined you on the boat?"

"No, I had to spend long voyages out at sea like you heard Molean complaining about and hardly made a weighing at the scales."

"Your son repairs your nets. How long has your good fortune been running?"

"Repairing nets is one of the many duties of a deckhand. He has always repaired them. My good fortune, as you call it, has only been the past two years or so."

He lowered his voice. "Your nets are, in fact, charmed, but not any mermaid. Your son has the ability to enchant them."

The Captain looked about wide-eyed and gave him a squinted one-eyed stare. "Are you saying that my son is a warlock?"

"People use that as a rather negative connotation. I prefer the term wizard, sir. But he knows not of his ability."

"And you do?"

"Yes. As he tied the knots in the strings, he probably kept wishing the fish would be happy to be in your nets, or would not resist them, and that the nets would be strong enough to hold them. His charms are the strongest I have ever detected from an untrained person."

"How do you know this?"

Zarlaam leaned closer. "Magic leaves a trace that can be detected by a person who knows. I could detect it the same way I know you have in the tackle box on which you rest your feet, three hundred eighty-seven gold crowns, ninety-three silver, and a few hundred odd copper coins."

Kalthazar jerked up and searched about again, eyes wide.

"No one can hear us. I made sure of that. I have the ability to read minds to an extent, sir. You thought of it when you worried what it would cost you for him to have this education. You also want him to have a better life than you have had."

"That is the dream of every father."

"And a good father you are to dream so."

"What good will you teach him?"

"I have a handful of apprentices I am teaching. We, magical users, are greatly outnumbered in this world. We must study and use magic in secret because not everyone understands it and the good it can be. Your son has the potential to become a strong wizard. We also provide a well- rounded education in grammar, mathematics, science, etiquette, history, and more."

The captain sat scratching his chin. "What will this education cost me?"

"He will live on our estate, Paxtirea, and we will teach him. Most of his necessities will be provided for. You will need only to provide for clothing and other essentials. Fifty crowns will suffice for the first year. He will be allowed to return during the summer to visit and fish with you."

"I want him to have an education that will make a gentleman of him."

"Our teaching will help him along that way, sir. He will be taught many things that would help him to be a gentleman."

"Gerak!" the Captain shouted.

"Aye, Captain?" The lad's voice came from down in the hold. A moment later, the boy stood before his father.

"Did you finish mending the nets, boy?"

"Aye, Captain."

"Get your kit together. You are going with this gentleman."

The boy looked from his father to Zarlaam and back. Then he turned without a word and went below. Kalthazar pulled out a key from his pocket and opened the tackle box. He unlocked a strongbox down inside it and pulled out a leather pouch. He handed it to Zarlaam.

"Teach him well, sir,"

"He will return to you next summer. Captain, I know you don't trust banks, but may I suggest using one if in the event you are lost at sea? That way, your son would have something to inherit."

"I'll manage my money myself, sir. You teach my son and make him a gentleman." He picked up his bottle.

"I meant no offense. We do our best towards your son, Captain."

The boy returned with a bundle in the form of a bedroll under one arm and a cloth bag in the other hand.

"Gerak, you mind this man, behave, and learn everything you can from him, son."

"Aye, Captain." Gerak walked over to the plank and left the boat.

"It's been hard on him losing his mother."

"You will not regret making this decision, Captain. Your nets will slowly lose their charm. Gerak will be able to improve them next summer."

"Just make a gentleman of him."

"Until the next time we meet, sir. Also, you will want to not drink as much as you have been in your grief for your wife, Captain."

"That some of your wizard's magic?"

"Magic should be used for the good of all. I am merely trying to share the good."

"Teach him well," he said as he set the bottle down on the deck and leaned his head back to look at the sky.

Zarlaam nodded and left the boat. He found the boy waiting a slight distance down the dock.

"Gerak, I am Zarlaam. I will be your teacher for the coming winter season. First, there will be one rule above all that you will obey while in my charge. Never pull your knife on anyone except in self-defense. Do not use it against one of my other apprentices or anyone in my household. Understood? We do not allow fighting among the apprentices. You will need to put your seafaring ways behind you, or I'll dismiss you from our presence and send you back home. You must choose to get along with them all."

"Aye, aye, sir."

"Excellent. You will always address people in a polite and respectable tone of voice, not what I endured earlier."

"Aye, aye sir."

"This way to my coach, young man."

The boy followed him silently. Bershome stood near the coach talking to Heroct. He noticed Zarlaam first.

"Master Zarlaam, I have gotten most of the supplies you asked for."

"Excellent, Bershome. Now, I would like to introduce you to our new apprentice. This is Mister Gerak Kalthazar."

Bershome smiled broadly and held out his hand. "Bershome Paxtare, sir."

"Gerak," he responded as they exchanged a firm handshake.

"Turn your bags over to Heroct, Gerak. He will secure them up top, and we will be leaving," Zarlaam said.

"Oh, Master Zarlaam, have I got a story for you." An excited joy sparked in the Bershome's eyes as he bounced on his toes.

"Excellent. We can use a bit of entertainment for the ride home."

"But when you hear it, you will not want to go home right away."

"We have been on the road for over three weeks with over a week to go. I long for the comfort and familiarity of my bed chambers. However, as excited as you look, I think you want to tell me now."

"About thirty miles north of here is a village called Natudix. The villagers claim that a curse has been put on them by a witch."

"Bershome, there are many a superstitious person who claimed to be cursed by a witch when many a time they have simply been a victim of unfortunate luck or their bad judgment."

"But sir, the gentleman said that he had visited the village and that it is caught in a perpetual winter. It has been snowing in their village all summer."

Zarlaam stood looking at Bershome a moment with furrowed eyebrows. He feared the lad had been taken in by a tall tale even though he knew him to be level-headed.

"Who told you this, lad?"

"Mister Houson, from whom I purchased our supplies. He told me, sir."

Zarlaam raised his eyebrows at this news. He knew the man to be a forthright person and not likely to mislead a young boy with a tall tale.

"Garsel," Zarlaam said to his driver, "Do you know the way to this village, Natudix?"

"Yes, sir. Bershome has provided me with a detailed map. It is not far off our road home."

"Let us visit this place of perpetual winter."

They climbed aboard the coach. Gerak sat beside Zarlaam while Bershome took the seat facing the rear. The coach started with a jolt.

"Bershome, advise Garsel that we are not in such a hurry, please."

The lad slid the panel behind him aside and tapped the driver on the leg.

"Not so fast, sir. Master Zarlaam says to slow down, please."

The coach slowed but continued to rock and bump as it traveled down the road.

"Gerak, do you understand why you are going with us?"

"I heard you and the captain talking. You think I'm a wizard."

"Yes. You have an undeveloped natural ability to perform magic. Under our tutelage, you will harness that ability and learn the skills necessary to control and use it."

"Will I be able to read minds as you do?"

"Excellent question. I see you are sharp-minded yourself. That is an ability of skill developed by many years of study that not all wizards achieve. Also, a person can block it with training. Only time will tell what your abilities will be."

"Oh."

"First, we need to educate you as to the rules of magic usage. Bershome, the first rule, if you please." Zarlaam pointed at him.

"Magic is to be used for the benefit of all. It is not to be used to harm a person or for wrongful gain."

"Why do you think that is so, Gerak?" Zarlaam asked.

"Because not to follow that rule is wrong," he said with a shrug.

"Why else?" Zarlaam looked at the lad over his spectacles.

"To seek wrongful gain of property or money or to harm a person is a violation of the law of the land."

Zarlaam nodded. "Yes, it is also a betrayal of your fellow mankind. Such a person is not worthy to use magic. Rule number two?"

"Magic is never to be performed in the presence of non-magical people," Bershome quoted.

"Why is that, Gerak?"

"I don't know, sir." He shrugged.

"It is because not all people understand magic. Many people fear the unknown and what they do not understand. As magic users, we are often blamed for the forces of nature. Some wizards and witches have been burned alive by mobs of villagers because they thought a curse had been cast by them, or they caused a drought. Some wizards and witches have used magic for ill gain. But most do not. Rule number three?"

"Avoid evil magic."

"Why would we do that, Gerak?"

"I don't understand the rule, sir."

"The entire world is interwoven with magic. Not all are aware of it. Magic has many forms. There are working spells to help make our life easier or better. There are also potions for health, medicine, and charms for protection. On the dark side of magic, there are curses and poisons. Many a witch are known to create love charms or potions. These are spells intended to affect the heart or mind to make a person fall in love with someone in particular. They are spells that influence the free will of a person. Such magic is not proper to use because it violates a person. Dark magic can also enter into the realm of demonism. There are evil spirit beings. Any attempt to control an evil spirit can result in calamity. Thus evil magic must be avoided."

"How can someone tell if a particular spell is evil?"

"Another excellent question, Gerak." Zarlaam raised his hand and tapped the air with his index finger. "The answer is: Moral Conscious. A person with a good moral conscious will recognize an evil spell or potion by knowing the intent of it. Also, they may tell by the nature of the incantation. This is some of which you will learn."

"How can we protect ourselves from evil magic?"

"There are a variety of ways. These you will learn in time. Bershome, the fourth rule?"

"Never use magic to wrongfully impose upon a person's free will."

"How can you do that, Master?"

"There are spells that can be used to calm a beast or make them obey you. Such spells should never be used against a fellow human because it is a violation of their very person. It is worse than robbing someone at knifepoint or brutally beating them."

"Rule five: Harm no one with magic."

"That is an easy one to understand. How will I learn to do magic of my choosing?"

"To use magic, we have different tools. The magical ability lies within the wizard. The individual ability to perform magic differs in strength from person to person. You may not be able to perform a spell at first. But with practice and learning, you can master it. Many spells can be made easier with the use of elements or ingredients. Most can be used with the aid of a magically enhanced staff such a mine or Bershome's." He leaned his staff out for Gerak to see it better.

Gerak looked at the staff a moment. "Will I get one?"

"Yes. Now, just because you get a staff does not mean you will be able to instantly perform magic openly. It is a learned skill that will develop and grow as you study."

"How do I make a staff?"

"Well, that requires very advanced skills in magic. We have a friend that makes them for us. Once you have a staff, it will grow with you. Its power will strengthen as you learn."

"On another note, Mister Kalthazar, I expect you to conduct yourself with high moral standards at our home. You are no longer a sailor. Profanity is not allowed."

"Yes, sir." The lad nodded.

CHAPTER FOUR

The coach slowed to a stop. The lads watched as Zarlaam made ready to disembark. Heroct opened the door, and Zarlaam motioned for the boys to go first. They climbed down quickly, eager to stretch their legs and rub the sore spots on their bottoms. They were not expecting the sight they discovered. They had stopped short of a village. He looked around them, and the countryside was green with vegetation and summer life, and the temperature was a bit warm to their liking directly in the sun. Not thirty feet away, the landscape changed radically.

Zarlaam stepped down from the coach to look at a line that existed as if drawn distinctly with a stick in the dirt. Across the line from where the coach sat, the village was in the middle of winter. A hundred yards across the village, green leafy trees grew. They looked all around and could see the area of the village was the only thing affected by the snowy weather.

The village was covered with a light coat of snow. Icicles hung from every house and tree limbs. Dead corn stalks, from a previous summer's season, stood in a garden plot. It was a radical contrast to the corn stalks that stood green and growing a few feet away. Smoke rose in slow curls from the chimneys of the houses.

He watched as a man chopped on one of the few remaining trees next to his house. Snowflakes from its boughs showered him with each blow of the axe. Another man ripped the pickets off of a fence and gathered them in his arms. He carried them inside his house. A third man, bundled in heavy winter clothing beneath a coat, walked towards them.

Zarlaam pulled his cloak from the coach, and Heroct helped drape it over his shoulders.

"We will be going in to visit. You and Garsel may stay here with the coach in the warmth."

"Thank you, sir." The guardsman smiled.

The villager approaching them stopped a few feet short of the line of warmth. He looked longingly at it a moment and then at Zarlaam.

"Greetings, sir," Zarlaam said.

"Hello, I would welcome you to our village, but I must advise you that a curse has been cast upon us. If you have food supplies for sale, we would be interested in them if you are asking a reasonable price. Our funds as a community have grown a bit thin."

"Unfortunately not, sir." Zarlaam stepped across the line into the chill. The ground crunched under his foot, and a chilling wind whipped at his hair. "My, that wind does have a bite to it. If you would like, I could send my coachmen and companions for supplies." He held out his hand, and the man shook it.

"You aren't afraid of the witch's curse on our village?"

"The extent of her powers could not encompass myself in her spell. As most likely, it does not affect the people living here either."

"I am afraid that is not so. When we realized the curse on us existed, the Rokberson family packed up in their wagon and rode out as if the countryside was on fire. Just around the bend on the way down the hill, their front right wheel came off, and they all died when the wagon rolled down the hillside. We all fear for our lives at the aspect of leaving."

"I suspect it was neglect of the wagon wheel that killed them, not a witch's spell. How is it that you have crops growing just outside your village?"

"Harome Jerty fancies Arleta, the innkeeper's daughter. He comes up from across the valley and has planted them for us."

"He will be harvesting them soon from the looks of the crop. Do you perchance know where this witch is, sir?"

"Certainly." He pointed over at the graveyard. "At the far end. That headstone by itself. Arleta found it in her hut when she discovered the witch had died."

"When was that?"

"Middle of last winter. This cursed winter hit us like a blizzard and snowed us in not a week before she died. Franklin, our blacksmith, returned from a trip come normal springtime and informed us that our village was the only place afflicted so."

"When was her body discovered?"

"Arleta found her just after New Year's day before we knew about the curse. Otherwise, we would have burned her hut down with her in it."

"That sort of action may have turned out to be a bad decision on your part."

Zarlaam walked over to the small cemetery outside the afflicted area. The wind that taunted his hair ceased. He went to the headstone and examined it. He also made a visual note that the line of the winter affliction stopped at the little picket fence around the small cemetery.

"I see her name was Fredean Winters." He looked over the village with a slight smile. "A fitting spell," He smiled and muttered more to himself than the man standing before him.

"Fitting curse, you mean! She has all but murdered us after her death."

"How did your people treat Miss Winters?"

"She grew up here. She and her mother were witches. They lived about a mile out in the woods in a hut her mother built decades ago. She went away for a long time but came back shortly before her mother's death."

"I ask again, sir. How did the people of the village treat her?"

"Oh, we were nice to her. Sometimes the kids would harass her when she was going through town. She had weird ways about her, you know. She wasn't quite right in the head. She was always talking to herself and making funny signs and hand gestures all the time. Many times someone would find her lurking about the village in the middle of the night. They would catch her in the act of scribing strange symbols on the houses. Some times with blood. "

Zarlaam crossed back over into the winter air.

"Have you a tavern? I could use a hot drink."

"The Inn has a tavern." The man stared at him but shrugged. He turned and walked away, shaking his head at Zarlaam's casual acceptance of the circumstances.

Zarlaam turned and saw the boys standing back beyond the boundary of the winter's chill. He motioned for them to join him. "You may come with me, gentlemen. It is a bit chilly."

Bershome calmly stepped into the chilly area and turned up his collar against the wind. He stepped several times as he smiled at the sound of the crunching icy ground beneath his feet and shook his head. Gerak was a bit more cautious, setting one foot in before stepping forward.

"How can this be, Master?" Bershome asked.

Zarlaam looked to see that the man was out of earshot. "Very powerful magic. Lady Fredean Winters was quite capable of casting this spell. I had met her many years back. I sensed such power in her. Let us stroll up to the tavern."

As they walked, Zarlaam would point here or there, and the boys would look. Bershome commented on the wards set in places that could only be detected by the symbols that Fredean had drawn on a fence post or the corner of a house.

From inside a house, villagers pressed their faces against the windows, watching them as they strolled casually past. "Fredean has protected this village well. Her wards are everywhere," Zarlaam whispered. "I can sense a lot of magic cast about. All are good omens to protect against illnesses and evil."

They arrived at the inn. Ice and snow covered the sign on the front of the building, to make it unreadable.

Bershome hurried up the couple of steps to open the door for his master. They hastened inside. The warmth was comforting after the freezing temperature outside. Several patrons were gathered into two groups on opposite sides of the room. Zarlaam stepped over to a nearby empty table and sat while the boys looked longingly at the fireplace, where one group of people sat with hardly an inch of free space between them. Some of the people were dressed in what looked like practically every piece of clothing they owned. Others were wrapped in blankets or quilts. Their faces were haggard and hungry. The lads joined their master at the table.

A redheaded young lady came over and placed a tablecloth over the table when no other table in the place had one. Then she curtsied. The boys took full notice of her and sat tall and straight. Bershome turned down his collar and neatened the front of his coat.

"Good day, your Lordship. How may I serve you, sir?"

"What do you have hot to drink and eat?"

"We have tea, mead, ale, and hot buttered rum, sir. We also have a stew, freshly cooked this morning if ye might be a bit hungry."

"Excellent, we will have hot buttered rums and the stew."

"I'll return with it shortly, sir."

Zarlaam leaned forward and spoke in a whisper. "She is a fetching young lady. Would not you gentlemen say so?"

Their only responses were to grin broadly and nod vigorously. Something under Zarlaam's hand on the tablecloth caught his attention. The cloth was a coarsely woven of white cotton with little colorful pink flowers sewn into it. His finger lingered over a place that had been repaired. He smiled, glanced at Bershome, and nodded. He tapped the cloth at the repair. The lad slid his hand over to the spot on the cloth. His face puzzled a moment, then he smiled and withdrew his hand.

"It is quite faint, Master Zarlaam, but it is there."

"Yes, but a mending spell was used."

Gerak showed no interest in the issue as he watched the young lady.

"Mind that you don't stare, Mr. Kalthazar," Zarlaam leaned closer to him and whispered.

The boy diverted his eyes and held his head down, ears turning red. She returned with three steaming mugs. She placed a mug close to Zarlaam's hand, leaned close to him, and whispered, "I beg forgiveness as to the condition of the cloth, sire."

"Oh, that is quite all right, child. I have a mending or two of my own on my robe. May I ask who made this lovely table cloth?"

"My mother, sir. God rest her soul."

"Yes. I gather you repaired it?"

"Yes, sir."

"Excellent job, almost undetectable."

"Thank you, sir. I'll fetch your stew."

She returned with three bowls of stew and a plate with small pieces of bread on it. She stood beside Zarlaam until he had tasted it.

"Excellent flavor. Wouldn't you gentlemen say so?"

"Yes!" Bershome almost shouted.

Gerak stared at the sparseness of the meat and vegetables. "Yes," he mumbled.

The boys began to wolf down the stew.

"Manners, gentlemen," Zarlaam spoke as he raised his spoon.

The boys stopped. Bershome sat erect, and Gerak watched him for cues. He switched his overhand grip on the spoon to imitate the underhand grip Bershome used. Zarlaam smiled and took another bite. The young lady lingered nearby. When Zarlaam finished his meal, he laid his spoon beside the wooden bowl. The girl stepped up as she twisted a small towel in her hands.

"Excellent. Thank you." He smiled and took the cloth gently from her and wiped his mouth as she flushed beet red for forgetting to provide them with napkins. The boys then used the towel in spite of the fact that they had already used their sleeves.

"I'm so sorry I forgot your napkin, your Lordship. We don't get nobility very often. Around her they us3 their shirt sleeves or the tablecloth. "

"No need to apologize. You provided it in a timely manner. May I ask the name of our lovely hostess?"

"Arleta Harsumg, your Lordship." She curtsied slightly.

"Miss Harsumg, that was an excellent meal and was well served. I shall recommend your establishment to all my friends who chance to travel this way."

"Ha!" a man across the room snorted.

Zarlaam turned to look at a gaunt-faced man near the hearth. "You doubt the word of a gentleman, sir?"

"No, your Lordship. I doubt the fact that anyone would come traveling here ever again."

"Why? You have a charming little village."

"With a charming big curse on it."

"Personally, I like the winter, sir. But I can see how you would not." He turned his attention back to the girl. "Miss Harsumg, I understand you had the misfortune of discovering the deceased, Lady Winters."

"Yes, sir."

"Is it possible for you to take me to her home?"

"Do you think you can remove this curse?" the man asked. Everyone about leaned closer to hear his response.

"Lady Winters was a very powerful witch. This weather spell is evidence of that for certain."

"I'll say she was."

"I'm inclined to believe she was upset with the people of this village before she died. Thus her casting of this spell."

"Can you break this curse?" the man asked again.

"I don't know this spell. I cannot."

The man hung his head, and his shoulders sagged as if Zarlaam had cast a heavy burden on him.

"I can perhaps find a way that it may be removed. Would you take us to her home, Miss Harsumg?"

"I can't, sir. Father has forbidden me to go there again."

"Perhaps I may have a word with him?"

"He is ill in bed, sir. I have to attend to the tavern."

"Oh, I see. It also wouldn't be very neighborly for us to rush out into the cold. Now would it?" Is there not someone you could trust to fill in your duties for a little while?"

Her glance skittered about the room. "Father said I cannot leave."

Zarlaam stood. "Perhaps you can give us directions."

She leaned close and whispered, "She has traps about, sir."

Zarlaam removed his coin pouch from his pocket. He took two gold coins out and handed them to her. "This should pay for our meal, and I offer another for your services as a guide." As she accepted the coins, he grasped her hand with his other one, and smiled up at her.

She looked at the coins when he released her. "Oh, this is too much, sir."

"I really enjoyed my meal and am happy with the price."

"I'll go speak with Father." She hurried from the room.

"You, sir," he nodded at the outspoken man. "May I ask your name?"

"Rantond Kessler."

"I would like to enlist you as a guardian, sir."

The man wiped his mouth with his hand, stood, and stepped over closer. "What have you in mind, sir?"

"I wish for you to look after Miss Harlow's establishment and protect her interest and patrons. Are you a trustworthy man?"

"I'm as trustworthy as anyone here."

"Excellent. Since you are vouching for the entire village, I believe Miss Harsumg will be relieved. Because I am creating the require-ment of your services, I shall pay you when we return. Providing, of course, she is satisfied with your services."

"Aye, sir." He sauntered over and leaned against the customer side of the bar.

Arleta returned and stared at Rantond.

"This gentleman has agreed to watch over your establishment," Zarlaam said.

She eyed him a moment. "Stay out of the mead, Rantond Kessler. Poppa is coming down."

"I trust he will behave. Lads, open the door for the lady, please. Lead the way, Miss Harsumg."

Gerak and Bershome rushed to open the door for her, bumping shoulders as they did. Arleta wrapped a shawl over her head and marched through the open door. She stepped briskly through the village to the east and stopped just short of the edge of the snow. Zarlaam stepped past her and crossed the invisible barrier. He held out his hand.

"I assure you it is safe, Miss Arleta."

She shivered once before taking his hand. He squeezed her trem-bling hand, and she stepped across the line. Without looking back, she led the way down the trail through the woods. Before long, she stopped beside a tree with a bucket sitting underneath it. A weedy clearing stood beyond the tree. She pulled a bundle of straw from the bucket of water and slapped it against each side of her feet.

"You need to do this also, sir,"

Zarlaam followed her instructions. "Bershome," Zarlaam asked, "what grows in this field?"

The boy looked about and smiled. "Tangleweed, Master. I speculate that the water in the bucket has rosemary in it to ward off the weed from your feet."

"Excellent. You have identified the menace of the plant and the cure against it."

"I've never seen such a thing, Master Zarlaam," Gerak said, scratching his head.

"Now that you have entered into the world of magic, many things will be new to you. You have lots to learn. But worry not; in time, you will know much, much more."

"What if I chose not to use the witch's water?"

Zarlaam smiled. "You may attempt to cross the clearing without it." He held out his hand as an invitation.

Without hesitation, Gerak stepped out ahead of the others. The weeds merely snagged his feet at first. But after a few strides, he became trapped. The weeds entangled his entire lower legs and stopped him. He looked at Zarlaam in shock.

"It is an enchanting little plant. Would you not agree, lad?" Zarlaam smiled. "Especially when a person deliberately cultivates a field of it."

"How do I get out of this?" Kalthazar asked. The young lad's eyes grew rounder, and his breathing quickened.

"Fighting it will not help. The weed will entangle you even more. Bershome, if you would, please assist our friend."

Bershome had treated his own feet already and walked over with the bucket in his hand. He slapped Gerak's legs with the wet bundle of straw, and the weed proceeded to untangle and release the lad's trapped limbs.

A cluster of trees stood at the far side of the clearing. A barrier of briars and vines grew in a wall around them four feet high. Between two close trees was a picket fence gate. Arleta tapped an old limb knot on the tree to the right three times with her hand, and the gate opened of its own will. She led the way in, and they found a large hut made of thatch with a very large garden.

"Bershome, check out the garden and show anything of note to Mister Kalthazar. Miss Arleta and I will check the hut for wards of protection.

"She said I should always put the bag on this post on the hook by the door," Arleta said as she reached for burlap sack.

"Excellent."

The boys headed for the garden. Arleta hesitated at the door.

"She was your friend, was she not?" Zarlaam asked.

"Yes, sir."

"How long has she been teaching you magic?"

Arleta stared at him; her eyes wide open as her face paled.

"No cause for fear, child. I am a wizard and practice magic too. I noticed the table cloth that you had repaired was touched with a mending spell. Either you or your mother had used the spell."

"I'm not a witch, sir."

"I understand your reluctance. Such a claim would not make you very popular in your village. I believe you have the potential to be a good and powerful witch. I felt it in you when I held your hand. The world of magic is your proper place."

"I cannot. The people of Natudix would burn me alive."

"I propose a solution. You can come with us and study more as an apprentice."

"Father needs me. Harome has asked me to marry him. I don't want to die as a lonely, old, crazy, woman like Fredean."

"Miss Winters chose her solitary life because she liked it. I know of an entire village where everyone practices magic on a daily basis. You are fascinated by the things you have learned from Ms. Winters and want to know more. I do not believe that a life in Natudix will make you happy."

"Well."

"Let us investigate this residence. Please tell me all that you know about the things inside."

Arleta slipped inside and eased over to a table cluttered with jars and papers. She proceeded to tell him the name of different ingredients in the jars and the potions Fredean said they could be used in.

"Where are her potions and spell books?" He sat in one of the two chairs in the hut.

"She hid them beneath her bed."

"Bring them to me, please."

She knelt beside the bed and pulled out a large book. The uneven pages revealed various objects such as feathers and plant leaves protruding from them. He accepted the book from her and laid it in his lap closed. He waved his hands over it, and the book opened. Many pages flipped from right to left until he was looking at a page with a white feather attached to it by a thread. He read the page. "So, that is how she did it," He said with a wide smile.

"Did what, sir?"

He closed the book and smiled at Arleta. "Did you find a paper of bequeathal?"

"What is that, sir?"

"Did she leave a will?"

Arleta stepped over to a cupboard and pulled a piece of paper from a tall vase. She handed it to him. He read. "She has willed everything to you."

"I don't know what to do about it."

"She had the king's title to fifty acres. She speaks of it here."

"I don't want it."

"She enjoyed your company. Did you not enjoy learning from her?"

"Well, yes, but..."

"I can understand how being a witch would make you an outcast in your own village. Particularly now. There is good and bad magic, just as there are good and bad people all over the world. Fredean was an old woman tired of being mistreated by some of the villagers." He handed her the will.

"She had done a lot of things for the good of them all. I observed her wards and spell makings of protection all over the village. Granted, she has done a bad thing to all of you with her last spell. She may have been wanting to teach them a lesson."

"She has killed five people, and my father is going to die soon too." Arleta sat in the other chair, tears streaming down her cheeks.

"I suspect the Rakordson family was simply victims of a broken wagon wheel at the wrong time. They were driving a heavily loaded wagon and in a hurry. The wagon rolled on top of them."

"She warned me you would come."

"Did she?"

"She wrote me a letter. She didn't give your name, but she said a great wizard would come to take me away."

"May I see it?"

She produced the letter from her pocket.

"Arleta, always wear the amulet you find with this letter. It will protect you until a great wizard comes for you. With him, you will have a better life. Now, go east from the door to the seventh guardsman. Then south to the next and three to the weak flank. Beneath the soil as if it were fertile lies your legacy." When he finished reading, he looked at her. "Do you know what that means?"

"No, sir. But she was always talking in riddles."

"Master," Bershome spoke from the door.

"What have you found, Bershome?"

"She had a productive garden at one time, now neglected. The remnants from last year's crops still remain. They were mostly vegetables, but she also planted many potion ingredients among them."

"Because to an unknowing person, they would appear to be weeds. Have you seen a spade, lad?"

"I wasn't looking for one, sir. I'll see what I can find."

"Thank you. Arleta, are there any other books or writings of Miss Winter's?"

"I have one book underneath my bed that father doesn't know about, and she had a box of loose parchments and scrolls. Are you going to take me away from my father?"

"There will be no force behind anything concerning you. I would take you only if you choose to go of your own free will. Please bring out the box. With your permission, I wish to take them with me to learn from her. I promise to return them to you."

"What can you learn?"

"There were some charms she cast about your village I failed to recognize. Witches and wizards learn from each other as well as by our research and experimentation."

"Master Zarlaam," Gerak whispered hoarsely from the doorway. He had a shovel in one hand. He grasped his fishing knife in his other.

"What is it?"

"Someone is riding about the outer fencing. We hear the hoof falls."

"Where is Bershome?" Zarlaam stood, his staff in hand.

"He stands guard at the gate."

"Let us join him. Arleta, this is your property they trespass upon."

A horse nickered from a slight distance.

Arleta stopped at a tree near the hut and plucked a couple of apples from it. She pushed past Gerak and Bershome.

"We are in no danger." She faced them. "It is only Dallietano."

Bershome lowered his sword a bit. "Show yourself, sir. We mean you no harm."

"He will not likely come out with you here." She stepped out in the clearing and held out her offering. A strip of land about ten feet wide lay between the brier barrier and the field of tangle weed.

Dallietano nickered. She turned to her left to face the noise.

"They will not harm you. They are my friends." She turned her head toward Bershome. "Put your sword away, please, sir?"

Bershome hastily sheathed the weapon. She looked at Gerak. He cast the shovel aside and tucked away his knife.

"Come on, boy, they are friends," she coaxed in a sweet voice as if calling a small child.

Slowly bushes moved, and a head appeared among their foliage. Arleta clicked her tongue at him softly. Everyone stood in amazement at the size and beauty of the creature as it cautiously stepped out of the woods. It stopped halfway to her. It looked at her, then them, and back at her.

"Tick, tick, tick," She clicked her tongue against the roof of her mouth. "Come on, Dallietano. They will not hurt you."

"How long have you known this unicorn, Arleta?" Zarlaam asked, keeping his voice soft.

"Since he was a colt, about two years. His mother was killed by a leopard last year." She walked over to him, holding out the apple.

Bershome eased back into the yard. He returned with several apples.

"Mister Kalthazar, what do you know of unicorns?" Zarlaam asked.

"They are in fairy tales mothers tell their children, sir."

"You think they are things of myths, eh? Do you believe your own eyes?" Bershome asked as he held up an apple for him to offer the magnificent beast.

"I have seen many magnificent beasts swimming the ocean. I'm talking about whales large enough to swallow the Scallywag swimming past us calmly as you please. But nothing have I seen has been as beautiful as this."

Arleta stroked the beast's neck as it munched on the apple. "He may not like you. It took a few times before I was able to pet him," she said.

Bershome unbuckled his sword belt and laid it on the ground. He held out his apple as he eased towards the animal.

"Hello, Dallietano, I have an apple also."

The animal looked at him and laid his ears back. Bershome stopped moving. The unicorn sniffed the wind to catch his scent. It raised its ears, and Bershome stepped inches closer. It stretched out its neck and sniffed his apple. Once he was within reach, it took the apple.

Kalthazar eased forward.

"Gerak, a moment," Zarlaam said. The lad stopped and looked at him. The wizard scratched his chin through his beard. He moved his lips in a silent spell as he pointed the top of his staff towards the lad. A mist smelling of roses emitted from it. Zarlaam sprayed him up and down. "This may help." The wizard smiled.

Gerak turned and approached the unicorn as Bershome petted the animal. It sniffed his hand and snorted. He remained still with the offering held out. The unicorn laid back its ears and would not take his apple.

"That's okay, Dallietano. He has an apple for you," Arleta coed him. The animal did not move.

"Here." He passed the apple to her. She offered him the apple. After a couple more sniffs, it took the apple.

"Will he let us ride him?" Gerak asked.

"No," Arleta's sharp tone rang out through the air.

"Why?"

Zarlaam stood beside him. "While the creature will allow us to feed him or maybe pet him, to ride a unicorn is a rare privilege indeed. They may allow it when there is a need to carry a person from danger. They're enchanted beasts. Only the purest and truest of hearts may sit astride a unicorn with his consent."

Arleta looked at him wide-eyed.

Zarlaam stroked his beard. "I'm surprised he is allowing this many of us near him as it is." He stepped around the others. "Ah, he has an injury."

"Where?" Arleta asked. She hurried around the unicorn to its right flank where Zarlaam stood. The lads joined them.

"It appears a large cat of some nature attacked him." They all looked at the claw marks on Dallietano's right flank.

"Arleta, do you know what and where the ingredients are for a poultice?"

"Yes, sir, I'll go make one." She hurried away.

"Gentleman, let us return to the yard. Dallietano will follow us."

They led the way, and Zarlaam walked beside the beast behind them. The unicorn went to the tree and selected an apple to eat. Bershome disappeared inside the cottage to assist Arleta.

A few minutes later, Arleta came out and carried a wooden bowl and a rag. She spoke to and stroked Dallietano before she applied the medicine. The animal turned to watch her as she pressed the concoction of herbs against his flank. He whinnied in discomfort but stood for her administration of the treatment.

"Mister Bershome," she said, "would you use the scythe hanging on the wall and cut an opening in the backside outer fencing to allow him to come in and eat from the trees?"

Bershome's smile stretched across his face. "Your request is my desire, my Lady." He hurried away. Shortly they heard Bershome hacking on the fence.

"Mister Kalthazar, do you like riddles?" Zarlaam asked.

"I guess," he shrugged.

"What would this riddle tell you? Go east from the door to the seventh guardsman. Face south to the next and move three to the weak flank. Beneath the soil as if it were fertile lies your legacy."

The lad thought for a moment. "Soldiers and sailors stand guard at their post. I'd say, from the door, seven fenceposts to the east, turn to the one south of it and three away from that post toward the shortest length of the fence."

"Have you a spade?"

"Beside the gate, sir,"

"Miss Arleta, may we assist you in taking possession of your inheritance?" Zarlaam smiled at her surprised expression.

"Please." She nodded as she stroked the unicorn's neck. "You will need to be more careful, Dallietano. I cannot come here very often to check on you."

Gerak picked up the shovel beside the gate. He looked at the sky and then faced the hut. His forehead wrinkled.

"Is something the matter?"

"The garden is west of the hut. I assumed post in the riddle would be a fence post for the garden because the rest of the area around this hut is fenced in by briars and brambles strung between trees."

He rushed past them to the opposite end of the hut only to return still frowning. "I see no fence post in the briar fencing here. If the trees are the post, there aren't enough."

"Actually, it is in the garden," Arleta whispered to Zarlaam as she suppressed a snicker.

"Please encourage him," he whispered back.

"May I show you the door?" she asked Gerak.

He turned to her. "You know where it is?"

"Yes. It is near the far end of the garden fence. She used half a door for a gate."

His face flushed, and he slipped past them again to the garden. He started at the door and counted the posts. Then he stood at the seventh one and looked across the garden. He counted the number of posts either side of the seventh post.

"There are nine posts to the east and eight to the west. We go three to the west. He walked around and started digging at the designated post. After a few minutes, he had a hole two shovels deep and then hit rocks. He stopped and examined the obstructions in the soil.

"Is there a problem, Gerak?"

"Rocks, sir."

"Did you expect her to make it easy for you?"

Gerak grunted, pulled the rocks out by hand, and resumed digging. Shortly his shovel struck a metallic object. He dug it free with his hands and heaved out a metal chest. It was about a foot square and a foot and a half deep. It was silvery and shiny in spots where Gerak had rubbed it in digging around it and handling it. Arleta remained standing beside Zarlaam as she looked at it. Bershome had finished his task and joined them.

"You are a good person to be her friend, in spite of the attitude the villagers had towards her. She wanted you to have it," Zarlaam reassured her.

"I just don't feel quite right." She shook her head.

"Understandable. If you wish, we can rebury it, and the person that pays the taxes on her land may one day discover it and gain the fortune inside. The chest alone appears to be of quite a value, considering it looks to be made of silver. It is even more valuable to the right person if it has any magical properties."

"It is almost as if I'm taking advantage of her in her death." She looked down.

He put a hand on her shoulder. "She had no family, and only you as a friend. She has willed all her belongings to you out of your friendship and her love for you."

"I suppose it would be foolish not to accept it."

"Do so with a clean conscience, child. You have done her no wrong."

"Very well. Would you gentlemen carry it for me, please?"

The boys grabbed a handle on each side and followed her into the hut. They set it on the table where she cleared a spot. Then they stood back to see its contents. Arleta found a rag and wiped most of the dirt off the chest.

"My, I never knew she had this. It is beautiful." The solid silver chest was engraved with vines and blossoms. Around the outer border, strange runes were carved into it also.

Zarlaam put his hand on the boy's shoulders and nodded for them to step outside. "Let's give her privacy," he said.

Shortly Arleta came outside carrying a glass tube sealed with a cork stopper and wax containing a rolled parchment inside.

"Ah, the title to your land, I presume?"

"Yes, sir, you would not believe how deep that chest is."

"It is a magical trick to make it multidimensional."

"Multi what?"

"It is a very complicated spell that allows the box extra space inside. Now, I saw a potion in her book for winter illness. Would you assist me in making a batch for your father and the others?"

"Yes, sir. But I think she already has a batch made."

"I wonder if she dates her batches. Many potions cannot set on the shelf very long. Especially in the summer heat."

"She has," Arleta paused, and her bottom lip quivered as she steadied her emotions. "There is a root cellar where she kept things."

"Please bring up the potion."

Arleta went inside and rolled a rug back to expose a trap door. She opened it and climbed down inside.

Zarlaam watched down in the hole and saw Arleta wave her hand over a candle she picked up, and a flame popped up to cast light into the dark cellar. She found three bottles and passed them up to him. They were cool to the touch.

Bershome returned inside and gave her a helping hand in climbing from the cellar. She smiled sweetly at him.

"Thank you, sir."

"You are most welcome, my Lady."

"Interesting," Zarlaam said, looking at the bottle. "Bershome, read this paper she has tied to it. My old eyes aren't so great for reading without help." He held the bottle up for Bershome to read.

"Medicine for winter illness. Take a teaspoon in the morning with a mug of water and again that night for four days. Sleep under covers to break the sweat. No good after summer's end."

"She must have made this just before her departure," Zarlaam speculated.

"Is it safe to give it to them?" Arleta queried.

Zarlaam removed the stopper and sniffed the contents.

"Yes, it has a distinct odor when it goes bad. This is still good. She took precautions to keep it cool in the cellar. You can administer this to your father and friends."

Arleta took a great breath and sighed in relief. She closed the trap door and covered it back up.

"Arleta, I notice how you lit the candle in the cellar. Can you do other such magic?"

She blushed a bright red. She had been caught unconsciously using magic and hesitated to answer.

"Allow me, please?" He waved his hand and pointed behind her. She turned to see a candle sitting on a shelf behind her ignite. He snapped his fingers, and the flame went out.

"Bershome?"

The lad waved his hand and pointed at the candle as well. The flame popped up again. He snapped his fingers, and it extinguished itself.

Arleta looked at them wide-eyed. "I never tried it from across the room."

"Feel free to do so. But you must focus only on the candle, less you catch the house on fire."

"Oh," she said and faced the candle slowly. She closed her eyes a moment and then waved her hand slowly. The flame flickered and perked up. She giggled slightly at her accomplishment. But the snap of her fingers failed to put the flame out. She stood puzzled.

"I always blew out the candle," she defended her failure.

Zarlaam snapped his fingers to kill the flame. "You could learn many, many, more things about magic if you wish."

"Fredean's books are hard to understand. Besides, Father will not allow me to bring them home."

"As I told you earlier, I bring gifted children such as yourself to Paxtirea Estates and teach them how to use magic for the good of all. You have the potential to make a good witch."

"Do you think so?"

"Yes. You could come, study with us during the winter and return to be with your father for the next summer."

"What does it cost?"

"If properly managed, I think Miss Fredean has left plenty enough for you to afford several years of education."

Arleta stood in silence, twisting the hem of her apron in her fingers.

"You need not decide this minute. Shall we return and help your friends bring an end to their winter captivity?"

"You can end the spell?"

"No, but they can."

"How?"

"You will see in due time."

Gerak had been leaning in the doorway, watching everything.

"Master Zarlaam, will I learn to light a candle as easily as that?"

"Yes, Gerak, in due time. Miss Arleta, if you will secure everything in your chest you wish to take, we can return to town with it."

She secured her inheritance, and Zarlaam added the spell books and scrolls to its contents. The lads grasped the handles and carried it out. Arleta paused in the doorway a moment to look about before closing it.

"I can cast a locking charm on it if you like?"

"Thank you, but no. Jason and Barney will probably burn it down if they cannot get inside."

"I can make them not want to mess around here. Nothing harmful, just enough to scare them." Zarlaam offered.

She smiled with intrigue at his offer. "What will you do?"

"I can make the picture on the wall scream when a person other than yourself comes near it."

She clapped her hands and chuckled. "Please do."

The four of them returned inside the cottage. All watched as Zarlaam took an old painting down from the wall. It was a picture of a young noble woman sitting on a bench in a flower garden.

"People do not realize that an artist actually captures a minute piece of a person in their work. This artist was very good." He cast his spell, and a mist emitted from the end of his staff and engulfed the painting. She turned her head from looking out across the painting to face Zarlaam.

"Can you hear me, Fredean?"

"Yes, sir."

"Miss Arleta would like for you to watch over her house. Kids will come and be up to mischief. You have permission to warn and frighten them by shouting and screaming. You may even threaten to cast a curse of warts on them if they do not leave this house alone."

"But, I cannot cast magic."

"True, but a boy poking around where he does not belong will not know that. We will place you so that you can see out the window and watch the door being opened."

"Thank you."

"Thank you, Miss Fredean." Arleta said to the painting.

"My pleasure, lass. Do I know you?"

"I was a friend of Fredean's"

"That's nice. Friends are our most valuable treasure."

Zarlaam placed the painting on the shelf.

"How did you know it was Fredean?"

"I assumed it would be her or her mother. I also know she was once the wife of a nobleman. That is an expensive painting by a well-known artist."

"Can any painting be animated?"

"This is a high-level spell which is easier to do it when the artist is painting the picture if the magic is woven when the painting is made. The personality and other attributes of the individual are actually captured in the art. The paintings also know not to be animated around non-magical people. This lady is limited. She is really more of an animated puppet with limited intelligence."

"I think I resent that remark, sir," Fredean responded. "One should not talk about another in front of them as if they are not there."

"I beg forgiveness, Lady Fredean." Zarlaam bowed slightly.

"Apology accepted. My, my, this place could use a good cleaning maid."

Arleta smiled feebly as she closed the door. The group followed her to the village. When they arrived at the edge of the village, Arleta stopped and looked at Zarlaam.

"Master Zarlaam, would you mind hiding my chest in your coach for a little while?"

"Certainly. Lads, have Garsel and Heroct stash it inside."

The group returned to the inn and saw everyone sitting in the same place they had been when they left. Rantond was still leaning on the bar. He stood tall with a smile as he anticipated payment from Zarlaam. Arleta went to her father, who had come downstairs in her absence to watch over his pub.

"Father, you should be in bed."

He whispered to her hoarsely with a smile, "I had to keep Rantond out of the mead."

"Mister Harsumg," Zarlaam spoke, "I would like to have a word with you in private if I may, please." He studied the pasty-look of the man's skin.

"Are you a wizard, sir?"

"Yes, sir."

"Can you undo the curse that Fredean has set upon our village?"

"Unfortunately not, sir. Only your own people can break this spell, no one else."

"Then she has murdered us all." He lowered his head, shaking it. "Young Harome is a good strong lad, but he cannot farm enough. We will all starve to death or die of lung fever. We have three people afflicted now."

"Only if you choose to do so."

"How do you mean that?"

"I suggest that you gather everyone over by the cemetery. In fact, all of you people, hear me." He raised his voice and spoke to everyone. "All of you join me at the cemetery. The entire village must come."

"Why should we do that?" Rantond asked.

"To admit your sins against the woman and ask her forgiveness."

"She is dead. Do you think her ghost is haunting our village and will remove the curse?"

"That can only be learned at the cemetery."

"I ain't going to the cemetery. She put a curse on me," a little boy said.

Zarlaam looked at him. "What was her curse, young man?"

"She said my teeth would fall out for throwing a dirt clod at her. See?" He smiled widely and exposed his missing two front teeth.

"How old are you?"

"I'm seven."

"She made no curse on you. She merely spoke the truth. Did not your parents tell you that you would lose your baby teeth for new ones to grow in?"

"Oh yeah?" another young lad piped. "She cursed me and caused me to break my arm." His trousers were tattered and torn at both knees.

"I wager young man that you are a rough and rowdy young fellow who takes risk doing things that your parents are constantly spanking your bottom for. Correct?"

The lad looked down at the floor without response.

"You are a bit clumsy too."

"That he is," a lady sitting behind him spoke.

"She only said that to frighten you because she knew you would hurt yourself one day. I will wait for all of you at the cemetery." Zarlaam turned to his young companions. "Shall we go, gentlemen?" he spoke to his charges and walked out of the inn. The lads caught up with him quickly.

"Bershome, Gerak, this is an example of how magic can be improperly used as an evil against people."

"How did she do it, Master?" Bershome asked.

"I'll explain in due time. Ironically, her greatest feat here is not this spell of perpetual winter. It is the power of fear over the people of this village. This is why we magical people have such a problem co-existing with the rest of the world. They fear us and our powers. Her spell is actually harmless enough. It only affects the village area. But their fear forces them to remain inside its boundaries and not leave. They would have all eventually starved or died of winter sickness."

They continued walking until they were at the cemetery. Zarlaam stood at the foot of Fredean Winters's grave. Before long, the villagers started gathering near the last house a few yards away. They moved towards the cemetery in a mass group. It was a populace of mixed ages. Everyone thin and pail. Arleta helped her father walk in front of the group. Everyone spread out just inside the line of winter surrounding the village.

"Ladies and gentlemen. Rest assured that all of you may safely step across the frozen line and join me here around the dearly departed lady's grave."

"It's fine, Daddy. I've already been past it."

Slowly one person stepped across and then another. Finally, everyone was in the cemetery.

"I saw where Miss Fredean Winters cast many spells and charms about your village. All were for your protection. They are on your fence posts and house walls. For example, I detected wards against evil, protection against ailments, and protections against death in childbirth." He looked at a young woman holding a baby. "You were afraid of her because you did not understand her. She was old, and I fear her mind was slipping in the end. You parents said things behind her back, and your kids heard it. That is why the kids were mean to her. You would only have something to do with her if you needed her skills in making medicine and healing. She lived a lonely life because of you people. All she ever wanted was to be accepted into your village as a friend. Miss Arleta was her only true friend."

Everyone stared at the ground in shame.

"You two lads. Step up front here and give Miss Fredean your most sincere apology," Zarlaam ordered firmly.

A woman pushed the reluctant lad with the broken arm. He looked about and hung his head low and mumbled.

"Louder, young man. I cannot hear you. How can you expect forgiveness from her if you will not admit how wrong you were?"

"I'm sorry I was mean to you, Miss Fredean," the lad shouted.

"I'm sorry too," the other lad said.

One-by-one each person stepped up and offered their apology. All except Arleta. As the last person, she stood beside the headstone weeping.

"Miss Harsumg, have you any words to say?"

"I'm sorry I let everyone here be mean to you, and I'm sorry I let my father keep me from coming to you and helping you when you were ill. You were a sweet person and should not have been left to die alone."

"I believe that about covers it," Zarlaam said.

Everyone turned around and looked at their still frozen village. Then they looked back at him.

"You leaders of the village must now decree to move the boundary markers of your village to include this cemetery and Miss Winters's grave."

"What?" one man said, "Why didn't you just tell us that back in the inn?"

"Because you would not have learned the lesson that you should not be mean to other people because they are different. I think it would be best that today's lesson always be in your minds as you go about your lives in the future. Personally, I would not tell this story to travelers. They would think of you as an unfriendly village and spread the word that you should be avoided. This would harm the commerce and growth of your community."

Several people nodded in agreement.

"Now, you can move your boundary markers." He stepped close to his companions. "Lads, you will find a stone among the markers with carvings on them. Bring them to me.

Several men separated from the group and headed for the two markers at the edge of the village. They had to fetch picks and shovels to dig up the stacked stones. Most everyone followed to help but Arleta and her father. Even the children helped carry what they could. Zarlaam slipped over to Arleta's father and spoke to him.

"Mister Harsumg, may I discuss with you about Arleta going with me to further her education. She has the ability to be a good magical person."

"Why? So she could end up old, alone, and crazy like Fredean?"

"So she could learn more and help people. But we teach more than just magic."

"I can't afford to pay for such a thing."

"She has her own means now. Miss Winters has bequeathed all her belongings to Arleta."

"Has she now?" His eyes brightened up.

"Yes, sir. Had I not arrived here, your daughter could have been the only survivor of this occurrence."

"Will you teach her to be a lady?"

"She already is and carries herself as one. We provide a rounded education to help her be a better one, sir. She will return to see you in the summer, and you shall see for yourself. The final decision is up to Arleta, of course."

Arleta watched as the village begin to thaw when the final stones were put in place. A rattle of rigging from down the road attracted their attention. A tall, muscular young man came riding up in a wagon pulled by a single mule. He stopped beside Zarlaam's coach and climbed down. His attention became fixed on the stream of water in the middle of the road coming from the melting ice and snow. Arleta walked over to him, and they spoke quietly.

"What do you want to become a witch like crazy Fredean for?" he shouted.

Arleta put her fist on her hips and stared at him. "She was not crazy."

"Only a crazy woman would put a curse on an entire village and try to kill everyone.

"She cast the spell to teach them a lesson. Not to kill them."

"Yes, and I suppose the Rakordson family learned it too."

"Their wagon wheel broke and fell off. It was an accident. You saw it yourself."

"I'll not have a witch for a wife!"

"As you wish, so be it!" She turned and stormed over to join Zarlaam and her father. "Lord Zarlaam, I will go with you."

Zarlaam looked at the lad beside the wagon as he stood with his fists on his hips and mouth agape.

"Would you like a little more time to talk to the young man and perhaps leave on a better note?"

"He hated Fredean. He talked as bad about her as everyone else. I have no regrets about anything concerning him."

Zarlaam faced her father. "Mister Harsumg, Miss Winters left a will that gives all her possessions to Arleta. As her father, you may take possession of the land in her absence and begin farming it. I would suggest you keep everyone away from the hut the lady lived in."

"What about Dallietano, sir?" Arleta asked.

"He will be fine. I have some friends that can help relocate him to a place that I know about where he will be much safer. I will make arrangements on our way home."

"Who is Dallietano?"

"A friend of Miss Winters, sir. Nothing you need to trouble yourself about. Miss Arleta, would you like to gather your things and leave with us or make your own travel arrangements?"

She looked at her father. He smiled at her and nodded his head. She clutched him in a hug. Zarlaam stepped away to allow them privacy.

Harome approached him. "Hey, old man, are you the one filling her head with this nonsense about witch's curses and such?"

Zarlaam smiled at him. "No, sir. Miss Winters started teaching her the blessings of magic many years ago."

"You can't take her with you."

"It is an issue between Arleta and her father. She is a free person and has a mind of her own. I believe you have made your feelings clear to her."

"You a warlock?"

"No, sir. I'm a wizard."

"Are you in the habit of running around casting curses on people too?"

Zarlaam gripped his staff tight. "Miss Winters did many good things for these people, and they repaid her with rudeness and cruelty. She chose an improper way to teach them a lesson in manners about not being mean to people just because they are different."

"You call that a lesson in manners? Five people died because of her. How many will die from sickness because of her?"

"Miss Winters caused weather to occur around the village. She did not make them load up in their wagon and ride it out of here at a neck-breaking speed. She did not sabotage their broken wagon wheel which caused their death. It was a result of their own actions. They suffered an unfortunate accident."

"She killed them just the same."

"You are a good man to do what you could to help out these people in their time of need. Miss Winters helped them many years herself. She did not wish harm on anyone."

"You defend her action because you are one of her kind."

Zarlaam sighed. "I am not defending her actions. But she was not evil. In old age, her mind appears to have gone a bit array. The people's fear caused them the greatest problem. The spell is broken, and the village is thawing out. The sick will get better because she left behind a potion for them."

"That is supposed to make everything okay?"

"I have heard it said; all is well that ends well."

"Tell that to the Rakordson family," Harome said, walking off.

Zarlaam sighed and walked over to where his coachmen had waited all along.

"Gentlemen, we will be leaving in a little while with another passenger. Miss Harsumg will be joining us."

Shortly, the lads helped carry a couple of bundles of her possessions from the inn to the coach. Arleta hugged her father a last time and stopped to look at Harome as he stood across the village talking to Rantond. He looked away from her and at Zarlaam. She turned towards the coach and wiped away a tear.

Heroct stood holding the door open for them to climb in. Zarlaam assisted Arleta into the coach, and she sat in the back seat. He joined her, and the lads sat in the front seat. A moment later, Heroct slapped the reins on the horse's backs, and the coach started with a jolt. They rode in silence for a ways to allow Arleta to compose herself.

"How long will it take to get to Paxtirea Estates, Master Zarlaam?" Arleta broke the silence.

"A few days. I have a favorite inn I like to stop at. The cook is an old friend of mine and makes an excellent shepherd pie. Also, I'll speak with him to make arrangements for your unicorn friend."

"I'm eager to start studying, sir."

"Excellent. Would you like to start now?"

"Can we?"

"Of course. It is better to begin earlier than later. Gerak, if you would tell Miss Arleta the rules of magic and reasons for them." Zarlaam looked at him as he spoke and leaned back to listen, but mainly to hear Gerak's retention of his lesson of the rules. The master gave him a nod and a smile with each correct one

Arleta turned to Zarlaam when Gerak and Bershome finished. "With such magic about, why do you teach it to people?"

"Because magic is beneficial to all when learned and properly used."

"How?"

"For example, the poultice you made for Dallietano. Without it, his wound could have become infected and caused his death. Or the infection would have made him weak, and he would be easier prey for a leopard or bear. You helped save the life of a beautiful and wonderful magical creature. You can make a potion to help a sick person, and they recover from their illness. While poultices and potions are more knowledge of plants and chemistry than magic, we work with those elements the most because we are approached for them by people."

"But how can a spell like the one you put on the painting be beneficial?"

"She guards your house. She could hold a message for a person and repeat it when they arrive. If such a painting were near the doorway, and it alerted you to an intruder, you could be better prepared to protect yourself. You will learn many spells. Some can disarm an assailant or immobilize them. Most of the spells you will be learning are useful aids in everyday living like the mending spell you used on your tablecloth."

"A mending on a cloth is weaker than the original cloth." Arleta said," Fredean taught it to me to make the mend as strong as the rest of the cloth. So you go around looking for apprentices?"

"Yes and no. I travel the country in the summer and sometimes discover a potential apprentice. I have been most fortunate this summer and found two."

Arleta looked at the lads and smiled at Gerak. He blushed and looked out the window.

"We will be learning together, then?"

"Time will tell. Initially, you will have similar studies, but you will most likely be more advanced in your knowledge because of what Fredean has taught you. Mister Kalthazar has not had the benefit of such teachings."

"What did you do, Mister Kalthazar?"

He stole a glance at her. "You can call me Gerak. I worked on my father's fishing boat. He is the most successful fisherman in our village," he said.

"You sailed on the sea? Did you ever see a whale? I hear tell they are as big as sailing ships.

"Yes, and they are. Some are even bigger."

She looked at him open-mouthed, then looked at Bershome, who nodded in agreement.

"Your father's success was mostly due to your assistance, Gerak," Zarlaam said.

"How so, sir?"

"Without knowing it, when you repaired the nets, you enchanted them so that the fish would not fight against getting caught."

"How?"

"What did you think or say to yourself as you worked?" Zarlaam gave him a lead for his answer.

Gerak thought a moment. "I thought about how strong the net needed to be to hold the fish, and it would be better if the fish didn't fight to get free."

"Your weaving magic into the nets without knowing is how I found you."

"How did you know?" Arleta asked.

"Magic leaves a trace that can be detected. It is like having a vase of flowers in a closed room. For a time after they have been removed, you can walk in and still smell them. Detecting magic is sometimes difficult, but the experience and knowledge makes it possible to do so. Bershome, how about you bring out your books and begin our lessons."

Bershome pulled a pair of books from under the seat. They had been hand bound with heavy leather covers. He opened one.

"This is a book on herbology, and the magical properties plants have. Also, it contains some of the potions they can be used in."

"I have assembled these books over the years. In due time you will have a copy you make yourself. Find the page about Gottcha Creepers. Gerak, the other book is about magical creatures. Open it to Gottcha Creepers also. Bershome, please read.

Gottcha Creepers plants are a root tuber that grows tall bushy vines. They have short spear-shaped leaves of bright, waxy, green.

Very small amount of poison from the thorns of the Gottcha Creeper root is useful as a laxative to loosen con-stipated bowels. Caution must be used. Large amounts of Gottcha Creeper can cause a woman with child to lose it or give birth too early.

Gottcha Creeper can be used with other ingredients to make a potion to return someone magically petrified to normal.

WARNING: The Gottcha Creeper can kill. They ensnare their victims and shred their flesh with their poisonous thorns as they struggle to escape. The decay of the bodies fertilizes the earth so their offspring can grow.

"Excellent, the next parts discuss the making of different potions. Now read your's, Gerak."
The lad looked nervously about and cleared his throat.

Gottcha Creepers plants are a root tuber that grows tall bushy vines. They have short spear-shaped leaves of bright, waxy, green. The female plant produces tiny red pear-shaped fruit that is fragrant and tasty to lure animals to them. Gottcha Creepers grow in wooded areas where patches of sunshine reach the ground. Offspring grow between male and female plants when their roots join.

When a clearing becomes overcrowded, adults will uproot themselves and crawl like worms to another area. Offspring are also known to migrate to crossbreed with other patches of Gottcha Creepers.

WARNING: Gottcha Creepers will kill animals attracted to their fruit. The decaying body becomes fertilizer to the soil for the young. Defense against Gottcha Creepers the spell; Struthen statta. It makes them raise their vines straight up and not move. A rejuvenation potion counters the poison."

"This lady and gentlemen, is an example of a plant that is also a creature. Many magical and non-magical creatures' parts can be used in potions.

"Bershome, have you a pebble?"

Bershome fished in his robe and pulled a pouch from his pocket. He opened it and dug around in it a moment to extract a pebble.

"Now, we will give you a practical demonstration of a spell." He nodded at Bershome.

The lad lifted his staff from between his leg and the wall. He stood it straight up and spoke. "Muttalo." He thumped his staff against the floor. Suddenly the pebble sparkled, releasing glitter dust. Quickly the glimmer dissipated. An eerie silence fell over the group. The coach made neither a creaking or rattling sound. The wheels rolled in silence on the gravel road. The horse's hoof steps could not be heard. Arleta and Gerak continued watching the pebble in his hand. Zarlaam raised his hands and held them over the lad's and clapped them quickly. Gerak and Arleta gasped. Arleta clapped her hands also. She giggled at the silence and harder when she couldn't hear herself. Zarlaam gestured for Bershome to cast out the pebble. The lad cast it out as hard as he could to get it as far from the road as possible. The noise rushed back into their ears.

"That was amazing!"

"Yes, Miss Arleta. Such a spell has many purposes. You can cast it on your bedpost and sleep peacefully in spite of the noises all around you. But caution must be applied. You must always keep the presence of mind and observe the rules of magic."

"How long will it last?"

"It depends on the strength of the caster. I used it once in the great hall for a couple of hours. I put it on my button for a nap in my chair. Practice and training lets you control the size of the area affected and the duration of the spell. You can actually make a bubble around yourself and a companion. You can talk, but no one else can hear you."

"A person could use that spell so he could move without being heard when hunting game."

Zarlaam looked at Gerak, "True, but he would not be able to hear an approaching danger himself and be attacked by a hunting lion or bear. Also, that wouldn't be very sporting. Now would it."

Gerak turned red-faced, sat back, and looked out the window. They spent the ride learning more about plants. Arleta showed an excellent knowledge in the field, pleasing Zarlaam.

CHAPTER FIVE

Their coach arrived at a village built along the bank of the river. The inn sported a sign of a unicorn's head. A portly man was standing outside wearing an apron. A cane made from a large, knobby root hung on his arm. He recognized their coach and beamed at them.

"Good day to you, Lord Zarlaam. I see you have been traveling again this summer."

"Yes, we have Mister Bozter. I have a coach full of companions today. We will need three rooms for the night if you please."

"Excellent. Your usual room is free, and I do have others available. Do come in, your lordship. I'll prepare you a table and attend to your needs personally. Hello, Heroct. If you take your coach around to the stable, my son will see to your horses."

The innkeeper bowed slightly and led the way inside. The spacious tavern held a dozen heavy plank wooden tables with benches. He quickly cleared away a table and motioned for them to be seated. Zarlaam and his apprentices settled at the table. Zarlaam glanced around and noticed a man sitting at a table near the hearth. The hood of his robe covered most of his face. A carved walking stick was leaning against the table beside the person. It was carved decoratively its entire length. Zarlaam studied him a moment.

"There are many travelers about this time of year. Would you not agree, Master Zarlaam?" Bershome said.

"Yes. I would say we are most fortunate to find rooms available. Mister Bozter, have you made your famous shepherd's pie today?"

"I make it daily and sometimes more than once, sir. However, it will be a good hour before the next batch is ready. Perhaps you would care for an ale and a chance to freshen up from your travels while you wait?"

"Excellent idea. Where are my manners today? My apologies, old friend. Please allow me to introduce my companions. May I present; Miss Arleta Harsumg. She is from the village of Natudix. Mister Gerak Kalthazar is from the seaside village of Galley's Cove. They are my new apprentices. You have met young Bershome before."

Mister Bozter shook each hand offered him and smiled. "Bershome, you have grown an inch or two, haven't you."

"I try to every day, sir."

"Did I hear correctly that you said she was from Natudix?"

"Yes." Zarlaam nodded.

"Tell me, lass. I heard a rumor just last week about a village of such a name trapped in a perpetual winter."

She looked nervously at Zarlaam for guidance.

"Actually," Zarlaam spoke for her, "I heard the same and went there to see for myself. It is perfectly normal now," Zarlaam said.

"Well, some people tell stories just to see if they can raise an eyebrow and earn a free pint of ale."

"Yes. Miss Arleta needs a room for herself. The lads here and one of my coachmen will share a common room. No reflection on you or your staff, my friend, but the other man will stay in the coach."

"I do understand, Master Zarlaam. I'll fetch you the keys, sir."

Arleta leaned over to whisper in Zarlaam's ear. He smiled. "You will be quite safe in your room, young lady. Unless you wish to share the room with Heroct and lads. I believe there is an empty bed left. There are usually four beds in a room at this inn. It is how they can make them affordable to common travelers."

"You shouldn't be such an expense on my account, sir."

"It would be up to you to allow other ladies to share your room. But you will need to take precautions to safeguard your belongings against theft. Mister Bozter cannot assure the quality of his boarders as he can his cooking."

"I shall reimburse you then, sir."

"We can settle it at a later time if you wish. Also, do you have a scarf or something you don't need that you wore recently. I'll give it to Mister Bozter to arrange for his son to help Dallietano move to a better place to live. It is a village called Woods Edge. It is quite a ways north of here."

She pulled a handkerchief from a pocket she had been using to wipe her face with occasionally.

"Does he, well," she hesitated.

He winked at her. "Yes. They both were once apprentices of mine."

A short time after they ate, Arleta excused herself and went upstairs to her room. Bershome watched the beautiful young girl as she ascended the stairs. He sighed and returned his attention to his master and Gerak's discussion.

Zarlaam yawned. "I believe we should all retire. I wish to be on the road before daybreak on the morrow so we might reach home before dark. I have some business to attend to with our innkeeper, and then I shall follow suit."

Bershome followed Gerak upstairs. Without pausing to think better about it, he stopped at the door before their room and knocked. "Miss Harsumg, it is Bershome."

She opened the door and smiled. "Yes?"

"If you wish, I could place a magical lock on your door," he whispered.

She looked over her shoulder about the room and back at him. "But there is no chamber pot in here. What if I have a calling in the night?"

Bershome shrugged. "I didn't think about that."

"I'll just put a chair under the door handle."

"We will be next door if you need us."

"What about my chest?"

"The compartment it is locked in is magically locked. Plus, Garsel will sleep in the coach. Either way, he or Heroct usually does when we travel. They are most trustworthy and capable of protecting it."

"I shall sleep more restfully then. I will see you in the morning," she said. He nodded as she closed the door.

Bershome found Gerak lying back on a bed looking at the ceiling. Bershome sat on the bed with a big sigh. Gerak rolled over and pushed into a sitting position and scowled with narrowed eyes at him.

"I'll bet you a crown I'll get a kiss from her first."

"Gerak, she is like you, coming to learn. You cannot afford such frivolous thoughts. I also conclude that you underestimate her. She will not be distracted by your flirtations."

"Any young lady can be persuaded with the correct attention."

Bershome stared at him. "That is a pretty good act you put on. You do not sound like a fisherman's son now."

"My mother made me read everything she could get her hands on. I'm not totally uneducated."

"But you know nothing of magic, herbology or potion-making. Concentrate on your studies."

"Mother was particular about what I read in books. The Captain taught me to read the sea and men." With that statement, he ended the conversation by blowing out the candle and lying down on his bed to sleep.

Bershome nodded but refused to pursue the topic any further. *Master Zarlaam, you may have a tougher time than you think in taming this one into submission. I think I'll keep an eye on him myself.* He crawled into bed and dropped off to sleep.

Gerak, more accustomed to the quiet of life on the sea, awoke in the night to hear an argument coming through the wall from Zarlaam's room.

"Zarlaam, these are valuable spells. The book is worth ten times the five crowns I am asking."

"Kieffer, they are evil spells. I would buy the book if I knew this was the only written copy, and destroying it would mean that they would never be used. I am merely offering to compensate you for the parchment you ruined making the book."

"You are disillusioned, Zarlaam. There are not two sides of magic, good and evil. It is all one magic. I seek out the stronger type of magic."

"You choose the wrong kind of magic, Kieffer. I'll have nothing further to do with you. Never seek me out again."

"Your loss, Zarlaam." The man left with a slam of the door.

Bershome snorted and turned but didn't appear to have awakened. Heroct snored on the far side of the room. *What was that about?* Kalthazar made a mental note of the man's name. He might need to remember it sometime.

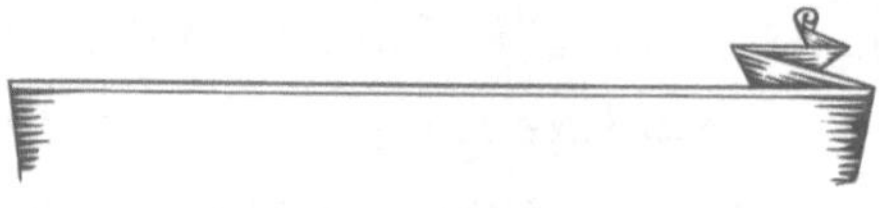

CHAPTER SIX

"Ah, we have arrived," Zarlaam announced, "This is the village outside the castle grounds here to the left."

Gerak and Arleta were straining to look across Bershome and Zarlaam to see over the six-foot walls. Moments later, the coach tuned onto the castle grounds entrance road. They leaned out their windows for a better look. Zarlaam and Bershome exchanged smiles, for they had witnessed the conduct before.

The mile-long cobblestone lane, wide enough for two coaches driving abreast, passed through manicured grounds studded with fruit trees spaced every few yards apart. Some groundskeepers pruned back the fruit trees. Others were spreading fertilizer off a wagon. A finely dressed old gentleman sat astride a stallion as he spoke with a worker. Garsel slowed the coach down as they approached the man on horseback. The gentleman turned his attention to the coach and smiled. He waved for the driver to stop.

"Welcome back, Garsel, Heroct," he bellowed to the driver and guard as he rode up to the coach and leaned down to see inside.

"Ah, Zarlaam, Bershome, how was your trip?"

"Excellent, my Lord. May I introduce Miss Arleta Harsumg and Mister Gerak Kalthazar?"

"Splendid, new apprentices, I gather?"

"Yes, my Lord."

"Welcome to the two of you. We will meet again later. You have lots to do get settled in. I'll leave you to your duties, Zarlaam. Bershome, we have a two-year-old I need assistance with tomorrow."

Bershome perked up with a wide smile. "Yes, Grandfather."

"Garsel, carry on."

Arleta sat wide-eyed at the encounter. Zarlaam noticed it. "Lord Paxtare is my brother. He makes it a point to know the name of everyone he meets."

Gerak jerked his head to look at Bershome with a raised eyebrow. Bershome noticed his connection of their last names. He smiled.

The exchange was missed by Arleta but not the master wizard. He studied Gerak with a casual air.

"Is everyone here a user of magic, Master Zarlaam?"

"No, Gerak, we will show you the Hall of Knowledge and training grounds. That is the only place where you will be allowed to perform and practice magic. Some of the villagers are magically inclined. I do not doubt that everyone in the village knows of our activities, but the Lord's servants are most loyal and do not speak of it in public. Some of the servants are magic users themselves."

CHAPTER SEVEN

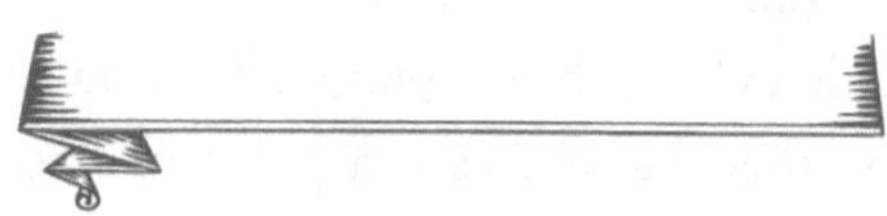

Their coach stopped in front of the manor. The lads waited for Zarlaam and Arleta to climb down.

"Bershome, why don't you show Arleta and Gerak their places in the apprentice wing, where they may refresh themselves? Then you can give them a short tour of the public portions of the manor. We can meet back in the great hall. It is almost lunchtime."

"Yes, sir." Bershome turned to face his companions as he walked backward towards the manor. "My Lady and Gentleman, if you will follow me, I'll start the tour. The Paxtirea estates and castle Paxtirea were established a couple of hundred-odd years ago. Initially, it was a single stone house a few miles west of here. Grandfather had to have it rebuilt for his new bride. The apprentice wing we are going to is the newest addition. Our current Lord had it built for the benefit of our apprentices. It can accommodate about forty apprentices at one time, but we would not turn more away. The largest group we have ever had at any given time is thirty-five."

"How many are there now?"

"Last year, we had eleven boys and thirteen girls."

"Where do they come from?"

"They are from all across the country. Most of them are children of magic users themselves. Others are ones recommended to Master Zarlaam by previous apprentices. Then there are those he chances to find such as you. We should have about twenty-six with you two. The rest of the apprentices will begin arriving this week. Unfortunately, we are not exactly sure who will show up."

They followed Bershome into the large receiving hall. A couple of small tables and several benches set against the walls in the room. Gerak and Arleta stopped and looked at a massive mirror. Several hideous masks representing different demons of ancient legends hung on the frame. They recognized a few from stories they had been told when growing up. The Devil was obvious. Bershome named: Ogre, Goblin, Monitor, Hydra, and Medusa for their clarity.

"Grandfather had it set here for a conversation piece. On All Hallows Eve, we will have a party, and people will get to wear the masks."

"Mirrors are expensive and rare, but one this size is even much more so. Where did you get such a large mirror?" Arleta stared at it.

"It was a present from one of Grandfather's league lords a few weeks ago as a peace offering. He and Grandfather had a few cross words." Bershome lowered his voice. "Grandfather thought it was strange for the man to give such an expensive present because he believed the man is plotting to kill us and take over our estates. Grandfather has his spies."

"Some of those masks are hideous."

"Yes, especially the devil at the top there. Master Zarlaam and I examined all of them and the mirror. They have magical properties, but we have yet to identify them or know they're what for. Master Zarlaam says they are harmless."

They followed him up a set of stairs to the second floor. He opened a door to a large long chamber. Wooden wardrobes six feet high were used to create cubicles with two beds and a table each. Two fireplaces stood equally spaced along the right wall.

"This is the ladies' dormitory. Miss Arleta. You will find the wash closets at the far end on the right. The chamber pots are on the left.

"I'd pick a bed close to the hearth if I were you. We'll be back for you after I show Gerak the boys' dormitory upstairs."

The boys headed upstairs, where Bershome showed Gerak a room identical to the one they left Arleta in. Gerak counted twenty beds in the room.

"Heroct and Garsel will bring up your baggage. You may select any bunk you want. Except, Martello and I always take the first ones in the chamber," he looked at Gerak. "Some people prefer the ones closest to the fireplaces. We are farther north than where a few of the apprentices live. Winter is a bit colder here, and they aren't used to it."

"You live in the dormitory?" Gerak asked.

"All the apprentices do." They met back on the second floor with Arleta.

"How long have you been studying magic, Bershome?" Arleta asked.

"Since I was about ten. Nowadays, I mostly assist Master Zarlaam in his teachings. He sometimes has to leave during the winter study period."

"You are quite experienced then. Would you help me if I have troubles?"

"Yes, helping everyone is part of my responsibilities. Shall we go down for lunch?"

They headed downstairs and entered the great hall. Two tables, thirty feet long, sat in the room. At the far end of the room sat another table at a right angle to the long tables. Several people were seated on the right near the head table.

"Come on down and have a seat." He gestured for them to use the opposite side of the table he walked down. "Hello, everyone."

Most of the people simply acknowledged his arrival by raising a hand or giving him a nod.

"We are a bit casual for lunch around here in the summer providing his lordship is not having visitors. Please, have a seat."

Platters of food crowded the table. One platter held trencher bread loaves about eight inches in diameter. One held roast beef, potatoes, carrots, and beets. Another platter was a mixture of pears, cantaloupe, grapes, strawberries, and other fruits. A fourth platter had cheeses on it. Bershome picked up a loaf of bread and cut it in half with a long knife provided with the bread and handed it to Arleta.

"Here is your half a trencher, my Lady. Gerak," he passed him the other half.

He took another loaf and cut one for himself. They scooped out the soft bread inside the thick crust and had a bowl. The platters were slid down the table so the newcomers could serve themselves. Bershome cut a chunk of beef off the roast.

"Care for some beef, Miss Arleta?" he smiled at her as he speared the chunk of meat.

"Thank you." She held up her bowl for him.

"Just help yourselves to whatever else you want," He served Gerak some beef as well and then himself.

"Welcome back, Lord Bershome." A scullery maid stood by his elbow with a pitcher in each hand.

"Thank you, Oralette. What is the juice today?"

"We have peach, pear, or apple cider."

"I'll have pear. Miss Arleta, Gerak, name your poison."

"Peach, please."

"Yes, peach, please," Gerak said.

Heroct and Garsel arrived while they ate. Bershome slid the platters down to the new arrivals.

"Your bags are in the dormitories. We set them on the first bed," Heroct said. The men accepted a polite smile and a nod from Arleta, for they caught her with her mouth full.

"If you put your bags on a bed, our servants will arrange their contents into the adjacent wardrobe for you. Arleta, the first two bunks are reserved for the older lady apprentices. They act as big sisters to control the heathens," Bershome told them.

"Oh, my chest?" Arleta asked.

"It is locked in Master Zarlaam's office," Heroct said, "He will help you with arrangements for it."

"Thank you."

Oralette brought ales to the driver and coachman. Bershome's grandfather and Zarlaam arrived and sat at the head table. Oralette served them drinks and fetched plates of food. When Bershome had finished eating, Zarlaam caught his eye and beckoned at him. He rose and stepped over to the master.

"You need to take our new apprentices into town and get them robes. Mister Kalthazar also needs trousers and tunics, at least three apiece. Give this to him. It is from his father. Miss Arleta has her own coin." Zarlaam set a pouch of coins on the table.

"Yes, sir." He returned to the table and saw they were almost done eating.

"When the two of you are finished, we will be going to the village."

"Why? We just arrived."

"We need to get your training robes. Master Zarlaam has our apprentices wear them to help keep their regular clothes clean and for identification purposes."

"Why?"

"It helps prevent making the mistake of using magic in the presence of visitors that are not supposed to be around the training area. Sometimes kids wander. You do not use magic if you see anyone in our area not wearing a robe."

Shortly, Bershome walked them down the long drive to town and guided them to a shop where they were met by a scrawny older lady.

"Afternoon, Lord Bershome."

"Hello, Mrs. Jackson. I have two friends I wish to introduce to you. This is Miss Arleta Harsumg and Mister Gerak Kalthazar. They are new apprentices and need robes for training."

She looked Arleta up and down and took her hand. "My, you are a pretty young lady. I see you aren't some simple city raised girl. You've earned your living. Step right over here, young lady, and let me measure you. Bershome, you better catch this one while you can."

Both of them turned bright red-faced.

Bershome turned his back on the ladies and pulled the pouch from his pocket. He held it so no one but Gerak could see it as he whispered, "Master Zarlaam said this is from your father and suggested you get three pairs of trousers, tunics, perhaps undergarments, and at least three robes. I would recommend adding a suit of clothes for formal occasions. Her prices are very reasonable here. There are other supplies you will need also."

Gerak took the pouch and slipped it in his pocket. "Thanks." He looked about in an awkward manner in spite of Bershome's discretion.

"Think nothing of it." Bershome slapped his shoulder, turned his attention back to the ladies.

"You are still growing, young lady. I'll add an inch or two to the length so you can get an extra year's use out of them. Mind you don't spill acid on them."

"Thank you. I need three robes. Oh, that is a lovely hunter's green cloth."

"Yes, I just got it in this week."

"I want six yards, please. I also need thread of the same color, white, and black for sewing and shears. I forget to bring any. Oh, you have ribbons. I'll have yellow, green, blue, and red. How about a couple of yards of each?"

"This is going to take a while," Bershome said. "How about we go next door, Gerak?" They left to enter a shop that handled dry goods.

"Hello, Bershome."

"Hello, Mister Jackson. Has Master Zarlaam sent you his order for supplies yet?"

"I got it just a little bit ago. I have most of the items." He pointed to a group of wooden crates. Bershome stepped over and gave it a casual look over. There was a stack of parchments, ink bottles, quills, limestone chunks to be used as writing chalk, and packets of unknown contents.

"I'll have the rest in a few days."

"Thank you, sir. Please, allow me to introduce one of our newest apprentices, Gerak Kalthazar. Gerak, if you give Mister Jackson a list of anything you want, usually, he can get it in a few days."

Gerak stepped close to him and whispered, "Does he?" Gerak hesitated.

"Yes, he is one of the few magic users in the village," Gerak said softly.

"Sir," Gerak kept his voice soft, "Do you have any books on magic that you would be interested in selling?"

The man stepped close and spoke so no one else could hear. "Magic books are rare and expensive, lad. I have my own book that I have written myself. All of Master Zarlaam's apprentices have one. We add to it over the years. Sometimes the old master sends us scrolls of spells and potions he has students write up for us to add to it. We go back to it now and then for reference and usage. So, it isn't for sale. Besides, I have another son that may have a need of it when he's older."

"Oh," Gerak said with sagging shoulders.

"Don't be discouraged, lad. You will have your own soon enough. You will also have your special notes to go with them."

Gerak turned to Bershome. "Would you let me use your book so that I may copy it?"

Bershome was surprised at the request. "Gerak, you need to follow Master Zarlaam's study schedule. Your abilities as a wizard need to be exercised and developed. It is like growing up. You crawl, you walk, then you run."

"Aye, lad," Mister Jackson said. "I remember the first time I tried to levitate a pear. It shot up like it was catapulted. When it hit the rafter, the splatter went all over the room and got everyone. Ha, ha, ha. It took me all day to clean up the mess."

"Spells can go wrong like that?"

"Oh, yeah! And potions too. Master Zarlaam had to forbid one girl from making potions. Gerladine, I believe her name was. She started studying the same time I did. She was good at spell casting. But every potion she mixed went awry. One made a cloud of noxious fumes and ran us out of the Hall of Knowledge for a couple of days. But the last potion was an outrage. She was making a plant growth potion that turned out to be very excellent. She dropped a plant root in it as a test. It started growing like crazy and managed to fill the Hall with a wild-growing weed. The darn thing had branches the size of my arm." He grasped his bicep to stress the diameter of the limbs. "It took over a week to hack and chop it up to get it out. The darn thing grew almost as fast as we could chop and carry the pieces off until her potion ran out. Master Zarlaam loves telling about that one."

"Has he said whatever happened to her?" he asked, looking at Bershome.

"Baron Cox married her after he made her swear never to mix a potion."

"I remember him," Mr. Jackson smiled. "He was with the master his last year back then. It was a pity he wasn't very good though."

"Magical strength varies among us," Bershome responded.

"Hello," Arleta said from the doorway.

"Hello, please come in, my Lady," Mister Jackson turned to take care of his new customer.

"Mister Jackson," Bershome spoke up, "allow me to introduce Miss Arleta Harsumg. She will be joining us this year."

"I would definitely allow you to bring around and introduce me to any lady this pretty, Bershome."

Arleta cast her glance at the floor and cleared her throat. "Thank you, sir. It is a pleasure meeting you."

He took her hand and bowed over it. "The pleasure of your acquaintance is all mine, Lady Harsumg."

"It's Miss Harsumg, sir. Fortunately, I'm here to inform Gerak that your wife is ready to do business with him. I apologize for taking so long."

Gerak smiled in reply and stepped next door.

"I see you have quite a bundle to carry there. Let me get my son to assist you, Miss Arleta."

"Mister Jackson, I grew up helping my father run an inn and a tavern. I do thank you for the offer, but I'm not a delicate flower, sir."

"Bershome, if I were your age, I'd grab this girl and hold on to her. She will make a fine wife for you."

Arleta's face flushed deeper, and Bershome's ears grew so hot he feared they would burst into flames. "I'll assist her, sir." He gave the man a wink. "She needs studying supplies as well."

Before long, the three of them were headed back to the manor. Once on the Paxtirea estate grounds, Bershome used his staff to levitate the bundles of goods just ahead of them to their amusement.

CHAPTER EIGHT

The next day, Master Zarlaam sat in his open sanctuary, the shade of a pear tree, reading. No one ever disturbed him when he was on his bench.

Several wagons in a caravan turned up the road to the castle. Each wagon driven by a man in a blue uniform of a transport company advertised on the side of the wagons. Zarlaam saw most of his apprentices riding in the backs of the wagons on benches as they returned from their summer's visits at home. He knew some would have improved their skills, while others had spent the time working with their parents, farming, or doing other tasks to help support their families. He also knew some would bring him new spells and potions.

The first wagon was occupied by one of his oldest apprentices of Bershome's age, Martello. With him was a young lady Zarlaam didn't recognize. He raised his eyebrows. *Who had Bershome's friend brought with him?* The other wagons carried more of his apprentices. All of them waved at him as they rode by. He returned the waves as each wagon as it passed. He knew the apprentices would be taken care of by the house staff.

The wagons then disappeared around the castle toward the stables. A short time later, Zarlaam noticed Martello standing outside the staff entrance. He would look at Zarlaam, down at his feet, scuff at the stone with his shoe, and look across the orchard and back at his master. He fiddled with a rag in his hand. With a sigh, Zarlaam closed his book, raised his hand, and beckoned him over with a wave. The lad hesitated a moment and then ran the fifty yards to stand before him.

"Hello, Mister Lynstrom. Did you have a good summer?"

"Yes, Master Zarlaam. I apologize for disturbing your reading, sir."

"That's fine, young man. We couldn't have you wearing a hole in the stepping stones."

"Was I that obvious, sir?"

"Martello, your presence alone told me you have an urgent matter you wish to speak to me about."

"Yes, sir. I think I found a witch. She wants to learn magic."

"I'm always receptive to good news. How old is she?"

"She is just turned fourteen."

"How is it that you think she is a witch?"

"I saw her unknowingly use a mind spell on her little brother. I detected many traces of magic in her house. Here, feel this." He held out a handkerchief.

Zarlaam took the cloth. It had been carefully embroidered with little roses in excellent detail of red petals and green leaves and stems. He could detect traces of magic in it. "Yes, this cloth was sewn with magic. It is a simple binding spell to prevent the unraveling of the embroidery work."

"She made it, sir."

"Has she had any teaching of magic? Is she an acquaintance of a practicing witch?"

Martello looked at his feet. "Not that she knows of, sir." His excitement still kept him shuffling from one foot to foot.

Zarlaam did not like the idea of hurting the lad's feelings. He chose to begin letting him down easily.

"Mister Lynstrom, not everyone that develops a slight magical ability can become a master of it. You also know I test every candidate personally. I cannot give you any assurances that your friend is of the magical type. Particularly at her age. You may have brought her here only to face disappointment."

"I understand." Martello's face lost its joyful look, and his words came out flat.

"Can her family afford to pay her expenses?"

"Yes, sir. Her dad is my father's new partner."

"I hope you haven't built up her expectations. For a young lass of fourteen to start studying now puts her behind in proper development, and she may not mature completely either."

"You didn't find me until I was fourteen, sir. She is very smart,"

"Ironically, my boy, intelligence does not assure an ability to use magic. I gather you have been tutoring her this summer?"

"I showed her a bit of potions making."

"Excellent beginning. And the rules?"

"Absolutely, sir."

"Well, then perhaps you should introduce us. I'll meet her in my study. However, before that, I want to thank you for having so many of our apprentices gather at your house before finishing the trip here."

"Lord Paxtare will like it better, sir. The men driving the wagons will be hauling full loads back with them. I arranged a business venture with my father. He liked the goods I took home last spring."

"Excellent thinking, young man. I hope it is prosperous for you."

Martello hurried into the castle. Zarlaam gathered himself together and grasped his staff. He proceeded to stroll along, carrying his book and the handkerchief. He found Martello and the young lady standing at his study door.

"Master Zarlaam, may I present Miss Freya Oxmore. Freya, our mentor, Master Zarlaam."

Zarlaam bowed in response to her introduction and curtsy. "Please, come on into my study," he said, opening the door. He walked over to his bookcase and slid the book into its empty slot. He indicated for her to take a seat. He noticed that Martello had closed the door and remained outside. He settled into his chair and looked at the young lady as she sat with her back straight, legs crossed at the ankles, and hands cupped together in her lap. She tried to hide her nervousness. Her clothing told him her father prospered well in his business. Her naturally curly long hair fell over her shoulders and cascaded down her back.

"Miss Freya, Martello said you made this handkerchief. Would you tell me what you said or thought as you made your stitches?"

"It was a little poem my Grandmother taught me. This little stitch of string, I sew in love with ease. Fray not in time for me, if you please."

"Is she still alive?"

"No, sir."

"Do you know if your grandmother was a witch?"

"No, sir, not that I know of. But she always had little poems for things she did."

"Can you tell me another?"

"She had a poem for mending. This stitch in time will save me nine. Fix this tear that is wrong and make my mend just as strong."

"When would she say them?"

"She taught me to always to say them as I made the knots to finish the sewing."

"Did she have any books or parchments that she kept hidden from everyone?"

"No, sir."

"Did she ever mix strange herbs and potions?"

"She would make medicines from the strangest weeds sometimes when we were ill."

"Did she ever put candles in or around drawn symbols on the floor or walls?"

"Not that I recall."

"Your grandmother was what I call a passive witch. She did indeed know and use magic. She may have been taught it or merely developed some of the knowledge on her own. The mixing of medicines she could have learned from anywhere or anyone."

Freya sat wide-eyed as she absorbed the information.

"Martello thinks you were able to use a mind spell over your younger brother. Tell me about it."

"I didn't know it was magic. He is a bit of a pest at times. I stare at him with a stern face after I tell him what he should or should not do, and he behaves." She shrugged.

"Is he always looking at you when this happens?"

"No, sir."

"Now, do you think it is a magical power that you are welding over him or his knowledge that you will smack him on the back of the head a good one if he misbehaves?"

"I always thought it was the smack on the head that enforced his behavior."

"You smack him less nowadays?"

"Yes, sir."

"I am inclined to agree. He is learning not to be such a pest," he said. He stood, walked around the desk, and held out his hand. "I need to test if you truly have any power. Roll your sleeve above your elbow and give me your hand, please. Close your eyes. Now think of a full moon shining in the night. It shines on your flower bed. Do you see them?

"Yes."

"What color are the flowers?"

"They are pink, red, and violet."

"The pink ones are growing poorly. Think of you pointing this hand at them and wish them to be well."

"I wish..."

"Silently, please."

"Oh, sorry, sir."

"That's fine, think just of the flowers, nothing else."

He lay her hand in his, and he grasped her thumb between his thumb and index finger. Then he grasped her elbow with his other hand. He pulled up her hand and placed her extended fingers to his forehead.

"Concentrate on the limp flower pedals. Wish them well as you mentally point your hand I hold at them."

She concentrated as he instructed. After a long moment, he released her hand and stepped backward with a smile. Although she failed to notice it, his forehead had slight glowing spots from where her fingers had touched him.

"Are your fingers tingling?"

"Well, a bit."

"Is it a good tingle or a bad tingle?"

"It is a good one."

He opened his desk drawer and pulled out a bleached parchment. He placed it on the desk before her.

"Place your right hand flat on this." He set his candle stand with lit candles beside the paper. "Now close your eyes. Think of the shadow of your hand on the parchment without your hand over it. Think hard. Think to yourself, shadow stay, shadow stay, shadow stay. Do you see just your shadow on the paper in your mind?"

"Yes, sir."

"Keep your eyes closed and remove your hand."

She pulled her hand, and he smiled at her shadow still on the paper.

"Open your eyes, Miss Freya."

"Ah!" she gasped and put her hand over her mouth in surprise.

"Miss Freya, I am happy to inform you that, with teaching, you could make a fairly strong witch. Place your hand back over your shadow and reclaim it. Say, shadow come back."

She did, and the shadow was gone when she removed her hand.

"How did I do that?"

"You have the power of magic within you. I merely helped you concentrate and focus it to do your bidding."

"I never knew."

"Many magical people never know they have such power. Usually, it begins to manifest itself as early as the age of ten and as late as fifteen. If it is not developed with teaching and practice, it will eventually fade away. Martello said you have been helping him make potions. What kind?"

"One for removing warts, one for skin blemishes, and another for sour stomach."

"That lad has a talent for plants and potions. However, potions are more chemistry than magic. Now," his voice took a serious tone, "what are the rules of magic?"

She quoted the rules as if she were reading them from a book.

"Do you understand the rules?"

"Yes, sir. Not everyone can do magic, and our lives could be in danger if we are observed when using magic. Also, we should not harm anyone with magic," she explained.

"I expect the rules to be obeyed. Especially when you leave here. You would be putting your very life in danger. I will not be around to protect you."

"Martello was very adamant about the rules."

"Has he taught you anything else about magic?"

"No, sir."

"Are your parents prepared for you to become a practicing witch?"

"My mother passed away many years ago. My father told me to get any kind of learning I can."

"I brought two other new apprentices here this week. You will have a couple of friends your age to study with."

"Will I not be able to study with Martello?"

Zarlaam smiled. "Certainly. Did he mention a necessity of funds for your expenses?"

"Yes, sir. I brought money with me."

"You will be able to purchase most of your supplies in town here."

"Martello helped me get some already. Thank you for allowing me to study here."

"Rather sure of himself, was he?" He stepped around the desk and offered his hand. She placed hers in his and stood.

"You are most welcome. I will allow you the privilege of announcing to your friends that you will be studying with them."

He gestured towards the door with his free hand. She walked with a spring in her step as she left his office. Cheers broke out in the hallway before the door had closed behind her.

CHAPTER NINE

Gerak sat on his bunk, reading the book about enchanted creatures. The door to the dorm burst open, and a roar of noise came from several kids shouting at once.

"I get the fifth bunk!"

"I get the ninth bunk!"

One boy came running in to stand beside Gerak's bunk and looked at him in shock. Then he threw the bundle in his arms on the empty bunk across the space from Gerak's. The lad looked to be a touch shorter than Gerak and was a bit heavy-set.

"Hello, I'm Willard Glasslow." He offered Gerak his hand. Gerak took it and gave him a single lift and jerk down. The lad held a staff in his other hand. Gerak noticed the intricate carvings down its length.

"Gerak Kalthazar."

"Hey, Willy, did you get us..." another lad came up and noticed Gerak. He was much shorter and thin as a rail.

"Gerak, Jartus Fletcher." He pointed to the new arrival. "Jartus, Gerak Kalthazar. Jartus and I were hoping to get the space here together."

Gerak smiled slightly. "I was told I could bunk anywhere."

"Yes, that is normally so. But you see, we have had this space for three years running."

"I don't blame you. I'll wager this will be the warmest spot in the chamber on a cold winter's night. Short of sitting on the hearth."

"Would you be willing to change bunks and let us have our space together?"

"You can have a space together anywhere you want." He looked back down at the book. "Except for this one. I'm here."

"Let's go, Willy. The next one is free."

Willard grabbed his things and gave Gerak a hateful look as he left.

A tall, hardy-built lad older than Gerak walked by, but he stopped and looked at the empty bunk and then at Gerak. He stepped up beside the empty bunk.

"This bunk taken?"

Gerak shook his head without looking up. The lad dropped his things on the bunk and walked toward the wash chambers. Gerak looked at the back of the boy and then the staff he left lying on the bunk. It intrigued him that a piece of wood could be carved with runes and enchanted to create more magic.

The rest of the boys milled about the dormitory and visited.

CHAPTER TEN

Everyone gathered in the dining hall. All the children stood dressed in their best formal attire behind their benches as Zarlaam arrived dressed in a smart light green suit with a vest and dark green cloak. He stood behind his chair at the head table and surveyed the room. He had twenty returning apprentices and three new ones. Lord Paxtare arrived dressed in a fine blue-grey suit and vest. He stood a moment and surveyed the room before he sat.

"Please be seated," Zarlaam said. Scraping and thumping sounds filled the room as the apprentices sat at their tables. Zarlaam waited until everyone was adjusted to their comfort. "Ladies and gentlemen, for those of you who haven't met them, we have three new apprentices: Miss Arleta Harsumg, Miss Freya Oxmore, and Mister Gerak Kalthazar. Let us give them all a welcome to our family."

Everyone clapped.

"I know you have spent the afternoon settling in and getting reacquainted with your friends. In the morning, I shall be making a trip to visit our friend and supplier Kasfas. If anyone wishes to order any supplies, please present your list and funds to Bershome by first thing in the morning. After breakfast, everyone will assist Mister Lynstrom in harvesting our special garden on the grounds while I am away. Bear in mind these are ingredients that we need for our potions and such. Try not to cross-contaminate them. Purity of ingredients is important in potion-making. Hopefully, the remainder of our friends will arrive tomorrow."

"Let us thank our host, Lord Paxtare," he gestured to his brother in the center of the head table, "for providing us with the means for us to study our magic and our fabulous banquet this evening." Thunderous applause echoed around the room. They began their feast.

CHAPTER ELEVEN

The youngsters waited for their master to climb down from the coach. Heroct lent him a hand, and Zarlaam moved away from the door to stretch the kinks out of his body. Bershome dismounted from his horse and tied the reins to the coach. He stood beside the door to assist the ladies stepping down. Heroct gave him a smile and a quick wink.

"Hidey ho, Master Zarlaam," a scrawny man spoke from his perch on a large limb about ten feet above them. Behind him, one could see the makings of a treehouse in the massive oak.

"Salutations, Kasfas."

"I heard you found three new apprentices this summer."

"You do get around for a gentleman living out here in the middle of the woods."

"Oh, I haven't left home in months, sir. Oralette told DeLeanna. DeLeanna told Lucar. Lucar told Mondal, and he came by late yesterday."

"You have quite a network for news collection."

"Well, when a visitor drops by, we talk, and I learn the news. I have been extremely anxious for you to come calling because I have the most wonderful thing to show you."

Zarlaam's expression took on a slightly worried look. "We will be right up."

Kasfas turned and disappeared among the foliage of the tree.

"Children, be cautious. Kasfas is not the most careful wizard with his potions and notions. He also has a peculiar sense of humor. A few visitors have been known to get bitten by the seemingly most innocent item."

"In other words, look but don't touch," Arleta said.

Zarlaam nodded. He turned and walked around the little garden beneath the tree to the backside, and they followed. A long stairway made of stout living vines provided access to the treehouse. All about the limbs of the tree hung various things on twine. Some were in clay jars, simple glass bulbs, cloth, or leather pouches. Many herbs and other plants had been cut and hung on the limbs to dry.

Inside, innumerable jars and bundles of ingredients cluttered every wall shelf and flat surface in the shop. Zarlaam saw Gerak and Freya walked in with their hands in their pockets. Arleta had her fingers interlaced and held to her chest.

Zarlaam introduced his newest apprentices. They exchanged handshakes, and Kasfas stopped without releasing Arleta's hand. His eyes widened, giving him a bug-eyed appearance on his skinny face.

"May I ask what your necklace is made of?"

"I made it from horsehair," she spoke, slightly defensive as she placed her hand over the locket hung against her chest.

"I must apologize, but that is not normal horsehair. Is it?" He twisted his head a bit sideways and stared at her with a single squinted eye.

Arleta looked at Zarlaam. He smiled and nodded slightly with a wink.

"Well, it is actually hair from the mane of a unicorn."

Unbelievably the man's eyes grew wider still.

"Kasfas," Bershome interrupted. "Oralette sent you this basket of cinnamon rolls."

But the man would not take his eyes off the necklace as he held out his hand for the basket.

Zarlaam cleared his throat. "My dear friend. We have come today in need of staff's for my new apprentices, sir,"

Kasfas returned to reality. He faced Zarlaam and smiled. "Sorry, Master Zarlaam, I don't make staff's anymore."

Zarlaam squinted at Kasfas with a furrowed eyebrow and a frown this time.

"I have something better, sir." Kasfas walked around him and opened a cabinet. He returned with a cloth bundle about twenty inches long. He placed it in the only empty space on the counter. He waved for Zarlaam to come over as he unrolled the cloth. Within the roll rested several sticks that varied in diameters, lengths, and colors of wood. Each was tapered to a rounded point and had been etched with runes and carvings. Everyone crowded around to see them. A couple of the sticks were crooked, and others were straight.

"Wands?" Zarlaam's eye opened wide, and both eyebrows stretched for the top of his forehead. "I thought the art of wand making was lost when the Romars invaded!"

"Well, Master, they have been gone over a century. Anyhow, shortly after your visit last year, an old friend came by. Do you recall Waylan the Wanderer? He was here once when you visited ten years ago or so."

Zarlaam shook his head.

"No? Never mind then. He has been traveling far, far southeast and encountered a wizard that makes them. He managed to buy a book of instructions. I'll have you know, he wanted a pretty hefty coin for it too. I have managed to make these since then."

Kasfas lifted one that was a mixture of colors of dark red wood with black irregular lines on it. "I made this one for you. It is briar root, like your staff, and the core is a hippogriff feather."

"I have several decades of use with my staff, my friend. I have also spent many, many hours enhancing its power. It is an essential practice of a wizard, so to say, for his staff to grow with him. Where a wizard develops, the staff and the wizard develop together."

"Would you like to try it, sir?" He held the wand by its pointed end in a gesture for him to take it with his other hand supporting it in the middle as if he were offering Zarlaam a dagger.

Zarlaam narrowed his eyes and leaned back a bit, but took the wand. He propped his staff against the counter and stepped away from everyone. He slid his index finger slowly down the wand's length and then held it pointed up. He twisted it slowly in his fingers, examining it further. Then with a flourish, he whipped the wand in little circles and pointed at the floor. A stream of red sparks ejected from its end and encircled a tiny dark spot on the floor.

A small tree sprouted from the floor. The little tree grew and spread out a foot in diameter, sprouting limbs and foliage. Blossoms burst open in a beautiful display of pink colors. Their sweet fragrance filled the room. Everyone clapped at his display of magic. Zarlaam then jerked the wand up and down. The tree shrank instantly to about half a foot in height.

"Bershome, kindly take this tree outside and plant it for our friend. Kasfas, you definitely have something here."

"Glad you approve. Unfortunately, it takes about two weeks to make a wand. I go through a tedious selection process to make them."

"Is it harder than making a staff?"

"Oh, yes. The purity requirements of the wood and components are most stringent. The merging process is grueling. I have hardly had time for anything else. I've been thinking of stealing one of your apprentices."

Zarlaam gave him a single squinted eye stare. "How many have you sold?"

"Yours will be the second."

"Will I be able to make a tree grow from nothing?" Freya asked.

"No," Zarlaam said, "Magic cannot produce something from nothing. You can expand what already exists." He watched her sag in disappointment as he spoke. "Nor can I, child. I saw a seed on the floor and made it grow. Even I cannot create a tree from nothing. In time and after lots of study, you would be able to accelerate the growth of a plant."

She smiled in her understanding.

"His was a very complex spell," Bershome said as he lifted the tree.

"Mister Kasfas, let's get wands for my apprentices."

"Miss Arleta. I wish to propose a business deal. I'll swap you a wand for your necklace."

She still hesitated as she clasped it in her hand and shook her head.

"Shall we see how her fitting goes first, Kasfas?" Zarlaam asked.

"Yes. Please sit here on this stool, and we'll go through our list of questions," Kasfas said as he turned and snatched a parchment from the shelf where the wands had been stored. "I have instructions here as to how to determine which wand is best for you." He glanced over the paper and set it aside.

"Let see," he began muttering to himself as he made a notation on the paper. "Birth date, age to date, night or day, and his list went on. He scribbled her answers on the parchment and referred to his formula in his book. After a moment of thinking and scratching, he lay his quill down and smiled. He picked up a white wand and held it up for her.

"Ivory wood with wood nymph hairs. I cannot guarantee it, but this is the closest I have for what the book says. If it works, I'll let you have it for a discount until I can make the proper wand for you."

Arleta grasp it slowly and examined the tiny intricate runes carved into it.

"Let's give it a test, Miss. Have you a spell in mind?"

"I only know one. It is to change the color of flowers and fruit."

"Excellent spell for a beginner. Here is a squash. Now the wrist motion is as important as the incantation. Now swish it back and forth twice like this and then touch it."

She cleared her throat and pointed the wand at the squash. With a sideways flick, she spoke. "detba rouge." Then she touched it.

The quash rocked slightly, and the yellow color was swept over from one end to the other by a faint red. She screeched and giggled with glee. Everyone applauded her accomplishment.

"Now, flick the wrist to cancel it."

She complied, and the squash returned to yellow. "I did it, Master Zarlaam. I can change its color."

"Very excellent performance. You show great promise. But how did you do it before without a wand or staff?"

"Ms. Winters had me hold and rub it with my index finger."

"Oh," was his only response, and he smiled.

"Your wand for the unicorn hairs, and I'll throw in ten pounds of parchments, a bottle of ink, and a dozen quills. It is about all that you will need for the first year of your studies."

"I wish to keep the locket."

He nodded with a wide smile.

"Miss Freya, is it?" Kasfas questioned, looking at his next client. He motioned for her to sit on the stool and took her information. He worked his formula. He then selected a wand. "Willow wood with a pixy wing core."

Freya took her wand and looked at the vegetable, eager to perform magic.

"ditba rouge ." She swished her wand.

POOF! The squash disappeared in a puff of smoke. Everyone stepped back in shock.

"Miss Freya, your pronunciation was incorrect." He placed another squash on the counter. "Try it again, but it is pronounced; detba rouge. It is a short e not an i."

She tried it and was able to succeed on the next attempt.

"Excellent," said Kasfas with joy. "Now, young man, your turn."

He measured Kalthazar and ran his formula. He consulted his paper and scratched at the formula again.

"Well, young fellow, I don't have a wand best matched for you yet. I do have a couple in the box curing. Perhaps let us try this one. It is a red oak with hippogriff feather.

Kalthazar took the wand and looked at the squash.

"Would you repeat the spell for me, please?"

"Detba rouge."

"Detba rouge," he repeated. He cast the spell. With a single sideways motion of his wand and flicked it.

The squash shriveled and turned black.

"HMMM," Kasfas mused. "Let us try one of these." He pulled a black box from under the counter and opened it barely enough to slip his hand inside. He fumbled around a moment and then pulled out a wand.

"Ah. I'm really not sure of this one. I haven't had it curing but one day. Instructions call for three days to a week. But they are kind of iffy on that point." He held the wand out for Kalthazar. "hickory with powdered dragon scale core." He handed it to him and produced another squash from under the counter.

Gerak successfully changed the new squash red with his wand.

"Well, Kasfas, it appears that wands are as picky about their wizards as staffs are," Zarlaam announced.

"Yes, they are. Now Miss Arleta," he said, rubbing his hands together. "Have you decided about the offer?"

"Could you make me a wand from some of Dallietano's mane hairs?"

"Who is Dallietano?"

"Oh, sorry. He is the unicorn that these hairs came from."

"You are an interesting young lady. You perform magic the first try with excellent discipline and know a unicorn by name. I gather you have befriended him?"

"Well, he lets me pet him, and he eats from my hand. Master Zarlaam has seen him."

Kasfas unconsciously looked to Zarlaam and got a nod for confirmation.

"Your formula doesn't include unicorn hair. I will attempt to make you a wand from it. But I cannot promise that you will be able to use it as effectively as this one."

She removed the necklace and handed it to him.

"What is this locket on it for other than a ward of protection?"

"I would like it back, please. A dear departed friend gave it to me."

Kasfas removed the locket from the braided hair necklace, and she pocketed it. He put the unicorn hair cord on a shelf. "Now, Miss Freya, your wand is fifteen, and Mister Kalthazar yours is twenty.

They started digging in their pouches for the payment.

"Mister Kasfas," Bershome spoke. Would you fit me for one?"

He took to the stool, and when done Kasfas, looked at him discontented.

"I don't have one for you, lad. It calls for a wood and core blend I do not have, but now I know exactly what you need."

Crestfallen, Bershome looked at the others as they prepared to pay for them. He slipped his hand up and down his staff.

"Wands look like they would be much more..."

"Convenient?"

"Yes, sir."

"A little bit easier to use as well. I'll have more in a week or so. How about your wand, sir?" he looked at Zarlaam.

The master wizard looked at it in deep thought.

"Bria Saorga," he said, and the tip began to glow and emitted a light that was good for seeing at night. "Well, it has its potential. I can see its better aspects. But I like the feel of my staff in my hand. I'm used to it."

Suddenly the wand levitated, and he held out his and with fingers spread apart. It spun end over end slowly and disappeared.

"But I would be making a hypocrite of myself in front of my apprentices if I refused to try it. What do I owe you for it, sir?"

"Twenty, sir."

Zarlaam pulled a parchment from inside his robe. "We need to gather some supplies as well, my friend."

Kasfas took the parchment and examined the list.

"Bat wings, dried snails, toad eyes, tangle weed, Wolfsbane, bitter weed, monk's hood. My, my, this list does go on and on."

"We have many potions to learn this winter."

"I don't have everything here, but my supplier, Giled Haru, will be coming next week. He usually has a very good stock. I would be willing to deliver them then."

Zarlaam leaned close and whispered. "And take opportunity to peddle more wands to the rest of my apprentices?"

"I can only hope, Master." Kasfas was mentally counting the coins the visit would put into his pockets.

"Well, I will prepare my apprentices for you so that they may try to have the funds available. You will be most likely to sell one to every apprentice. You will be taking their staffs in trade to defray the expense because you could reuse them? But I must insist on a better price for them all. Say a quarter less?"

Kasfas's smile dwindled slightly at his suggestion. "It takes over a week to make a single wand, Master."

"We cannot compromise the quality for volume, my friend. We have a couple months before the supplies get scarce."

Kasfas cocked his head slightly and nodded. "I take my wand-making more serious than my staff-making, Master."

Zarlaam smiled fatherly. "I wonder if your teacher had anything to do with your dedication to quality and performance?"

"Yes, he did, the old goat," Kasfas picked at him with a smile of affection.

"Ladies and gentlemen, we shall put away our wands; less someone accidentally sustains an injury. We will get better acquainted with them during our studies. Bershome, help our friend gather the supplies he has and make note of what we still need."

"Yes, Master Zarlaam."

"Mister Kasfas," Kalthazar spoke after all the supplies were gathered, "I could gather the information from all the students for you, and you would know what wands to make in advance."

"Excellent idea." The old man's eyes brightened.

"Could you spare five pounds of parchment and two bottles of ink and six quills for the service?"

"Quite a businessman, aren't you. But you have a deal. I'll write you the instructions on the information I need for each person."

They were headed back to the castle before too long.

"Gerak, the book, please? Let us review more on creatures."

They settled into a study mode as each read about different enchanted creatures, and they discussed them. This made the ride home pass more quickly. As they had hoped, the remainder of the students arrived.

CHAPTER TWELVE

Eager to get the information on the other students, Gerak went straight to the dorm with his supplies and put them in his wardrobe. He took his instruction sheet, parchment, quill, and ink bottle. He found a group of boys watching one boy making a star cluster appear in the middle of the dorm.

"Gentlemen, I am Gerak Kalthazar. Master Zarlaam's supplier, Mister Kasfas, is making wands instead of staffs. I am assigned to take measurements for any person that would be interested in getting one."

"What is a wand?" the youngest lad asked.

"This." Gerak pulled out his wand and showed it to them. "They are more powerful than a staff."

"Amazing!" One lad reached for the wand. Gerak pulled it back close to his chest.

"You have to be measured for your specific wand."

"Show us how it works."

"It works just like your staff does. I would demonstrate it, but I don't know enough magic yet."

"How much is the old buzzard going to charge for them?"

"I don't know. Mine cost me twenty crowns."

"That is outrageous!"

"All I can say about it is he is the one that makes wands and sets his prices. I'm just taking the information he needs. Master Zarlaam has persuaded him to take your staff's as partial payment on them."

"I'll wager some of that coin goes in your pocket," one accused.

"None, whatsoever. He gave me writing parchment and ink for gathering information for him."

"Well, measure me up and let's see what he makes for me," Trejann said.

Everyone then proceeded to consent to the measuring. Gerak was at it until supper time was announced.

CHAPTER THIRTEEN

After breakfast the next morning, everyone went to the dormitory and fetched their study supplies. In the Hall of Knowledge, Zarlaam waited in front patiently as they all found seats to their liking. He noticed Gerak move a younger boy so that he could sit near Arleta.

"I see everyone is eager to begin learning. Please recite the rules of magic." He thumped his staff on the floor, and two large banners unrolled from the ceiling and hung behind him. "Everyone in unison: Rule number one."

Then everyone read the rules aloud together.

"Now, for the new apprentices, I will explain more rules concerning conduct here about Lord Paxtare estate. Please ask questions if they are not clear to you." Zarlaam explained all the rules covering where they could and could not practice magic and what to do if visitors were about. They weren't allowed to pull magical tricks on the castle staff. In the end, punishment would be dished out for misbehaver.

Once all the rules were covered and questions answered, Zarlaam moved on to the next topic of the day. "Last spring before your departure, I asked all of you to be on the lookout for new spells and potions during your summer break. In due course today, you will each have the opportunity to present them to me. I will decide if it is appropriate to share with our companions. In the meantime, you will be making a potion."

Zarlaam smiled at the excited looks on everyone's face. "Put away all materials except parchment and quills. Here on the slate board is your first potion. It is a medicine for curing croup and coughing. The weather will be changing soon to cold and dampness in which nature brings sickness. Martello and Bershome will be instructing you while I receive your new findings in turn. Young Mister Willion, if you would be so kind as to follow me to my study, I will see your findings first. Bershome, you and Martello, you have the class."

Zarlaam left the classroom, followed by the apprentice.

Bershome picked up a couple of boxes with jars of ingredients as Martello stood and stepped forward. "We have one cauldron per pair of apprentices. Most of you are teamed up already. Miss Freya, I'll assist you myself."

Snickers slipped out from a couple of younger apprentices.

He turned the slate board so the class could see it. "Here are the ingredients list and procedures. Write down the ingredients and instructions in your book. Once everyone is done, we will begin the process of making the potion. This way, everyone will have reviewed it once through before mixing ingredients. Bershome is putting boxes on each table with your needed ingredients. The jars and pouches are marked with their contents. Measure all ingredients first to the precise amounts specified. Follow the directions you have for mixing and simmering the potion."

During the procedures, Bershome noticed Arleta showed Gerak how not to contaminate the different ingredients when measuring before mixing. He concluded her time with Miss Winters had provided her with valuable knowledge. He also felt a touch of resentment of her and Gerak being paired together. It took hours for them to mix the potions. Several batches had to be thrown out because Martello was dissatisfied with them for poor mixing procedures, and the apprentices had to start over.

During the morning, several apprentices rotated out to see Master Zarlaam. They would carry out a pouch or folded up parchments with them. Some returned with large grins of satisfaction. Others returned disappointed. Zarlaam joined the class at lunchtime.

"Ladies and Gentlemen," Zarlaam said, "Before we take lunch, I have an announcement to make. Several of your classmates have brought us a few new spells; six in all, and five new potions."

Clap, clap, clap. He waited for the round of applause.

"Yes, I thank all of you for your efforts. Some of the discoveries this summer were inappropriate or too dangerous and will not be added to our books. We have a prize for the best spell discovered. It is an enchanted night lamp. It goes to Mister Willems for his spell on making water cold and even freezing it. That will be a valuable spell in the heat of summer when a cool drink of water will be most refreshing."

Everyone applauded as the lad stepped up and claimed his prize.

"Just tap it three times for it to glow. Twice and it stops."

"This prize of a small silver encased hourglass goes to Miss Arleta Harsumg for giving us the five new potions."

Arleta sat in shock a moment as everyone applauded. She then remembered the books she had given Zarlaam to look over.

"Also, Mister Kasfas, our principal supplier, has a long lost magical tool revived. He is now making wands. They are much more convenient than staffs. He will be visiting us in a couple of months, and each of you will have the opportunity to purchase a wand. He has agreed to take in exchange your staffs for those of you who possess them. Unfortunately, it will not be an outright exchange, but it will keep the cost down somewhat. Personally, I have chosen to keep both. I do prefer my staff. It is, after all, a handy walking stick."

"Anyone who hasn't seen Mister Kalthazar for him to gather your information for our wand maker may do so sometime any evening. He has agreed to help Mister Kasfas. He will collect the necessary information to determine the type of wand you will need."

"After lunch, we will be separating into two groups. The gentlemen will be staying in the dining hall with Bershome for etiquette training, and the ladies will go up to the dormitory for some training of their own."

"Mister Martello. How do we stand on our potions today?"

"Several were successful the first go. The others are slow because they had to start over. "

"May we neglect them to take lunch?"

"Yes, sir, All are completely mixed and need simmering."

"Then let us go dine." They all left the classroom and went to lunch.

CHAPTER FOURTEEN

All the students remained in the great hall after lunch. Bernary, the head of staff, came walking into the dining hall, followed by an aged well-dressed lady as the servants removed the dishes at the end of lunch.

"Ladies, please follow Lady Esmeralda upstairs to the dormitory for training. Gentlemen, all of you mongrels will gather around here at this table. Divide yourselves evenly on each side of the table."

He stood at the end of the table with a stern expression as they shuffled about for a seat. The older boys were the farthest away from him and had forced the younger ones to take seats close to their instructor. Bershome and Martello did not sit down on the benches. Gerak realized it and stood from his seat.

Bernary stared at each and every boy as he waited for the ladies to leave and the servants to clear out the remains of lunch. Eventually, all the boys caught on to the older boys actions and stood behind the benches.

"Well, it looks like you did not forget everything while you were away for a few months. I could not believe what uncivilized heathens you have become. Every one of you were here last year but one. Only that person has any form of an excuse for misbehavior. Mister Kalthazar, today is your last free day of sins without penalty." A very brief smile flashed across Bernary's face as he looked at Gerak, and it turned into a scowl instantly as he looked about the boys.

"I saw people using their utensils incorrectly, handling food with their fingers, slopping juice from your glasses on the table and yourselves. Someone," he looked sternly at a twelve-year-old, "dropped food under the table. But worse of all, I saw the most horrid habit of people speaking with their mouths full of food. You are here at the grace of Lord Paxtare, and I will not tolerate you misbehaving and embarrassing him in the presence of his visiting dignitaries. His Lordship expects me to ensure that there are no problems in his home and especially during his meals. I will have proper conduct and manners from you mongrels."

He scowled at each boy individually until they looked down in shame. Bershome and Martello winked at him. Bernary raised one eyebrow and continued.

"Remember, nothing goes on in this castle that I do not become aware of. First of all, there will be no sneaking of food from the dining hall or the kitchen. I will not have roaches and rats in this castle. Anyone breaking that rule will be on kitchen duty for a week. Anyone brought to my attention by my Lord for misconduct will be dealt with by either Master Zarlaam or myself in his absence. I believe a few of you remember some of the punishments used last year?"

The servants had returned with fresh dishes for the boys to use in their lessons. They stood a few feet past Bershome as they waited on Bernary's cue.

"Now, be seated quietly."

Scrape.

"What was that? It is rude to scrape the bench on the floor and interrupt his Lordship's conversation with his guest. Get off those benches!"

Scrap, scrap.

"I have all afternoon allocated to teach you mongrels manners. Until you can be seated without noise, you will repeat your lesson. Be seated."

It took another try before they accomplished the desired standard.

"Finally! If I hear a single scraping during a meal, you will all be repeating this lesson. And it will be on your time, come a Saturday or a Sunday."

Bernary proceeded to run through all his rules of table etiquette and manners of conduct before he declared his class at an end.

"Mister Bershome. If you will, lead them upstairs to the dormitory for the next session, please."

Bershome led the boys out of the dining hall and upstairs. They encountered the ladies filing down the stairs. "Good afternoon, ladies," he spoke. They all smiled and waved at one another as they passed. Bershome could not resist giving Arleta a wink. Her smile widened when he did.

He looked back and noticed Gerak was behind him and must have interpreted her smile as being directed at him and smiled back. Bershome didn't smile as he unlocked the door once they arrived at the dorm.

"In you go, gentlemen. Stay in a single file against the wall center on the hearth."

Mister Bernary came walking into the dormitory with a very hostile face. "Listen to me, you mongrels, I will not tolerate you trying to turn Lord Paxtare's home into a pigsty." He proceeded to run down the rules written on parchment and attached to the inside of every wardrobe on the door.

"Every morning, when you rise, the first thing you should do is make your beds up nice and tidy as you will be instructed here today." Bernary pointed his thumb over his shoulder at the bed behind him without turning around. "That bed is a disgusting shamble and is not acceptable."

Bershome saw Gerak's face turn beet red. He looked at the bed where he had pulled the sheets and blanket over it. The pillow lay on top.

"I will demonstrate the correct way to make a bed."

With Bershome's assistance, they stripped the bed down and proceeded to make it according to Mister Bernary's specifications. Afterward, he had everyone making up their beds. He inspected every bunk in the dorm. Only two of the older boys passed the first inspection. Martello and Bershome sat chatting while most everyone else had their bunk stripped down and remade.

CHAPTER FIFTEEN

Zarlaam strolled toward the dining hall for breakfast the next morning when he encountered Gerak standing in an archway near the dining hall.

"Good morning, Master Zarlaam."

"Good morning, Gerak. Is there something I can do for you?"

"Well, I'm not sure. I have gotten all the information Mr. Kasfas is needing. But I uh..."

"You aren't sure how to get it to him?"

"Well, yes, sir," he said as he looked down at the floor.

"I have an idea. I'm sending a man tomorrow to fetch the remainder of the supplies I ordered. You can send your papers with him."

Gerak looked up with a smile. "Thank you, sir. Oh, are there any of the staff and servants that you think would want to be measured for wands?"

Zarlaam paused a moment and looked at the lad.

"I'll ask them. If there are any, I'll let you know."

"Thank you, sir. What about villagers? Do you think they would be interested?"

"I admire your dedication to your task, young man. You have earned your fee already. I think it wiser you concentrate on your studies while we let Mister Kasfas work on his capital pursuits."

"Thank you again, sir," Gerak said and walked away.

Zarlaam watched the lad as he went into the dining hall. Zarlaam took note of his disappointment. Gerak confused him. His habit of reading a person's open thoughts did not cause him any guilt. He could judge a person's character by catching unprotected thoughts. He had detected a desire in the lad's mind to know all the magic users in the village and estate. But not the reason. *Is he stronger than I detected? Is he that capable of concealing his thought already?* He followed the lad into the dining hall.

That evening, apprentices sat about the man hall studying or talking. Some played board games.

Bershome moved his queen and set her down with and rap of finality. "Check and mate in two moves, Ole Chum." He grinned at Martello.

"My rook will take your queen."

"You can't move it. It blocks my bishop from mate on your king. You have one free space place to put your king. I'll take your rook and have checkmate."

Martello sighed and laid his king down. "Good game. You must have been practicing this summer to beat me so quickly."

"Bershome," Arleta spoke up from across the table, "Would you mind teaching me the game?"

"It would be a pleasure, and I'll have you winning against Martello by the end of the year. Perhaps the first lesson tomorrow night?"

She nodded.

"That sounds like he thinks poorly of your skills," Freya teased Martello.

"I started teaching Martello when he first arrived, and now he is formidable. I've been playing since I was six. With us, the winner often depends which of us has the first move."

"I intend to learn enough to beat you, sir," Arleta said.

Bershome chuckled as he put the pieces in the box. "That is a day I'm looking forward to."

Arleta smiled at him. "I think I have copied enough for my book tonight. Good night. Ready, Freya?"

Freya closed her book and looked at Martello. "Yes. Care to walk us up?"

"It will be my pleasure." He rose and left with the ladies.

Bershome collected the board and box to put on the shelf as he looked about the hall. Two young apprentices were busy writing away. He stepped over to see and noticed they were copying from their spellbooks.

"Making a copy of your books, lads?"

One looked up at him. "Yes, Gerak is giving us a pence per page."

"Is he now?"

"Yes."

"Does he provide the parchment paper and ink?"

"No sir,"

"I'll have a word with him. You will finish this page and do no more for him. He needs to be writing his own book like you did. Understand?"

"Yes, sir." They lowered their heads.

"No harm done on your part, lads. Just no more." He headed up and found Gerak on his bunk reading a book. Bershome looked at the cover as Gerak stole a glance at him over the top of the book.

"Words of the Brotherhood. That is good reading, Gerak."

"I thought it would be interesting. It's full of dribble about bleeding hearts and giving away what you have to poor saps that don't deserve it."

Bershome lowered himself onto the foot of Gerak's bunk. "It is about loving and helping one's fellow man. It's is about dealing fairly with all and teaches principles of being a good person and living a proper life. By all means, do finish reading it."

Gerak looked at him a moment as if he was analyzing the statement.

"The real reason I came to talk to you is that you need to write your own book of spells and potions. There is no high road to learning. You must do the work yourself. You will learn it better. Many scrolls are written in ancient languages that you need to learn. Also, if you encounter something you don't understand on a page, you can ask someone and put in your own notes for years later, lest you forget. The lads are finishing the pages they are on. You are forbidden to have apprentices to do it for you." He stood to leave and stopped. "Also, a pence per page is taking advantage of them. Give them a crown apiece for what they have done, and thank them for all their efforts."

"That is a bit much for simply copying down spells." Gerak's tone bit at him.

"Call it the price of learning, and do as I say." Bershome smiled at Gerak's scowl.

He slammed the book closed. "That may be a paltry price for you to pay, but not so for me."

"Why do you say that?"

"You have the entirety of your grandfather's estate to draw from."

"Actually, I do not. I live here with the apprentices for a reason. I have fewer funds than you have for the year. Grandfather believes I should understand the value of a coin and the work people put into earning their living. I work hard every summer like a common laborer while my room and board are calculated as part of my wages." Bershome stepped close and held out a hand, palm up. I have calluses just as you do. I'm not a pampered nobleman's grandson." He winked at him and left for his bunk.

CHAPTER SIXTEEN

One afternoon, Gerak wasn't ready to go to the dorm yet. He casually strolled through the manor out of general curiosity looking things over. He encountered a couple of servants going about their evening responsibilities, and a student passed him headed for the dormitory. He smiled and nodded but did not stop. When he arrived in the main hall, he saw he had that part of the manor to himself. He could not detect any noise from the kitchen as he stepped into the entrance hall. He stood and looked at the haunting mirror. He studied everything in it from the furniture about the walls behind him to the fading sunlight reflecting through the window behind him. The haunted mirror curved from the middle and backward as he looked along its width to the outer edge. This made the mirror reflect absolutely every bit of the room. He noticed that he could see two other mirrors in it. One was on the wall adjacent to the mirror. But the other one was in the next room. He went to it and examined it. This mirror appeared to be normal, but he noticed he could see the haunted mirror and another at the far end of the main hallway. This mirror was curved as well. In it he could see a glass door cabinet in the main dining hall. From the reflection of the cabinet, he could see the kitchen door. Through the kitchen door he could see another mirror. He went back to the haunted mirror.

The kitchen mirror was tiny in the haunted mirror as seen through the other mirrors. But he could see the kitchen sink window through the reflections. He wondered what more he could see if doors were opened at the right time.

Gerak stepped up on the bench in front of the mirror. He grasped the devil mask. It lifted free of the wooden peg it hung on. He sat on the bench and examined it. It was carved from wood. Leather straps on the back formed a web to hold it on the head. He found strange carvings all over the inside of the mask. He had seen similar carvings on staffs.

He put the mask over his face and tied the strings behind his head to hold it in place. He was surprised at how much he could see when wearing the mask. He leaned back against the mirror as he looked up at the ceiling and fell backward off the bench. He jumped to his feet and looked about. He stood in the entry hall, but behind the bench he had been sitting on. Yet the bench sat against the mirror. He stepped over the bench into the hall and faced the mirror. He did not see his reflection.

So, that is your secret.

He stepped up to the bench and reached out to touch the mirror. His hand went beyond the glass. He wondered if the reflection was true.

A pot rattled in the kitchen. He wondered if other people could see him. He headed into the kitchen. The door was propped open with a stool to allow more air in to cool the room. He poked his head in and saw a cook putting wood into the fire. The man rose and walked over to the table. He hummed softly to himself as he worked and returned, kneading a large batch of dough.

Gerak leaned across the table and lowered his head so that he knew he was in the old man's line of vision. The man suddenly stopped moving. He glanced around the room. When he saw he was alone, he shrugged and resumed working.

Gerak walked around the table and stood close to him. "Can you hear me?" he whispered.

"Do what?" The cook looked in Gerak's direction, blinked, and searched the room. The man reached over and grasped a large knife from a group lying on the counter.

Gerak slipped out of the kitchen back to the hall. He stood looking in the mirror as he removed the mask and saw his reflection reappear.

A pot rattled in the kitchen. Gerak quickly put the devil mask back to its place and returned to the dorm, taking his time to avoid attracting attention. He had a lot to consider.

CHAPTER SEVENTEEN

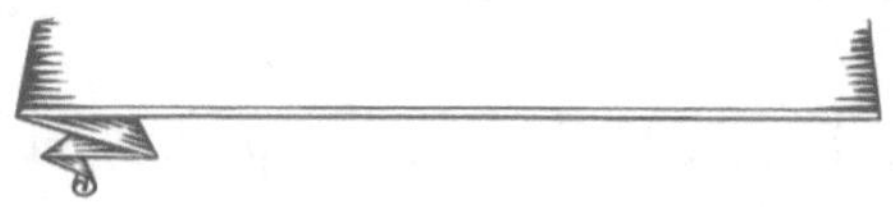

A few months later, the apprentices headed to lunch, and a few noticed Master Zarlaam and his lordship had visitors. Mr. Kasfas was seated beside the master at the head table. The buzz of whispered conversation among the apprentices reflected their excitement. All knew he had most likely completed his making of wands for them. All lingered at the table in anticipation of when the master would make his announcement.

Once Bershome was finished eating, he turned sideways on his seat and gave his master a wink. The man made a slight gesture with his fingers to beckon him. He stood and strolled over to the head table. He gave a nod to their visitor. "Mr. Kasfas, your presence has caused quite a stir among the younger ones." He shook the man's offered hand after checking what might be hidden in it.

"Bershome, Mr. Kasfas has brought the remainder of our supplies. Would you have them unloaded and take an inventory?"

"I'll take the entire rabble with me to give peace in here, Master."

"Excellent idea, sir." The man nodded.

Bershome went to the table and leaned over to speak softly. "We all need to leave quietly and help unload our supplies Mr. Kasfas had delivered. Also, you need to go fetch your purses."

"Did he bring our wands?" one whispered.

"We will find out when he joins us. Now, out you go quietly, please."

He repeated himself to the next portion of apprentices down the table and followed them out. A wagon was parked near the hedge access way to the Hall of Knowledge.

"Everyone grab a bundle, box, or whatever is in the wagon and carry it inside. Do not open anything up, less you spill the contents." The last thing on the wagon was a black box with a hasp and lock on it. He put two lads to handling it and placed it on the master's desk. Once inside, they all started jabbering about the new wands and speculating what type of wood they were made of.

"Our lessen will resume as of before lunch," Bershome announced and received collective groans of protest. The master arrived to his rescue, followed by his companion. "Bershome, This afternoon we will forgo our scheduled lesson and allow Mr. Kasfas to conduct his business." Everyone erupted with cheers and clapping. He waved his hand quieting them down. "Yes, yes, we are all excited. Before we begin," He looked about with a squint-eyed stare across the room. "We will have no silly spell casting inside the hall. Once everyone has their wand, we will go out to the stone garden and get acquainted with them. Mr. Kasfas will call you by name, and you will transact your business to return to your seats and act like civilized heathens."

Bershome sat in the back with the master and the already holders of wands to watch the rest get their new toy.

Bershome was the last name he called out. "Your wand was particularly hard to make, my Lord. It is Olneya wood. That desert iron wood is very hard to craft with, and it has hippogriff feathers for a core. It promises to be quite powerful. If it accepts you."

Bershome smiled at him and leaned close to whisper, "You wouldn't do that to me, now would you, sir?"

The man looked at him with a dropped jaw, and Bershome laughed.

That afternoon they enjoyed the spell casting and were surprised at the greater strength the wands had compared to their old staffs.

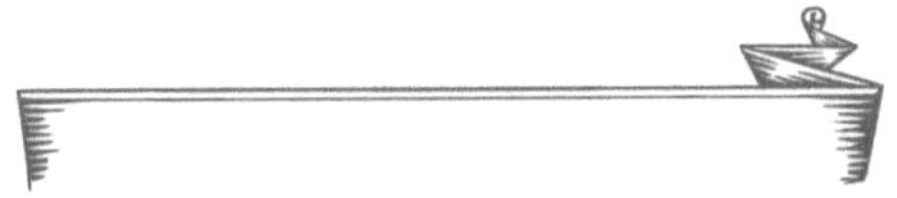

CHAPTER EIGHTEEN

Most of the apprentices were sitting about the great hall in little groups, studying their lessons, or socializing. Martello, Freya, and Janara were engrossed in the chess game between Bershome and Arleta.

Bershome moved his queen. "Check and mate in two or three moves, depending on your choice of moves."

Arleta looked at him and then studied the board. "No. I can block it with my bishop."

"Illegal move. He is blocking my rook from checkmate."

"Well, I can block with my queen or move my king."

"Moving your queen gives you one extra move. Then I take your bishop and have you in checkmate."

Arleta laid her king over on the board. "You win again, sir."

"Despair not, sweet lady. You are getting better. This game lasted twice as long as the last one."

"I'll beat you yet, sir." She wagged an index finger at him.

"I'm looking forward to the day, madam."

"My turn, sir," Janara announced.

Arleta forfeited her spot at the table, so Janara would be in the center of the group.

Jartus ran into the hall. He rushed over to Trejann and leaned across the table. All the apprentices watched as he spoke.

Bershome paused, placing his pieces on the board to see what had Jartus so excited.

"Guess what."

"You can turn your hair green?"

"No, silly. What is worth five crowns apiece?"

Trejann stood, showing wide-eyes at the question. "Where?"

"Snipe Grove, of course. Same place as four years ago. Mister Gerkmere, the herd master, just told me he spotted three last evening."

"But if we can catch four, we can pay Mrs. Jackson to make them into a stole and get over fifty crowns." The lads grinned at each other for a moment.

"Catch what," Gerak asked

They looked at him and spoke simultaneously. "Snipes."

Bershome and Janara turned their heads away to look at Martello. She slapped her hand over her mouth as he pressed his lips together hard and fought to restrain a snicker.

Freya and Arleta cocked their heads, and they looked at Bershome for an explanation. He put a finger to his mouth to keep them quiet. "Listen."

"What is a snipe?" Gerak asked.

Jartus sat down across from Gerak and stared at him.

"You have never heard of snipes?"

"No." He looked back and forth between Trejann and Jartus.

Janara explained. "It is a little critter about the size of a grown rabbit. They are brown when young but turn snow-white as they get older. Noble ladies pay premium prices for things made of their fur because it is so soft."

Bershome stared with furrowed eyebrows at Arleta and shook his head when she gasped.

Trejann said, "They are more skittish than a rabbit, slow as the dickens, and easy to catch. When you scare them, they pass out like an opossum. Besides, you have your wand and can stun them. You just grab them by the back of their neck and stuff them in a bag."

"Hey," Jartus slapped the table. "Tomorrow is Friday. We can go hunting tomorrow night."

"Yeah, but two people aren't enough. Hey, Chal, wanna join us for a snipe hunt?"

Chal shrugged, "Naw, I gotta study my math."

"Can I go?" Bodle asked.

"Uh, sorry, fellow. Master Zarlaam says you must be twelve or older to go. How about you, Gerak?"

"Ah, man," the lad responded with drooped shoulders.

"I will for a cut in the money. But why tomorrow night?" He smiled.

Bershome pressed his fist against his mouth. Janara scrunched her eyes shut, but she stuck her tongue out a tiny bit between her lips. It was obvious she was biting it. He watched Freya and Arleta exchange knowing looks and nod.

"Snipes don't come out 'til dark. It is best to hunt under a full moon because their fur practically glows. But we need to leave early, so we will be set in place come time to start the hunt after sundown. Trejann and I'll be the beaters, and you can catch them."

"What is a beater?"

"The snipes are in a grove of oaks. We will put you in place on the north side, and we start beating the bushes and making noise to drive them to you."

"Why the north side?"

"The prevailing winds are from the north right now. We have to take the horses to the south side because snipes hate the smell of horses. They won't smell them, and our beating the bushes will help."

"You can call them to you. Do this." Trejann worked his jaw up and down, causing his tongue to slap against the roof of his mouth to make a smacking sound.

Gerak tried it.

"Wet your tongue."

Gerak repeated the sound. "You got it, buddy. Practice it, though." Trejann clapped Gerak on the shoulder.

"Count me in." Gerak held out his hand, and both lads shook it to seal their agreement. "Tomorrow night, then?" He closed his book and headed for the dormitory as he practiced smacking his tongue.

"Tomorrow night," Jartus said.

After Gerak left the hall, Arleta asked. "What is so funny about snipe hunting, you guys?"

Bershome shook his head, chuckling, as he set his pieces on the board. Janara snickered. Arleta grabbed her by the throat. "Tell me now."

"Okay." Janara whispered. "First of all, there is no such animal. Second, after they drop Gerak off north of the grove, they come riding back with his horse, and he has to walk home in the dark."

"Awh, that's mean," Freya said.

"Not really," Bershome stated. "It is harmless fun. And it's almost a rite of passage for guys around here. Even Janara and Wanlae went snipe hunting. We got Trejann, the same year with them."

The girl nodded when Arleta looked at her.

"Unless it starts raining like when you took me," Martello stated.

"I couldn't predict the weather. I did go fetch you, my friend."

"I was soaking wet and practically home by then."

"Back when I was twelve," Bershome said, "Marlon and Legser took me a good day's ride south. It took me all night and half the next day to get home. Fortunately, about mid-morning, a carriage of ladies came passing by. Marlon's and Legser's mothers and girlfriends were coming for a visit and found me. They dressed those guys up and down royally for taking me so far out. Since then, we named a particular spot of trees Snipe Grove. It is on the main road north and about a three-hour walk away."

"Gerak is not going to like it, Bershome." Janara warned.

"He will have to accept it as a joke and live with it."

"Trejann, Jartus." Bershome beckoned them with a wave.

The lads came over grinning but lost them under Bershome's stern stare. "Are you two prepared for the consequences?"

"He ain't gonna do nothin."

"Okay. Whatever happens, it's on the two of you."

The next day, Gerak could be heard testing clicking his tongue, and everyone that knew would snicker. After supper, the lads left for the hunt. As expected, the two returned without Gerak.

Four hours later, the apprentices were still gathered in their usual spots when the front door slammed with a loud bang. Bershome turned and sat straddle of the bench to watch Gerak come stomping into the hall. Bershome raised his arm and held out his hand. "Stop, Gerak." The boy knocked it down and kept going. Bershome leaped to his feet and followed him.

Gerak reached across the table, grabbed Jartus's tunic, and was about to punch him when Bershome grabbed his free arm.

Gerak stared at Jartus and shoved him away. He glared at Bershome.

"Have a seat, Gerak."

He jerked his arm free and stood unmoving as he stared at Bershome.

"Listen to me before you say or do anything. Snipe hunting is a joke. Everyone here who has been sniping hunting, stand up," he called out.

All the lads but Edrick stood. Wanlae and Janara stood also.

"See? You aren't the only one that was taken in by the joke. I went hunting too, but I had to walk all night to get home. Martello there," He pointed over his shoulder. "got caught in the rain, and I had to go fetch him. It is a rite of passage around here. In a year or two, you'll get a chance to take someone new."

"It ain't funny." Gerak stared at Trejann and Jartus.

"Did anyone in Galley's Cove send you looking for scales to weigh anchor or a bucket to catch wind spill from the sails? How about a box of fish hook eyes?"

Gerak looked at him a moment and blinked at Bershome's knowledge of those jokes. Then his face softened. "The Captain sent me looking for a fish hook straightener." His voice dropped to a whisper.

"How many other fishermen did you ask before you figured it out you were looking for something that didn't exist?"

"Most all the boats in the harbor," he almost whispered.

"It was a rite of passage to becoming a fisherman. You just went through ours."

"Hump," Gerak grunted.

"You can plot a payback on them. But," he raised his hand and held up a warning index finger. "you cannot harm them or damage anything."

Gerak grinned.

"But be careful. Chal, tell Gerak what happened when you filled Janara's wardrobe with frogs?"

"The maid opened it, and they escaped. She ran out screaming in horror. Janara and I spent two days catching them all, and I spent a week in the kitchen, working. Lord Paxtare had a party that weekend, and I thought Mister Bernary tried to work me to death scrubbing pots and dishes. He does not allow usage of wands."

Everyone laughed. Even Gerak.

"Have some juice, Gerak. You must be thirsty from your trek home." Bershome slapped him on the back and then pointed at Trejann and Jartus. "You two have horses to unsaddle."

The lads stood and offered Gerak their hands. "No harm done. Eh, Gerak?"

He shook each one's and sat down at the table.

Three days later, Bershome choked on his morning eggs as the dining hall erupted in laughter. Trejann entered, sporting a head of hair colored a ridiculous shade of pale blue. Jartus' hair practically glowed a bright green. They took it in stride and laughed along with the crowd. They smacked Gerak on the back in congratulation. "Good one, G."

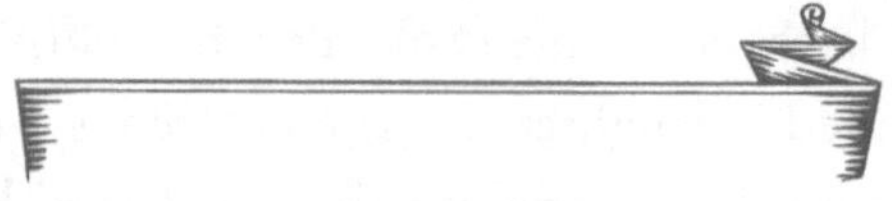

CHAPTER NINETEEN

Bershome was helping everyone work a new spell in the Hall of Knowledge when the door opened, and Afreck stepped in.

"Bershome, sir, his Lordship needs you."

"Keep working your spells. Trejann, Janara, I need you to help them while I'm away. Bershome followed Afreck as he headed to the castle at a brisk pace without a word. Bershome saw a group of soldiers gathering near the stables with their horses. Afreck led the way straight to Grandfather's office. A ragged-looking young man dressed in common farmer's clothing sat across from Grandfather.

"Bershome," Grandfather said, "This is Lenaredal from Kittwick Village. Raiders hit them this morning and took livestock and three girls. I want you to hunt them down and return the girls to their families."

"Were there fatalities, sir?"

"Two. Most of the villagers were in the fields. The Captain is getting the men ready with a couple of days rations for them. I'll send a cook and supply wagon to follow you within the hour. Make haste, son. But be careful."

"Afreck, have my horse saddled while I get my armor and battle kit."

"Already being done, sir."

"This lad needs a fresh mount as well."

"It is being saddled, also, sir."

Bershome hurried to his private bedroom in the family wing. He was half undressed by the time he got there. He pulled out his undershirt and chainmail armor. He tucked his wand in the special pocket in his vest. He changed into knee-high thick leather boots and grabbed a cape. Once he was dressed, he grabbed his weapon roll consisting of a long sword, a pair of horseman's axes, a quiver, and a bow. He grabbed his shield and helmet. He rushed back to the office.

"Lenaredal, which way did they head out from your village?"

"They left by the north road."

"How long after they left did you ride out?"

"They were still in sight when father sent me."

Bershome scratched the side of his head. "They will have five-hour head start by the time we get to your village."

"Father sent Cigl to shadow them from a safe distance."

Lord Paxtare stepped around his desk and held out his hand to Bershome. "Take care, son."

Bershome took his hand and pulled him into a hug. "We have the best soldiers short of the king's army, Grandfather. I'll be back in a few days. After they run the livestock a couple hours, they will be forced to slow down. We may find them by nightfall."

"Take our banner. I want all to know we take care of our own," Grandfather ordered.

Afreck took the banner from its stand in the corner and headed outside.

"Let's ride." Bershome nodded at the lad.

"May the gods be with you, son."

"I'll pray in the saddle, Grandfather."

Bershome hurried out to where a man held his horse's reins as it stood at the head of a double column of twenty men holding their spears in their stirrups and pointing at the sky. He quickly stashed his weapons and shield in their harness behind the saddle

"Where is this lad's fresh mount?"

"Here, sir," Mr. Henson called out as he came forward with a horse in tow.

Bershome mounted Rhubarb and faced the lad. "Lenaredal, you ride just behind me less I make a wrong turn." He raised his voice to address the soldiers. "Men, we must rely upon speed today. If your horse goes lame, drop to the wayside, and let everyone pass. His Lordship is sending a supply wagon behind us. We will start at a canter to warm the horses up and gallop once we are on the road. Mr. Henson, send a dozen remounts and four guardsmen with the wagon in case this pursuit goes on into tomorrow."

"Aye, sir."

Bershome started Rhubarb at a canter as the apprentices came from the classroom to head for lunch. He saw wide-eyed faces as he passed them by. He made a slight head bow to them and turned his head forward.

"Where are they going?" he heard one person ask. Bershome did not make or hear a reply.

Many villagers stopped and bowed as Bershome and his men galloped past. Some shouted blessing at them. They knew something was up for Bershome to be in armor leading a force of soldiers. From there, the men rode at a good gallop eastward. A few miles later, he took the road north. Any travelers that spotted them coming gave up the road for the column of soldiers. After about three hours of hard riding, they reached the village. Bershome saw that a couple of the thatched houses the raiders set afire had burned to the ground and were a heap of smoldering logs. Most everyone came out at the sound of the thundering horse hooves. Bershome reigned Rhubarb to a halt near the middle of the village.

"Mister Thatcher?"

"Here, your Lordship." A man in his fifties came running up. "Bless you, sir, for coming so quickly. They headed north. They killed my wife and Kelly, our black smith. They also took three of our girls."

"We will do our best to bring them back unharmed. Is Cigl a cool-headed lad? Will he not try anything until we catch up?"

"Aye, I told him not to do anything but follow and not be seen. He will stack stones if they change off the main road. He should come out to the middle of the road when he knows you are coming. I'll come with you."

"Sir, I understand your anxiety for your loved ones. But this is a job for my soldiers and me. My men are strong and well-trained."

A woman pushed a bread roll into his hand. "Here, you must eat to save you strength."

He took the bread. "Thank you."

"Please bring my Sarah back to me."

"We shall do our best." He bumped his horse lightly and started moving through the crowd of people. Everyone quickly cleared the way for them to pass. Bershome was at a gallop by the time he reached the edge of the village. They rode hard for another three hours during which the wind began blowing against them, and he slowed down to a trot.

Then the rain came at them like a moving wall of darkness. Suddenly, they were being pelted fiercely. Bershome gathered his cape, tied it closed on his upper body, and pulled the hood over his head. The raindrops were small and hit his face with a piercing sting. He held his gloved hand up to shield his face to little effect. He realized his horse had slowed to a walk. It held its head down to look at the ground and let the top of his head and neck take the brunt of the assaulting pellets. He pulled out his wand.

"Shieldor maxum." Bershome cast a shield spell the protected himself and Afreck. Bershome looked behind at his men. Most had taken up their shields for protection against the torturous pelting. Lenaredal was laying forward on his horse's neck and had his head covered with a blanket someone had given him. He was relying total-

          LARENCE LEE

ly on his horse's instinct to follow Bershome's. Bershome leaned towards his captain.

"Afreck, the men cannot take much more of this. We need to get in the woods for a bit of protection and wait this one out."

"Regrettably, that is the wisest decision, sire."

"Lead them in. I'll make sure no one misses the turn." Afreck dropped back and turned to the woods as he shouted the order to his men. Bershome stopped in the middle of the road and watched everyone follow the captain. He brought up the rear. The men quickly dismounted and tied their horses to trees with their rumps to the wind. Afreck gathered the men together to talk to them.

"You two men, take three spears to the road and drive them in the ground. Make a tripod. Tie them together and lash a shield to them for our sergeant to see. You stand guard at the edge of the woods to see that he does not miss our sign. Gorki, Frankil, get the tarp off the packhorse and get it tied up to some trees to make a headcover and windbreak. The rest of you men gather the driest wood you can find. As soon as we get a fire going, I'll break out the whiskey skin and give everyone a ration."

Lenaredal stepped up to him. "Is there anything I can do to help, Captain?"

"My men are trained for this. Try not to get any more soaked than you are. I think the best thing for you to do is find the biggest tree close by and put your back to it to block the wind and rain off ye."

Bershome stood back out of the way and let Afreck handle things. When the windbreak and headcover were set up and everyone that could gathered under it, a meager fire was started. But all were happiest when the Afreck hefted the skin on his shoulder and gave out their ration of whiskey.

"Gorki, go relieve Efard on guard duty. Keep an eye and ear out. Matok, Radon, you two warmed up yet?" They nodded slightly.

"Good, get axes, and make a path for the wagon to come in past us here. Then start making a clearing for the tent for when the Sergeant arrives."

"Captain, I think he would have done a smart thing like we did and gotten out of the rain."

"That is why you are not my Sergeant, Radmon. You can rest assured that wagon will be arriving here even if he has to walk out front on that muddy road pulling the reins of the horses to lead the way."

"Captain?" A voice came from the dark.

"Who speaks?"

"Gorki, sir. I have lad name Cigl Thatcher, sir."

"Bring him in, and get back to your post. All it takes is half a minute for a rider to miss that sign by the road."

"Not a chance. We put it in the middle of the road, Captain."

Lenaredal's twin brother stepped up under the cover. He was drenched and shivering. Lenaredal threw his own blanket over his brother's shoulders and pulled him closer to the fire. Afreck poured a drink for him.

"Here, lad, this will help warm up your blood."

"Did you find them? Is Jenni alright?" Lenaredal pumped Cigl for information.

"Easy, lad," Afreck said, "Let him warm up a minute. He didn't even have a blanket."

Lenaredal dropped his head down. "Sorry, sir."

"Cigl, while you warm the shivers out of yer body, this is Lord Paxtare's grandson, Bershome," Afreck said.

The lad bowed.

"We can wait until you get the feeling back in your body and are ready. We would like to hear what you have for us," Bershome said. "Meanwhile, I want you to know your father did the wisest thing he could by sending young men out like he did. Anything else would have only caused more senseless deaths. I know it isn't a comfortable riding a plow horse still in his riggings. Both of you have done your father and village proud. This damned rainstorm is something we could not have predicted or overcome. It is actually a blessing. Rest assured, those bandits are held up in the woods just like we are."

Finally, Cigl spoke. "I did like Father told me and never let them see me. Just before the rain hit, they sent two riders back to watch the road behind them. I saw the storm clouds coming from my hiding spot in the woods."

"They must have also. They were making sure it would be safe to go aground in the woods."

"When the rain caught up to where we were, they turned back riding hard. I tried to follow, but it was storming something fierce. I stacked a pile of stones up beside the road to know where I turned back. They are about a quarter-mile farther."

"How far do you think that is from here?"

"I reckon three miles or so, m' Lord."

Bershome and Afreck exchanged thoughtful looks.

"How good a look did you get of them? Could you tell how many there are?"

"Sorry, m' Lord. Best looks I ever got was peeking over a hill in the road. Closest I got was a quarter-mile away."

"You did a fine job."

"This storm will wash out all tracks, sir. How will we ever find them?"

"How about you and your brother get here in the middle of the windbreak and get some rest. Let my captain and myself do the worrying here on out. Wellom, bring some bread and meat to these lads."

"We need more wood, men," Afreck stated loudly. Several turned and headed out in the woods.

"Captain, come have a word with me." Bershome left the protection of the cover and prying ears. They walked into the wind a ways, and Bershome stopped and cast his shield spell.

"Afreck, I think we need a bit of quiet scouting done." He started to unbuckle his sword. Afreck lay his hand on Bershome's to stop him.

"Nay, sir, this calls for a soldier. Time I earned my pay." Afreck removed his sword and grounded it.

"How far do you think they are?"

"Like you and the lad said, within a couple or three miles. Hold my cape, please, sir."

Bershome held the man's cape while he proceeded to remove his chain mail. Once the cumbersome armor was removed, he quickly undressed, and Bershome tucked his clothes in his cape to keep them dry. Finally, Afreck stood with only a six-inch blade dagger on a string around his neck.

"If you are not back in an hour, we are coming after you in force."

"It could be farther, sire. Give me at least three hours. I'm not quite as spry as I use to be."

"Just be careful, and don't try to fight them all yourself."

"Aye, sire," Afreck said. He looked as if he was bending over, and a gray wolf suddenly stood before him. It looked back at Bershome and trotted northward.

Bershome walked back to the camp and heard the arrival of the supply wagon.

"Where is the captain?

"He went that way with his lordship."

"We are glad you caught up, Sergeant," Bershome said. "Get under the cover and dry out a bit. Wellom, go take down our sign by the road."

"Is Captain Afreck about, sire?"

"He went out on a scouting mission."

"Oh, I'll get the men to setting up the tent right away."

"Not before you thaw out and have a ration."

"I can do it at the same time, sire. Giving orders helps stir the blood." The sergeant began spouting orders and instructions.

Bershome smiled and poured his drink. Torches were dug out of the wagon, and they started putting up the tent.

"Nathanial? I'm surprised grandfather sent you along to cook."

"It was a last-minute change, my Lord. Baron Westley stopped by on his way to the capital. They had managed to outrun the rain coming south. His Lordship had us load extra firewood, so I'd have plenty dry enough to cook with and feed you properly."

"How long do you think it will take to get something hot in these guy's bellies besides whiskey?"

"I'll make small pieces of the meat and potatoes. About an hour after the water starts boiling, sire."

Two men brought a large pot and metal rod tripod to set up over the fire. Another followed with a table, and more brought boxes of supplies. Nathaniel started working right away. The men stockpiled his firewood along the back of the overhead. The pot was filled part way with water from a barrel. Nathanial started chopping potatoes, onions, carrots, and radishes like a mad man.

The men went to the tent with their bedrolls. Nathanial was happy about that because it gave him a lot more room beneath the overhead. The fury of the storm subsided, and it settled down to a steady rain.

Unknown as to their origin, the Thatcher twins were given Bershome's and the sergeants' bedrolls. Bershome and the Sergeant chose to sit on a fire log, stood on its end, and watch the cook. Neither would bed down while Afreck was out scouting. Bershome did not realize it, but as he sat with his feet spread wide and rested his elbows on his legs, his head slowly sagged down, and he fell asleep.

"Captain," the sergeant spoke.

Bershome jerked his head up and jumped to his feet. He swayed unsteady a moment as a hand grabbed his arm.

"Steady, sire."

"What took you so long? It must be almost morning."

"The ladies are but a little behind me, sire. I need to dress lest I be exposed to them indecently."

"What?" Bershome asked as he handed Afreck the bundle of his clothes he had kept handy. "You made them walk in the rain?"

"Hell, they have been running all the way," he said as he dressed quickly.

"How many bandits are there, Captain?"

"Not exactly sure, sire. But there are two less. I took care of them while I was looking for the girls. I got to their camp just as the storm let up. I found the girls all tied together under a canvas. I cut them loose to get them ready for us to make a run, and the oldest one let me know they would not wait for a single minute. They followed me out to the road and headed south. I stayed with them in wolf form in case they were discovered missing."

"Sergeant, double the guards," Bershome ordered. "We need some blankets for the girls. See if any men will volunteer theirs. Afreck, you timed your return well. Nathanial has a stew ready."

"I know. I smelled it a quarter-mile away in spite of the rain. But my nose is extra sensitive in wolf form."

They laughed as Bershome handed him a cup with some whiskey. "Warm yourself up with this. Sergeant, let's go catch the girls."

The man gulped down it, and they went out to find the girls. They were about a quarter-mile away. The girls stopped and stood in fright at the sound of the men coming at them until Bershome spoke.

"Jenni, we are soldiers here to rescue you."

The smallest girl simply collapsed in relief and the complete loss of her will to go on. The Sergeant picked her up. Bershome gave his cape to Jenni and carried the other girl for the walk back to camp. Nathanial served them hot stew as they sat at the fire to warm up.

"We are extremely grateful for your rescuing us, me Lord," Jenni said when she finally stopped shivering against the cold.

"We are all too glad it was a successful rescue. Captain Afreck did the hard part. It appears the rest of us came along for the ride."

They laughed.

"How did you know to come so quickly?"

"Actually, you have the Thatcher men to thank for that," Bershome said and proceeded to explain the run of events after the girls were spirited away by the bandits.

"Lenaredal is here?"

"Yes, he and Cigl finally took my advice and went to try getting some sleep. Which is what I suggest you ladies do as soon as you warm up. I know I'm hungry. Cookie must have thought sleep was more important than food and didn't wake me."

"What will you do now that we are here?"

"I still have a band of outlaws, robbing and murdering innocent farmers and families that must be dealt with. You ladies will stay here with the lads and a couple of guards. At daylight, we men will do the rest of our job. By the way, did you happen to count how many there were?"

Jenni sat looking at him for a moment. "Nine, I believe. I'm sorry I didn't think to do so, sire."

He patted her shoulder. "Worry not about it. You were terrified and afraid for your life."

Her lower lip quivered a bit as tears swelled up in her eyes. She turned her head away. "I'm sorry. I swore I wouldn't give them the satisfaction of seeing me cry or show fear."

Bershome pulled her to his chest and held her. "You have been brave enough to carry you through the worst. It is over now. You are entitled to shed as many a tear as you want."

"I did it to help the little ones be strong."

"You did a good job."

She raised her hand and pointed to one that had fallen asleep with her bowl in her lap. Jenni set her empty bowl on the table and picked up the little girl. Bershome grabbed one of the lamps and led the way for them to the tent. The bedding available was sparse, but the girls settled down to sleep quickly. Jenni chose to lie down beside Lenaredal to sleep.

When Bershome returned to the overhead, he found Afreck sleeping the same way he had. The Sergeant and Nathanial had moved the pot from the fire to the edge of it to keep it warm before they sat with their backs to the windbreak against a tree behind it and nodded off themselves.

Bershome walked out and checked the guards.

"At least the ladies are safe, and the rain let up, sire."

"Yes, But we have the gruesome part of our job yet to do. Those outlaws need to be brought to justice for robbery, kidnapping, and murder."

"It will be daylight in a couple or three hours."

"Yes. We need to be moving out before daybreak. The outlaws will probably make a run for it when they know the girls are gone, and two men are dead."

"How far will we pursue them, sire?"

"Until justice is done."

"Thank you, sire."

"Why do you say that?"

"I grew up like them, poor farming folk. The baron we served under did not care as such for us."

"Those farmers are like you are. All part of our extended family. Each member of the family has responsibilities. Their taxes help provide for your wages. It is our duty to look after them. Go get a bowl of stew for yourselves." Bershome said and returned to the overhead and found Cigl leaning over the pot for a smell.

"Serve yourself, Cigl," Bershome whispered.

Cigl got a bowl and scooped out some.

"How did the girls come to be here, sire?"

Bershome pointed to the sleeping captain and continued whispering, "Your information was very good." Bershome relayed Afreck's story. "That Jenni is a strong-willed lass."

"Aye, sire, I think that is why Lenaredal loves her so. They are to be married after harvest."

"Well, I suppose I need to arrange them a gift."

"You have given them a big one already, sire."

Bershome smiled and got himself some stew.

"My guards and I have everything under control. Why not get yourself some more rest. Come daylight, I want you to ease on back home and let everyone know the girls are safe. We will bring the rest of them along after we capture the outlaws. I can't leave them to do harm to other farmers and villages about the country."

Cigl simply nodded. Bershome walked about the camp and checked the livestock to kill time. When he felt it was the right time, he when in the tent and woke the soldiers quietly so as not to disturb the girl's sleep. The men all came out to have stew for breakfast. The noise awoke the captain.

"Keep it down men, the outlaws will hear you five miles away."

"Sorry, Captain," a couple apologized, mainly for waking him up.

Bershome spoke up. "Gather round men. Eat while you listen. The most important reason we are here is done. We have the ladies under our safe protection. You can thank Captain Afreck for doing your jobs in the night while you slept. We now need to do the law enforcement part of our job. We will ride out in ten minutes and capture the outlaws. Then they will be carried to justice. I would prefer to take prisoners. If they resist, you may use whatever force is necessary. We will leave spears here in camp. This is going to be sword work today. Eat up your stew and make ready to ride quietly. I will give each of you a stone. It will have a silence spell for about a ten-foot area around you. We will go in two ranks and circle the camp. When we are ready, toss the stone away behind you so you can hear any orders given when we take the camp. Three men spread out along the line of livestock to keep their alarm from waking the camp." He turned to Afreck. "Have you anything to add, Captain?"

"I want no one to escape. Bailey, you and Wellom will remain here to guard the camp. If we are not back in four hours. Break camp and follow us. The lads can get the ladies home when they wake. The rest of you men have nine minutes."

The men hastened their preparations and were ready. Bershome handed Afreck a potion bottle. "I know you didn't get much sleep. This rejuvenation potion will give you an energy boost and help your strength hold out." He proceeded to drink his potion, as well.

"Thanks, sire. I'm afraid I'll need it before the day is done."

They readied their own horses. Bershome told Bailey his plans for Cigl come daylight. He did not expect to see him when they returned.

When all were ready, they rode out on a muddy road and kept the horses to a hard walk to prevent one from falling or breaking a leg. In no time, Afreck signaled a halt. He divided the men into two groups to surround the camp. Afreck would lead one group, and the sergeant led the other. Bershome didn't argue when asked to bring up the rear. He knew Afreck was politely insisting on allowing his men to do their job. They drew swords and slipped into the woods as the sun's rays started peeking through the trees. They surrounded the camp quickly. The soldiers used their swords to poked against each bandit and wake them up. Only one resisted.

"Like hell," he declared, but the soldiers knocked him down a couple of times with the flat of their blades and some hard kicks before he surrendered.

"Bind their wrists and feet, men. Drag them to the center over here." The prisoners were all collected together. "Empty their pockets and search them for weapons."

One soldier got a blanket, and all possessions were dumped on it. Pouches of coins were emptied for all to see. One man had a particularly large pouch compared to the others.

"Roll that man over." Bershome stood over the man and looked at him in disgust. "How is it that you carry more coin yourself than the value of that entire village other than the people themselves, yet you rob and murder for more."

The man stared at him with scowls and faces of hatred.

"How many people have you killed for that bag of coins?"

The man turned his head and spat.

"Wait a minute. I remember you. This is not the first time I have seen you lying on the ground tied up." The man squinted at him. Then his eyes widened in recognition of Bershome. "Apparently, you didn't learn the lesson my soft-hearted Granduncle tried to teach you."

Bershome looked at the other men and recognized none of them. "I see you put together another crew of bandits."

"Yea, two of my last crew were killed by wild animals. The rest deserted me."

"You will not be set free this time. You shall see justice for your crimes today. All of you are guilty of murder, robbery, and kidnapping. Men, throw these mongrels across their horses and tie them down. They do not deserve to ride in the saddle like men."

"What about their saddles, sire?"

"Put them on the horses. We don't want the animals getting sores from hauling these sacks of dung. Tie them good, less they fall off and cripple the horse."

"Sergeant, get two men to gather the livestock and head them back to the village."

"Aye, sire."

When the prisoners were loaded, Bershome led his men back to camp. They had caught up with the men leading the livestock along the way.

"Press on to the village, men. At this pace, you will be spending the night on the road," Bershome said as they rode past.

The girls were awake and up. Nathanial was loading the wagon.

"Captain, let's break camp and head home."

"Aye, sire. First, half you men strike the tent and get it loaded. Four more of you to the overhead. You rest, guard the prisoners."

Nathanial got a bowl of stew and handed it to Bershome.

"Good idea, sir."

"Men, when we are all load, but the cookpot and bowls, all of you get more stew," Bershome shouted. He took a sip of the broth in the stew. "This stew warms the cockles of a man's heart, Nathanael."

"It is the radishes and onions, sire."

"Sire?" one of the prisoners called out. "We haven't eaten but one bisque since yesterday."

"Why not? You had enough coin to buy a feast for the king's entire court."

"How many bisques do you have, Nathanial?"

"Thirty or forty, sire."

"Raydof. Take bisques and tear them four ways. Give each prisoner a bite."

"Aye, sire."

Bershome walked over to where Lenaredal and Jenni sat holding hands. They stood up and bowed.

"Lenaredal, that is quite a brave, strong girlfriend you have there."

"I know, sire."

"Promise me you will put her and your children first in whatever you do. Never strike her or them in anger. Do not let the sunrise or set without letting them know you love them."

Lenaredal looked at Jenni. "I promise, sire."

"As a wedding present, you may your pick one of the horses and saddles from among the prisoners. We will move the prisoner from the horse you choose."

"I, I," Lenaredal stammered.

"Thank you, sire," Jenni said as she stepped up and planted a kiss on Bershome's cheek.

"Oh, my. Cherish her, my man. She has soft lips." He nodded his head towards her. "Go on and choose your horse."

"That was a kind gesture, Bershome, sir," Afreck whispered in his ear from behind him. "They will probably sell it for a couple of cows and a hardy plow horse."

"Think that is a good start for a marriage?"

"It is more than just a promise to love her. Well done, sir."

Bershome kept his voice low. "We will hang the prisoners at the village after they dig their own graves."

"Aye, sire."

"Also, after we break camp, send Sergeant Taylor on home with a spare mount and have him tell Grandfather all is well. We will camp at the village tonight. It is too far to push on with the wagon today."

"Good choice, sire."

Bershome sat against a tree and watched everyone while Afreck and the sergeant checked the camp for forgotten equipment. The men gathered around the cookpot and got a bowl of stew.

"Captain, have men carry the little ones on their horses. I wouldn't want one falling off riding bareback."

The smallest girl walked up to Bershome and curtsied. "Can I ride with you, your lordship?"

"Under one condition."

"What would that be, sire?" Her surprise was obvious.

"I need to know the name of the lady I am honored to carry home from her rescue.

"I'm Junie-Ann, sire." She curtsied again.

Bershome bowed to her. "It would be my honor to have you ride with me Lady Junie-Ann. Did you get enough breakfast?"

"Yes, thank you. But it had too much pepper in it."

"That is to help you fight off sickness from getting cold and wet last night."

"Oh."

"Sire, we are ready," Afreck announced.

"Lady Junie-Ann, your ride awaits you." He picked her up and carried her to his horse.

They mounted up and rode to the village by mid-morning. Everyone crowded around to greet them. Bershome handed Junie-Ann to her mother, and she clutched her in a strong hug.

"Thank you, thank you, thank you," the woman kept saying to him as she cried openly.

Bershome dismounted and received a hug from everyone that could get near him.

"That is the bastard that killed my wife," Bershome heard a shout. He saw a man with an ax in his hand. Bershome rushed over as the man raised the weapon.

"STOP." Bershome caught the axe as the man started to swing down with it. "Stop, sir."

"He killed my Gurtty."

"And he shall pay for his crime today. I cannot allow you to use your axe on him. You could injure the poor horse, sir."

The man looked at him in shock at the reasoning.

"Also, I cannot allow you to take vengeance. He will be properly hung by law. Captain, take the prisoners to the graveyard and put then to digging graves."

The men moved to get the prisoners away from the mob.

"Ladies and Gentlemen. I assure those men shall pay for their crimes before sunset. But I cannot allow a mob killing. They must be hung in accordance with the law. First, they will dig the graves needed. I believe you need two for your departed beloved."

"Yes," a couple spoke.

"My men and I will be spending the night here in your village if you don't mind."

"We will be honored, my Lord. But we are a small village and are limited in houses. I shall give up my humble home for you, sir."

Bershome smiled and nodded. "Thank you for the offer. I don't wish to offend you, Mr. Thatcher, but it is not necessary. We have a campaign tent and will set it up nearby."

"Then, we will give all of you a feast fit for a king."

"We would be honored, but you will spoil my soldiers. A wholesome meal would be best."

"We will see they do not go to bed hungry."

"Excellent. I need to check on my Captain's progress."

Bershome went over to the graveyard. The soldiers were standing or sitting in a large circle about thirty feet from the graves being dug. All of the prisoners were cooperating but one. It was the leader.

"I mean it. I'm not digging a grave."

Captain Afreck grabbed him by the hair and jerked his head back. "You have two choices. A just and swift death with a proper burial or his lordship will drag you behind his horse until you are dead. As muddy as the road is, you will slide pretty well. The rocks will be the bugger, though. I think you will eat a pound or two of mud in the process. When you are dead, he will probably just throw you over is a field to feed the vultures. To them, meat is meat."

The man looked at Bershome and saw his look of disgust he showed on his face. "Captain, send a man for my horse and a rope."

The thief took the shovel and went to work. "Would you at least untie my hands?"

"Those men are having no problem with it." The man did as he was ordered.

Bershome stepped up to the captain. "Captain, remember we need two more for the villagers they murdered. Make that man dig one himself. Also, let's send half the troops over to put up the tent. Have Nathanial offer help to the village cooking supper for our men."

"Aye, sire. Men, every other one starting with Wellom, go set up the tent. We are spending the night." The men looked at each other and divided up for the job.

"By the way, Captain, where is that bag of coins off the bandits?"

"Under Nathanael's seat in the wagon, sire."

"Tonight we will give it to the village. After the men get the tent set up, let's have them cut poles for the lost houses plus one."

Afreck smiled. "I like that idea, sire."

Bershome went over and watched the men set up the tent. While they worked, he pulled a couple axes and saws from the wagon.

"Sire?" Bershome turned to face Mr. Thatcher.

"I want to thank you for the gift you gave my son."

"I didn't give it to him. I gave it to the both of them. If they call off the wedding, I expect the horse and saddle back," He smiled.

Thatcher smiled as well. "I doubt that will happen. They have been in love for years."

"Question, sir."

"Ask away, sire."

"How many poles do you need for a house?"

"I haven't counted."

"Also, I would like to borrow several axes. I'm going to have my men cut poles for three houses."

"We only lost two, sire."

"You lost two and need one for the newlyweds." Bershome winked.

Thatcher's mouth moved a couple of times without sound.

"Your thanks is not necessary, sir. I couldn't have my soldiers lying around being lazy all afternoon. We need to know what size poles and how many."

"I'll make a list of what we need." The man walked away with a slightly dazed look on his face.

Bershome enlightened the men after the tent was erected and passed out the tools. A couple of men fetched ropes and horses for dragging trees out of the woods. After a while, a soldier came over from the graveyard.

"Sire, the graves are done."

"I see no need to make a spectacle of it. Tell the Captain to proceed with the executions and burial. The leader and one other will bury the rest."

Bershome leaned back against the cook's wagon and watched. Captain Afreck was efficient. In ten minutes, outlaws were hanging from nearby oak trees.

"My Lord?" A young lady, his age, stood a few feet away. She held a bottle and a mug. "Father thought, perhaps you would care for some wine."

"Thank you."

His hand shook slightly when he held the mug as she poured the wine. After he took a drink, she put a hand on his arm.

"They were murderous outlaws, sire. They would have killed again. You did what was right and saved more lives. We all thank you for it."

He pressed his lips together to prevent his lower one from quivering. He couldn't look at her. He simply nodded and looked at the wine in the mug.

"Thank you, young lady. This is good wine."

"We buy it from your estate, sire."

Bershome smiled looked at the label on the bottle. He chuckled slightly. "This wine is three years old. It is a blend of red and white grapes. It was the bottom of the last to the two vats of the season. Glen, our brew master, had the idea of mixing them. This turned out pretty good."

"We have enjoyed it immensely. We will serve you more with supper."

"Yes, please, but this is enough for me right now."

"If you are hungry, I can bring you bread and cheese."

"I don't think my stomach could handle it."

"It is awful that you had to do this at your age."

"I hope it is awful for me every time it happens."

She squeezed his arm slightly and left.

An hour later, the last of the graves were being filled.

Captain Afreck put the rest of the men to cutting trees. Bershome was impressed at the way the men worked. They cared about the job. Once a tree dropped, men swarmed up on it and removed the limbs, and cut the log to length. Another tied the rope to it and the horses and dragged it towards the village. Every man from the village stepped in and worked also. Some of the ladies carried around buckets and served water to any man that was thirsty.

Mr. Thatcher came walking up to Bershome. "Sire, we have enough for four houses now.

"Men!" Bershome shouted, "We have enough. Finish the tree you are on and cut down no more."

"Yea!" several men shouted and returned to work.

"Well, sir, what you have leftover, you can use as firewood or be ready for the next wedding. My men need to wash up from all that work. If you keep the ladies away from the creek, they will do it there."

"I'll get soap for them."

The men followed the last log out of the woods. They stopped and gathered their gear and followed Bershome and Afreck to the creek.

"Gentlemen, I want to thank all of you for your hard work. We will wash up here, and the village is serving you supper to show their gratitude. All I ask more of you is that you mind your manners."

"We will, sire," several said.

The smell of food from the village made the men hungry. They washed up quickly.

"Gentlemen," Captain Afreck said, "You still represent his Lordship. We will have full dress for supper, less helmets, of course."

He heard a few groans, but the men complied. When ready, they fell into two ranks. Bershome sent one on an errand to the wagon. The rest followed Bershome and Afreck into the village.

The village had gone all out. They had set up plank tables in the grass, and every chair and bench was set out for them. Two open pit fires had been set up for roasting a calf and a goat. Nathanial's cook pots were used for boiling up sweet corn, potatoes, onions, carrots, and making gravy. Kegs of ale and bottles of wine sat in several places along the table. Mr. Thatcher stood beside the chairs in the middle of the tables. Bershome and the Captain headed toward him. The soldiers filed down both sides of the tables. Bershome looked up and down the tables. All waited for him to sit first.

"Mr. Thatcher." He signaled for the man to take the seat beside him. The man moved and hovered over the chair a moment until Bershome was seated. Everyone took a seat. The man that ran Bershome's errand set a bag beside his chair and found a seat for himself. Thatcher took the goblet in front of him and stood. He held out the goblet as he spoke.

"Lord Bershome Paxtare, gentlemen, soldiers," He looked up and down the table. "we people of our humble village of Kittwick wish to thank you for coming to help us in our greatest hour of need. We thank you for rescuing our children. Without you, we surely would have lost them. We appreciate you helping us bring justice for our loved ones. Thank you from all our hearts. We also thank you for helping us rebuild our lost homes. You have done in one afternoon what would have taken us two weeks. We thank you again. Sire, we wish to thank you, my Lord, the most for your thoughtfulness in having your men do this. It shows us humble people that our Lord and overseer and his grandson care about our welfare. Gentlemen, we toast you and to your good health."

Everyone toasted with raised glasses and took a sip. Thatcher sat, and Bershome stood. He rested his hand on his goblet without lifting it.

"Mr. Thatcher, ladies and gentlemen, Captain Afreck, and soldiers. It is with a heavy heart I stand here. Heavy on it is your loss of loved ones, which the outlaws killed with no respect for life. Heavy on it is the fact that I had to stand for justice and condemn those outlaws to death. Don't misunderstand me. They deserved the sentence passed on them, and it was just."

He picked up the bag. He dumped the coins out on the table. "They had more money on them than all of us combined. "I give your village their spoils, for from where they were taken we know not. It will not return your loved ones to you, and I mourn them with you. It worries me that such men are out in this world, and I know more of the responsibilities expected of myself and my grandfather, Lord Paxtare. Your act of gratitude touches my heart and makes me appreciate my purpose as a nobleman. You soldiers should feel it as well. Thank you, men, for your diligence and professional conduct. You rode through some of the nastiest weather I have ever been in with only cold, soggy rations to sustain you." He embellished the truth to make the village appreciate their efforts more. "You conducted yourselves well and captured the outlaws. You handled the gruesome task of your duty professionally and then sweated and worked hard to help these people in their need to rebuild their homes."

He lifted his goblet. "I thank you, men, and I salute you." He took a sip of his wine while standing. "Ladies and gentlemen of the village of Kittwick, I wish to thank you for this banquet. Just don't serve too much wine and ale to the men, please."

Everyone laughed lightly. "Captain, care to say a word?" Bershome said and sat down.

Afreck stood up and cleared his throat.

"I'm not a man of eloquent words like his Lordship. I'll thank you for preparing this fine food and to you men, job well done." He raised his goblet, drank, and sat down.

Bershome took a baked role from a platter and took a bite. That was the signal, and everyone began filling their plates. The sun set on the banquet, and lamps were brought out. Bershome and the Captain chatted with the village leaders a while after they had eaten their fill. The ladies started cleaning up, and most of the soldiers drifted to their tent.

"Mr. Thatcher, thank you again for the fine and filling meal. We will break camp in the morning and head home."

"Sire, I hope it is a long time to come, but you will make a fine Lord one day."

"I hope so. I know I am being taught by the finest."

"He is doing a good job. Please give him our thanks."

"I shall."

He stood to leave and shook the man's hand.

"Sire?" a female voice came from behind him.

Bershome faced her. "Yes, Miss Jenni?"

"I just wanted to thank you again for all you have done."

"It was my pleasure, and you are welcome."

Suddenly she reached up and grasped his head in her hands, pulled him down, and kissed him fully on the mouth. "I'm really grateful."

"That just made it all worthwhile. Thank you."

"Good night, sire." She turned and ran off.

"Good night, Mr. Thatcher," he said, walking off to the tent without looking at the man to hide his flushed face.

A guard stood outside the tent. A single lamp provided a dim light just enough for a person to see and not step on any of the men. A bedroll was laid out for him. The space around it was a bit larger than the way the men were crowd along the tent's length. He removed his boots and sword. Sleep came quickly, but nightmares haunted his dreams.

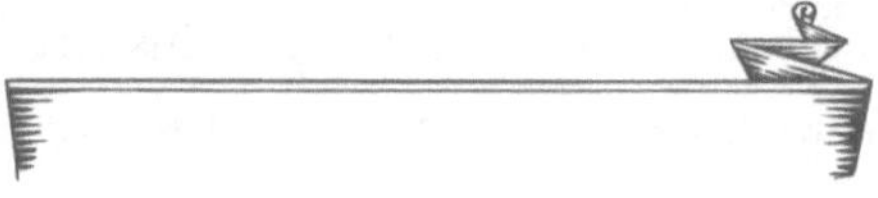

CHAPTER TWENTY

Roosters crowed at the morning sun. Bershome lay quietly as some of the men started waking up. A couple showed signs of a hangover. One man jumped up and ran out without his boots. He returned a few minutes later, wiping his mouth on his sleeve.

"Drank too much last night?" Captain Afreck accused from his spot near Bershome.

The man nodded without a word.

"We break camp in twenty minutes, men," he said as he pulled on his boots.

Bershome followed his cue and left the tent with his bedroll as the captain was bumping sound sleeper's feet. He chose to start his day saddling Rhubarb.

"Morning, sire," Nathanial called to him as he walked past the cook's wagon.

"Morning, sir. Have we any bisques and cooked meat to make breakfast out of?"

"Aye, sire. The village ladies insisted I take them."

"Good. Have it ready along with a ration of whiskey for the men. Captain Afreck intends to start loading up in twenty minutes."

The man threw back his covers and grabbed his boots. "That man is not one to dilly dally around when there is a long road ahead of him. Next time, I'll remember to have his Lordship send a helper with me. Twenty minutes to make food for over twenty men is not easy for one man."

Bershome strolled over to his horse as he figured Nathanial was talking more to himself than to him. He could still hear the man prattling on as he reached Rhubarb.

"Morning fellow, did the men give you enough grain last night?"

He talked to the animal and stroked his neck. By the time he had the horse saddled, the men were taking down the tent. He led Rhubarb over to the wagon and saw Nathanial cutting slices of meat for serving. Bershome took a bisque out of the basket and ripped it open like a book. He grabbed a couple of pieces of meat and stuffed it in the bread.

"Thank you, Nathanial," he said before he took a bite.

"A bottle of wine is under the seat of the wagon, sire."

"Uh hmm," he responded, taking another bite. He pulled out a bottle of wine, looked in the crate, and found no corkscrew. He looked all around and saw no one from the village, so he took out his wand and cast a spell that made the cork pop out. He deftly caught it in the air with his wand hand. After a drink to wash down the dry bread, he stepped over to Nathanial.

"You forgot the corkscrew, sir."

"Nay, I keep it in me pocket to keep soldiers from stealing the wine."

"Care for a sip?"

"Ah." He took the bottle and drank a belt. "I see a lack of a corkscrew can't stop you."

Bershome washed down his last bite of food and poked the cork halfway in the bottle, and set it on the table. "Give that to the Captain, please."

"Aye, sire."

Four men came carrying the tent on poles like a man on a stretcher. They were followed by several more carrying poles, tent stakes, and tools.

"Ready for the tent, Cookie?"

"Just a moment." He climbed it the wagon and moved a couple of things. "Toss it right here."

The men hefted the tent up shoulder high and flipped it over in the wagon.

"Bread, meat, and ration of drink for breakfast." Nathanial pointed to the table.

Several headed to the table.

"Breakfast is after you are saddled up," Captain Afreck's voice halted them in their tracks. They turned and headed for the horses.

"What about the spare saddles from the outlaws, Captain?"

Afreck looked a Nathanial and the wagon. "You got room, Nathanial?"

"Not really, Captain."

"Saddle them up."

"First two men to get saddled, hook up the team to the wagon."

Captain Afreck stood a few feet from the table. He spotted the bottle of wine and took it. After taking a belt, he replaced it on the table.

"His Lordship said the rest was for you, Captain."

Afreck nodded slightly as he watched the men. The picket line was taken down after all the spare mounts were tied to each other in groups, and then each group was tied to a soldier's horse.

Afreck picked up the keg and set it on the back end of the wagon. He started filling cups with drink and setting them on the table. The men formed a line at the table, and Nathanial passed out bisques and meat like Bershome had eaten.

After half the men had food, Afreck ordered, "Choke it down, men. We ride in ten minutes."

Bershome heard a man mutter, "Does he ever do anything in thirty minutes?"

"No, I do it in nine minutes."

"Damned, he has good ears."

Everyone laughed. When the last man was served, Afreck took some food himself and the wine.

A man came walking over leading a horse and handed the reins to the Captain when he had eaten his last bite. Afreck handed the man the bottle. He drank the last few swallows and dropped the empty bottle in the wagon. Nathanial put the remaining food in baskets and set them in the wagon. One soldier came back, carrying several empty cups and gave them to the cook. Another man loaded the table.

Captain Afreck walked around the area looking for anything the men had left behind. "Who dropped a knife?" He stepped a few more paces. Every man began checking his gear. "And a glove?"

Two men ran over to him a claimed the items. The captain mounted his horse and rode over to Bershome.

"Ready when you are, sire."

Bershome turned his horse and headed for the road.

"Column of twos, spare mounts in the rear behind the wagon," Afreck ordered as he followed Bershome with the bannerman carrying the standard beside him. They rode through the town, and people stepped outside and bowed to Bershome on his way by.

"Thank you again, sire. Blessings be upon you all."

A mile down the road, Bershome spurred his horse to a canter. He kept the pace steady all the way home.

He slowed when he entered the village outside the estate and walked them to the stables. The Captain took Rhubarb's reins from Bershome when he dismounted.

"We will take care of Rhubarb. His Lordship will be waiting for your report, sir," he said softly, "I'll give him my report later."

"Thanks," Bershome muttered. He took the standard from the man carrying it and headed for the castle. He met his grandfather halfway there.

"Ah, Bershome, thank you for sending me the message. I was worried. The sergeant told me everything. You are back in time for lunch today."

Servants stopped and stood with their backs to the wall and bowed their heads as they passed.

"I wanted you not to worry, Grandfather."

"Where are...?"

"Justice was served, Grandfather."

The old man nodded in full understanding of what Bershome meant.

"We brought back the horses they had. Except one, I gave to Lenaredal as a wedding present. One of the kidnapped girls is promised to him. We can expect a wedding invitation soon."

"What of the coin you confiscated?"

"I gave it to the village."

Bershome received a smack on the back. "That was a nice gesture, but the coin would have been good to help pay the expense of the campaign."

"I didn't think of that, sorry."

They entered Grandfather's office, and Bershome closed the door. He stepped over to the armoire and poured two drinks of brandy. He handed one to his grandfather and sat down across the desk from him and silently looked at the glass as he swirled the amber liquid slightly.

"Two of them were younger than I am, Grandfather," he said and took a drink. Bershome could not stop his hand from shaking.

"Lad, they were outlaws that participated in robbery and murder of unarmed peasants. They would have turned bad as the rest of the lot. You could have brought them here, and I would have done the same or them taken to the magistrate. Either way, the results would have been the same. What you did was not wrong."

"I made the decision and ordered their hanging. It still feels horrible."

"I hope it always does, son. I pray your heart never becomes calloused to it. I was almost thirty years old at my first hanging. It bothered me for a month with nightmares and foul stomach. Every now and then, they wake me up sweating in my sleep."

"You never mentioned it."

"It is not something one discusses openly. I'm not proud of it. But it had to be done."

Bershome finished his drink. "I stood over by the wagon like a coward and made Captain Afreck handle it. I watched as they swung with their legs and their feet twitched."

"It wasn't cowardly, son. You handled the unsavory task best you could. It is tragic a sight for watching. You will never get it out of your mind. But you will go on with life. What do you say, you go join your friends and eat lunch."

"I don't have much of an appetite."

"Force yourself to eat something. Pick your favorite food. Go and study magic. Go to the stone garden and cast some spells for fun. Interact with other people. They will know you are in pain and want to help you through it. Don't shut them out. Eventually, it will pass to just a memory you only think of occasionally."

"What if it were someone I knew, one of my friends?"

"Your friends are not evil, son. And you would have brought them back here for a magistrate to do his job."

"Yes, that is what I would have done."

"I ordered water drawn for you when the lookout spotted you in the village. They should be finished, and the water is hot. Go take a bath and put on fresh clothes. Lunch will be ready by then."

Grandfather stood and walked around the desk. When he opened the door, a soldier, Bartholomew was standing outside.

"Hello, Bartholomew, what may I do for you?"

"I wish to resign my service, sire."

"Why? Because of the hanging?" Bershome asked.

"Oh, no, sir. I've seen worse in my time. My father was a blacksmith, and I know the trade. Kittwick needs one."

"You wish to leave us then."

"Aye sire. There is a lady in the village that took my fancy. I've already spoken with Captain Afreck."

"You have been a good soldier, Bartholomew." Grandfather offered his hand. "We will miss you. Take your horse, saddle, and gear. The shield and tunic with our crest belong to the family. Stop by to see me before you leave. I'll give you severance pay."

"Thank you, sire. I'm honored."

"Bartholomew, you are bound by your word of honor to keep our family secret here," Bershome informed him.

"Yes, sir. I'll never mention to anyone. It has been an honor serving you, sire, and you as well, Bershome, sir." He held out his hand and received a shake from them both.

Bershome found a hot bath in his private quarters and fresh clothes laid out on his bed. He stripped down and slipped into the large copper tub to soak. The hot water eased the tension out of his body and relaxed him. He was lying back almost asleep when someone knocked on the door.

"Who is it?" Bershome shouted as he grabbed the soap and rag off the stool sitting beside the tub.

The door opened without his invitation. Bernary stepped in.

"Ah, Mr. Bernary."

"Lord Paxtare was afraid you fell asleep."

"Almost." Bershome began scrubbing his face vigorously.

Bernary closed the door while Bershome scrubbed his body and lathered up his hair with the soap. Bernary stepped over and picked up a bucket. He dipped it in the tub, and Bershome leaned forward to have his head rinsed off. Bernary traded the bucket for a large towel and held it up for Bershome. Bernary wrapped the towel around him as he stepped out of the tub.

"Thank you very much, sir. I'll be dressed shortly," Bershome said and effectively dismissed the man.

"Glad to have you back safely, Bershome, sir," he responded as he headed for the door.

"Me too Mr. Bernary. Me too."

Most everyone was well into their meal when Bershome arrived feeling like a new man. He headed for his usual seat beside Martello. As he sat, he heard someone tapping his goblet with a utensil. Everyone became silent and faced the head table where Grandfather was standing.

"I wish you all to join in welcoming Bershome home in healthy condition."

A round of applause filled the room.

"Ladies and gentlemen. Three days ago, many of you saw Bershome and our soldiers ride out. He was going to answer a call for help to the village of Little Kittwick. Outlaws had hit the village. They stole livestock, murdered two people, and kidnapped three young girls. Bershome and my men rode hard and fast to get to the village five hours behind the outlaws. They rode on another three hours and ran into the hellish rainstorm you witnessed that same afternoon. After being pelted by the harsh rain, they took shelter in the woods. Instead of letting the foul weather deter them, Bershome sent Captain Afreck out to make a reconnoiter of the road ahead and found the outlaws. He succeeded in rescuing the ladies that evening. The next morning, Bershome led our soldiers and captured the outlaws. They returned the ladies home safe and serviced justice to the murdering outlaws by hanging. This is some of the responsibility of our position in society. Our extended family, the town of Little Kittwick, called for help, and we answered them. Let us raise our glasses in toast to Bershome for taking command, accomplishing a job well done, and returning home with no injuries to any of the rescue par-ty."

All toasted him. Bershome actually felt relief at his grandfather for removing the burden of telling the story repeatedly himself. He looked at the man after he sat and received a wink from him. Bershome looked at the roasted chicken and beets on the platter and realized he was hungry. No one spoke to him as he ate. The dining hall thinned out of occupants. Martello, Freya, Arleta, and Trejann lingered by to wait on Bershome.

Bershome pushed his empty plate away and took a glass of fruit juice.

"Bershome, did you get to use any magic during your trip?"

Martello's question shocked him. He smiled. "Yes, as a matter of fact, I did."

"Master Zarlaam would be pleased to know," Arleta said.

"What is the study this afternoon?"

"Spell practice in the stone garden."

"Good. I could use some spell casting."

They left together for the garden. The class was already there, and they sat on benches or lounged on the grass. Zarlaam arrived at the same time.

"Master Zarlaam, May I have a word with them? I think you will like it." He received an approving nod and stepped out in front of everyone. "Afternoon, everyone. Anyone caught falling asleep will wake up as a rabbit," he threatened them. A couple of lads sat up where they lounged. "During my trip, I had the opportunity to use magic. If not for Martello asking, I would not have thought to tell you about it. I was able to do so only because of the trust we have in our soldiers. Always bear that in mind when you are away from here."

"The first spell I used was a shield spell. Shieldor maxum."

"You used it against the rain?" Janara interrupted.

"Precisely. I was able to shield Captain Afreck and our horses as well. Next, I cast a spell of silence on rocks. Each was only good for about ten feet. I gave these to the soldiers when we went into surround the camp of the outlaws. We were able to keep the element of surprise and capture them. The men were instructed to toss them away when we attacked so they could hear orders. Lastly, I had to open a bottle of wine without a corkscrew."

Everyone laughed.

"Excellent, Bershome," the master stepped up beside him, and Bershome surrendered the group to him. "He used helpful magic, and still, he maintained his secrecy. But we don't need corks popping out of bottles in the dining room." He waged a finger back and forth with a smile. "This afternoon, I want you to use the spells you are weak with producing."

Bershome sat back against a tree and enjoyed watching them foul-up spells and half-heartedly restrained his laughter. It was the weekend, and everyone not taking remedial training would be out hunting ingredients for potions, relaxing, and playing games.

After practice, Martello pulled Bershome aside for a talk.

"We had three more incidences in the dorm while you were gone."

"What happened?"

"Well, Jartus's boots ended up hanging in a tree. We found my spellbook floating against the ceiling yesterday morning. Dorantal's hair turned orange while he and his bunkmate were the only ones in their cell."

"That is a line of sight spell." Bershome reached up and scratched his head. "They didn't see anyone casting the spell?"

"No." They looked at the instant it started changing. No one was near their cubicle."

"It's not uncommon for the guys to pull pranks on each other."

"I know that. But it's just peculiar how these happened. You had to be there to understand."

"What did Master Zarlaam say?"

"I didn't see a point in telling him. I've been trying to catch the culprit myself."

"Thanks," Bershome slapped his arm. "I'll take over now."

CHAPTER TWENTY-ONE

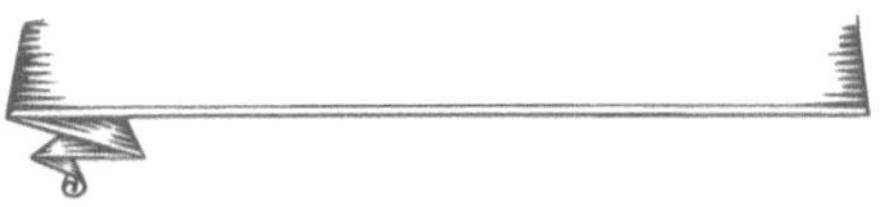

One morning, Bershome was pulling up his pants when the chamber door eased open, and a draft came in. He stepped over and closed it with a pause to check if the latch was faulty. He found nothing wrong and finished dressing.

"Has anyone seen my spell book?" Trejann called out. "It was here a minute ago. Who took it?"

Bershome walked down the chamber to see Trejann rummaging through his wardrobe. "What's the matter?"

"My spellbook disappeared."

"Did your cellmate, Gerak, see it?"

"He left a bit ago." Trejann shrugged.

'Did Gerak have it when he left?"

"Did I have what?"

Bershome turned to see Gerak standing behind him and glanced down at his empty hands. "Trejann's spellbook disappeared."

"So, you just automatically accuse me because I sleep in the bunk beside him?"

"No." Bershome shook his head. "I'm accusing no one, but I must ask if you saw or took his book."

"I don't have a need of it. He let me copy all his spells and potions when I first got here."

"Well, that was nice of him."

"I found it." Someone shouted from the washroom.

Trejann and Bershome rushed to the washroom and pushed aside a lad holding the door of a toilet, pointing inside. There, they found the book stuck in a chamber pot. Trejann grabbed it and lifted it. Fortunately, the pot was empty and clean.

"Who would do something like this?" He looked up at Bershome then around the gathered lads.

Bershome looked for a face with a telltale sign of guilt or satisfaction. Only one person wasn't there, Gerak. He went back to their cell and saw Gerak pulling his own spellbook from his wardrobe. "Gerak, if you don't mind my asking, where were you before I spoke to you a moment ago?"

"Not that it is any business of yours. I stepped out. I wanted to see what the sky was like today. Those windows don't show enough. Ask Martello. He saw me return."

Bershome nodded. "Okay, thanks, Gerak."

He stepped out into the walkway and raised his voice. "Listen up, all you hooligans. Whoever pulled this little stunt? You don't mess with a fellow wizard's spellbook. It will get you a one-way trip home when I catch you doing something like this again. Rest assured, you will be caught. Master Zarlaam and I know spells you do not. Now get yourselves together, and let's get down for breakfast. It is not proper to interrupt his Lordship's meal with you mongrels making noise getting to your seats." Bershome was the last to leave and trotted down the stairs to breakfast

CHAPTER TWENTY-TWO

That afternoon, Bershome followed everyone filing into the dining hall for lunch and discovered his grandfather sitting at the main table and chatting with a middle-aged nobleman. To the right of the nobleman sat a lovely young lady. She perked up and smiled widely when she saw him walk into the room.

All the chairs at the head table were taken by the estate supervisors. Mr. Henson sat next to the young lady. Bershome caught the casual hand signal from his grandfather. He walked up to the head table and nodded at Zarlaam.

"Afternoon Grandfather, Barron Westler, how nice of you to visit." He offered his hand to the man and received a hearty handshake.

"Hello, Bershome. You remember my daughter?"

"You offend me, sir." He pressed a hand to his chest and smiled, "No one can forget such a lovely lass as your Agatha. What a pleasure to see you again. You are looking divine as usual." He released the baron's hand and took his daughter's.

"Thank you. I insisted Father bring me along today so that we could visit. It has been months since we spoke."

"I'm delighted to see you as well. I apologize that I 'm not able to get out as much for socializing nowadays. Uncle and Grandfather keep me fairly busy."

"I hear you have a new stallion. I would love to see him."

"I have a few duties to take care of right after lunch but will come looking for you as soon as I can."

She took a deep breath and let it out hard through her nose as she looked at him with pleading eyes. Bershome patted her hand, and she smiled. He nodded to his grandfather as he turned to take his seat next to Martello. He placed his right fist upright on the table and cupped his left over it. He made the left-hand motion twice and looked at each student. He watched them pass the signal down the table until all apprentices and made the signal. Several took long looks at the head table in acknowledgment that visitors were about, and no open magic would be practiced today.

"Well, there goes an entertaining afternoon of watching apprentices messing up spells in the rock garden," Martello muttered to Bershome.

"Speak for yourself. I have to go show off a horse and entertain the lady. What shall we have as a substitute teaching for the afternoon?"

"How about tomorrow's math class."

"Is Rakord teaching?" Bershome threw a harsh whisper down the table to a lad several people away. "Hey, Rakord?"

Rakord looked at him with raised eyebrows as he took bites of a chicken leg.

"You ready to give the math class for tomorrow?"

The lad nodded.

"Good, you are giving it this afternoon."

Rakord forgot to chew for a moment.

"You ready?" Bershome asked again.

Rakord nodded again. Bershome gave him a wink and a thumb's up. "Math lessons this afternoon, pass it around."

In hardly a minute's time, everyone knew of the schedule change and why. There were several long faces all around the table. Bershome noticed Arleta and Janara kept talking in hushed whispers as Arleta stole looks at Agatha. Rakord was the first one finished eating and hurried out.

Bershome meandered over to the Hall of Knowledge in time to see Rakord writing on the slate board with a piece of chalk. "Rakord, I apologize for pulling this on you."

"No problem, I was fully prepared two days ago."

"Usually, Baron Westler never stays more than a few hours. I expect him to be gone before long. We will be back on schedule tomorrow. Tell everyone else for me, please. I have to go socialize."

"Hey, who is she?"

"You met her once last year, Baron Westler's daughter, Agatha. He fancies her marrying into my family."

"Ooh."

"Please, keep them busy and out of trouble, Rakord?" Bershome said. He walked out of the building and crossed paths with everyone headed in. Arleta made it a deliberate act to not look at him. He removed his robe and straightened at the wrinkles in his tunic on the way back in the manor.

"Kayla," He caught the attention of a maid and handed her his robe. "Would you please have this returned to my bunk? Thank you very much."

"Certainly, Bershome, sir."

He caught up with the Baron and their guest as they strolled towards the stables.

"Bershome!" Agatha squealed. She grabbed his arm and locked it in the crook of her own, and pulled him close to her. She guided him a little distance from the barons and whispered in his ear.

"My birthday is next month, Bershome. Would you come to my party?"

"Well, I'm not sure what my schedule is for next month."

"Oh, please? I would be terribly broken-hearted if you missed it. You have to come and protect me from Lord Gavi's son, Eli. He has been hinting about making a marriage arrangement for my hand with Father. I cannot stand him. He hardly ever bathes. I'm going to be sixteen, you know."

"Yes, I will try to be there. I already have your present selected."

"What is it? Tell me, please?"

"I can't do that. It would spoil the surprise," He made a mental note to remember to get her a present.

"Give me a hint, then. Is it made of wood, cloth, or leather?"

"Now, Agatha. It would not be proper to tease you about such a thing. And if you guessed what it is, there would be no surprise for your birthday."

They arrived in the stable and stopped in front of a stall occupied by a two-year-old stallion. The beast was solid black except for one white front sock. It backed away from the door of the stall and bobbed its head up and down as it neighed in protest of the presence of strangers.

"Steady, Rubarb, steady." Bershome spoke in a calming voice to the horse. "My friends just want to look at you. I apologize, Baron. I'd rather not bring him out of his stall. He is still a bit high spirited and spooks very easily."

The man appraised the horse from over the stall door.

"Lord Paxtare, that is one fine horse. I'll give you two hundred crowns for him."

"He isn't mine to sell. He belongs to the lad."

"Bershome, two hundred crowns."

"Sorry, sir, I have put forth a lot of time with him."

"Three hundred."

"I can't sell him so soon, sir."

"Damned, you drive a hard bargain. Three hundred-fifty."

"He is not for sell, sir."

"What? I have offered nearly twice his worth!" Baron Westley turned to Lord Paxtare. "My Lord, talk sense into the boy."

Before his grandfather could speak, Bershome did. "I'll make you an offer, Baron. How about I allow you to bring one of your fillies over for breeding with him next season? Half the usual fee."

The old man looked at him and broke out in a smile. "What would you charge for breeding more?"

"Sir, I need to see if he is any good first. If he cannot be properly broken, he is worthless, and any colt of his could be just as hard to handle. I'd really hate to geld him."

"Either way, I'll hold you to the half-price breeding." The man held out his hand and showed a grinned. Bershome sealed the agreement with a handshake. His grandfather winked and smiled.

Agatha captured Bershome's arm again. "Bershome, let's walk through the orchard, please?" She guided him out of the stable, leaving the barons to discuss the attributes of the stallion themselves.

When they were alone, she leaned her head against his shoulder. "Bershome, you know I so love to be in your company."

"You are a pleasant person to be around yourself, Agatha."

"Then why do you not come over to visit more often?"

"I have responsibilities here that require most of my time."

"What occupies your time so, that silly bunch of apprentices of your uncle's?"

"My Grandfather keeps me quite busy. He expects more of me every year."

"Or is it that redhead I saw near you on the bench during lunch?"

"Near me? She was, what, across the table and three, four people away? She is here to study. She has no interest in me."

"So, you knew immediately who I was referring to.

"She is the only redhead in the castle other than a couple of servants."

"I saw the looks she was giving me."

"I don't know what you are talking about, Agatha. She doesn't even know who you are."

"Well, I know what she is, and she sees me as competition for your attention."

"Agatha, she is the daughter of an innkeeper. We are nobles."

"You are a fool to think that will stop her. Many a commoner has used her feminine wiles to successfully capture a nobleman."

"Enough of this, Agatha. At the rate you are going, I'm afraid you will be challenging her to a sword fight on the green next."

She stopped him, grabbed the front of his tunic with both hands, and pulled him to her until their noses almost touched. "That would be one way to make certain she knows you are mine."

"Agatha, we have been friends all our lives. You will be a nice catch for whatever man wins your heart. But I am not going to be getting married for a while."

"How do you know you have not already taken my heart?"

"Because you have never professed your love for me, nor even tried to kiss me in all these years. I intend to be of a proper, mature age when I choose to wed."

"You say that like I should expect to be a withered old maid before you do. Please tell me, and I'll wait for you."

"Agatha, I cannot make any such promises. We know not what the future holds."

"Well, do not wait too long. Father may marry me off for some political alliance."

"I hope he takes your feelings into consideration before he does."

"So," she pulled him again, so close their noses touched. "you do care about what happens to me."

He tilted his head down until their foreheads made contact to avoid any attempt for her to kiss him. He looked her in the eyes. "You have been a very dear friend all my life."

"We could be more, Bershome."

"I have already told you, Agatha."

"Promise me you will consider me first of all the women in the world."

"You share the top of a very short list. Tell me, Agatha, are you doing this because your father wants a stronger alliance with my grandfather or because you truly have feelings for me?"

"You know Cheryl will be turning sixteen in two months." She avoided the question.

"Yes, I'm well aware of that. It means her father will be parading her around here soon also." He stepped back from her. "Both of your fathers need to learn to get along. They think they can gain an advantage by an alliance with my grandfather with us marrying. You two girls used to be very good friends. What did she do to cause you to hate her?"

"She planned a party the same day as mine to try to steal you."

"That was over a year ago. She said she made a mistake and apologized."

"She has done it since then also. I think she has a spy in our household. Watch and see. I'll wager you get a party invitation on the same day as my birthday."

"Like I got from you last year on her birthday?"

Agatha snorted and looked away. "She had it coming."

"Why? Because her party last spring conflicted with yours?"

She stole a sideways glance at him. "No." He knew she lied. "Before that."

"Why are you girls fighting? I say it's because your fathers are."

"You can marry only one, Bershome."

"That decision is years away. You and Cheryl need to stop your petty, jealous squabbling. Get back to being friends."

"Then promise to always be my friend."

"That is a promise I will make with one condition."

"You would put a condition on our friendship?"

"You must promise that when it happens, you will never try to come between me and the woman I do marry."

She turned her back to him and tilted her head so her nose rose higher in the air. "You put an unfair restriction upon our friendship. Besides, you make me think you have already chosen her."

"No. I know not yet who the lady may be, or when I'll marry. But I would truly hate the loss of your friendship. Are you happy about the loss of Cheryl's company? Have you considered friendships may be all we ever have?"

"Well, I do see your point."

"I am going to persuade her to come to your party next month. If you turn on her, I will take it to be a personal affront. I hate being caught in the middle of petty squabbling between the two of you when it is caused by your fathers. You asked me to attend your birthday party. I will if you will send a nice legitimate invitation for Cheryl to be there as well."

"What if she refuses?"

"Then you have been the better person by offering a hand of friendship to her, and she refused it. What you should concentrate on is when she accepts it. The two of you have mending to attend."

"You are that certain she will accept?"

"Yes."

"Oh, I see. You are going to blackmail her into attending my birthday party, or you will not attend hers."

Bershome smiled.

"And you will insist I attend her party. You are putting a very high price on your friendship. What will you do if we all decide not to pay the price?"

"Look at what I am asking. Be friends again. Friends enhance our lives. I do not think it is a high price."

"I understand your argument. I simply resent you being so right." She tilted her head back and looked down her nose at him.

"I wish to ask another favor of you. If you say no, I will accept and respect your decision."

"First, you force me to do your wishes with blackmail, and now you ask a favor?" She squinted at him. "You don't deserve it, but I will allow you to ask."

"May I bring some of my friends? They don't get away from here much during the winter."

"What? There must be thirty of them."

"Not all, I was thinking of just the ones closer to our age. Say, fourteen and up? If you feel this is imposing on your good nature, I will withdraw my request."

"Well, I have heard it said: the more, the merrier. Fourteen and up."

"Thank you. My friends and I will be most appreciative. Now they are common people, and their presents will be basic but creative."

She laughed. "Tell them presents are not required. I invite them to share the frivolity as friends."

Bershome kissed her hand. "You prove yourself the better person already, Agatha."

After the baron and his daughter left, Bershome returned to class, took them to the rock garden, and watched spell casting practice.

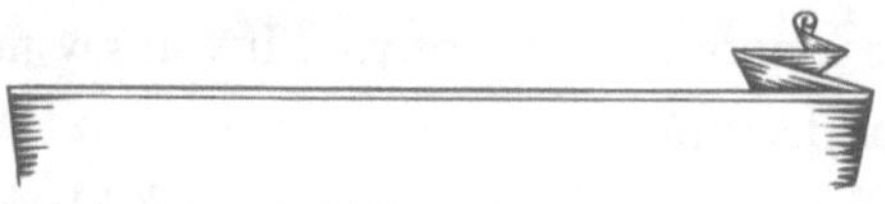

CHAPTER TWENTY-THREE

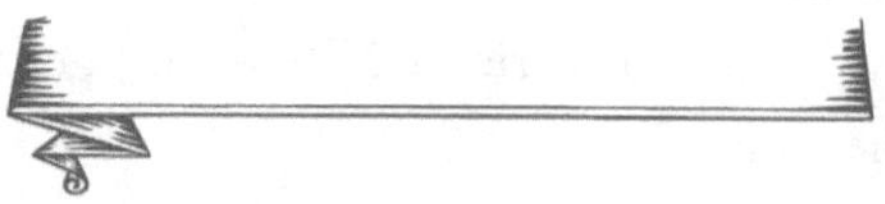

Zarlaam stood at the head table. "Today, my apprentices, you will go to separate training lessons. Ladies, you will go upstairs to the dormitory for tutelage under Lady Esmeralda, and the gentlemen will go to the practice grounds for weaponry training. Mister Leaves will be the instructor. Let us have a hearty breakfast and go to your training once you are finished."

Some of the lads teased back and forth about beating one another. Bershome sat at the table as he waited for the last lad to finish eating. He had arranged for Martello to hold all the boys in the dormitory. He moved over and sat with his back to the table beside the scrawny lad.

"Idreck, if you slip that last biscuit in your pocket and eat it before lunch, I will not tell on you. Just be sure you do not leave crumbs in your pocket."

The lad grinned. He stole a glance over his shoulder to make certain Bernary was not in the room. His hand snaked out, and the biscuit disappeared. "Thank you, sir."

"Run upstairs and ask Martello to bring everyone down to the front door."

The lad dashed out of the room. Bershome strolled out to the main entrance of the manor. When the group arrived, he led them to the practice grounds past the stables. Mr. Leaves was a middle-age gent about six feet tall. His dark hair formed a line around his head as if someone put a bowl over his head and cut away any hair that stuck out. Bershome watched as Mister Leaves took over. This was going to be fun.

"Good morning, lads. Grab a stick from the barrel and line up over here in pairs facing each other. I recognize all of you but one." The man stepped in front of Gerak and looked him up and down. "You are going to grow up to be a good-size man. How old are you, lad?"

"Fourteen, sir,"

"Have you ever wielded a sword before?"

"No, sir."

"Staff?"

"No, sir."

"Mace, shield, or a bow?"

"None, sir."

"How about that knife you carry?"

"I've learned a few things about how to use it."

"That how someone gave you that scar?"

"No one gave me nothing I didn't work for."

"Step over there, lad." He pointed towards another man. "Now, all of you know the exercise drill. Bershome, if you will walk them through the warm-up."

"Okay, lads, both hands on your sword. Over your heads. Bend down and reach for the ground."

Mister Leaves walked over to Gerak. "Lad, Peter here will give you one on one sword training. As it is, the smallest lad over there could make mincemeat of you."

Gerak snorted his disbelief at the thought.

"Size and muscle are not the only thing useful in wielding a sword. My kid sister could cut you to ribbons."

"I doubt that."

"Spunky, are you? But you know not what you are talking about."

"Prove it."

Bershome snickered. *Here we go.*

The soldier stepped back with a wicked smile.

"All right. Bershome, change of schedule. Everyone formed a circle. Jartus, come over here, lad. Gerak, go to the center of the circle."

The shortest lad in the group marched over, and the man bent down and whispered in his ear.

"That wouldn't be very fair, sir. He hasn't had any training."

"Everyone gets a first lesson."

"But, sir…"

"You have your instructions."

Bershome pinched his lower lip.

The two strutted to the middle of the circle about thirty feet across. Jartus stood with his stick held out. Gerak held his with the tip touching the ground.

"Never drag your sword in the dirt, young man."

Gerak raised his stick and dusted it off.

"First rule is you fight as gentlemen. No biting or hitting in the groin. If your opponent falls down, no kicking him." He looked at Gerak as he spoke and stepped back.

"Gerak, raise your sword and attack, Jartus."

"This isn't a fair-sized match, sir," Gerak said.

Laughter rippled through the apprentices assembled at the edge of the circle

Jartus rushed forward and struck Gerak on each side and once on a leg before Gerak managed to move to try to block a strike.

"Ouch."

"Get him, Jartus. No mercy," Willy encouraged him.

In the next minute, Gerak had been hit a dozen times and managed to block only two strikes. When he attempted a swing at Jartus, it was blocked, and he was hit again. Jartus made a final hard thrust into Gerak's mid-section.

Gerak doubled over with a grunt in pain as he fought for air.

"Stop."

Jartus stepped back several paces and stood ready.

Mister Leaves put his hand on Gerak's shoulder to steady him.

"Okay, the show is over, back to practice, lads."

"Hey, Gerak, no hard feelings, hey?"

Gerak only managed a red-faced nod. Bershome signaled all the boys to move back over to where he had them before.

"When you get your wind back, Gerak," Mister Leaves said, "go ask Mister Peters to teach you to defend yourself. Just for your information, Jartus was last year's champion for the young lad's group."

After a morning of combat training with every hand weapon in the arsenal, the lads returned to the manor. When they arrived, Lady Esmeralda had the ladies assembled on the courtyard where benches had been arranged. Bershome stepped aside to the side and allowed the apprentices to come forward and fell in at the rear of the line.

"Now ladies," Lady Esmeralda said, "we will practice the first-aid that we have learned this morning. Come here now, boys. We are waiting to treat your wounds. Form a line. No pushing." She motioned the first lad to move forward. "Ladies, what have we here?"

"Bloody nose," several said.

"How do we treat it?"

"Cold compress," Sallessa said.

"Tilt the head back and put gauze in the nostrils," Arleta said.

"Excellent, have a seat over there, lad." Lady Esmeralda called up the next lad.

"This one?"

"Black eye and bruised face. Slap a piece of steak on it for a while or ice in the winter." Janara piped up.

"Good, have a seat, lad."

"Ah, Jartus. I see no marks on you."

"I have bruises where I can't show you, my Lady."

"Behave, young man, or we will give you treatment for a broken nose."

"I have a bad bruise on my thigh from a mace."

"Oh. Ladies, how do you treat an injury from a spiked mace?"

"Pack the wound with a poultice."

"Why?"

"To prevent infection."

"Have a seat."

Chal stepped up with gauze in his nostrils and bloodstains on his chin and shirt.

"Oh, my, a genuine broken noise."

"Yeth, bamb."

"I see Mister Leaves has already straightened it for you."

"Yeth, bamb."

"Did you also bite your tongue?"

"Daff drust, bamb."

"What should we do for him now, ladies?"

"He will have a beautiful pair of black eyes."

"Concentrate, Helna."

"Ice pack and a steak patches over the eyes," she said.

Every boy was subjected to the scrutiny of the teacher and her students.

"Ah, Bershome, hiding in the back?"

"Minor bruises and nose bleed, Madam. Besides, the troops come first."

"Spoken like a true noble, Bershome. But how did you get a bloody nose?"

"Sucker punch by ambush."

"Arleta, you get a bloody nose." She turned her attention to everyone. "Ladies, each of you have a subject. Let us practice putting a splint on a broken limb. Pay attention, gentlemen. You may need to do this yourself one day."

Arleta looked up at Bershome's face and saw traces of blood in his nostrils, lines in the dust on his face, and a linger of moisture in his eyes. "I gather you took a staff thrust to the nose, my Lord." She smiled.

"No," he whispered, "it is that my eyes are so ashamed of their unworthiness to gaze upon such beauty as you. They weep for forgiveness."

Her cheeks flushed rosy as she lowered her own eyes and turned her head away. "I've never been complimented in such an eloquent manner, my Lord. However, you have my blessing and permission to gaze to your heart's content."

"My heart feels such elation; it may burst with joy."

"Oh, don't let that happen, my Lord. I only know how to set broken noses and splint broken bones."

"Dine with me tonight, and all will be fine."

"Have we not been dining across from each other all along?"

Bershome took a quick breath and let it out with a huff. "You make it sound so casual."

"Well, we are apprentices and friends. Let me get a wet rag to clean you up."

The lads each suffered through having splints put on their arm or leg for a supposed broken limb before anyone could go to lunch.

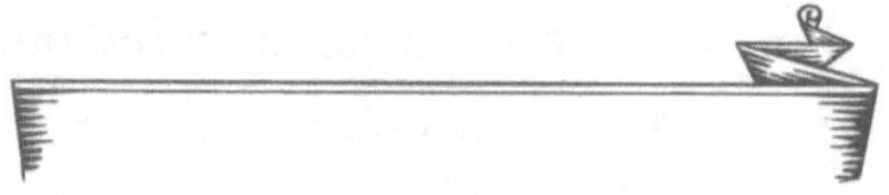

CHAPTER TWENTY-FOUR

The next morning, Bershome was the last one leaving the dormitory for breakfast. He closed the door and strolled down the stairs. He met Shyla walking up them.

"Pardon me, sir, but Baron Smiley and his daughter have just arrived."

"In time for breakfast? Hu boy."

"Would you like for me to take your robe back upstairs, sir?"

He released a deep sigh and removed the garment. "Thank you."

He made a quick mental review of the day's schedule and was relieved. No magic lessons would have to be rearranged. He set his shoulders and went into the dining hall. Baron Smiley and Cheryl sat at the head table with his grandfather. All seats were occupied at the table. The estate staff had saved him again. He smiled. Cheryl cocked her head sideways and returned the smile.

"Good morning, Grandfather, Baron Smiley," He accepted the baron's handshake. "And good morning, Lady Cheryl." He looked at the baron's daughter. "You are looking as beautiful as ever."

"Just for you, Bershome," she smiled and batted her eyelashes several times.

"How about we take a walk after breakfast, my lady. I have a new stallion to show off."

She smiled wider and nodded as he walked away to take a seat beside Martello. Across the table sat Freya, Arleta, and Janara. Bershome dug into his breakfast as the girls watched.

"Martello, I need you to keep the heathens down to a reasonable riot today, please," Bershome said between bites.

"Sure."

"Bershome, who are the visitors?" Freya asked,

Bershome paused with a fork full of food just in front of his mouth. He sighed as he lowered his fork and looked at his plate. "The only answer that comes to my mind is to say they are another part of my nightmare."

Those sitting close to him burst out laughing at his analogy.

He looked at Martello and the ladies. Arleta tilted her head and showed him a pressed lip frown as an expression of sympathy. He shrugged and resumed eating. After breakfast, Bershome went to stand beside Cheryl. She had finished eating and waited for him.

"Are you ready?" She smiled at him.

"Yes."

He offered her a hand. They walked out past the remaining apprentices that were still eating. A couple of the younger ones stole a look at them and snickered. He chose not to speak until they were outside.

"Lady Cheryl, I must ask. Did you travel half the night from your home or camp outside our door until time for breakfast?"

"No, silly. We were but a couple of hours down the road at an inn when we were awakened out of our sleep by the most awful ruckus. The innkeeper's son and daughter-in-law were carrying on about something he had done. Father decided since we were already up, we should continue our journey home. I insisted on stopping by."

"Well, you are a most pleasant surprise to find at our breakfast table." He guided her into the stable and approached Rhubarb's stall.

"Thank you. We enjoy visiting here because everyone is always most friendly to us."

"We enjoy visits from our friends and neighbors."

"Oh, my, he is a beauty," she whispered.

Bershome appreciated her knowledge of horses. He grabbed the horse's halter and stroked his nose.

"What did you name him?" She raised her hand, allowing the horse to get her scent.

"Rhubarb, because of his bittersweet spirit."

"Is he saddle-broken yet?"

"Yes, but he is a touch rebellious."

"You have to bring him over to let me ride him after he settles down. Please?"

"Certainly. He should be ready before long."

"Speaking of visits, I wish to invite you to my birthday party."

"Interesting, are you not planning a party on the twenty-fifth of next month?"

"No. Should I?" she asked and grinned at him.

He looked at her with a raised eyebrow. She looked away at Rhubarb and tried to act innocent. "I will attend your birthday party, only under two conditions."

"One that I be civil and go to Agatha's party and play nice. What is number two?"

"You invite her to your party."

"You expect her to play nice, I gather?"

"You, Agatha, and I have been friends our entire lives until this past year."

"It was she who chose not to accept my apology. Father forced me to have the party on that date."

"Your fathers have been fighting border squabbles for decades. They always keep it down to small bands of men here or there and spread them apart so as to not make it an out-right act of war. They are spreading the hate that drives them into your hearts. Do you know how much it pains me to see my two most favorite friends not speaking to each other?"

"Her father is trying to poison you against my family to prevent you from considering me worthy of courtship."

"What makes you say that?"

She looked about them and leaned close to him to whisper. "I have a spy in her house."

"She suspects such."

"Well, she will never know for sure."

"Cheryl, I wish for you ladies to make amends and be friends again. It weighs heavy upon my heart. For some day may come that friendships are all we have."

"You speak as if you are choosing never to wed."

"I intend to be more mature when I take a wife."

"Are you considering me as a prospective wife?"

"You share the top of a very short list."

"Share?"

"All ladies who know are on it with equal standing. For now."

"How can I move closer to the top?"

"Are you asking me because you truly have affection for me or because your father is pressuring you to marry me for his political alliance and gain?"

"I have always had feelings for you, Bershome."

"Friendship is one thing. But you have never openly declared anything more."

She looked away without a word.

"Please promise me one thing?" He asked.

"What would that be?"

"Promise that you will be a friend to the lady I choose to marry as you have been my friend, no matter who she may be. I would hate to lose your friendship."

"That could be difficult, Bershome."

"Even when I fall in love with a woman, I will always cherish your friendship."

"Your wife will be jealous and hate me."

"I hope if you are her friend also, then there would be no cause for jealousy. Promise me?"

"You do push. I suppose you demanded the same of Agatha?" She poked a finger at him.

"Yes, because I want you two always to be my friends and be friends for each other again. You enjoy the company of each other and have fun together."

"Yes," she smiled. "Remember, when we tied you up and stuffed you in the barrel and rolled you around in it?"

"Yes. I also remember I could have drowned when it got away from you and hit the pond had it not turned upright in the water. Especially considering I was the only one of us that knew how to swim at the time." He raised his hands shoulder high.

"We thought you would get free of the ropes in time."

"You had me tied with hatchet knots."

"They were not. We untied them ourselves."

"After I spent half an hour on my head in the barrel floating around until Mister Hanson rescued me."

"You were so red-faced when you came out."

"Yes, I was. But not near as red as you two were when Mister Hanson finished scolding you both."

Cheryl reached up and petted Rhubarb. "He is a beautiful beast."

"Yes," Bershome almost whispered as he watched her.

"Father has hinted that he may marry me off to another for alliance purposes."

"I hope he takes your feelings into consideration before he decides."

"So do I. Otherwise, I have no idea what will become of me."

"Posh pot, Cheryl. I know you better than that. In the long run, you will marry the man you want and have your father thinking it was his idea to begin with."

She smiled at him. "Father is probably boring your grandfather to death with his business ideas. I think we should go rescue him, and Father and I head on home. We have been on the road for a month coming back from the capital. Father had to go see the king about a trade license of some nature."

Bershome knew the intent of their visit had been accomplished. Her father had put her up for courtship.

"Now, may I ask a personal favor about your birthday party? He presented the same request he had with Agatha.

"Certainly, your friends are my friends. But, I get at least two dances."

"I promise. Thank you."

They chit-chatted casually as they meandered back to the manor. Her father was sitting in the study with his grandfather.

"I told the Prince we needed to build better roads like the Romarts did." Baron Smiley said.

"And how did they build those roads?" Lord Paxtare continued without allowing an answer, "By conquest and on the backs of slaves. Our forefathers were some of those slaves."

"There are countless heathen, barbaric tribes in Aflantika that run around practically naked and half-starving to death."

"And there they should remain on their continent. We should not oppress them and drag them up here when we barely do well enough to feed our own. I cannot condone slavery."

"Neither would I, Father." Cheryl spoke up before he could counter in the argument.

"How is the horse?"

"He is magnificent. Father, shall we leave our friends to go on about their planned business of the day and continue home? I so miss my own room, my own bath, and most of all, my own bed."

Baron Smiley glanced at Bershome but betrayed nothing of his thoughts. He rose to his feet. "She is as pushy as her mother was.

But sweet as an angel, though," he hastened to add as he smiled at Bershome.

Bershome and Lord Paxtare escorted their guest out and watched the coach leave.

"Interesting visits this week," Lord Paxtare said.

"Yes, Grandfather. It seems that many young lasses are coming of the marrying age this year."

"Yes, I expect more this winter."

"Definitely. According to my count, there are two other daughters that have not announced themselves yet, the twins. Perhaps we should put them all in a pit and declare the last one standing the winner."

"Oh, if you want a sparring partner more than a wife, I believe Mister Leaves's younger sister is widowed and available again."

"I was being facetious, Grandfather."

He reached over and rested his hand on Bershome's shoulder and sighed, "I know, son."

"Besides, she is five years older than I am and can still beat me at swords. I can't see marrying a woman who can beat me at swords."

They laughed.

"How goes the teaching?"

"Math and English today."

"Well, I've my own math work to do. I have to tally the books."

Bershome wandered over to the classroom and sat in the empty chair in the back of the class. He only half-listened to the assignment Lady Esmeralda presented.

"Now take the paper from the bowl and tell no one what you have for your work. Your one double-sided parchment is due Monday."

The bowl was passed around the room, and everyone took a folded slip of paper. When the bowl reached the back, Bershome moved to take it, but Lady Esmeralda took the bowl first.

"You need not participate, Bershome."

He nodded absentmindedly. "Oh, I need to speak with everyone before you dismiss them." At the end of the class, she turned them over to him. He dismissed the younger ones and waited until they left.

"I have some good news for all of you. I have been given permission by a couple of my friends to invite you older apprentices to two birthday parties. The first one is on the twenty-fifth of next month. The other is two months later."

"Do they have anything to do with the ladies that have visited this week?" Trejann asked.

"As a matter of fact, they do. Both ladies' fathers are bannermen to my Grandfather."

"Who is the first one that visited?"

"Lady Agatha Westler. The second one was Lady Cheryl Smiley. They understand you have limited funds and need not worry about a gift. If you can give one, it is your choice."

"What if we pool our resources and give her one gift from all of us?" Arleta asked.

Bershome smiled and held his hands out palms up. "Work it out among yourselves. I'll offer to match half what you pool together. Remember, they are non-magical people."

"How old are they?

"They are both turning sixteen."

"That means they are eligible. Do you have any designs pertaining to them?" Trejann asked.

Bershome blew a huff of wind. "Everyone ready for supper?"

They all filed out, and Bershome surveyed the classroom before he closed the door and locked it. He turned around and found Chal waiting on him. "Ready for supper, Chal?"

"Yes, sir."

"You can call me, Bershome, Chal."

"May I ask you a question, Bershome?"

"Certainly," he said and walked down the path, but he realized Chal was not following. He stopped and looked at the lad.

"Can we talk here?"

"As you wish." Bershome pointed to a bench beside the path. They sat together.

"What does love mean to you, and how do you know you are in love?"

"Has one of our ladies caught your fancy?" Bershome reached up and ruffled his hair.

"No, this is for my paper next week."

"Hmm. The best way I can describe love is to compare it to a butterfly. It is a very fickle and elusive creature. It is also very delicate and easily damaged or lost."

"What do you mean by that?"

"It is one thing for a guy to fall in love with a girl. But for love to be complete, she needs to love him also. That is the fickle and elusiveness. Once you know a girl loves you, you must treat love gently. Girls have problems telling a guy they love him. They are afraid of being hurt. That is the delicate part. You have to pay attention to things they say. Girls don't directly tell you how they are feeling. It is what they think about something. You are supposed to remember what they have told you in the past and arrive at the correct conclusion." Bershome gazed into the distance and gathered his thoughts.

"Females have very complicated emotions. They can be worrying about many things at the same time. Such as what you think about them? What are they going to wear at the next social gathering? Do you think they are prettier than their main rival? Will you be a good husband? To win a girl's love, you must first choose to be her friend. Spend time to get acquainted and to understand her first. Somewhere along the line, she may fall in love with you also."

"How do you hint to a girl you are attracted to her?"

"Compliment her casually and often. Tell her you like her hair, her dress, her laugh. Even if it is like an old hag's cackle. Women are vain and want you to notice their beauty. Let them know you think they are smart. Complimenting lets them know they have your attention. The most important time to give them a compliment is when they look their worst or when they are not feeling their best. How they react to your compliment lets you know a bit about what they are thinking of you."

"What kind of girls are you attracted to?"

"How long does this report have to be?" Bershome cocked his head and looked at Chal.

"Double-sided page of parchment."

Bershome sighed. "First of all, I have heard it said beauty is only skin deep. True beauty is shown by the soul of a person. What they do and how they conduct themselves shows a lot about a person. The type of woman I find attractive is smart, self-reliant, trustworthy, honest, sociable, generous, and has high moral standards. I mostly listen for their laugh. You can tell a lot in a lady's laugh. Now, if the young lady is pretty, it only makes things better."

They heard a giggle from beyond the nearby bushes.

"But a lady should not be a sneaky girl eavesdropping from behind bushes," Bershome spoke so that whoever hid in the bushes would be sure to hear.

The bush shook, and they heard the tapping of several shoes on the stones as someone ran off towards the manner.

"Chal, who put you up to this?"

"Lady Esmeralda." The lad pulled a scrap of paper from his pocket. "See?" The paper said: Interview Bershome. 'Ask about love and what he looks for in a woman.'

"Let's go eat. What is that woman up to?" He mused over the question as he headed for supper.

The cooks had made roast beef. Bershome joined his friends at the table.

"Bershome," Arleta said as he cut a slice of roast and put it on his plate. "I have a question for you if you don't mind."

"Challenge me." Bershome cut a slice piece of roast and put it on his plate.

"How would you resolve a difficulty between two arguing factions over a border issue?"

Bershome did not look at her. "Freya, what is your assignment?"

The two girls snickered. "I'm supposed to ask you what you have to say about taxes and the responsibilities of nobility."

"It appears I know what my weekend is going to be like. Everyone is going to be following me around and bugging me with questions."

"Sorry, Bershome. It is our writing assignments we need to turn in on Monday."

"I wish you all well on your spelling and composition. What you don't know is that Grandfather put Lady Esmeralda up to this task. While the bunch of you are writing a simple paper for grammar study, I am being tested on politics, philosophy, government, personal ethics, and no telling what else."

"Oh, sorry," Arleta offered her sympathy.

"Thank you, but an apology is not necessary. I have been tutored all my life for a position of responsibility."

CHAPTER TWENTY-FIVE

Bershome nudged his horse, and the caravan headed to Lady Agatha's party. Several apprentices pulled out their spellbooks to study and practice. The effort was short lived because the pace the driver set made riding too rough to read by. They told stories to one another or sang.

Halfway through the day, the caravan was rolling along a hill-crest. The Lieutenant pointed down the hill into the woods. Bershome followed his finger and saw several boxed-in wagons sitting in among the trees. There were people milling about between them. A couple of ladies stood beside fires, cooking in kettles hung from metal rod tripods.

"Gypsies, on Paxtare property, sir."

"Let's have a visit with them." Bershome maneuvered his horse out of the caravan, and the lieutenant followed.

"Drive on, Jerrod. We will catch up," Bershome told the lead wagon driver. They rode at an easy pace to the camp to avoid causing alarm. About halfway there, he glanced back over his shoulder and realized that the lieutenant had signaled two soldiers to follow them. The men were spreading out from behind him to get a better fighting advantage if necessary. The soldiers had their bows in their hands held down by their side without drawn arrows. They would not act aggressively. He nodded and smiled in approval at his lieutenant.

He surveyed the camp. There were about a dozen wagons in the group. Only a few women were visible from his location. No men or children were out in the open. Bershome suspected a bow was aimed at him. It was difficult to tell how many people were in the camp.

"Hello, in the camp!" He spoke loudly as he stopped about ten feet from the closest person, a young dark-haired woman stirring the contents of the kettle. She had watched him descend the hill. She faced him and curtsied.

"Good day, m' Lord."

He bowed over the saddle horn and smiled at her. "Pardon me, my lady, but is your clan leader here abouts?" He looked her in the eye. She struck him as a fetching young lady his age. A middle-aged man hurried through the camp.

"Greetings, Your Lordship." The man stopped beside the young woman and bowed.

"Mind if I ask the name of your clan, sir?"

"McGiddens, sir."

"Hmm, I know of a Donyat McGiddens clan. Any relations to you?"

"He is my cousin, sir. I'm Willar McGiddens."

Bershome dismounted his horse, handed the reins to his lieutenant, walked up to the man, and removed his glove. He held out his hand for a handshake.

"Well, sir, if you have seen them in the past two years, they might have mentioned the Paxtare estates in conversation. I'm Bershome, and you are on our land."

"The name is familiar. No offense intended, sir, but my cousin put the name to a venerable old man," Willar said.

"That would be my grandfather. Mind if I ask your travel plans?"

"We are headed south to Messedia for an entertainment in four days. But one of our wagons crossing the river down that way," he jerked his thumb back over his shoulder, "broke an axle, and we need a couple of days to repair it."

"Sorry to hear that. You will be pressed for time. Could we offer a hand? My men would gladly assist you."

"Oh, I appreciate the offer, sir, but we have more hands than can do the job already."

"I'll tell you what, about a mile south, back the way I just came, stands a massive oak tree. It died just this past summer. You will find plenty of firewood from it. I'm sure the core of a larger limb would still be sound enough for making an axle."

"Thank you, your Lordship. We are most grateful."

"The hunting in this area is fair. Deer are present. You may take one for your clan. But you will find boar mostly. There are some pheasant and turkey as well. But they like the brushy country a few miles south."

"Thanks, sir. We will only hunt what we need, your Lordship."

"If you want to buy beef, sheep, or goat, you can send a rider down my back trail which follows the river. Our home is half a day's ride by horse. How are you set for grain and flour?"

"Fair, sir."

"If you look for Mister Hansen, our stables master, he can direct you to the man to sell you goods and staples. We also have an excellent blacksmith if you need something for that axle.

"I'll be coming back through in a few days. It would not hurt for you to stop our by our castle and see what we have that you may need. If you leave someone with the broken wagon, I'll see to it they get help. Our craftsmen are some of the finest."

"Thank you. We appreciate your kindness, your Lordship." He bowed.

"It is an honor to meet another member of the McGiddens." Bershome offered his hand, and they shook again.

"My Lady." He nodded to her and returned to his horse. Bershome and his guards turned and galloped away to catch up with their friends.

"That was nicely done back there, lad. I like the way you laid down the rules about buying our livestock instead of helping themselves," the lieutenant said.

"I saw it work for Grandfather years ago. Seemed like the thing to do."

CHAPTER TWENTY-SIX

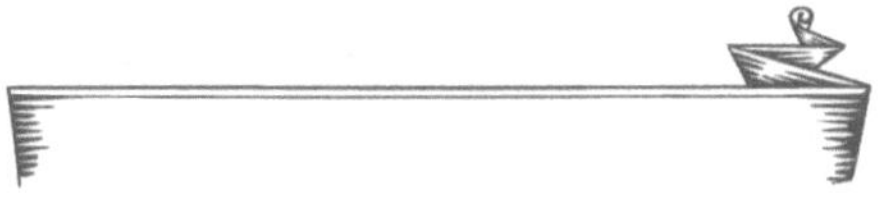

The lead horsemen spread out and slowed their pace so that they were flanking Bershome and the lieutenant as they approached the castle, and dropped back as they reached the receiving party at the door of the manor. Baron Westley was standing with Agatha by his side to greet Bershome. Behind them stood the household staff, ready to answer the baron's beck and call. With a look and a wave of a hand from the baron, the stable boy ran up and took the reins from Bershome as he dismounted.

"Thank you, young man. He is high spirited. Watch he doesn't hurt you."

"Salutations, Bershome! Welcome to our humble home."

"Greeting's Baron, Lady Agatha." He shook the baron's hand and kissed hers."

"How was your travel, lad?"

"Quite pleasant, Baron." He added with a whisper, "But I had the advantage of my own horse. Baron, may I present the commander of my guards. Lieutenant Swann."

"Your Lordship." The man clicked his heels and bowed slightly.

"Lieutenant Swann, see my commander, and he will make arrangements for your men."

"You are most accommodating, Baron. Thank you," the man said and stepped away to handle his duties.

"Bershome, you timed your arrival well." Agatha smiled. "Bring in your friends and let us dine. Our cook announced supper is ready just a few minutes ago."

"Have any other guest arrived yet?"

"A couple. Most live close enough to travel here in half a day, and as my invitation said, the festivities will commence at noon tomorrow on my birthday."

"There are those who would not spend a night in my house, Bershome," Baron Westley said.

"That is a pity, Baron, for I know you are most pleasant and generous to your guests."

"Thank you, Bershome. Remember, you and yours are always welcome here."

"Thank you, sir. Speaking of friends, please allow me to introduce my companions."

Bershome turned and beckoned his friends to approach with a wave of his hand. He proceeded to introduce them one at a time as they filed by and shook hands with Baron Westly and Lady Agatha.

"You have quite a passel of friends, Bershome. Agatha let me know they were coming. We have arrangements for the ladies in the manor and a tent over there for the lads. I hope they do not take offense."

"I'm certain it will be fine for us."

"Oh, not you, m'lad," he whispered, "we have a room ready for you."

Bershome whispered back. "Thank you for the consideration, and please take no offense, but I wouldn't feel quite proper, sir. I'll stay in the tent with the lads also."

The Baron smiled. He smacked Bershome on the back. "Let's us go dine for the evening, lad." He walked beside him into the manor with Agatha just behind them, and the remainder of the group followed. Bershome followed the baron to the head table.

"Earl Sweeney, you know Lord Paxtare's grandson, Bershome." The baron made the introduction to an elderly man seated at the far left of the table.

"Don't get up, my Lordship." Bershome shook his hand with a smile.

"How is Lord Paxtare, lad?"

"He is doing fine, working hard, and healthy as an ox. I'll let him know you asked."

"That old goat will probably outlive us all."

"I hope so. I'm rather attached to him, sir,"

"Come visit sometime, Bershome. I want you to meet my twin granddaughters. They are all growing up lovely and well mannered."

"I'll vouch that they were the last time I saw them. Excuse me, sir. I'll leave you to enjoy your meal."

"They will be here on the morrow for the party."

"Excellent." Bershome nodded and sat between Agatha and her father. Everyone else filled in the spaces along the other tables. All the tables held massive platters piled with food. Each table had a roasted pig, a roasted lamb or goat, piles of beef, and chicken. There were platters of trenchers, cheeses, boiled potatoes, mashed potatoes, bowls of butter, beets, cabbages, carrots, radishes, pears, peaches, apricots, plums, and more.

"Tell me, Bershome," Agatha whispered to him, "why did you bring the little redhead?"

"She is in the age group we agreed on. Do I detect a hint of jealousy?"

"Of course not." Agatha tipped her head upward and turned her face away.

"But gosh, she does care," he whispered in her ear.

"It's just that I always thought it would be just us, Bershome. Now every time I see you, that redhead is around.

"She is an apprentice of my uncle's and a friend. Besides, I've only seen you twice this year. Today is the second time."

"We aren't little children anymore. I can't just go to your place and spend a week at a time frolicking in the fields and play bowl or charades. I stay pretty busy nowadays. Father was ill for a week, and I had to run things around here. He is worried about passing away and leaving me all alone. He is afraid I'll fall prey to an evil husband. That is another reason he is pushing your grandfather about us getting married. Do you think she is prettier than me?"

"No." He took a bite of food and detected her smile from the corner of his eye. The conversation was light for the rest of the meal. Bershome mopped the last of his gravy up from his plate with the remaining piece of bread and leaned back with a satisfied smile.

"Did you save room for the chocolate pudding?" the baron asked. "Agatha made it herself. She is quite a cook, m'boy."

"I'll have to try it, sir."

Little pudding cups were brought out at the baron's wave. After the head table was served, the pudding was offered to the rest of the room.

"Mmm, Agatha this is divine and smooth on the pallet." Bershome inhaled the pudding.

"Ah, Barron," Bershome leaned back in his chair and rubbed his belly, "You do serve your guests well."

"Only the best for you, Bershome. Now tell me," he whispered in his ear, "have you seen any lassie prettier or handier in the house than my Agatha?"

"I can't say that I have, sir."

"She will make a fine wife. Lord Dresmore's son has been coming around the past year to spend time with her."

Bershome furrowed his eyebrows as he tried to place the name and man.

"I expect him to make a proposal before long, but enough about that. Bobby, How about a little violin music to entertain us while we let out feasting settle in our bellies."

The family minstrel produced his violin from a pouch on the back of his chair. He struck up a mellow tune and played it very well as he moved about the room and up between the U-shaped table arrangement.

Afterward, Janara asked for a special tune. He stepped over close to her and began playing. Janara sat with her eyes closed through the first set and began singing a melody of two young lovers. Trejann joined in and sang the boy's part, and everyone sang the chorus.

Bobby played a few more spirited tunes, and the Baron finally called out thanking him. All clapped, and he took a bow.

"It was a lovely evening with you here, Bershome. I need to retire and start early in the morning. I gather you need to help your friends get settled in?"

"Uh, yes, sir. Please excuse me." Bershome turned to face Agatha. "Thank you for that excellent pudding. He moved to place a kiss on her cheek. She turned her head and gave him a full kiss on the lips.

He looked at her a moment and could not help his blushing. "That is a first in many years. Last time you did that, it was to make Lady Robin jealous."

"I'm full of surprises, Bershome. I have other tasty things just for you. It is a pity you will be sleeping in the tent," she whispered.

He whispered back. "For some reason, I think I will end up in less trouble that way."

Agatha looked away a moment and back to Bershome. "I think the little redhead is jealous."

He didn't look as he pressed his mouth close to her ear to whisper. "And you are loving it. Lady Agatha, would you be an angel and show the ladies their rooms?"

"Certainly, Bershome. I'll put her in the room we saved for you right next to mine. I hope she isn't a light sleeper. I do believe our house is haunted."

"Beware, she has a very powerful amulet of protection, dear."

He walked over to the table where his friends sat. He made it a point not to look at Arleta directly.

"Ladies, our hostess will be showing you to your rooms shortly. I recommend you insist on sharing two or three to a room so they will have others for new guests arriving. By the way, this castle is not haunted. Gentlemen, we will be sleeping out in the tent the baron has provided for us. So if you are all through eating, we may take our leave." Bershome looked the guys over and gave his head slight jerk to his right. They all rose and followed him.

Bershome led the way outside to the tent. The tent was about fifteen feet wide and thirty feet long. Planks had been laid down to make a floor. Bits of grass poked up between the boards. Two open-grate metal fire pits sat near each end of the tent. In the middle rested a narrow table with a bowl of fruit, bottles of wine, a pitcher of water, and several mugs. Beds had been set up along each side the length of the tent. The first two bunks had all the guy's kits sitting neatly in a row. A servant boy of about sixteen placed a log in the farthest fire pit. He faced them.

"Sir, Baron Westly told me to fetch anything you wished to make your stay pleasant."

Most of the lads jumped over beds to lay claim to the ones closest to the fires. Bershome walked up to him and offered his hand. "Bershome Paxtare. What is your name?"

"Larly, sir." The lad seemed taken aback by Bershome friendliness and almost missed the handshake.

"I see you have the north end closed up on the tent."

"Aye, sir. I also moved the planking to hold down the sides."

"Excellent idea, if the wind says calm, it will be quite warm in here. How long have you been out here, Larly?"

"Since the tent was erected and beds brought in. I prepared them for you. I can fetch more covers if you think you need more."

"You missed out on supper."

"My work was not completed, sir."

"You have done an excellent job. Go get something to eat."

"I, I cannot, sir. I'm here to attend to you gentlemen's needs, sir." Bershome smiled.

"Larly, one of my friends is still hungry. I think he has a hollow leg where his food goes to instead of his belly. He needs a single plate with a nice portion of roast beef, oh about this big," he gestured with his hand, "gravy poured over it and some mashed potatoes, plenty of butter, green beans, a couple or three rolls. What other vegetables do you like, Larly?" Bershome saw Larly licked his lips slightly.

"I'm a bit partial to beets, sir."

"Excellent, add plenty of beets for you. I see we have wine for you to wash it down with."

"Anything else, sir?"

"I think that will fill a grumbling belly."

"I'll be back right away, sir." The lad slipped past him and hurried out of the tent.

"How could you torture him like that?" Martello asked as he examined the wine bottles."

"What do you mean? It's his supper he is fetching."

"You think he won't eat while he is gone?"

"If he didn't understand my words, he may gobble down a roll and stuff one in his pocket while the cook makes the plate. Do you notice the scent of pear in here?"

"Hey, come to think of it. That Baron is pretty good to scent the air with it."

"He didn't. I think the lad gobbled down a pear and is burning the core to hide what he did. Poor fellow."

"That is nice of you, Bershome."

"Has everyone found the bunk they want?" He looked about.

"Bershome. There's no corkscrew for the wine."

"Jacks, I'd figured you would notice. Does a simple cork in a bottle stop you?"

"You said no magic."

"We are alone. Are we not?"

Wands appeared from inside vests and up sleeves instantly. The corks had no chance as they shot out of the bottles by themselves. The wands became invisible as quickly as they appeared.

"Discretion, gentlemen, the chamber pot is in the little tent outside with no heat. Also, we don't need a drunk knocking over the fires and burning the tent down. Larly is a diligent lad and has worked hard for your comfort. I would be quite dissatisfied with you if you cause him to look bad in the baron's eyes."

Everyone nodded in agreement. Larly returned with a large plate covered with a bowl turned upside down. Bershome saw breadcrumbs on in the corners of his mouth. He winked at Martello.

"I hope this is satisfactory, sir."

"Larly, I'm sorry if you miss understood me. I consider you my friend."

"Thank you, sir. I am honored." He looked downward as he spoke. He held out the plate as Bershome poured a mug of wine.

"Have a seat here on this bunk by the fire Larly and enjoy your supper."

"Sir?" he asked.

"You are my friend. The supper is for you, Larly. Sit and eat, please." Bershome spoke as he held the mug out to the lad. "This bunk will do nicely," he gestured with his hand.

"Here, sit, Larly." Jartus patted the end of his bunk for Larly to sit on.

The lad sat down and uncovered his supper. He picked up the fork and looked about. Bershome stepped past him toward the front of the tent. He faced his friends.

"Gentlemen, now we review everything Lady Esmeralda and Mister Bernary taught us about etiquette and how to conduct ourselves in during the party and when dancing with the ladies."

"Ugh," a couple guys groaned, but gave their attention to him.

Bershome was about finished with his skit of the wrong things not to do during the party when the baron arrived. Bershome stepped to block the man's view of the tent.

"Bershome, m' lad. I wanted to check on you before settling in for the night. I really wish you would take that room."

"Baron, your man Larly, has done an excellent job keeping the fires stoked. We are cozy as a hound dog in a hay pile, sir. He even set planks on the bottom edges of the tent to keep out the wind and the bunks on them to hold them down. Smart lad you have there, sir."

Bershome stepped aside as the baron glanced down at the planking with an expression of enlightenment. Larly had quickly set his plate aside and picked up a log to be right on cue with it at the fire. Bershome noticed Jartus had pulled the plate onto his lap as if he had been eating.

"Boy, I don't want any of Bershome's friends getting a chill in the night. You understand me?"

"Yes, Baron. I'll fetch more wood shortly, sir."

The baron smacked Bershome on the back. "You send Larly for anything you wish."

"I will. Thank you, Baron. You bundle up against the cold going back in, sir."

The baron surveyed the tent and left with puzzled smile on his face after looking at Jartus. Bershome tied the tent flaps shut, and Larly let out a nervous sigh.

Bershome patted the lad on the shoulder. "He will not be back tonight. Go finish your supper," he whispered.

"Now, where were we, gentlemen?"

He was answered with more groans.

"In summary. Your conduct is a reflection on me, my grandfather, and Master Zarlaam. Mind your manners, hands off the inappropriate places on the ladies. Easy on the wine. I don't need you stumbling about the dance floor and embarrassing us all. It is dark out, and the sun rises early. I'm going to bed."

"Yea," was a lame cheer, and a couple of handclaps from some of the guys.

He picked an empty bunk, removed his boots and sword before he crawled under the covers. Larly turned down the lamps and slipped out with the dishes to take them back to the kitchen.

CHAPTER TWENTY-SEVEN

Crowing roosters announced the dawn. A couple of lads slipped on their boots and rushed out to relieve themselves.

Larly slept fallen over from a sitting position on a bunk with a quilt around him for warmth. He had stayed up most of the night attending the fires. The pits were half-filled with ash and coals. A couple of lads stuck some logs in the coals to revive the fires.

Gerak returned to the tent and jumped back under his covers. "Damn! It's cold out there!"

Larly bolted upright. He dropped the quilt on the bed and moved to tend the fires. "I'm sorry I let the fires die down, sirs," he muttered.

"Larly," Martello said, "You did an excellent job."

"Here, here," several spoke up.

Bershome pulled on his boots and made his rush to the chamber pot. "Larly." Bershome beckoned when he returned. "Good job last night. We could use a couple of pots of wash water and towels.

"The Baron has arranged for you the use of the downstairs washroom, sir. I'm to show it to you."

"Excellent. One, two, three, four." Bershome pointed at guys as he counted. "Larly here will escort you to the washroom. Act like civilized heathens and keep the riotous noise down."

"Anything else, Captain?" Gerak asked as he stood with his toiletry kit in his hand.

Bershome ignored his derogatory tone and stepped aside to let them out.

Larly returned. "Sir, his Lordship says there room aplenty in the manor. You may wait in the common hall and get out of this chilly wind."

"Let's go, guys. Thank you again, Larly. Go now to get your breakfast. The bunks can wait," he said, heading into the castle.

"Ah, Bershome. Have a good night's rest?"

"Excellent Baron. Larly was most diligent keeping the tent warm."

"Good, good. Breakfast will be served shortly, and then Agatha has a full day of activities planned. I have obligations that require me elsewhere. I'll leave you young ones to have your fun."

The lads had washed up and dressed in their finest clothes. The ladies were clad in their best. Arleta sported the new long-sleeved dress she had made of the emerald-colored cloth she had bought when she first arrived. It was obvious she had shared the material because bits of it showed up in accessories on some of the other ladies.

Agatha wore a golden-yellow dress with her short sleeves, which were gathered and puffed out above the biceps. The neckline was cut lower than anything Bershome had ever seen her in and displayed a suggestive, but respectable, amount of her cleavage.

Bershome sat between her and her father at breakfast. Agatha kept leaning forward in Bershome's direction with an excuse to speak with him or her father.

"Father, what time will the minstrels be arriving today?"

"Malcolm promised me by noon sharp."

"We cannot have a party without them."

"What do I pay Bobby extra for then?" he asked.

"His folk songs are not fit for party dancing. A violin and lyre for music just will not do."

"If I may offer," Bershome spoke, "Jartus plays a very good flute that he did bring with him for entertainment on the road. Jacks carries rhythm well on a drum, and a large pot could suffice. Livonia is good on a harpsichord and sings like a bird. You heard Janara last night."

"There you go, Darling. You will want not for music, and the entertainment will not suffer."

She dropped her voice. "They are guests, Father. They should not have to perform."

"Agatha," Bershome cut the baron off, "I'm certain they would be delighted, if not honored, and not mind at all. In fact, I'll sing you a song in honor of your birthday."

"Then, you need not worry until noon, Dear." Her father smiled and dismissed the issue by taking a drink of his wine and turning his head to the Lord Sweeney.

Agatha sat back in a huff.

"Agatha, I assure you, we would consider it a privilege," Bershome reassured her.

She placed her hand on his and gave it a squeeze. "I suppose the minstrels will be arriving with a company of the stage players."

He returned the squeeze. "All will be alright."

Agatha was tense the rest of the morning as she rearranged the dining hall into a ballroom. Bershome and his buddies lent a hand to the house servants and helped muscle the large tables out into the corridor and arrange the chairs along the walls.

"Lady Agatha," Denniks, a servant, rushed in from outside, "A coach arrives."

"Oh my, we aren't ready yet. Why did Father leave so soon?"

"Agatha," Bershome laid his hand on her arm. "I'll receive your guest for you. Shall we, Denniks?"

"Oh, bless you, Bershome," she called to his back.

He headed out and met the coach arriving at the door, turning up his collar against the wind. A wagon piled high and covered with canvas followed the coach.

The coach driver and escorting soldiers were dripping wet. Bershome recognized the family crest painted on the side of the coach. He opened the door as the footman bent over to set the step-stool in place. A flood of muddy water rushed out and drenched the man.

"Oh, my goodness! I'm sorry, I didn't expect the water," Bershome apologized.

The footman stood, showing a smile. "Quite all right, sir. I couldn't get any wetter."

A man stepped down dressed in a stuffy-looking suit with a high collar and scarf puffed out at his throat. He was muddy up to the knees and dripping wet as well. Four more men in the same condition followed him out of the coach.

"Hello," Bershome said to each stranger as he stepped down.

A sweet familiar voice came from within. "Hello, Bershome."

"Salutations, Lady Cheryl." He bowed. Then he took her hand and helped her down.

"Bershome, fancy you greeting arrivals. Where is the Baron?"

"He was called away. Lady Agatha is handling some last-minute decoration arrangements. Who are your companions?"

"Unfortunate travelers. It appears they are Lady Agatha's playwright troop. They lost their coach when a wheel broke in the river. They were trying to drag it out in the rain when I came by. I offered them a ride."

"Pardon me, your Lordship. Is it possible to move our equipment inside before the rainstorm catches up with us again?"

"Go inside, and I'll get some people on it. Cheryl, get your men in front of a fire before they catch their death of a cold."

"Yes, inside everyone," Cheryl ordered.

"We will get the horses in the stables, my Lady."

"Make hast and get warmed up, Jeb."

"Yes, my lady."

Bershome followed Cheryl inside and found the troop circled around the fire. Servants came rushing in with blankets to cover them.

Agatha turned around and walked toward Cheryl and Bershome when they entered the hall and stopped. To Bershome's surprise, she curtsied and bowed her head.

"Lady Cheryl, from the depths of my heart, you are most welcome in our home."

Cheryl returned the act of reverence. "I thank you from the depth of my soul, Lady Agatha."

The ladies rose and moved forward to embrace in a strong hug and kissed each other's cheeks. Bershome proceeded to clap his hands.

"I also wish to thank you ever so much for rescuing my performers."

"The pleasure was all theirs." Cheryl looked down at her soiled pail green dress from where the men had accidentally gotten mud on it.

"Gentlemen!" Bershome raised his voice above the noise, "We need every able-bodied man outside before the rain arrives."

"Carefully, sirs!" The troop leader spoke out, "It is very delicate equipment."

Every lad and male servant filed outside. The driver of the wagon had already started unloading and stacking items on the ground.

Bershome helped carry the heavy harpsichord inside. The troop leader took control and ordered the placement of the equipment. The two ladies had disappeared, and Bershome's friends were helping the servants put the finishing touches on the hall preparations.

"A coach arrives, sir," Denniks said.

Bershome rushed out and met another coach. This coach was not as wet. He opened the door and was attacked by a fluffy blue mass clutching him in a hug.

"Bershome!"

"Lady Robin." He gasped and staggered backward to regain his balance and keep from dropping the young girl."

She proceeded to smack his cheeks repeatedly with kisses. He managed to set the nine-year-old down and extracted himself from the embrace.

"Cedric, bring in my present for Lady Agatha," she said as she took Bershome's arm and headed inside. Her footman followed with a large package.

"Lady Agatha, Lady Cheryl!" she shouted and ran to embrace each one.

Bershome noticed Cheryl was wearing a dark blue, clean dress.

"Place the box with the others in the corner, Cedric."

"A coach arrives, sir."

Bershome headed out. When he opened the door, the storm pelted him hard. The servant followed and tried to hold up a cloth of some type to shield him. Bershome opened the door but could not see inside for the rain was in his face.

"Climb in, Bershome," someone ordered. So he did.

"Hello, Ladies Gertrude and Ella," he said, looking at a set of twins dressed in lavender, "Lieutenant Arthur. Taking a holiday from the king's regiment?"

"Yes."

Bershome turned back to the twins. "I saw your grandfather just this morning. He left with Baron Wesley."

"Yes, they are plotting a business adventure together. How are we going to get inside without taking a bath in our clothes?" Gertrude asked.

"I'll have the driver pull around to the south entrance. The castle walls may shield you some."

"I'll tell him, sir," Denniks said from outside the coach.

"And get yourself inside, man," Bershome said.

The coach lurched forward, and they traveled around the castle. The kitchen door opened, and servants came out carrying tablecloths as rain shields. The riders quickly leaped from the coach and rushed inside.

"My, what a storm!"

"Your hostess awaits you in the dining hall, ladies and gents," Bershome said.

"Oh, Mistress Danar," Bershome said to the head cook as he removed his dripping jacket.

"Yes, me Lord?"

"I know you are very busy and all, but could you send hot cider, rum, and food to the stables? There are cold, wet men out there."

"I have plenty made up, but no one to take it out."

"Gather it up in baskets with some mugs, and I'll get a couple of someones for you."

He headed out to the dining hall and found everyone standing about or sitting in wait. None of the noble ladies were present.

"Where is Lady Agatha?"

"She ran from the room in tears, that direction," Athur said.

"Oh, oh." He shook his head. "Excuse me, Athur. Martello." He beckoned his friend over. "The cook has some things for the drivers and coachmen. Would you see they get to the stables for the cold and wet? Take Trejann to help you." He dropped his voice so only Martello could hear. "Go ahead and use a shield spell from the rain."

"Right away." He grabbed Trejann and left.

"Sir," Bershome approached the troop leader. "Are you ready to conduct your performance?"

"Yes, sir,"

"I'll bring out our hostess, and you may commence. How much stage area do you need?"

The man stepped out to mark the spot. Bershome added another step and turned to face the room.

"Ladies and gentlemen. Please arrange the seating starting here in rows for observation of the performance. Your entertainment will begin as soon as our hostess returns. Everyone may take a seat, and please be patient. Please leave the front row with two empty seats, and all eyes stay forward to the stage when we come out."

With a bit of light conversation, they began arranging the chairs in the front row and benches behind.

"Miss Harsumg, please have the cooks bring out hot drinks and snacks for everyone."

"Bershome!"

He turned to see two young men come from the kitchen, dripping buckets of water from their clothes.

"Hank, Sylas! Shuck those drenched overcoats and get by the fire. We will have some hot cider out for you in a moment."

"Where is Lady Agatha?" Silas asked, looking about.

"Holed up in her chamber. I was about to go fetch her."

"Oh, I gather things are not going well in the house of Westley."

"Just the party. Her performers were late and the storm early. We will have entertainment as soon as she joins us."

"There are cold, soppy, souls out in the stables. Lucas refuses to run in."

"I don't blame him. I got caught in it also. We are sending hot food to them."

"Hello, beautiful lady," Halte said as he turned his attention toward Arleta.

"Hot cider, sir," Arleta said, holding up a tray.

"Thank you ever so much. I never knew an angel could look so beautiful."

She smiled and stepped away.

"Simmer down, Halte." Bershome placed a hand on his shoulder. "She is under my protection, not that she needs it," Bershome said.

"Aye, sir."

Bershome caught up with Arleta, took the tray, and winked at her. "Please take a seat. Miss Harsumg. They are about ready." Then he leaned to whisper in her ear. "You are a guest, not a servant."

"I was just lending a hand," she whispered back.

He handed the tray to Halte. "Pass these out to the rest of the guests and behave."

"Aye, ya spoilsport." He followed Arleta to offer her a drink and sat beside her.

The guest settled into quiet conversations and enjoying the refreshments as the troop made final preparations to begin.

"What may I do to assist, sir?" Denniks asked.

Bershome looked at Denniks a moment. "Have two servants, one on each side ready to serve her ladyship and the others more refreshments as soon as she is seated. Then the troop will get started."

"You owe us one, Bershome," Martello whispered in his ear.

He looked at his dripping friends. "Name it reasonably, and I will pay it. Pick a seat and have some hot cider."

The outer kitchen door slammed.

Bershome stepped into the kitchen doorway and saw a dripping Larly holding a massive bundle of a quilts.

"The tent blew away," the lad said, "I managed to get all the gentlemen's things in, though. I imagine the remaining quilts and beddings are scattered across the province by now."

"Put that bundle down over there," the cook said, "and get by the fire. I'll get you some hot cider,"

Bershome shook his head and chuckled at the irony as he walked through the dining hall to Agatha's room. He knocked lightly on the door. Lady Robin opened the door a crack.

"Bershome."

"How is Agatha?" he whispered

"She was almost settled down. Your knock started another bout of crying. She refuses to come out."

"Let me have a word with her."

She let him in, and he saw Agatha sobbing face down on the bed.

"Ladies," he whispered and waved for them to come close. The twins, Cheryl, and Robin approached. He spoke softly, "would you please go take your seats, and I'll bring her out shortly."

Each touched his arm as they left. He walked over and sat on the bed. He stroked her hair a moment then patted her back.

"Agatha," he whispered.

"What?" the bedding muffled her voice.

"Rollover and look at me, please."

"No."

"All await your presence. The troop is ready to perform. Your guests are seated and ready to watch it."

"It is all a total disaster."

"No, it is not. All is ready for your arrival to begin."

"It is going to be bad."

"I can't hear you. Roll over, dear."

"No. I look horrible."

He grasped her shoulder to roll her over himself, and she fought his gentle pull. He got a firm grip and heaved her over. She grabbed a pillow and hid her face.

He took her hands in a firm grip, pulled them away, and pinned them to the bed. She had released the pillow, but it still hid her from him. He grasped it with his teeth and tossed it away with a swing of his head.

"Now," he looked at her puffy face and red eyes, "I can hear you."

"It is a total disaster. I'm too embarrassed to show my face to everyone. Nothing is ready. My guests are having to come in through the servant's entrance. It is all a horror."

"Hank and Silas arrived. Lucas is waiting out the rain in the stables. All your guests and their servants have been served hot drinks and refreshments."

"You are wet."

"And you are beautiful."

"Huh?" she stared at him.

"I said you are beautiful."

"You lie. My face is puffy and tear-streaked, my makeup is a mess, and my eyes are blood-shot. I look like a haggard old witch."

"And you are still beautiful," he bent down and gave her a soft, lingering kiss. When he drew back, she gasped a deep breath.

"That was much better than the kiss this morning. Give me another." She licked her lips.

"Got your breath back?"

"Enough for another kiss," she whispered."

"Under one condition," he whispered back."

"Name it." She gasped as she watched him lick his lips.

"You wash your face and join your guest at the party."

He lowered his head to kiss her. She turned her head away. "Must you always have conditions to everything you do?"

"Not always. I just want you to have an enjoyable birthday party and show that sweet smile."

"No."

"Lady Agatha, you are born into a family of nobility. Nobles do not surrender to adversity. They do not cower when they have setbacks. They hold their heads high, do the best they can in a dire situation, and dog it until they conquer it. Nobles do not cower for their shortcomings; they overcome them and show appreciation to those who help them."

"I can't."

"Why not? You were doing very well in the beginning today. You just became a bit overwhelmed."

"I can't, silly, because you have me pinned to the bed. So either give me another kiss or let me up."

He smiled. "That is the Agatha I know." He gave her lips a quick peck and rolled off her.

"Hey, that wasn't fair!"

"You have guests waiting." He fetched a damp washcloth and held it out to her. She cleaned up before the mirror. "I still look dreadful."

"No one will notice. Hurry."

She walked over, pinned him to the wall, and laid a long, seductive kiss on him. When she pulled away, they both sucked in deep breaths.

"Hoo," she blew out a breath and fanned herself. "I'm ready to conquer the world now."

He tucked her arm in his and escorted her to her seat. Servants offered them drinks and cookies. Bershome nodded to the troop leader to begin.

They enjoyed a comedy about a rowdy lad always getting into trouble and his love. She learned to tame him to make a proper young man of him before she would consent to marriage. By the end of the play, Agatha was back to her normal self. After a proper round of applause, Agatha stood and faced everyone.

"Ladies and Gentlemen, I wish to thank all of you for your patience and help earlier. Alas, again, we work a little for our fun. If we put the seating against the walls, we will have a dance floor."

Everyone worked, and the floor space was opened up. The musicians pulled out their instruments and made ready.

"Ladies, since this is my party, I can play with the rules. Our first dance is ladies' choice." She slipped her arms around Bershome's to declare her choice. "I believe we have enough space for eight couples. This dance is called The Queen's Review. Ladies to my right, gents to the left."

Everyone scrambled for a dance partner. Bershome saw Jartus hooked Robin's arm as she hurried past. "May I have this dance, my Lady?" Bershome noticed how she smiled and pulled him in line.

"Maestro, if you would please," Agatha asked.

The violin and harpsichord struck up a merry tune. Bershome tapped a foot to pick up the rhythm. Agatha and he stepped out to meet in the middle and faced down the line. He bent his arm at the elbow and held his hand out palm down. Agatha placed her hand on his. They looked at one another and stepped out together in a halting step as they paused in front of each couple. They reached out a hand toward the next person and brought it back to touch each other's hands as if they had taken something from the person in the line and presented it to their partner. When they reached the end of the line, they faced each other with both hands clasped, then they backed away to join the line. The promenade progressed until everyone had passed in review. Because of the size of the hall, everyone faced the stage and walked back up the floor.

Bershome stepped in a circle with Cheryl. "I'm glad to see you and Agatha are getting along again."

"We made up weeks ago. We felt guilty and wrote letters. Thank you."

Bershome was surprised and almost missed a step as he returned to Agatha. "You sneak," he accused when she was in his arms again.

"Me?" She laughed as he let go and move to Elena.

He circled Elena with a smile and a hello and went back to Agatha.

"Yes, Cheryl told me the two of you made up weeks ago."

"Yes," she said, then circled Jartus.

Bershome stepped toward his next partner, "Hello, Robin. That is a lovely powder blue dress. Almost as lovely as you. You ran off before I could tell you."

"Thank you, Bershome," she said, blushing as they circled, and he danced away to Agatha.

"I think Cheryl and I are actually twin sisters separated at birth. Her letter arrived the day I wrote mine," Agatha said.

Bershome stepped over to Arleta.

"Arleta, I thought Halte would steal you for a dance."

"He lost interest in me." They laughed together.

Such was the way conversations went. Brief little exchanges as they danced around. Afterward, the dances were more personal.

Agatha, Cheryl, Robin, and the twins kept Bershome on the dance floor while most of the people took breaks and let others dance. Bershome flopped in a chair and refused requests. He observed Jartus did well to monopolize Robin's attention while Gerak sat the entire time sipping wine.

Halte joined Bershome. He had a handkerchief wrapped around his left hand, covering his knuckles.

"You were not kidding about the little redhead, m' boy."

"How so?"

Halte held up his left hand. "I simply lay my hand on hers in her lap. She gave me a sweet smile and rapped me on the knuckles with a very sharp knife."

"I warned you that she did not need my protection."

"You could have warned me she was armed."

"I didn't know. She must keep it in that wide waist belt on her dress. You were warned she could take care of herself. You have to pay her respect. "

"Aye, paid in blood." He raised his bandaged hand.

They both laughed.

Later Bershome spoke to Arleta. "Did you actually rap Halte on the knuckles with a knife?"

She blushed bright red and looked at him. "I didn't look at the blade and failed to realize the cutting edge was down. I was so embarrassed I couldn't look at him."

"Well, whatever you do. Don't apologize for it."

She burst out laughing.

"Ladies and Gentlemen," Agatha spoke up for everyone's attention, "Our head cook has informed me, she has a feast fit for the king ready. And now we need to work for our supper. If you would, please help me."

All the lads headed into the hallway if by an unspoken order and carted the tables in as the ladies grabbed the chairs, and they reestablished the dining hall into its original order of tables in a U shape. Bershome had a small table brought from the baron's study and set it in the middle of the open area of the hall with one chair beside it. He took Agatha's hand and sat her down at it.

She looked puzzled. "Am I being sat here by myself as a naughty girl for punishment, Bershome?"

"Certainly not. You have presents to unwrap."

"Oh."

Several people formed a line and passed all the packages from the corner to the table."

Agatha made a big to-do over each present. After her gifts were opened, the servants brought in the feast of finely roasted lamb, every vegetable in the garden, sausages, four different breads, and peach cobbler for dessert.

After the meal, most of her guests departed.

"I gather you will be spending the night again with us, Bershome?"

"Yes. Is that room you offered me still available?"

She looked at him sideways. "As a matter of fact, it is," she said with a smile.

"Good, the lads and I will need to use it."

"All of them? Whatever for?"

"The storm blew away the tent."

She put her hand over her mouth in surprise. "Why wasn't I told?"

"You had enough disasters to deal with at the time."

"Only problem is we don't have enough bedding now." She pressed a hand against her chest.

"Yes, we do."

"It all must have gotten soaked in the rain."

"You're man, Larly, a dandy and diligent servant that he is, saved our things from the storm. Also, we have a bedroll for each of us in the wagons we came in."

"You do plan ahead, don't you?"

"I didn't think it would be right for us to descend upon you like an invading hoard of relatives expecting all the amenities of royal visitors. After all, I practically forced my friends on you."

"It has been a pleasure to be in their company. I want to especially thank you for taking over and salvaging a wonderful party out of my disaster."

"Nonsense, it was all your planning that made it so grand. You just needed a little help getting it started."

"And you helped so well." She leaned her head on his shoulder.

"It was my pleasure."

Arleta walked over. "Pardon me, Lady Agatha."

"Yes, Arleta?"

"I wish to ask a favor. Well, I ask for all us girls."

"Yes?" she smiled pleasantly.

"We just love your dress and were wondering if you would share the pattern with us."

"Absolutely. How about I make a copy of it and send it to you?"

"Well," she looked down a moment.

"Yes?"

"We were sort of wanting to have dresses made like it before the next month. We love the sleeves and the way you gathered the skirt at the waist."

"Excuse us, Bershome. It is time for us women to talk." She stood up, took Arleta's hand, and tucked it in her elbow as they walked. She waved a beckoning hand to the others. "Ladies, ladies, please come also."

Martello moved to the vacant seat next to Bershome. "Tell me, ole chap, what about tonight's sleeping arrangements? Larly says the tent blew away."

"We have the bedrolls in the wagons out in the stables. There is one bedroom available we can all camp in, or there are these tables in here."

Later, Bershome and several lads found space enough and settled down in the room for the night. Before he fell asleep, Bershome felt an urge to use the chamber pot. He didn't like the idea of using the one in the room and having it sitting there all night. He decided to use the one in the common washroom. He slipped out. After he had taken care of his business, he went to the kitchen for a drink.

He found no one in the kitchen and helped himself to a glass of wine. He sat at the table and took a sip. As he took another, he heard a noise coming from the pantry. He stopped with the glass just at his mouth.

A muffled female voice laughed, "You have never done this before. Have you?"

Bershome stole over to the pantry.

"I like the name Gerak. It is very manly."

Bershome opened the door. He discovered Gladis, the cook's helper, lying back on a pile of grain sacks. Gerak was standing with his shirt removed and a hand on his belt as he looked at Bershome.

"You need to go back to our room, Gerak."

Gerak looked him and at Gladis a moment.

"Now, Gerak," Bershome emphasized his order.

Gerak fastened his belt and grabbed his shirt off the floor. He stormed over to Bershome, who stepped back from the doorway to allow him to pass.

"She has my coin."

"Consider that a payment for a lesson learned. I'll talk to you later about proper moral conduct. I hope you haven't done such a thing at my house."

"Even a dog knows not to mess where he eats." He made a nasty snarl.

"Good to know you are at least as smart as a dog. Go on. I'm right behind you."

Gerak turned and stomped away as he put on his shirt. Bershome turned his attentions to Gladis. She was busy getting correcting her clothing.

"I suppose you will tell on me to his lordship. Unless," she exposed a healthy sight of her leg and looked at him, "you want a taste yourself."

"No, I don't. You should be ashamed of selling yourself in the baron's house. You will tell Lady Agatha yourself first thing in the morning and save me the trouble."

He closed the door on her and returned to the bedroom. In the dim lantern light, he could see the snarled stare Gerak had for him before he rolled over to put his back to him. He knew Gerak was coming of age, but he needed to learn when not to give in to his urges.

CHAPTER TWENTY-EIGHT

Sometime in the night, the storm moved south. The morning sun rose to a clear blue sky. Bershome sighed. At least the trip home would be easier. He glanced around the room. Everyone was cheerful at breakfast, but looking forward to returning home. Bershome sat between Ladies Agatha and Cheryl as they ate.

"I think you ladies could have at least let me know so I would stop worrying."

"We thought you should suffer for putting conditions and demands on your favors," Agatha informed him.

"Yes, it seemed only fair," Cheryl said.

"So, it was your bond for revenge on me that brought you back together as friends?"

"No, that just made the pie sweeter," Agatha smiled.

"I shall suffer it gracefully for the sake of your friendships. But I am happier about it than the two of you combined."

They both turned and placed a kiss on his cheeks at the same time. "Thank you, Bershome," they said simultaneously.

"I expect both of you will be at my party the month after next. Right?" Cheryl asked.

"Yes," Agatha and Bershome said.

"I see most of my friends are finished, and we really need to start for home."

"As I am," Cheryl said.

"I shall be left all alone again."

"You have another dress to design and make in time for my party, Agatha."

Agatha whispered in Bershome's ear, "She doesn't know I already have one. It's your favorite color too."

Bershome smiled and stood to leave. "Ladies, my men have left for the stables. I'll return as soon as I have checked on them." Bershome stepped over to where his friends sat. "Ladies and gentlemen. We need to gather up our things and make preparations to leave. I'll get our rides ready, and we can meet back here to make our fare-thee-wells."

Bershome happened to notice Gerak's hateful scowl as he spoke. He turned and walked through the kitchen to get to the stables. Gladis looked down shamefully when she saw him. In the stables, he found his men rigging the horses to the wagons.

"Did you gentlemen get enough breakfast?"

"Aye, sir."

"Excellent. Rhubarb, are you awake?" The horse called back with a nicker in response to hearing his name. Bershome petted his nose and got his saddle. "You ready to go for a ride?"

Before long, their modes of transportation were ready. Bershome tied Rhubarb's reins to the back of a wagon and returned to check on his friends. When he passed through the kitchen, he saw Gladis washing dishes. She gave him a hateful stare, and he noticed her red eyes and a bright red handprint on the side of her face. He entered the dining hall and found everyone standing around Lady Agatha.

"Seriously, I want to see all of you at Cheryl's party. You are wonderful people, and I enjoyed your company.

"I'm glad you feel that way," Bershome said, "I think they are good friends as well. I also want to thank you for allowing me to drag them along."

"You didn't drag us," several girls protested in one voice.

"Either way," Agatha said, "I enjoyed having you here for my party and am glad to make new friends. That is what life is all about, family and friendships." She smiled at Bershome and blew him a kiss as he backed out the door to head for home.

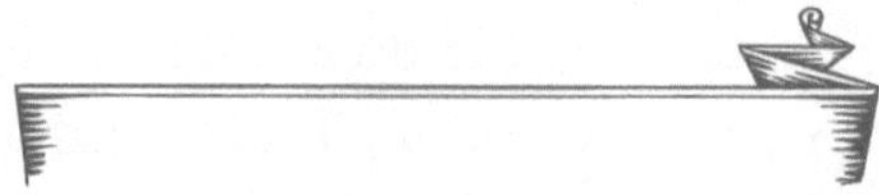

CHAPTER TWENTY-NINE

Bershome watched as Martello walked over to the table shared by Livonia and Trishta. He looked at their potion.

"You are doing good. I see you are cutting the pieces of that root smaller for the best results."

"Thank you, Martello," Livonia said with her hand over her mouth to hide her irregular teeth. With her other hand, she slipped a small folded parchment into his hand. He tucked it into his pocket and moved to the next table.

"Jocelt, you put too much sulfur in your potion. You will have to start over. Measure your ingredients carefully."

"How can you tell?"

"By the color and the smell. It is now poisonous. Throw it out, clean your cauldron thoroughly, and start over."

"Ladies and Gentlemen," Martello spoke loudly, "Measure your ingredients precisely. This potion is a medicine, but if you mix the wrong amount of the wrong ingredient, you will poison your patient, and they will die."

He sat down at Bershome's table and slipped the note from his pocket.

"Oh, bother," he said softly after reading it.

"What's up?" Bershome asked.

Martello slid the note to Bershome, who read it and smiled. "What are you going to do?"

"Bershome, please don't think I'm a shallow person. She is a sweet girl but is just not the right person for me."

"She is fourteen. If she were living in a small village instead of a large town, she would be considered of acceptable age for marriage."

"Yes, but not to me. She knows I'm with Freya."

"You can't blame the girl for trying."

"What should I do? She could ruin it for me with Freya."

"Reassure Freya and let Livonia down gently."

"Would you tell her for me?"

"What? She could transfer her attention to the closest guy." Bershome whispered harshly. "I don't need her causing me problems. I have enough coming as it is."

"I know." He made a wide grin. "We need her to get distracted by Gerak."

"That is an idea, but don't you think that would be a little bit cruel to her?"

"It would be better than bluntly telling her to leave me alone. Besides, she is still young enough to get over it. Who knows, maybe they will take a liking to each other." Martello thought about the idea and looked over at Gerak, stirring his potion. "You will owe me one, Bershome."

"Me, owe you?"

"Watch this." Martello stood, walked over to Gerak, and looked at his potion. Bershome gave full attention to Martello's actions.

"You are doing good, Gerak. What did you do to get it to mix so well?"

"The root was thick, so I split it lengthwise after I cut it."

"Your potion needs to simmer a while before you add the next ingredient. How about lending a hand and tell Livonia your secret."

"Sure," he said with a shrug and took his spoon out of the potion.

Bershome walked over to check another apprentices' progress as he stood so he could inconspicuously eavesdrop on Livonia and Gerak. Bershome noticed how her face flushed a bright red. Gerak, however, appeared to be ignorant to her reaction of his presence alone and indifferent to the effect it was having on her.

She tried to follow his instructions and cut her finger. "OUCH."

Gerak grabbed a rag on the table and wrapped the injury tightly as she stood crying.

"Just hold this tight." He wrapped her other hand around the rag and wounded finger. She started to sway and fell backward. He managed to catch her before she hit the floor. Gerak held her in his arms as he looked about.

Bershome could tell he was confused as to what he should do. Bershome stepped over to lend a hand. "Take her to the servants. They will know what to do."

Gerak carried her from the classroom as Martello fetched a rag and cleaned up the blood. He returned to checking the progress of other apprentices. When he was through making a round of the room, he sat at the table with Bershome.

"Now, we wait," he smiled.

Gerak returned later and went straight to his bench to finish his potion. Martello stepped over to check with him.

"Thanks for helping Livonia for me, Gerak."

"Think nothing of it, sir."

"Just call me, Martello, Gerak. I'm an apprentice here, same as you. I see your potion did not suffer from neglect. It should still turn out to be good."

"I was worried. These procedures are rather specific."

"How is Livonia?"

"Mister Bernary took her and said Mrs. Pilliat could mend her finger right away, and it will be just as good as before. Tell me," he dropped his voice to a whisper, "do all girls faint at the sight of blood like that?"

"Only the more delicate ones, Gerak. Livonia's father is a prominent businessman in her town, and she has lived a sheltered life. Unlike some of the farm girls we have around who can kill and dress a chicken for dinner. She is pretty smart, though."

Later, Livonia returned to the room by herself. She spent more time watching Gerak than paying attention to her potion. Unfortunately, Martello had to inform her it was ruined and to throw it out. He and Bershome exchanged knowing looks that their seed of conspiracy had sprouted exactly as they wanted.

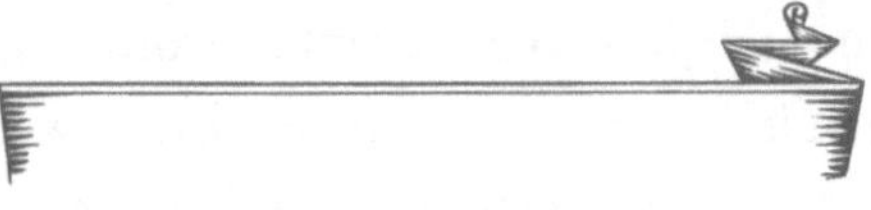

CHAPTER THIRTY

Festivity filled the dormitory while the apprentices dressed for the costume party. Gerak watched as the others dress and head downstairs. Willy was a scarecrow with straw sticking out every opening of his clothes and under his dog-chewed hat. Jartus was a sprite with fake pointed ears and a flute.

Jartus stopped in front of him as he and Willie headed out. "Get a move on, man. All the best masks will be taken."

"I already made me one."

"Oh, so that is where you have been sneaking off to after lessons. Great! See ya!" the lad shouted as he dashed off.

Gerak waited until everyone left the dormitory before slipping on a black robe and red cape. He pulled the devil mask from his wardrobe and put it on. His final prop for the costume was a small three-pronged pitchfork with exaggerated widened points that looked like spearheads. The polished metal mirror in the washroom showed him a scary devil standing before it.

Gerak headed downstairs. He managed to slip down unnoticed and moved around the outer edge of the people in the room as they danced or move in rhythm to the music. He saw a portly man in his forties holding the devil's mask he had made to replace the original one. He was in an intense whispered conversation with the man beside him, holding the monitor mask. Gerak slipped over to stand beside the enchanted mirror and watched the crowd. When he felt no one was watching him, he hunched over to be hidden by close bodies and stepped over the bench and into the mirror in one smooth motion. He vanished from the room. He stood in the mirror and stepped from it. He checked to see he had no reflection and moved among the people trying to avoid contact. Wanlae stepped backward and bumped into him.

"Oops, sorry," she said and turned to see who she had bumped. She stared at an empty spot where someone should have been. She shrugged and turned back to her conversation.

Gerak boldly stepped up in front of the man with the replacement mask he had made.

"Ferlacs, I tell you this is not the real master mask. It is a fake," he whispered.

"Does that matter? We can still kill the three of them and seize the estate.

"I cannot become invisible. I have to kill the baron where everyone can see him simply fall over dead, and then I appear across the room suddenly and be innocent. I, for one, do not want to face that old wizard and his magic. The lad is just as good. Do you want to be a goat or a toad the rest of your life?"

"I have the strength of five men in this mask."

"Not unless I give it to you. I can't without the real mask. Brute strength is nothing compared to cunning and the magic everyone here knows. We haven't a chance. Even my soldiers waiting in the woods are useless unless we kill those three."

Gerak made a fist and stuck the baron in the face. His head bounced against the wall, and his eyes widened as blood trickled from his nose. Gerak drew out his knife and pressed the edge of the blade on the man's neck. The fat man quivered in fear. The man pressed back hard against the wall and held his breath.

Gerak whispered so that only the two men could hear him. "You dare plot to use my power for murder? What would it feel like to have your throat slashed open and not be able to see the devil that killed you?"

"Oh, please don't kill me. I have a wife and children."

"You dared to plot to kill your liege lord? Death should be your reward."

The monitor moved to draw his knife, but Gerak watched him. The man eased his hand over to his own knife, Gerak snatched it from its sheath and sliced into his arm with it. He poked the man in the belly hard with his own knife to pin him to the wall but not stab him. The monitor stood with one hand on his wound, and his hand shook in fear. The actions had caused Gerak to cut slightly into the flesh of the fat man's throat.

"Please, please, spare me. Please, please."

"I can kill both of you here, and no one would know it was I. But, this is a festive evening, and I am in a good mood. You will leave and never return to these estates. If you do, I will kill you before you get past the great hall. I am the master of the mirror. I control all its powers. Leave your masks here. I don't want to break up the set."

Both men nodded. When they felt the pressure of the knives disappear, they stood frozen in fear that the devil was taunting them and waited for them to move before killing them.

"Run, you fool," Gerak whispered in the fat man's ear.

The man ignored their wounds and bolted for the door with his henchman right behind him. Gerak found it hard not to burst out laughing. He moved about the room for a little while and would tease someone by tapping their shoulder and seeing how they acted when they saw no one behind them. Treats had been provided for munching on while the party ran. Gerak eased over behind Martello and Bershome as they stood holding their masks in their hands. A pair of beautiful wood-nymphs rather scantily clad in emerald green frocks had their attention. Everyone recognized them in spite of the green mask they wore. Freya and Arleta had made their costumes.

Suddenly Bershome and Martello both turned around and faced Gerak. He stepped back in alarm. The two exchanged looks and then back towards Gerak. Bershome reached out as if to grab Gerak, who stepped farther away. Bershome's waved his arm between them as he tried to grasp something, and then lowered his arm.

"Did you feel it, Martello?"

"Definitely, but what was it?"

"I don't know. It was like something powerfully magical came up behind us and disappeared when we turned around."

"Do you have ghosts in your house?"

"None have ever manifested themselves. But I wonder, considering the peculiar things happening these past few months. "

"Oh well, I'd rather be talking to the wood-nymphs."

The boys turned their attention back to the ladies. Gerak looked about to make sure he was not going to be seen. Satisfied, he slipped off the devil mask and broke the spell. He looked about and saw he was undetected. He slipped the mask back on and danced around the room. He gave Bershome and Martello a wide berth and approached the wood-nymphs.

"Ladies," he bowed deeply, "would you like to dance in the moonlight with the devil?"

"Cute pitchfork. Wait! Who are you? The devil's mask was given to a portly, older man." Freya asked with a smile.

"He was but an imitation. I am the real devil." He laughed hideously and shook his pitchfork.

The ladies stepped back towards Bershome and Martello.

"What?" Gerak asked with indignation.

"You can go someplace else, please." Arleta's voice shook.

"All I asked for was a dance."

"We promised these guys our dances."

"You can go away, devil," Bershome said.

"Your loss, ladies. I shall go conjure a curse to put on you that will turn your hair pink," Gerak said, throwing his hands in the air. He turned around and left them as he laughed again as he headed towards another group.

"That sounded like Gerak," Martello said.

"By golly, it did." Bershome said.

"Enough about him," Freya said. "I believe we gave up a dance with the devil for the likes of you two?"

"I shall not let you down my lovely wood-nymph." Bershome took Arleta's hand and sashayed her across the floor. Martello followed suit with Freya.

CHAPTER THIRTY-ONE

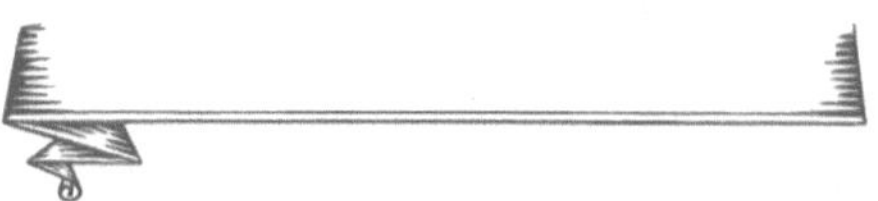

On a cold noon, a week before the end of the year, Bershome went to the head table, and Grandfather spoke with him. Then he had a word with the stable master and returned to join Martello and friends at the apprentice table.

"Miss Harsumg, I need to ask a favor of you."

Arleta smiled. "I will allow you to ask, sir."

"I have been assigned a ceremonial family task to accomplish this afternoon and request your company and assistance in doing so."

"What is this task?"

"I will enlighten you during our ride, my Lady."

"A ride? Do you know how cold it is out?" She crossed her arms against herself and shivered.

"Yes, my lady. I would encourage you to wear a coat, scarf, and gloves. I'm having the carriage brought out front after lunch."

"You are serious?"

"Indubitably so, my Lady." He nodded.

"Why am I going to risk my health in a ride to where you are not saying? For a reason, you specify not. How long is this ride going to take?"

"Perhaps an hour or two."

"I would be an icicle by then." She clutched herself again and shivered.

"A quilt will be provided in the carriage to help keep you warm."

"Freya," She leaned close to her friend "do you think I should go on a carriage ride with this shady fellow to a destination unknown for a purpose unexplained?"

Freya joined in the teasing. "As far as I have seen, he has always conducted himself as a gentleman, but I would not go without a proper escort. You know, for appearance's sake."

"My driver and footman will be with us, ladies."

"Lady Esmeralda would be a more proper chaperon," Freya said.

"I agree, Freya," Arleta said and looked at Bershome with her eyebrows raised.

"She is engaged this day and thus my reason for asking you."

"It was snowing like a blizzard when we came in from the Hall of Knowledge."

"That was hardly a blizzard. Besides, you were playing in a snowfall worse than that this past weekend."

"That is neither here nor there. I will be missing out on practice for three new spells this afternoon."

Bershome realized what she was doing. "Okay, I thought you might be interested. Since you're not, I'll ask Livonia." He shrugged.

Arleta frowned. "I did not refuse your offer, sir."

"You just decided to torment me to make me appreciate the inconvenience of going with me." He gestured with open hands to offer her a chance to defend her actions.

"I protest such an accusation, sir." She leaned back and crossed her arms. He saw she struggled to hide her mirth about it.

"Miss Harsumg, the adventure will reward you beyond your inconvenience." He said to give her a last chance.

"Very well, then. I accept your invitation."

He thumped the table lightly with his knuckles. "Thank you. You will not regret it. We will leave shortly after lunch."

She smiled and took a bite of bread.

After lunch, Bershome escorted Arleta to the carriage and assisted her up. She took a heavy quilt on the forward seat and unfolded it and noticed an ax and saw lying in the seat. He joined her and assisted with the quilt to cover their lower body and legs.

"Bershome."

"Yes, Miss Arleta?"

"Do I have a need to be alarmed?"

"Why do you ask?"

"What is the ax for?" She pointed to it.

"Oh!" He laughed. "That is for our task at hand."

The driver slapped the reins against the horse's back, and the carriage lurched forward.

"You are not providing much for reassurance here, sir."

"Okay, I'll tell you the story now. Many years ago, just after my grandfather was married, it came time for their first Hogmanay together; he went out to get a tree for them. It was the scrawniest, ugliest, most lopsided tree grandmother had ever seen. From the next years on, they always went together to pick the tree. My grandparents did it, and father and mother did it, as well, the first two years they were married. Mother passed away before their third year."

He sighed. "Since then, a visiting lady or Lady Esmeralda has gone with Grandfather to select the tree. That is why I asked you to escort me."

"You had to act so mysterious and couldn't tell me this in front of the others?"

"Well, I was a bit embarrassed to ask for help picking out a tree. Besides, you had your fun with the matter."

"Well, I guess I did."

"Until I called your bluff."

"Would you have really taken Livonia?"

"You bluffed, I raised, you folded, you will never know."

She looked to her left at the trees across the pasture. "Well, I don't think you played fairly."

"How so? You were giving me a miserably hard time about it."

"So, you think everything should be handed to you because you are a nobleman?"

"Definitively not. Every man should work and earn his way in life. You are the daughter of an innkeeper that only needs to worry about a small handful of people in her life plus her patrons for the day and evening. As a nobleman, I have many, many responsibilities to many, many people, from our stable boy, our house staff, soldiers, alliance neighbors, folks from many towns and villages, and up to the crowned king himself."

"How will you keep track of it all?"

"Hopefully, as well as Grandfather."

"That one." She interrupted him and pointed at the trees across the open field.

"What?"

"That tree right there."

He looked at the borderline of the forest. No particular tree caught his eye.

"Afreck, turn left, and go to the tree line."

When they stopped, Arleta leaped from the carriage without waiting for the footman. She ran a ways and stopped at a tree. She looked it up and down.

"Is that it?" He questioned.

"Well, it is a bit taller than I expected.

"It is every bit of twenty-five feet tall."

"Actually, over thirty, lad."

"How separate is it? Not another growing into it is there?" Bershome asked.

They looked at the tree on all sides.

"Arleta, let's step out there and look at the top half of it. We have a height limit of fifteen feet." They all walked out and looked at it.

"It is a pretty fir tree," Afreck commented.

"Thank you for agreeing," Arleta said.

"The top half definitely looks nice," Bershome said. He walked up to the tree with the ax resting on his shoulder and stopped to face her. "You are sure?"

She rocked her head to one side and then the other. "Yes."

He studied the tree a moment. "It will drop as we need it, out in the open, gents."

"Aye," both men said.

Bershome turned and hacked away at the lower limbs. His driver and footman dragged away the discarded boughs. Bershome stopped and looked at Arleta again.

"You are sure?"

"Even more so now."

"Please stand far enough away so it will not fall on you."

He chopped on the twelve-inch trunk. He cut the fall notch to drop the tree into the open and stepped around to the backside.

"You need to step over this way, my Lady," Afreck said and led her a safe distance to the side.

A little bit later, Bershome had the tree creaking and popping with every swing of his ax. He made a final chop and stepped back away from it as it leaned farther and farther. It popped and cracked as it fell, tossing a spray of snow and bouncing a couple of times, then rolling slightly toward Arleta and Afreck.

"Good job, Bershome," Arleta declared.

He stepped over towards her as he breathed heavy to catch his wind.

"Afreck, let's measure it and cut the limbs away from the lower part."

"I'll handle that, sir." He took the ax from Bershome. Before long, they had a long pole with a treetop.

"Bershome," Arleta said as she slipped her arm in his, "How are we going to get this monster to the castle?"

"We will cut the trunk to an acceptable length and tie a rope to it."

"But dragging it back will damage the beautiful symmetry of the tree."

"Who said we would drag it?" He smiled at her with mischief in his eyes. "You brought your wand. Did you not?"

"Yes. Oh! We are going to levitate it!"

"She catches on quickly."

"But we are outside the safe-haven of our training area."

"Well, there are certain advantages to being the grandson of the reigning lord." He smiled and wiggled his eyebrows.

The men cut the trunk off with a saw and left a couple of feet below the limbs.

"I see no one traveling about our property. Would you care to do the honors and move it over by the carriage, Arleta?"

She pulled out her wand and pointed at the tree. Her hand shook.

"Take your time," He whispered.

"It is so big. It must weigh a ton," she whispered back.

"Size of an object does not matter. It is simply a stick, just like in your lessons. Breathe, gather your willpower, and cast your spell. It is just a stick."

She cast her spell and swished her wand back and forth. The tree shook, and Arleta smiled wider. She muttered her spell again, and the tree floated off the ground. She started moving it towards the carriage.

"Just get it in the open, and I'll take over."

She cocked her head and set her jaw. Bershome raised his own wand, but Arleta stepped out and blocked him from the tree. She continued until she turned the tree and had the butt end within a couple of feet of the carriage, and she set it down.

All the men applauded her performance.

"Nicely done, my Lady." The men said.

"You only needed a little encouragement," Bershome whispered in her ear.

"Thank you." To his surprise, she pecked his cheek in appreciation.

Afreck tied a rope to the tree and the carriage.

"Shall we go?"

Everyone loaded up, and Bershome sat in the carriage facing the rear. He cast his spell and sat back to relax.

"Can you maintain the spell the time it takes us to get back?" She asked.

"Yes. With practice, you can handle a spell and do almost anything at the same time. It is a simple concentration. I saw one apprentice a few years ago that could make it look like he was casting three spells at the same time. But he could swap between them so quickly one could not tell."

Arleta looked back.

"By the way. Thank you for braving the life-threatening perils of freezing to death in a blizzard to help me select a tree."

They laughed together. When they arrived at the manor without incident, Bershome let the tree rest softly on the ground.

"Bershome, sir," Afreck stated, "we will get the carpenter to make a stand for it and let you know when we need it moved inside."

"Excellent looking fir, Bershome," Grandfather said as he came walking up. "Thank you, Miss Arleta, for assisting the lad for me."

"Oh, the pleasure was all mine, sir."

"The cook has hot cider on the stove for any who ask. It will help warm you up."

"Thank you, sir."

"Oh, Afreck," Bershome paused on his way to the door. "Ask the carpenter to retrieve the reminder of that tree trunk. I'm certain he can put the wood to use."

"Yes, sir."

Bershome followed them to the kitchen.

"Ah, Bershome, here is a cup of cider for you. Or would you rather have brandy to stir your blood back up?" Mister Masey asked.

"Oh, hot cider will do fine."

"My Lord," Arleta said, "Bershome told me a story about you in your younger days and your first Hogmanay with your wife."

He smiled and gazed at her "Yes, the tree was as sorry-looking as it could be after I dragged it to the house behind my horse. But Jolene put the flat side to the wall and decorated it up pretty. She draped ribbons and tied fruit in it. We lived a few miles from here in a little house hardly larger than this kitchen. We had moved out of father's castle to have a bit more privacy while our marriage was young. Those were much simpler times. She had hot cider waiting for me then too," he said with a glimmer of mist in his eyes.

"I want to thank both of you for including me in your family tradition." She leaned over to him and placed a kiss on his cheek.

"Oh my, such soft lips. Thank you for keeping us from having a lopsided tree."

She smiled at Bershome and took a sip from her cup. "I think I have time to rejoin my friends and get in on a couple of spell castings." She set her cup down and hurried off.

"She has a strong spirit like your grandmother."

"She has a touch of a mischievous streak, too." Bershome told him the hard time she had given him before she accepted the invitation.

"Now, that is my kind of lass." He laughed as he walked off to his study.

Bershome went out and moved the tree to the center of the dining hall after the carpenter was finished with the stand braces. It was ready for decorating that evening.

Everyone gathered for supper, and Grandfather stood to speak. "Ladies and gentlemen, as you can see, Bershome, with the help of Miss Arleta, has brought us our tree for celebrating Hogmanay and the bringing in of the new year next week. All about it are boxes of decorations. Anyone that would like to partake in decorating the tree, please feel free to commence once you have finished eating." He looked over at the apprentices. "If you wish to make a decoration of your own and add to our collection, we welcome it. If you want to hang one and keep it yourself later for remembrance, please do so. Also, if you wish to give out New Year's First Step presents, you may place them beneath the tree. As we herald in the new year with a party, we will dispense them during the merriment."

He sat down, and everyone applauded. A buzz swept across the room as everyone discussed the coming event.

"By the way, Bershome, when's your birthday?" Freya asked.

"Oh, it was about seventeen years ago. I was too young to remember it, though." He smiled mischievously at Arleta. She stared at him open-mouthed and appeared to be forming a remark.

He chuckled. "It is New Year's Day. Which makes it nice."

"Why's that?" Arleta asked.

"I get to have a party and get presents, even if no one knows or remembers."

They all laughed.

That evening, most of the ladies raided the wooden boxes and brought out the many decorations available while the lads sat back and watched. Every now and then, someone would throw in a comment or joke about a decoration. Many were simple colored, dried clay, wood, or leather, with a person's name cut into it. Wands were out and used to levitate ornaments high into the tree. The tree was decorated in a multitude of colors and differently-shaped ornaments and colored ropes around it every few feet. Everyone stepped back to admire the tree, but all agreed it need something for the very top.

Mister Bernary brought one last box the size of a loaf of bread from the kitchen and set it on the table before Grandfather.

"Miss Freya," Grandfather said in a deep, reverent tone, "Would you please honor my home by placing the top ornament on the tree?"

She placed a hand over her heart and stepped up to the box as he slid the lid back in its slot. She carefully moved aside the straw and gasped at the contents. She placed her hand over her mouth. "I'm afraid I would drop it, sir. I couldn't live with that."

The man smiled and stood. He lifted the ornament from the box and removed any hanging pieces of straw. It was a crafted glass star of a dozen spires sticking out in all directions from a center ball. He held it resting in one palm and leaned slightly against the other. Light from the candles and fireplace made it glitter in changing colors.

Bershome stepped up and placed an arm around her shoulders. "Let me help," he whispered. He raised his other arm and cupped his hand under her wand hand. "You know the spell. It is just a stick."

"It is too beautiful to call just a stick."

"You have been elevating ornaments over an hour already this evening without breaking a single one. This one is just as easy."

Her hand shook as she pointed her wand at the delicate glass star. The room was so silent everyone could hear her raspy breathing.

"Take a deep breath. Let it out easy. Look at it, not me. Now levitate it slowly as you already have been doing."

She took another deep breath and began her spell. Her wand hand quivered slightly as the star rose free of his hands and hung in the air. Then it rose near the ceiling and floated over the top twig and lowered without a bobble. When she dropped her hand, peopled in the room erupted with cheers and applause. Grandfather reached out to her, and she gave him her hand. He kissed it and thanked her. She still trembled as Bershome guided her back to the table.

The next day, everyone came in for lunch and discovered quite a pile of identically-sized and wrapped presents under the tree. Each had a small card tied to it with a name. Throughout the week, the pile grew in packages and assorted wrappings.

Grandfather stopped Bershome before he could sit for dinner two days before New Year's eve. "Have you decided on a companion for First Step Day yet, son?"

"Yes, sir."

"Good, good," he smiled and headed for his chair.

Bershome sat and waited for everyone to arrive. Arleta sat across from him, and he offered to pour her juice. "Miss Harsumg, I would like to invite you along for a visit to the village New Year's Day to assist me with presenting First Step presents. Would you be interested?"

"Yes. Thank you for inviting me."

"I figured I had better ask you before Grandfather or Master Zarlaam stole you."

"I didn't know I had a choice."

"You don't. Any more, that is."

"What if I change my mind?"

"I'll ask another lady immediately. Let's see," he turned his head to look down the length of the table. "I took Janara with me last year, Wanlae the year before..."

Arleta leaned against Freya and openly asked so he could hear. "If he mentions Livonia, do you think I should turn his hair pink?"

"Nope," he commented, "she went with me her first year here. She was so shy and scared being away from home."

"I know who." He jerked his head to gaze upon Freya. Her response was a wide-eyed, silent stare. Then he and Arleta looked at each other with their heads tilted down slightly and stared from beneath their eyebrows as if daring the other to say the wrong thing as they grinned.

"Well, I guess that settles that," Martello stated.

"Martello, 'ole boy. You have participated in the past. Would you and Freya care to join us? We will have plenty of gifts and doors to knock on."

He and Freya exchange looks, and she nodded. "Definitely, sir. By the way, ladies, It is a bit of tradition, all the apprentices go and help his Lordship on First Step day."

"Yes," Bershome piped, "We will have wagons rolling along down the streets with the gifts, and we will pass them out for him. The ladies carry baskets with paper wrapped shortbread for the children."

CHAPTER THIRTY-TWO

Gerak made sure he was not followed and no one was paying attention to him as he walked through the manor with his bag. When he arrived in the main hall, he looked all about and used the mirror to check that he was not followed. With a smile of satisfaction, he quickly slipped the mask from the bag and put it on. He quickly stepped over the bench into the mirror and back into the hall. He headed down the corridor to the Baron's study. The door sat open as the man usually kept it. Gerak leaned against the wall to eavesdrop.

"You know I have no objections to your apprentices, Zarlaam. Nor to your pursuit of teaching them magic. It does take a bite out of our coffers. I'm not complaining about that. Every time I see your apprentices come into the grand hall to eat with a smile on their faces a mile wide, I know they had a grand day. The joy I see in their faces gives me joy. Because I know we have caused it.

"I'm glad of that, brother."

"If Father had not understood how much fulfillment you received out of magic and saw the good of it, he would have refused to allow you to pursue your studies and not given me the responsibility of the estate. Very few people know I am the younger brother."

"That is because I hide behind my beard. I have no regrets, brother. You have done us all proud, and our wealth has prospered greatly. You know how to read and handle men. I am grateful you allow me my indulgences, for I am a far better wizard than I would be a governing Lord."

"I enjoyed studying it with you when we were lads. But the time came for me to learn other things. Bershome knows magic. I hope he can continue to learn more, but I need him to learn more of the family business. He has no brother to help him, like you did."

"He has been a help to me as he runs the training while I pursued more apprentices and magic. I appreciate your indulgences."

"I need him more. It would be unfair for me not to teach him all I can. The Gods will not let me live forever."

"I understand."

Gerak, in his boredom, as he listened to the men, let his arm swing across the threshold of the doorway. The room flashed a deep red color for an instant. Gerak leaped away from the doorway in shock and stopped with his back against the wall across the hallway.

Zarlaam and his brother were instantly on their feet. The Lord had his sword out and grabbed a bottle of wine while Zarlaam had his staff ready and cast a spell.

"What was that?"

Zarlaam continued his spell of detection and a sphere of pale blue light emitted from his staff for about five feet. He moved his staff about searching the room for a presence. "It was something foreign, brother. Possibly evil. But definitely a powerful magic crossed the doorway even if only for an instant."

"Should I cast about the wine to see what it strikes?"

"No, you would be wasting it, for I don't believe it remains in the room. The ward of detection would still glow red. Also, I detect nothing. I'll let you return to your ledgers, brother, and see if I can find the cause of this disturbance."

Gerak turned and rushed upstairs to the dorm. He took the mask off and stuffed it in the cloth sack. He slipped quietly into the dorm and went to bed. *So, Master Zarlaam, you put up wards of de-*

tection to protect yourself from magic. What magic is about that you are not telling us?

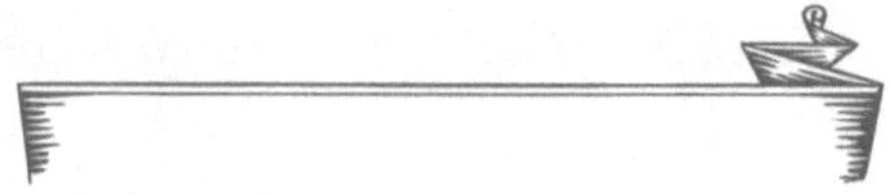

CHAPTER THIRTY-THREE

Several weeks later, everyone was in a festive mood as they gathered for lunch because of the new spells Master Zarlaam had given them to learn while he was away. Grandfather stopped beside Bershome as he headed to his seat at the head table and spoke softly. "Bershome, Martello, I need a word with you two in my office after lunch."

"Yes, sir," they said in unison. The lads exchanged looks with raised eyebrows.

"I didn't do it," Martello said to Bershome.

"Don't let it bother, buddy. He can't turn you into a frog; he isn't magical."

"Maybe this why he wants you too?"

"Naugh, he has some little project in mind for us. Besides, I'll tell him it is your turn to be a snake anyway."

"Gee, thanks for the vote of confidence, buddy."

"Hey, Wanlae," Bershome cast his voice down the table a few seats down.

"Yes?" she hissed at him with a wide smile and fluttering eyes.

"You will have the gang of miscreants to yourself for a little while this afternoon for the poetry reading."

"But I wrote a beautiful sonnet just for you."

"Martello and I have his Lordship's business to attend."

"Well, any excuse, I guess." She jerked her head away, and it tossed her hair around to slap her face. Then she looked back with a smile.

Naomi and Freya joined them in time to hear Wanlae's remark. "What was that about?"

"Wanlae being Wanlae," Bershome said with his smile pulled sideways as he reached for the pitcher and offered to fill their glasses with fruit juice and then his own.

"What is your poem about today, Martello," Arleta asked."

"The perils of having a friend who thinks you should be a frog."

He and Bershome cracked up laughing at their inside joke.

"Satire, I like the sound of that," Arleta said.

"Bershome, what's yours about?" Freya asked.

Bershome looked at her then Arleta with a furrowed eyebrow. "We have a call to duty by his Lordship. Martello and I have to miss class."

"Oh," the girls sighed in unison.

"But here, Arleta," He pulled a piece of folded parchment out and handed it to her. "I would like for you to share this one with the class for me, please."

"Freya, if you will do the same for me?" Martello handed her two pages of his own.

They busied themselves with lunch as the girls read the poems and giggled.

"This is sweet, Bershome. I'll never look at a muddy pig the same way again." Arleta managed to say between her giggles.

"Then, my intended goal is accomplished." He raised his hands, palm up, shoulder high.

"Why frolicking rocks, Martello?" Freya asked.

"Why not. Shouldn't they be allowed to play and have fun instead of just sitting there in the dirt all the time?"

"She said the poem was supposed to be about love."

"It is. I love rocks."

Freya closed her eyes and shook her head. "Boys."

"Want to read mine, Bershome?" Arleta asked.

"Later, if you don't mind. I'm trying to figure out what Grandfather wants with us."

Bershome finished eating and went to Grandfather's study to wait for him. Martello followed shortly. After a few minutes, the man arrived and shut the door behind him.

"Lads, do your magic thing and see that we are alone." He waved a hand back and forth as if fanning smoke.

The lads whipped out their wands and cast their spells. A blue haze moved around ahead of their wands, and they checked the room from corner to corner.

"Good." The man sat down and let out a deep breath.

"What's going on, Grandfather?" Bershome stood with his eyes squinted as he stared intently at the aged baron.

"We have had some strange things going on in the night lately. If I knew not better, I'd say a spirit has decided to haunt our home.

"What sort of strange things?" he asked as he sat a chair opposite him, and Martello settled beside him.

"Well, when Zarlaam is away like he is this week, the strange things seem to pick up. And they stop when he returns. The night cook says things move around in the kitchen on him when he is doing his night baking. Food disappears from bowls he just set down and platters on the table or from the pantry. He sets a bowl down, and when he turns back around, it's moved. I put some of the guards to walking about at night. They say they get tapped on the shoulder, and no one is there when they turn around. Also, doors mysteriously open and close in the dark. The animals in the stable get upset sometimes and wake the stable hands. They search and find nothing. The next morning we find no tracks of a mountain lion or wolves about."

"This is most unsettling, Grandfather. Why have you not spoken to me before about it?"

"It should not be worries of a growing lad, my boy. It is my duty as master of my home."

"You should not worry about it alone, sir."

"Well, a couple of weeks ago, Oralette, the kitchen maid, swears someone was in her chamber while she washed. Then last night, the worst happened. Witalem almost caught something messing with the door to the girl's dormitory. He tried his sword on it but missed, then something shoved him, and he almost went tumbling down the stairs."

"We can take turns patrolling the castle with the soldiers at night, sir. I'm sure Trejann and Jartus would be willing to join us."

"We just don't know what it is. I fear someone will get harmed or killed."

"We are all old enough to join the king's army. That means we are old enough to protect our own home."

"What about those funny capes you two have?"

"Our chameleon cloaks? Yes, we can use them to sneak around undetected."

"Now, I don't want you to endanger yourselves by trying to fight this thing alone."

Bershome waved his hand in the air and smiled. "Sir, we have an arsenal of charms of protection and defensive spells."

The old man smiled and sat straighter in his chair as if a great weight had been lifted from his shoulders. "I thank you, lads."

"I'll speak with the captain of the guards and work out a password in case we bump into each other in the dark. We don't need getting skewered by our own men."

"Yes, they will be jumpy enough after last night. Oh, let us not bother the other children with these matters. We don't need them screaming in the dark from nightmares. Just be careful."

"Yes, Grandfather," Bershome acknowledged his wishes as he rose to leave.

"Martello, you go to class, and I'll get with the Captain."

Bershome worked out the details with the captain and returned to class. The mathematics lesson finished early, and he stepped forward to relieve Trejann.

"Thank you, Trejann. Let us go ahead and retire to the castle early today and wash up for supper. I do need a word with Jartus, Martello, and Trejann. Thank you all."

The lads move up close to Bershome except for Martello. He lingered at the door and stepped outside to ensure they were alone. When he closed the door and stood with his back to it, Bershome spoke.

"Quickly, men, search the room for invisible intruders."

They all whipped out their wands instantly, and everyone searched the area around them. Bershome directed each to make sure no place was missed.

"Now gather close, please."

All assembled within arm's reach as he looked them over. He spoke in a low voice. "Someone or something has invaded our home. It is invisible and is haunting our servants and chambers. It is also disturbing the livestock out in the stables. Last night, it attacked a guard and almost shoved him down a flight of stairs outside the girl's dorm, which it was trying to get into. Thank goodness the door has a charm on it at night."

"What could this thing be?" Jartus asked.

"We have no idea. You two are supposed to learn about this next year, but Martello and I have chameleon cloaks. We can stand next to things while wearing them, and it is possible not to be detected."

"Wicked," Jartus whispered.

"It takes a sharp eye or magic to detect us. Usually, motion will give away the wearer."

"I can't wait to make my cloak," Trejann said.

"I've decided we will work with the guards at night. We will magically lock the outside doors and patrol the corridors with them. The guards patrol all night and sleep the next morning, but we cannot. We don't want anything to seem out of the ordinary. I think we should work four-hour shifts. Two at a time for half the night. Martello and I take the first shift tonight. We will wake you up at two for patrol until dawn."

"If you get separated, we will use a challenge and password like apple and pudding. That way, when a guard is coming upon, you can let him know you are no danger. These men have been searching for this thing for a while now. They are jumpy. No horsing around. You could get hurt."

"What if we find something?"

"Use your defensive spells. Petrify it. Levitate it. Push it away and slam it into the wall. Everyone will carry a charm of protection against evil spirits. You will feel it get warm against your chest if you encounter such a thing. Martello, can you make us each a small pouch of glitter dust?"

"Glitter dust?" Trejann questioned.

"Yes. Whatever this thing is, it is invisible but solid in nature. By chance, if you are sure you have encountered this thing, you can cast the dust on it, and maybe it will stick. You can see it to chase after it if necessary, but more importantly, you can aim spells at it."

The young men spent time discussing strategies. Bershome was hesitant about them carrying swords. Detection and capture were their intent, not to trying to kill it. He decided they would carry their training sticks as clubs. At the end, he made them all swear not to let any of the others know about the problem. They headed to the main hall to dine, and all the apprentices gave them looks of curiosity. Bershome knew his men would not compromise their secret or start rumors to frighten their companions.

Bershome lingered in the dining hall and visited with Martello and the ladies for an hour or so. Jartus joined them when his group retired upstairs. When the ladies decided to retire for the evening, Martello escorted them to their dorm, and he went up to the boy's dorm.

Bershome sent Janus out to the training field to fetch their sticks. He went to the boy's dorm to get their cloaks.

"Trejann, ole' buddy. Don't let the guys keep you awake, or it will be a long night."

"I'm gonna cast a spell and blow out all the candles in half an hour."

Bershome and Martello met with the soldier at the stables.

"Ah, Bershome. I feel a ton better knowing you will be patrolling with me tonight," John spoke when they arrived at the stables.

"Marvin," Bershome said, "don't feel left out. Not only is Martello good with his spells. You know he is a good swordsman."

"I know. I fought him last summer." The man held out his hand. Martello took it, and they shook hands.

"We will be under our chameleon cloaks and hugging the wall as we walk behind you. Sometimes we will stop and linger at passages to watch and listen. We have glitter powder to try to cast on this thing so you can see it. Remember, mistakes happen. We could accidentally dust ourselves or one another. Personally, if my friend dusts me, I will drop to the ground and call out. Then he will be a toad or a goat for a few days." Bershome smiled at his friend and wiggled his eyebrows up and down.

"The challenge before you swing your sword is apple. The password we will use is pudding."

"Why not apple and pie? There is no such thing as apple pudding."

"Exactly, everyone normally thinks of pie, not pudding. If you hear pie, swing away."

"Excellent, sir. I'll check in with his Lordship to start our watch."

Bershome turned and led the way back into the castle. When they entered, he walked close to the wall as he slipped the hood over his head. John proceeded on to the Baron's office and knocked on the door frame.

"Ah, John, ready for the night watch?"

"Aye, My Lord. Marvin, me and our shadows, sir." He spoke softly and gave the man a wink.

"Just be careful men, all of you," he spoke normally and glanced about for a hint of where the lads stood.

"Aye, my Lord." John nodded his head and returned to the hallway. Bershome followed him as he started his patrol. Marvin mounted the stairs to patrol the second floor. The servants were going about putting out the torches in most of the sconces and leaving about a fourth lit to provide a little light.

Bershome followed John's slow ambling walk. John had a habit of walking with his hand on his sword hilt and the other hand holding the sheath, so it protruded well out to his left. He walked his path slowly, going from one side of the corridor to the other as if a drunk would trying to stager down the hall. Bershome imitated his pattern in opposite so the corridor was fully covered most of the time. They checked all doors to see they were locked.

Halfway through their watch, John meandered around the dining hall. Bershome took the opposite side of the room. John hesitated at the door.

"John, all is empty," Bershome whispered.

John jerked with a slight start and chuckled as he opened the door. He lingered with it open, and Bershome slipped in.

The cook had looked up as John stepped in. His eyes popped wide open, and he snatched up a wicked-sized knife. "Behind you, John." The cook jerked up the knife to throw it.

"Wait." John threw up his hands in warning. "It's Bershome."

The lad jerked back his hood and smiled at the cook.

The cook slowly lowered his knife. "Damned, lad. You gave me quite a start," he said as he walked over to a cupboard, pulled down a bottle, and took a hearty snort. "I thought you were a demon or something."

"Sorry, Mister Mash. I'm patrolling the halls with John to try and catch your ghost."

"Well, you nearly became one, lad."

"Can't say that I would blame you for it, sir." Bershome whipped out his wand and searched the room. "We are all alone, gentlemen."

The cook went about the room, pulling knives stuck in the walls of the room. "I periodically throw a knife to see what I can hit."

"Well, I think you are safe enough, Mister Mash."

"Aye, but poor Oralette is still afraid to bathe at night. The creek is too cold for her to do so even in the daytime." He leaned forward to Bershome. "She is beginning to smell."

"I'll help her out," Bershome offered.

The cook picked up fresh bread rolls and tossed them to him and John.

"Oh, Mister Mash, you need not mention what we are doing. Grandfather wants it all hush, hush. No need to worry people any more than they are. Martello is patrolling with Marvin. We lads will be replaced in a bit by Jartus and Trejann."

"Warn them. I might not stop in time."

"We will drop our hood before coming in."

"Just hurry up and catch the damned thing. It gets hot in here without a door open."

They left the kitchen. Bershome thought he heard the thunk of a knife hitting the door a moment after they left. Marvin met John at the stairwell. They stopped and exchanged a few whispered words. The lads slipped off their hoods and joined in the conversation. John wanted to warn Martello about the cook.

After another full patrol of the castle, Bershome went in to wake up their relief. He cast a silent spell on his shoes to not make noise. He shook Martello awake. When he went to wake Trejann, he cast another spell of silence on Gerak's bedpost so the noise would not wake him. They gathered out in the corridor.

"Anything happen?" Trejann asked and yawned.

"No," Bershome growled softly.

"Good."

"If you go in the kitchen, be sure to drop your hood beforehand. The cook is deadly with throwing his knives, and he does it often."

"Why?"

"He is trying to hit something invisible. I was almost skewered by him when entering the kitchen."

The lads exchanged hands with the cloaks and parted ways.

CHAPTER THIRTY-FOUR

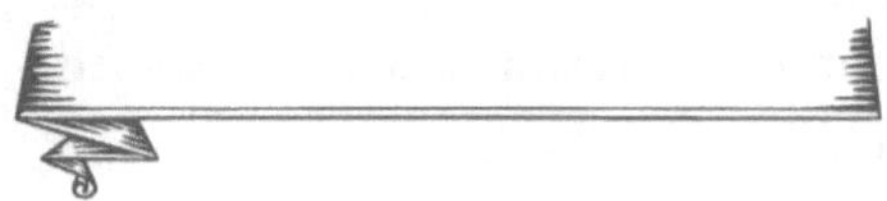

Morning came too early for Bershome. Trejann was shaking him hard to wake him.

"How did it go?"

"I think we wasted a good night's sleep, Bershome."

"How do you think the guards feel, buddy?"

"The same."

"Look at it this way, they felt stronger and braver with us trailing around behind them last night. At least I know I would."

"Good point."

Bershome went to the washroom and scrubbed his face to fully wake up. As he looked into the polished brass mirror, a thought struck him. He went and dressed quickly. "You ready, Martello? Let's go."

"Where are you off to in such a hurry?" Martello asked as Bershome flicked his wand at his bed, and in an instant, it was made up without a wrinkle to Mister Bernary's standard.

"I had an idea."

"What about?"

"Time."

"Time?" Martello asked as they left the dorm.

"Yes. The one thing we never questioned was what time frame the incidents occurred. For example, before or after midnight."

"Why would that make a difference? Ghost don't tell time, just night and day."

"Then why do people call midnight, 'the witching hour'?" Bershome headed to the family wing in long quick strides. Martello stayed right with him. They slowed down as they approached the guard outside his grandfather's chamber.

"Morning Jenson, is his Lordship up yet?"

"Can't say, Bershome," the guard said as he stepped aside to allow them past.

Bershome knocked on the door but did not wait for a reply as he let himself in.

"Grandfather," Bershome called out as he stepped into the chamber.

"Yes, is that you, Bershome?" the voice came from the wash closet.

"Yes, sir. I apologize for the intrusion."

The old man came out, tying up his undergarment at his waist. "Did you catch the damned thing?"

"Unfortunately not, sir. But I got to thinking."

"Oh, hell. We are in trouble now." The man smiled at him as he picked up his tunic from the dressing table. "Tell me, son."

Martello let out a snicker, and Bershome ignored him.

"I was wondering what time of night the strange things happened."

Grandfather looked at him a moment. "I think the guard was attacked about midnight. Oralette said it was after she finished cleaning up in the kitchen. That would be about eight. The cook said it was late in the evening, maybe ten or eleven."

"I knew it." Bershome declared with excitement.

"You knew what?"

"It is a person that has a damned good invisibility spell." Bershome pointed up with his index finger,

"You don't say? Who is it then?"

He waved his fist and finger about. "That is what I don't know."

"How is it you know it is a person?"

"He stays up late but goes to bed to get some sleep."

"Oh, it is a he now?" Martello questioned.

"Who else would be invisible and lurking in Oralette's chamber when she is about to bathe? She is a pretty woman."

"Good point, lad." His Grandfather stepped over and smacked him on the arm. "Now, how do we catch him?"

"We get Oralette to take a bath."

Both of them looked at Bershome with their mouths agape.

"I don't want to get the poor woman in trouble, but the cook mentioned it."

"I'll talk with her."

"May I handle it, Grandfather?"

"You planning to stand guard in her chamber while she bathes? I imagine she will have objections to that. Not to mention Marvin if he finds out. Remember, they are getting married next autumn."

"Oh, no, sir. I'll be outside it."

"Good. She can simply lock her door, and Marvin can stand guard outside with you."

"But that would be obvious, sir."

Grandfather sat in a chair with his shoes in his hand. "You want to set a trap if Oralette feels all right with it. However, if this thing is not a man, you could be endangering her life, son."

Bershome looked down at his feet in silence. Then he looked up at his grandfather's stern gaze. "Look at what it has done, sir. Mischievous things like playing with the cook's dishes, stealing food, trying to get into the girl's dorm. Tapping guards on the shoulder. He has moved a few personal items around the boy dorm as well. I just never connected them all. I think he only shoved the guard to get away."

"Only if she willingly consents. And I want both of you lads there with guards nearby." He pointed a boney, aged finger at him.

"Thank you, Grandfather." Bershome turned to leave.

"Bershome?"

"Yes, sir?" He paused with his hand on the door.

"Are you sure this will work?"

"I feel very confident about it."

"Then I'll leave the matter in your hands, son."

"Bershome, how did you figure this out?" Martello asked as they hurried along the corridor.

"It hit me when I was washing my face with cold water to wake up."

"Washing your face?"

"Yes. The servants carry hot water from the kitchen through the main hall to their chambers. Everyone there sees it. Then maybe tonight the voyeur will try to watch again, and we catch him."

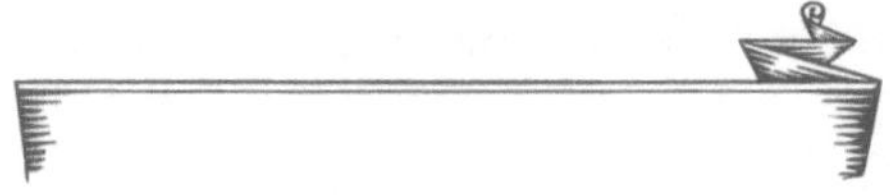

CHAPTER THIRTY-FIVE

Bershome and Martello lingered in the dining hall after the apprentices went to study grammar with Lady Esmeralda. Oralette and Shyla came out gathering up dirty dishes.

Oralette paused near Bershome with tray-load of dishes. "Are you not studying today Bershome, sir?"

"I will shortly. Sit your tray down. I wish to speak to you about something."

She set the tray on the table, made a slight curtsy, and stood before him with her hands cupped together in front of her. "What is your wish, sir?"

Bershome whispered, "Oralette," She leaned closer to him. "When was the last time you had a full bath?"

She stood erect, turned a bright red, and her bottom lip trembled. "I...I..."

Bershome saw tears welling up in her eyes. He held up his hand to stop her. "You are not in trouble of any kind. I know and understand why."

"Well," She looked over her shoulder. "it's still a bit embarrassing, sir."

"Not my intention to do such to you. I wish to enlist your help in getting rid of our castle's ghost."

She took a small step backward.

"I promise you will be in no danger. Please, sit, and let me tell you my plan."

She obeyed, and Bershome laid it all out for her and Martello.

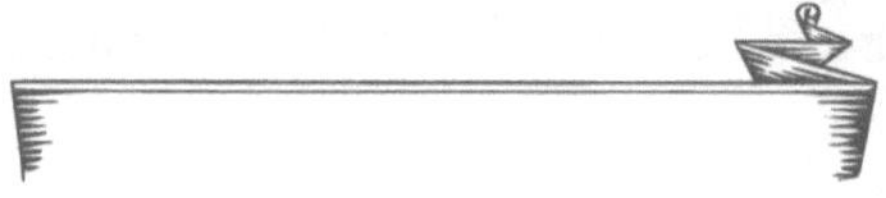

CHAPTER THIRTY-SIX

That evening, as usual, several of the apprentices lingered in the main hall studying. Lavonia helped Gerak with math, Jamie and Trejann were in a group with others chatting. Bershome was with his group as Arleta was explaining to him the grammar course he had missed out on. Oralette and Shyla came through the hall carrying steaming buckets of water to the servant's chambers. Bershome gave Martello a nodded.

"I didn't sleep well last night. I'll see you people in the morning." Martello stretched his arms out wide and faked a yawn.

"Walk me to our dormitory?" Freya asked him.

Martello offered her an outstretched arm, and she gathered her books.

"Arleta," Bershome said, "why don't you go too. You look a bit tired yourself." He saw the hurt in her face as she avoided looking at him with her downcast gaze and head as she slowly closed her book and left with them.

You worded that badly, m' boy.

Bershome looked at his book to pretend to be reading but noticed Gerak and a couple others left for the stairs to the boys' dorm. Bershome got up and went into the kitchen.

"Have you enough hot water, Mister Mash?" he asked after he closed the door.

"Aye lad. She can get in a good scrubbing tonight."

"Let's hope so, sir. Also, maybe you can stop wrecking the cabinets with your knives."

They cracked up laughing together as Bershome unfolded his cloak and put in on.

"Good hunting, lad."

Bershome slipped his way along the outer the walls and avoided contact with the remaining apprentices in the hall. The maids returned to the kitchen for more water. He tiptoed into the servant wing and found John and Marvin lingering in the hall and blocking the way to Oralette's chamber. No torches were lit beyond them in the hall. Only a single one burned halfway down the stairs.

He eased up near John as the man laughed at Marvin's joke.

"Apple," he whispered.

Marvin flinched as if he had shouted, but John handled it like a veteran with nerves of steel.

"Pudding," John whispered without taking his eyes off Marvin.

"I'll slip past you against the wall."

John shifted his stance, and Bershome squeezed past. John closed the gap behind him. Shortly the maids returned with more water. Bershome stood still on the opposite side of the door.

Marvin took Oralette's buckets, and she opened the door. "I could offer to wash your back for you, beautiful lady."

She opened it wide, and Marvin took the water in. "You will have plenty of time to do that after our marriage come autumn, sir."

He came back out and declared, "I'll do it as often as I can." He leaned toward her, and she gave him a quick kiss. "All is safe now." He winked at her and took a strange place step to the side. The ladies quickly stepped in and closed the door behind them. Bershome heard the click of the lock.

Bershome had planned for Oralette to slip Martello into the room and check it for intruders while the ladies were fetching more water. Then he came out with Marvin leading, and the ladies were locked safe behind the door.

Bershome leaned against the wall and opened his pouch. He held it ready in his left and wand in his right. Martello was to take up a spot down the corridor just past the stairs. He heard splashing of water and girlish giggling through the door. They kept it up for several minutes and, after a long pause, started again. They were louder this time, and the noise carried down the corridor.

Bershome almost missed hearing a noise that sounded like a scrape of a shoe against the floor. He stopped breathing for a moment as he strained to hear over the giggling within. Suddenly, he felt a presence.

A tiny green spark escaped from the keyhole in the door. Bershome thrust his left hand beyond his cloak, and a dust cloud of glitter exploded in front of him as it sailed through the air.

The glittering form stood taller than him had horns rising above the head. Startled, Bershome sucked in a breath. He cast a stun spell at the demon.

Red sparks struck it, and the demon was lifted off the floor and sailed back a few feet to land on its back. The moment it struck the floor, green sparks hit it from Martello's paralyzing spell. Martello stepped up and scattered his dust over the thing to expose it better.

"Well done, 'ole chap."

"It is a hideous-looking thing. Look at those horns."

Bershome knelt beside the head. "Careful," Martello warned, "we don't know how strong it is and if it can kill us."

Bershome ignored him as he grasped a horn and pulled on it. The head came off the body, and Bershome found himself looking at a wooden devil's mask from the mirror in the entrance way. "Grab a torch, and light it."

Martello fetched the burning torch and returned running.

"I never would have thought it was you, Gerak Kalthazar."

They stood over the unconscious lad.

"Go get the guards and tell no one," Bershome ordered as he removed the wand from Gerak's hand.

Martello rushed off and returned with the guards. Their leather armor squeaking as they ran.

John, Marvin, lock this one up in the dungeon. Use one of Master Zarlaam's enchanted locks. Magic cannot open them. His Lordship and Master Zarlaam will decide what to do with him. Also, tell no one about who or what it was."

"The lad ought to get a lashing for this."

"That is Grandfather's decision to make. I am going to bed." Bershome watched the men cart Gerak off. He knocked on the Oralette's door. It was quickly opened, and both ladies stood fully dressed with areas of their clothes showing wetness from their playing.

"Is it over?"

"Yes. Thank you, ladies, for your help. You may now bath in peace and safe comfort."

"What was it?"

Bershome smiled while turning away. "Something that will never bother you again."

"That is it, then?" Martello questioned him as they ascended the steps.

"There is nothing to do until the morrow, my friend." Bershome put the mask in his wardrobe, undressed, and went to bed.

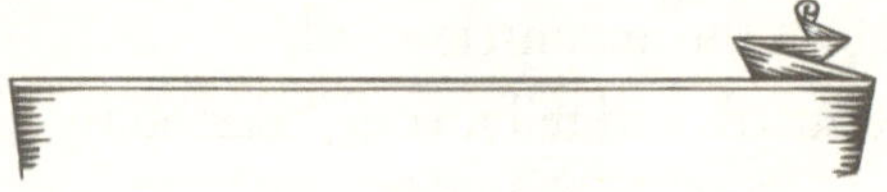

CHAPTER THIRTY-SEVEN

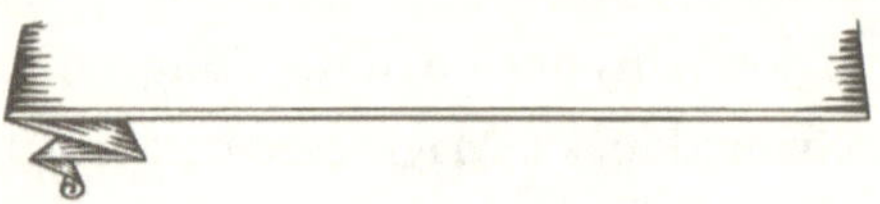

Trejann awakened Bershome the next morning. "What happened last night? You didn't wake me up for my shift."

"We captured, uh, the culprit."

"Wow. What was it?"

"Not what, but who, and it's something I would prefer not to discuss at this time. I'll have to deal with it when Master Zarlaam returns."

"Sounds like you don't want to do it."

"Not really."

Trejann leaned close and whispered. "That is the curse of being high-born, my friend."

"Tell me about it. Also, nothing about this entire matter is to be discussed with anyone."

"Good luck with it."

Bershome cleaned up and wrapped the mask in his robe. He headed down to breakfast with the rest of the guys.

While they went towards the dining hall, he headed to Grandfather's office. The door stood open, and the man was looking over his books. Bershome knocked on the door and stepped in. "Morning, Grandfather."

"Ah, Bershome, John informed me this morning you had an exciting evening."

"It definitely had a surprise in it."

"What would you recommend we do with the lad?"

Bershome unwrapped the mask and set it on the desk. "Personally, I'm thankful it is not my place to decide, sir. You and Master Zarlaam get to make that decision."

The old man chuckled. "The march of time and old age is inevitable, son."

"Aye, sir. I don't relish it coming."

"Fine, we will wait for my brother. After all, it is his jurisdiction. The culprit can sit where he is and spend time thinking about his sins."

"There is one consolation, however. We will now know part of the secrets of the mirror. Well, Gerak does. We need to lock this up in the vault for now. I recommend all the masks be put there."

"I'll have it done after breakfast."

"May I suggest one thing, Grandfather?"

"Certainly. "

"I told the soldiers to keep quiet about this."

"I'll put the word out to the staff."

"Thank you. I think it best."

"How about breakfast, lad?" They headed to the dining hall.

After breakfast, the apprentices headed to the Hall of Knowledge. When they all assembled, Lavonia had stopped at the door.

"What's the matter, Lavonia?" Bershome asked.

"Where is Gerak? He wasn't at breakfast. He was supposed to help me with my potions today."

"He received word that his father is ill and will be away for a while. Check with Chal. He is getting pretty good."

She dropped her shoulders and walked up to Chal. Bershome could tell she was not enthused about his idea. He thought for a moment to warn her about Gerak but dismissed the idea for the time being.

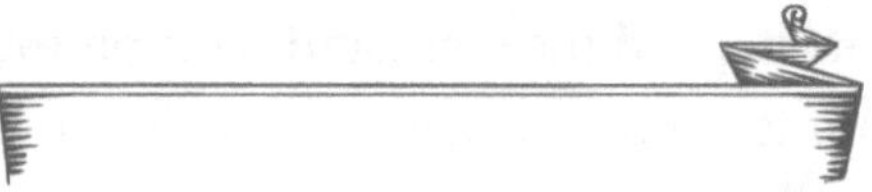

CHAPTER THIRTY-EIGHT

Arleta sat in the dormitory at her little table writing. Livonia sat down across from her.

"Whatcha doing, Arleta? Spring is in the air, and we should be outside."

"Writing a letter to Poppa."

"Can you help me?" she whispered.

"What do you need? Having problems with a potion?"

"No, a boy."

"Who? Martello?"

"No, he and Freya are goofy-eyed for each other. I am talking about Gerak."

"That is a hard nut to crack. Be careful. Personally, I don't trust him."

"Why?"

"He is the son of a fisherman. He practically grew up on a boat. They think they are rougher and tougher than other boys. I heard him talking about some of the fights he has been in with other sailors. Have you noticed he still carries his knife with him?"

"He is tall, tanned, strong, and handsome."

"There is still something about him I don't trust, Livonia. What do you need me to help you do?"

"I was wondering if you could help me look pretty."

Arleta looked her over as she smiled. "We can do something with your hair. "Here," she reached out and pinched her cheeks, "this will give you a bit of color. I have a blue blouse that would match your eyes. Let's try it on."

"Okay."

Arleta walked around the girl and examined her with a more critical eye.

"Let's see. Uh-huh. We can try to curl your hair. I have several nice ribbons. We can tie it up and let it cascade down the sides. I think a blue one would be best to accent your eyes. The yellow would show how blond your hair is. Now press your lips together hard a moment. Yes, that puts a little color in them. Pinch your cheeks here below the bones. It will give you face a little color. That's it. No, let's not smile so widely." She almost grimaced at the crookedness of the girl's teeth. "Now, you are frowning. Just curl your lips up here." She touched the corners of her mouth. "Uh-huh. Now, what can we do with your dress?"

Her dress was a simple, coarsely woven green cotton cloth. The neckline curved in the front and sported a simple narrow collar.

"We could use more ribbons. If we slipped them beneath your collar and let them stream down to about here." She indicated just above her breasts.

"What can we do about these?" Livonia cupped her breast with her hands.

"Sweetheart, nature has to do its work there. You are only thirteen. You must give it time."

"I'm almost fourteen, thank you."

"Give it time, and it will make a woman out of you soon enough. I have seen some girls put padding in their blouses, but it looked as phony as it was. And it would be a little too obvious right now. The boys would laugh at you. They don't understand such things."

Livonia sighed.

"Let me brush and try to curl your hair."

Arleta got her comb and brush. Livonia picked up her spellbook from the desk.

"Where did you get this? May I look at it?"

"Yes. An old witch named Fredean gave it to me. She lived outside our village."

Livonia began turning the pages as Arleta brushed her hair. After a few pages, she gasped.

She shrieked. "This is it! This is what I need!"

"What?" Arleta looked over her shoulder.

"A beauty potion. Right here in your book."

"Oh, I haven't looked at the book much. I guess it has been too soon after losing my friend Fredean. She gave it to me."

"Oh, I'm sorry."

"It wasn't a very pleasant affair. Everyone in my village was afraid of her because they didn't care to know her. She was a really sweet person."

"Yuck. That is awful."

"What is?"

"The ingredients are, listen to this, bat eyelashes, lizard lips, newt tongue, witch's weed, powdered seashells, and willow tears."

"What do you do with it?" Arleta asked.

"It has to be brewed and left to set a week?" Livonia said and groaned.

"I hope you don't have to drink it. It sounds awful," Arleta said.

"No, you spread it about your face under the beginning full moon. Oh goodness. You wear it for a full night. Then you wash it off with fresh goat's milk the next morning. At least that doesn't sound so bad." Livonia said.

"I'm not sure I could stand that. That sounds like it would be yucky going on and dry to a flaky crust."

"Well, Mother always said it is painful to look beautiful." Livonia sighed. "The beauty will fade with each wash. Using fresh goat's milk and clear water will help it last up to three weeks. That doesn't do me much good. It will be another week before I can use it again."

"What if we make enough to last a couple of months? You wouldn't have to make it as often." Arleta said.

"What are willow tears?"

"A weeping willow tree cries during the day. I wonder how you would collect such a small mist of moisture. Hmm. I seem to remember reading about a gathering spell to bring things together like leaves in a pile or the clutter of clothes strewn about a room into a basket. We would have to be careful not to harm the tree and get only the mist it gives out."

They turned through the pages looking for the spell.

"Here it is. It is a simple incantation. We need a flask and a funnel."

"It needs to be a crystal flask," Arleta informed her.

"How do you know?"

"Fredean told me when gathering components for potions, you need clean, pure containers to prevent contaminating them. Some components need special containers. You can use one made from gold, silver, copper, crystal, and glazed clay pottery, but never lead or bronze."

"Why would it matter? We mix them in a pewter cauldron."

"The cauldron is enchanted to be neutral to prevent it from affecting potions."

"How do you know so much already. I've been studying two years now."

"Fredean taught me a lot about potions for years."

"Is there a love potion in here I can use on Gerak? Oh, I love the way his name sounds. Gerak, Gerak, Gerak."

"Focus, dear. I'll go ask Master Zarlaam for a crystal flask."

"No, we can't let anyone know what we are doing."

"Why? Master Zarlaam encourages us to study and experiment."

"I want Gerak to be surprised. He will see I am prettier without knowing it and fall in love with me."

"You will have to do this every month."

"Not quite."

"The instructions were precise. It only lasts a month. And you have to do it under a full moon too. That helps because we have three weeks to gather the components for our first batch."

"That is too much work and too often. I have a cousin that knows a potion to mix with it that might make it permanent."

"Hold on. Master Zarlaam warned us about mixing potions."

"I'm going to test it."

"Where did you get such a potion?"

"My cousin lives way, way, south of here in Woods Edge village. He told me about it." Livonia said.

"Oh? Why is he not attending here?"

"Everyone in the entire village is a magic-user. They teach themselves. Besides, he is like twenty-five years old."

"I have heard of Woods Edge Village. A friend of mine named Dallietano moved to live near there."

"Is he good looking? How old is he?"

"He is..." Arleta thought a moment. "He's too old for you."

CHAPTER THIRTY-EIGHT

The next day, Arleta and Livonia walked across the grounds as they headed towards the river. The baskets they carried in one hand and blankets in the other made it appear they were going on a picnic. They passed a few other apprentices lounging about on a warm Saturday afternoon in the orchard as they studied, practiced their spells, or socialized. The river was half a mile away from the castle. They walked along the bank until they found the largest willow tree there. They set stones around a flask to make it stand. Livonia stuck the funnel in the neck of the flask. They stood back and looked the tree over a minute.

"Shall we do this?" Arleta looked at Livonia.

"Most definitely. Have you got the spell?"

"Yes, for the umpteenth time." She pulled the parchment from her pocket along with her wand.

"Sorry, I don't mean to be pushy."

"You are anxious."

Water and tree, sky and breeze
As cries the willow this time of year
Around the tree go round the breeze.
Breeze circle high, circle round
Circle closer coming down
gather wispy mist of tears,
into the funnel and not the ground.

A light breeze began circling the tree. They watched the leaves sway and flicker in the breeze for a few minutes. Livonia stepped close and looked down in the funnel.

"I don't see any in the funnel."

"That is why we brought the blankets and baskets of goodies. We need to wait for enough to gather."

They moved to beyond the boundary of the wind surrounding the tree and lay out their blankets and dug into the baskets for their lunch.

"Now, Arleta, which one are you going to choose, Bershome, or Gerak?"

"You want Gerak. I'll not interfere."

"You haven't seen how he looks at you. It's almost like a dog drooling for a prime steak. I wish he would look at me that way."

"I don't care for him."

"Why?"

"Because it is not love that I see in his eyes."

"How do you know?"

"Livonia, you have lived a sheltered and protected life. While there is nothing wrong with that, it has limited your knowledge of the ways of the world and the ways of boys becoming men. I have worked as a tavern owner's daughter and seen how boys and men act. Especially, when they are trying to get what they want from girls and women. Sad to say, it is not love, dearie."

"So, you think Gerak does not want to love you."

"Not in a marriage way. He is superficial and only looks at the skin beauty of the girl in front of him. He is not aware of, nor cares about the sweet loving soul that is your beating heart."

"What of Bershome?"

"He is a hard one to read. While he is pleased to be in the presence of a beautiful girl, he isn't quite sure of himself. He is well educated. I think he wants what all boys at his age desire, but he prefers to be honorable about it. I believe he would sacrifice himself for someone he loves. He is good looking, kind, sweet, considerate, strong, and loyal. He is the marrying kind."

"It doesn't hurt that his grandfather is rich either." Livonia grinned.

"That is a different problem in itself. Any commoner pursuing him could be considered a gold-digger. What chance do you and I have? We are not nobility." Arleta shrugged.

"He is a ruling Lord's grandson, not a prince. He can marry a commoner. We have hope."

"We?" Arleta looked at her with raised eyebrows.

"Well, you didn't outright say you wanted him."

Arleta rolled her eyes and waved her hands in the air in exasperation. "Livonia, make up your mind. First, you were after Martello, then Gerak, now Bershome? You are beginning to act like a trollop."

"I am not." She cried.

Arleta watched her a moment, shocked that her words had hurt the girl so. "I'm sorry, Livonia. I was trying to warn you what it would look like to others."

She looked at Arleta, wiped her tears, and regained her composure. "I just want to be like you and have a boy love me."

"How about we work on the beautiful part and let love take its natural course?"

"Okay. Oh, look! The flask in overflowing."

They hurried to swap an empty flask with the full one and put the stopper in it.

"If we get two flasks full, we will have enough for a year's worth of potion."

When the potion was finally ready, Livonia painted her face with it under the beginning of the full moonlight and slept with it. When she washed it off the next morning, she ran to Arleta to look at the difference.

Arleta looked her face over as she turned her head to look at one side and the other. "Livonia, your skin is flawless, all the blemishes are all gone. It is smooth and soft."

"That's all?"

"Yes. I think you have a good potion for blotchy skin treatment."

"But I'm not beautiful?"

"You are the same as you were, with clear soft skin,"

CHAPTER THIRTY-NINE

Master Zarlaam walked into the dining hall mid-way through lunch. All the apprentices commenced clapping and welcoming him home. The rest of the staff joined in.

"Thank you all. Quiet it down lest his lordship becomes jealous." Everyone laughed, and he took his seat next to his brother that Afreck had vacated.

After Grandfather finished eating, he left and paused to lay a heavy hand on Bershome's shoulder, and whispered to him. "We have business to attend to, lad." They headed to Grandfather's office. "After the apprentices return to studying, have guards bring up the prisoner."

Before long, Zarlaam came in and took a seat. Bershome updated him on the details of Gerak's activity while haunting the castle. Afterward, he stepped out and sent the men for the prisoner.

Zarlaam told them of his trip when they were interrupted by the rattle of chains. Gerak was standing in the doorway wearing leg irons and manacles."

"Bring him in, Captain, and close the door," Grandfather ordered.

Gerak stared with a sneer at Bershome as he shuffled into the room.

"Mister Kalthazar, you have caused quite a bit of havoc in my home," Grandfather said.

Gerak stared at him with his jaw clenched and lips pressed together. "What is he doing here?" He jerked his head at Bershome.

"It is his place to be here. Remember yours, lad. You are a guest in my house. It is not your place to question how I manage the affairs in my home. Also, he is the reason you are still here. If he had not convinced me to let your master handle this, you would be flogged publicly and run out of the territory."

Gerak lowered his head without a word.

"Mister Kalthazar," Zarlaam asked, "how did you discover the secret of the masks and mirror?"

"I put the mask on and leaned back against the mirror. I fell inside it. When I stepped out, I was invisible."

"Why did you not come forward with such information?"

"I thought I would have a little fun with it."

"Did you?"

"Some. But you should be grateful to me. I saved all your lives. The man that had the devil mask copy I made was going to use it to kill the three of you the night of the costume party."

"That is a fierce accusation, young man," Grandfather said.

"I heard him and his man talking about it, and I scared them off."

"Do you expect our gratitude after the way you have conducted yourself, terrorizing my night cook, sneaking into our maids' chambers while they bathed? Scarring my guards as they patrolled the castle, which I had to do because of your antics in the kitchen? There is no telling what other antics you indulged yourself in, either."

"I never saw her undressed. She began acting suspicious, and I left."

"What about nearly killing Wellom when you tried to shove him down the stairs?"

"He attacked me with his sword."

"We knew not what evil was haunting our castle. What would you expect him to do?"

Gerak looked at the floor. "What he did to protect his home, sir."

"Why should I allow you to remain here, Gerak?" Zarlaam asked.

"I'm truly sorry, sirs. I didn't think it was harmful. It was just a little bit of fun." Gerak sounded as if he was on the verge of tears.

"Well, Lord Paxtare. No one was actually harmed and no damage was actually done," Zarlaam spoke up. "What we have here, I think, is a case of poor judgment and adolescence mischief."

The men exchanged looks for a long silent moment.

Grandfather spoke. "Boy, you should be grateful to your betters here. Bershome kept the word quiet about you being our demon haunting the castle. Otherwise, the rest of the apprentices would be treating you like a leper."

Gerak looked wide-eyed at him.

"Bershome, fetch Oralette and Mister Mash. Gerak has apologies to make," Grandfather ordered.

He left the room and brought the maid and cook to the office.

"Thank you for coming, Oralette," Zarlaam said. "Mister Kalthazar wishes to speak with you."

Gerak glanced up at her and back down to the floor. "I'm sorry I frightened you. I'm sorry for trying to watch you bathe."

"Look a person in the eye when you speak to them, boy," Grandfather ordered. "That way, they can tell your sincerity."

Gerak turned to face her and looked up slowly. "I'm sorry I frightened you, and I'm sorry for trying to watch you bathe."

Oralette stepped over and slapped him so hard he staggered away and fell to the floor. She faced Lord Paxtare and curtsied. "Thank you, me lord."

He nodded. "Miss Oralette, please tell no one about this. I'm embarrassed enough as it is."

She curtsied and left

The soldiers helped Gerak to his feet. He faced the cook. "Mister Mash, I apologize for playing tricks on you in the kitchen."

"Lad, I'm not his Lordship, but I'd give you a punishment, and you would carry the scars for the rest o' yer life. Be thankful his Lordship is a merciful man." Mr. Mash bowed to Grandfather and left.

"Mister Kalthazar," Zarlaam said, "I advised we have a high standard of moral conduct here. You will not do magic for a month and report to Mister Henson for duty every morning. Remember this lesson. Go clean up and see him. John, if you will remove his shackles."

Gerak looked at everyone a moment. "Thank you for your forgiveness and mercy, sirs."

Lord Paxtare gave a simple wave of his hand to dismiss him.

CHAPTER FORTY

Weeks later, time drew near the last official day of training, Master Zarlaam stood at the front of the class. "Good morning, ladies and gentlemen. Today and for the next few days, in fact, we will be studying about making charmed objects. Who can tell me the purpose of a charmed object.? Ah, Miss Livonia?"

"A magically enchanted object can be used as wards of protection."

"Thank you. Nicely described. Yes, there are several types of charms. Some offer their protection constantly for the parameter of their magical strength. Others are made as a reserve of magic and are active only when invoked."

"What does a charm look like? Mister Jartus?"

"A charm can be made into anything. A ring, a necklace, a spoon, a rock."

"Precisely. Any non-living object can be made into a charm. What are the elements of a charm? Mister Trejann?"

"There are three components to a charm. They are; the object you are charming, the spell to invoke, and the binding incantation."

"Yes. The three elements are combined in several different ways. It all depends on the object, the spell, and the binding incantation. For example, a ring of protection like you would wear on your finger against evil spirits must be combined while the ring is being forged. Then you carve in the ruins of enchantment while chanting the spell.

"Today, we will have a test and play a game. The test is to flex our ability in magical detection. It is a difficult talent to master. Do not feel bad if you fail to detect the magical items properly. I, myself, must admit there are times when I have failed to detect or accurately detect magic or the spell involved. The best way to detect magic is with the development of what I call your seventh sense. It will grow with your magical skills."

"Jartus, here, distribute these pouches. In each, you will find a dozen red disks. You will use these disks to cast a vote on each item we test. There are three choices, yes, no, and not sure. This board is numbered one through twelve. It has pockets under each number. They are appropriately labeled. You will levitate your disk and float it over to the pocket for your vote. On your parchment, you may keep your personal score. Please write down the spell if you can detect it. Please do not invoke the charms.

"There are three rules to the game. No touching the disk to cast them as a vote. I wish for you to levitate them with your wands. No shooting them across the room at someone. We wouldn't want to put out an eye. Please, be honest with yourself in your vote. Is everyone ready to play?" He saw everyone nodding and smiling. Many had their wands in hand.

"The first item is a red disk. There is one charmed disk in your pouch. Find it and cast your vote to pocket number one. For some of you having difficulty, try laying your hand over each disk. Close your eyes. Open your mind and feelings. Can you sense something?"

A few isolated disks quickly floated across the room to the pouches under number one. Most of the others were slower.

As he saw the last votes cast, he pulled out the other objects and passed them out. Each item was numbered with a tag on a string. The first person tested the object and passed it on, then sent their vote to the board.

"Please be sure of the item number you are voting for."

Gerak, Kayla, and Idreck had trouble levitating disks and moving them across the room with accuracy. Bershome stepped over to each and assisted them. By the end of the testing, they were doing fairly well.

"Now, was that fun or not?" Master Zarlaam asked the class.

All the test items were returned up front, and he stepped up to the board.

"First, we had the disks themselves. Bershome and I personally charmed them this past summer and tried to make them as strong in magical properties as possible. Let us see here. One not sure. And it is a magical disk. The person in doubt is better than they think. They were actually correct. Give yourself a point. No, had three disks. Two of them are magical. The remaining are yes. One of which is not magical. Did anyone identify the spell? Valnessa?"

"It is a ward against evil?"

"Yes. Well done."

"Next item was an hourglass. One not sure. Nine for no, and the rest are yes. The hourglass is not magical. Thank you, Miss Arleta, for the loan. The fact that it glows in the dark is a natural phosphorescence in the sand."

"Item number three is a key. Eight votes no, and the rest are Yes. Fact be known, it is not magical."

"Item number four is a pocket watch. All yes. I am astounded and proud of you all. Afreck's watch whistles on the hour."

"Item number five is a parchment. Twelve not sure, Nine for no, and one yes. Oh, one of our missing magical disks. The parchment is nothing other than a recipe for a cake in written in the old Grumman language. Non-magical."

"Item number six is a mirror. All yes. Correct. Who identified the charm?"

No one raised a hand.

"If you hold it behind your head and tap it. It holds the vision of your hair you cannot see." He demonstrated it and showed everyone the reflection of the back of his head.

"Item number seven is a paperweight. One not sure, seven no, the rest yes. It is magical. Anyone identify it? Jartus?"

"Ward of protection."

"Yes."

"Item number eight is a lovely locket. One not sure. And the rest yes. Who identified the charm?" He glanced around the room. "No one? Do not feel bad. This charm is unique and special. It has wards of protection and is a spell enhancer."

"How does it enhance, sir?" Tigran asked

"Well. It is almost like a staff or wand. It was forged under magic and etched in ruins."

"How would you use it?"

"Miss Arleta, if you please?" He beckoned her to join him. "Use your repulsion spell to push the paper-weight across the desk."

"I don't have my wand, sir."

"Please try."

She held out her hand and muttered her spell, but the weight did not move.

"Now," he handed her the locket. Try again."

She tried again. The weight wobbled slightly and then slid slowly away from her. Everyone applauded.

"Such charmed items are difficult to make. It takes lots of preparation and advanced research. You also need a trustworthy blacksmith that will not sell you out to a mob for hanging. If any of you lads take up the hammer and anvil, you can consider charms such as this. I have two parchments of instructions available on making charms of this quality."

"Item number nine appears to be a wand. One not sure, and all the rest, yes. Now, now, who really tried? It is a stick with carvings on it. They mean nothing."

"Item number ten: a knife with elk bone handle. Only five for no, and the rest are yes. Who knows the charm?"

"Ward of protection," someone said.

"Correct."

"Item number eleven is a lovely cameo necklace. All yes. Anyone know the charm?"

"It is a love charm."

"Yes."

"Master, why would a person make a love charm?"

"If I wore a love charm when I got close to a person I was trying to buy something from and wanted a bargain, the charm would make them like me and possibly influence their decision to give me a better price. Also, it could have a calming effect against a hostile person."

"Item number twelve is two mirrors in a hinged frame. They are not magical. One yes, and the rest are no. I must ask of the person. Why the one yes?"

"When I opened it, I saw the reflection of myself, a magical person," Wanlae spoke up.

"Excellent perspective. I was hoping someone would catch my intent. Thank you. But all of you were correct. Was that not fun? Let's retire for the day. I heard the cook has made cherry tarts for dessert."

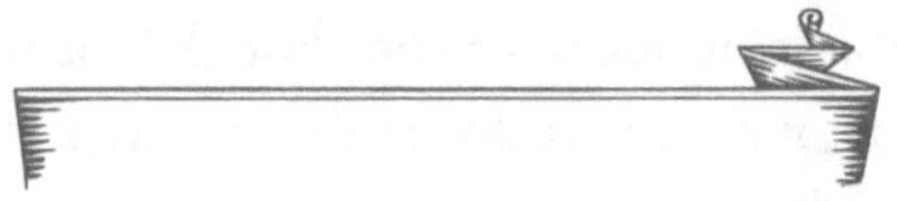

CHAPTER FORTY-ONE

A week later, Master Zarlaam stood before his apprentices. He looked at each face. He saw mixed emotions among them. Some were happy and eager to depart and return home. Gerak was not among them. Zarlaam read his emotions. They were not the sad feeling he expected. They were cold, almost angry. The lad's adjustment to the lifestyle on the estate and constant studying was a difficult accomplishment for him. Zarlaam figured that returning home would be just as difficult.

"Ladies and gentlemen, it is with great personal discomfort in my heart that I bid you all farewell for the summer. I wish you all good health and safe travel. Now I must remind you of the rules of magic. Repeat together."

Everyone quoted the many-times repeated rules verbatim in unison.

"These rules are for your safety and the safety of your families. If you simply must practice, find a secluded place in the woods away from everyone. Do not cast any curses on anyone, even if the village bully deserves it. In time, that person will get their justice due.

"If you can safely seek out new spells and potions, I would gladly review them. Please be wary of evil spells and curses. They are out there and do not belong in our world of magic. Magic is for the good of all. Harm no one. I am already looking forward to your return this fall after the harvest season. Send me letters. I cannot promise to reply to them, but I do find great joy in hearing from you."

Many of the apprentices departed in groups or with a family member who came to take them home. Zarlaam spent the morning seeing everyone off. He was standing outside the main entrance to the castle when he saw Kalthazar walking out carrying his kit and bedroll.

"Mister Kalthazar, I hope you have a pleasant trip and a good visit with your father."

Gerak paused before him. Zarlaam sensed he was gathering his thoughts and was conflicted with his inner emotions.

"I think it will be a brief visit, Master Zarlaam. I'll charm his nets again to help him."

"You fear that his drinking has worsened?"

Kalthazar shrugged.

"I attempted to help him with the problem. You must understand that your mother was the greatest love of his life. He misses her severely. He blames himself for not being there when she was ill."

"A fish cannot change his scales, sir."

"That is true. But a father can change his ways. He may have difficulty showing his love out of fear of losing his son."

"He cannot lose what he has driven away."

"Perhaps you could make an effort to mend what was lost, lad."

"Yes, Master Zarlaam."

"How are you traveling?"

"I have arranged to hire a horse in the village."

"Good trip to you, young man."

Kalthazar turned and waved as he headed down the road to the village.

Zarlaam had barely detected Gerak's thoughts. He had things on his mind more pressing than nursing his relationship with his father, but Zarlaam could not tell what the lad was planning.

"Master Zarlaam," a sweet voice interrupted his concentration.

"Yes, Miss Arleta?"

"Will you be traveling near Natudix this year?"

"Unfortunately not, my dear. I received a letter a few weeks ago, and my travels will be taking me a different direction this year."

"Oh," she said crestfallen.

"Go and enjoy your visit with your father. Harvest your garden of what has survived and bring us back what potion ingredients you can. I will gladly pay you for them."

"I'll see what I can do, sir."

Bershome stood behind her with her bag and trunk. He loaded them in a wagon she had hired. There were several barrels of wine, ale, and bourbon in the back, along with several rounds of cheese.

"I see you are hauling trade goods with you. Are you intending to travel alone, Miss Harsumg?"

"No, sir, I'll be traveling with Martello to his town and then home. The cargo will make this trip home quite profitable."

"I am afraid for your safety alone on the road."

"Martello said his father does business with a town near Natudix. I can travel with his teamsters there, and it is a short ride home. Besides, I do have a couple of defensive spells to help protect me if I need them. You and Bershome are good teachers, Master Zarlaam."

"Thank you, Miss Harsumg. I hope you have no need of them. Oh, don't forget your rosemary for the water that you need to get past the tangleweed."

"I have it in my bag, sir." She patted her purse.

She stole a look where Bershome was loading her things and lowered her voice to a whisper. "Also, Gerak will be traveling escort with us on his horse. Please don't tell Bershome."

Zarlaam thought a quick moment. "Arleta," he hesitated, "I am not in the habit of speaking ill of anyone. Just be careful with him."

"I have already considered that, sir. I have a spell just for him if need be. But I believe he will be a gentleman."

"Then I wish you God's speed in your travels."

Arleta accepted Bershome's help getting in the wagon, and she followed Martello and his wagon load of apprentices down the road. Zarlaam felt good about the safety of the caravan. Bershome stepped up next to him and returned a final wave to Arleta as she rode away.

"Where are we traveling this summer, Master Zarlaam?"

"I need to speak with you about that. Your Grandfather needs your assistance. I will be traveling alone this year."

"I hope you have a good adventure, Master Zarlaam. I suppose I should check in with him and see what he has scheduled. I suppose we will be checking on planters, herders, visiting barons, and such." Bershome hid his disappointment well as he watched the wagons disappear.

Zarlaam laid his hand on the lad's shoulder. "She will be fine, Bershome. Martello will see to that."

"I know. Gerak will probably ride along also because there is more safety in numbers, and he is turning out to be fair with a sword."

Zarlaam chose not to say anything about it. They went inside. Zarlaam went to his study and Bershome to find his grandfather.

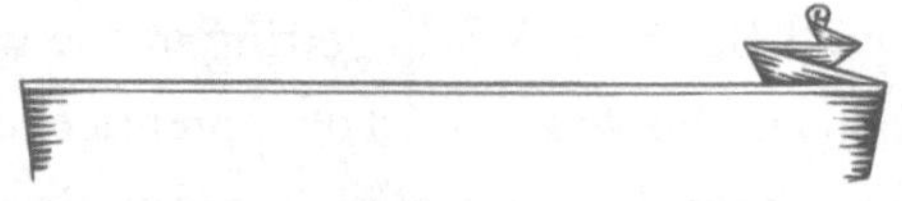

CHAPTER FORTY-TWO

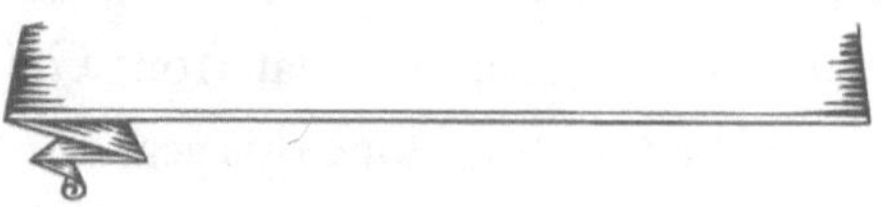

It was late afternoon when Arleta stopped the wagon in front of her father's inn and started to climb down. She selected her footing on the wheel but glanced up before continuing. She paused and exchanged looks with Harome. She looked a moment at his scowling face. He did not move to assist her in getting off the wagon. She still managed to gracefully get down then looked at him again.

"I remember a time when you would lend a helping hand to a lady, Harome."

He stepped close to her, and she felt old feeling tug on her heart. She thought she saw a waver in his demeanor when her perfume caressed his senses. His stone face softened for a flash of a second and then hardened.

"Fancy clothes and perfume don't change the fact that you are a witch. Witches ain't welcome in this town."

"I see you haven't changed. There is one thing to consider, Harome. My father owns half the property in this town. I don't think he has turned against me, and I doubt he ever will. I am still the same person I was before I left. Except I have learned a lot about many, many, things. Not just the stuff like Fredean knew." She stepped around him and went inside. A young girl about her age stepped from behind the bar and walked up to her.

"Good afternoon, me Lady. What could we do for you today? We have a stew started an hour ago, and it is about ready. Perhaps you desire a room for the night?"

Arleta looked at the girl and smiled. "Brita, I've only been gone nine months."

The girl looked at her, and her mouth dropped open "Arleta!" she screeched and grabbed her in a hardy hug. "I didn't recognize you." She released her, turned around, and shouted, "Mister Harsumg."

"Brita, I'll just go see him. Would you please keep an eye on the wagon?" Arleta patted her arm as she walked past to go around the bar to the kitchen. Her father entered the back door as he wiped his hands on a rag with traces of blood on it. His apron was streaked with blood. "Hello, Poppa."

"Arleta!" He reached out his arms to hug her and stopped himself as he looked at her in the emerald green dress. "Whoa, sorry, dear. I'm all bloody and greasy from dressing down a goat. I wouldn't want to soil your nice dress there."

She practically threw herself in his arms and gave him a crushing hug. "It will wash, Daddy."

He delicately hugged her back without using his hands. "Well, now step back and let me look at you. Is that hat what ladies wear nowadays?"

"Among other ones. My, have you been ill again, Daddy? You have lost a lot of weight."

"No, I have been healthy as a horse since the week you left. Fact of the matter is, I have been working my tail off. I never realized how much work you were doing around here. I finally managed to hire Brita to fill in for you. Baby girl, I'm sorry, but I need to finish dressing down this goat."

"I'll lend a hand."

"No, I can't let you soil that pretty dress with blood."

She tiptoed and kissed his cheek. "Okay, Daddy. I'll go change. Oh, I brought some supplies for you to sell."

"Good. Bring the wagon around, and I'll unload it."

Arleta found Brita carrying in a round of cheese.

"I figured you wanted these things brought in?"

"Yes, thank you. We will get what we can and take the wagon around back for Father to finish."

They carried everything inside but the larger wine and brandy barrels. Brita led the horse to take the wagon around behind the inn while Arleta took her things upstairs to change clothes and returned downstairs to find Brita in the kitchen with her father.

"Brita, I believe you offered me a stew when I first arrived. I am a bit hungry now."

"Oh, yes. Would you like bread or cornbread?"

"Cornbread, please."

"Sweetheart, you go on out and enjoy your dinner. I have a few more things to finish up out back and will attend to your horse."

"Thank you, Father."

Brita brought her stew, and Arleta dove in. By the time she was through, Brita and her father were finished with their work and came out to join her.

"Where in the world did you get all these goods, girl?"

"I bought them, Poppa. The estate where I'm studying has vast vineyards and orchards along with lots of dairy cows and loads of livestock like you would never imagine. His Lordship offered me a very excellent deal on it all. I figure the profit you make off this load will not only pay for my trip home but my next year of studies as well."

"It is good they have taught you something up there."

"No, Poppa, that was something I learned from you." She reached out and put her hand on his arm. He smiled and winked at her. "Dad, it is none of my business, but I was wondering why Harome was here earlier?"

Her father and Brita exchanged looks. "Me," Brita said.

"May I ask how long this has been going on?"

Brita looked down at her hands as she hesitated. "Last year, about a month after you left."

"Brita," she set her hand on top of the girl's, "please don't take me wrong here. If you think you and he will be happy together, I wish you all the happiness in the world. Harome is a good person and hard worker. It is just that I saw a side of him I didn't like and decided we needed to go separate ways. I am happy with my life as it is going."

"Thank you for understanding."

"Now, you two tell me all the gossip going on here and in the valley."

"Well, Fredean's house is either haunted or another witch has moved into to it," her father whispered.

Arleta absorbed the news and waited. "How do you know?"

"Jason and Barney went down there up to their old mischief. They found a hole in the brier fence of hers and sneaked in. They were trying to get in the house when some woman in the hut started screaming at them."

"What did they do? Don't tell me they burned the house down."

"Oh, no, it is still there. The woman scared them so bad they ran like they were on fire themselves."

"Good."

"I went down there, and she did the same thing to me. That is one foul-mouthed woman. She started chanting a curse at me, and I ran too."

Arleta struggled not to burst out laughing. "I'll go down there tomorrow and see what is going on. I think I know who it is."

"Well, I went walking about the place. That property has a lot of potential. There is a hardy creek running through it. If properly harvested, there be lots of timber. Then that land could be used for livestock grazing until the stumps are removed and then farming."

"That is good news, Father."

"I was thinking about hiring Harome and a friend of his to do the work for me."

"Could we discuss this later, Father? I am a bit tired from my traveling."

Brita sat back in her chair, then rose. "Excuse me. I have a customer that I have neglected." She walked across the tavern and spoke to a traveler sitting at a table near the hearth.

"Arleta, I am your father and can do what I wish to that land until you are married or come of age. I told you about it before doing anything out of my love for you. That and I don't want that woman to put curses on us."

"I love and respect you for that, Pappa. I want to look things over myself, first, if you don't mind."

CHAPTER FORTY-THREE

The next morning, Arleta awoke a little before dawn as she always did. She dressed, went downstairs, and started breakfast. She stoked up the fire in the stove and set a teapot on to heat the water. She found a large piece of salt pork in the barrel, cut off thin slices, threw them in a skillet, and set it on the stovetop as well. Her father arrived wearing a wide grin.

"It is nice to see you in here cooking. But I don't want you to live this life, daughter. Are they teaching you good things to help you become a lady?"

"Yes, Father. I am learning the most wonderful things. Not just magic and spells. Now, pass me the eggs, and I'll make your breakfast."

Brita had joined them by the time breakfast was ready.

"Here guys, you must try this peach marmalade. It is so divine. They make it right there on the estates where I stay and study."

Brita spread some of the peach dessert on a chunk of bread and took a bite.

"Umm." She looked like she would swoon to the flavor.

Later, Arleta took a bucket of water and headed out of the village. She stopped and talked to a couple of neighbors. When she arrived at the open field of tangleweed, she saw the old bucket was turned over, and there were distinctive gaps in the tangle weed. She pulled out the pouch of rosemary clippings and mixed it in the water. She splashed the water mixture on her shoes and walked slowly through the clearing. She could tell that someone had come into the clearing and ripped out the tangleweed by the roots to escape its clutches. She wondered if it were her father or the boys of havoc and mayhem. She smiled at the latter thought as she continued to the hut.

"Hello, Fredean!"

"Hello, who is there?"

"It is Arleta, Miss Winters. I have come to visit." Arleta went inside and found everything exactly as she had left it.

"Hello, Arleta. I have the responsibility to report to you that we had some riffraff attempt to come in here not long after you left. I scared them away by threatening to curse them. I heard a horse outside many times but never a rider. I think the horse was eating your apples from the tree. Then twice in the first week you left, someone tried to get in the house. I believe the first time was a couple boys, and then the next day, it was a man. The man wanted to argue that I was not supposed to be here, and the property belonged to his daughter."

"Yes, my father said you became very foul-mouthed and chanted a curse."

"Well, I apologize for not being lady-like, but you did ask me to protect this, uh, home. He was persistent, and I had to change tactics to convince him to leave. That is all it was. I am incapable of performing magic, you know."

"Well, thank you for doing such a good job."

"Many months ago, I believe it was about three weeks after you left, a young man came and said he was looking for Dallietano. He claimed to be a friend of yours and Zarlaam. He knew me by name, as well. We had a pleasant visit. He said Dallietano was a unicorn. But somehow, I already knew that the moment he said it."

"Yes, he is. My friend helped him move to a better place. He will be safer than being here. Speaking of moving, how would you like to move to a better place?"

"Please, may I. It has been horrible looking at this pigsty all these months, and I have been terribly lonely. Plus, I have been in absolute fear for my well-being."

"Why?"

"There is a very large ugly rat living under the bed over there. I think it is a girl and she has given birth to pups. Also, over to the left, somewhere that I cannot see, is another rat."

"We will leave it alone. I'll be taking you with me. Now, the first place I'll take you is my home here in Natudix. Then, I'll take you to the place where I am studying. It is a very fine estate. You will never have to see such as this hut again."

"Oh, I would be ever so grateful, Arleta."

"There is one problem."

"What would that be?"

"You cannot move or make noise. The people in Natudix are deathly afraid of magic or anything related to it. They don't know or understand, and they will fear you. They would burn you because they think you are a cursed abomination."

"Oh my."

"Yes, I'll spend a few days getting what I want from around here, and then I'll take you with me."

"Oh, Arleta, I would be so grateful to get away from here. I promise to behave and not let anyone see me move."

"Good. I was afraid I was going to have to hide you wrapped up. What I do not need is for you to start making noise around the wrong people."

"Oh, please do not cover me up. I don't like the dark."

Arleta smiled. "Don't worry. I'm going to go see what I can get from the garden."

"Dear, I'm afraid that it's been rather neglected."

Arleta went outside and examined the garden. She found the herbs and other potion components to be sparse. Common weeds had flourished in the absence of attention. She was happy to find the peach and apple trees prospering well. She gathered many things together inside the hut and from the cellar into crates and bags.

"Miss Fredean, I'll be going for the day and come back tomorrow."

"I thought you were going to take me with you." The painting pouted.

"In a few days, dear. First, I have to move things to my wagon to take them with me."

"It is not fair to get one's hopes up with a good promise and delay it at your convenience. Have I not done a good job as you asked me to?"

Arleta was shocked at the sensitivity of the painting. She almost laughed at the thought of it all but didn't want to be offensive to the one individual that she would be able to talk to about magic for the next couple of months. "My apology, Fredean. I will be taking you with me now. I will put you in my room until I leave, and I'll take you with me. You cannot speak or move unless we are alone."

"Oh, thank you. I promise to behave."

CHAPTER FORTY-FOUR

Gerak rode his horse slowly into Galley's Cove with his back straight and his shoulders square. He recognized several people but made no move to greet them. He dismounted the horse outside the Crow's Nest, walked inside, and stood with his hand on the handle of his dagger until his eyes adjusted to the dim light. He surveyed the room and then walked over to the bar.

Tell me, sir, is the captain of the Scallywag around?"

"Couldn't say, her captain doesn't come around very often nowadays."

Gerak smiled and left without a word. He took his horse to a stable and arranged a for a few weeks' stay. Then he headed down toward the wharf. He found the Scallywag tied up, and his father mending the nets.

"How good is the fishing, Captain?" Gerak spoke from behind his father.

"Not like it used to be," he said without turning around.

"Perhaps you need a deckhand that knows how to mend nets."

"I know how to..." the captain spoke as he turned around with a scowl on his face. His eyes widened as he looked at his son with a grin.

"Hello, Captain."

"Glad to see you, Gerak. Load me a needle."

Gerak set his kit and bedroll on the ground and proceeded to thread the twine into a mending needle.

"You look like they are feeding you well. You have put on a few pounds."

"Aye, and grown an inch as well, sir."

"Is that a sword you are carrying?"

"Aye, sir. They gave it to me. I'm fairly good with it too."

"What else are they teaching you?"

Gerak looked around and saw that no one was within ear shout.

"Lots of things. I have been reading great books and learning English composition, mathematics, geometry, social etiquette, politics, swordsmanship, military strategy, herbology, potion-making, and magic."

"What kind of magic?"

Gerak lowered his voice to a whisper. "Well, I can enchant your nets again so that they are stronger, and you can catch more fish."

"I could do with stronger nets," the captain grinned with a wink.

"Let me do the mending then." He took the needle from his father and proceeded with the mending. As he weaved the net, he spun his spell of enchantment. Captain Kalthazar sat back and watched his son mending the net. He noticed Gerak's lips moving as he worked. He also noticed that each knot the lad made sparkled like the sand on the beach a few moments before fading away to the brown of the twine.

"Does this magic thing really work, son?"

"Yes, but I cannot be interrupted when I'm casting my spells."

His father proceeded to thread twine on a spare mending needle. When they were through mending the nets, they loaded them back on the boat and made ready to sail with the morning tide. Then they sat on the deck and watched the sunset. Gerak noticed that his father had only a single glass of whiskey that evening before going to bed.

The morning sun rose to light the world of the coastal area of Galley's Cove. The Scallywag sailed out with the morning tide. Her single square sail was up, and a steady breeze filled it. The captain was at the rudder. Gerak acted as deckhand doing the job he knew and coiled ropes and prepared the nets for usage. They sailed northwestward for the captain's favorite fishing area. After Gerak finished neatening up the deck, he started to climb up to the crow's nest.

"Where are you going?" the captain asked.

"The crow's nest to watch for fish sign."

"Take the rudder, First Mate. I'll pull the first watch in the nest."

Gerak couldn't hide his shock as his father stepped away from the rudder and started aloft. Gerak grasped it firmly. He stood with his feet shoulder-width apart as he felt the rhythm of the water against the rudder. He stole a look at the crow's nest.

"Steer her ten degrees to the port, First Mate," the captain called down at him.

Gerak adjusted their course and looked up. He saw his father smiling down at him. Then the man turned his attention out to the open sea. They sailed on for a couple of hours. Several times Gerak saw his father lean forward or to one side to watch the water intently as if he saw signs of fish and the settle back in a relaxed manner.

"First Mate!" the captain shouted, "Steer fifteen degrees to starboard."

Gerak adjusted their course as the captain came down.

"Make ready to cast the net," he ordered as he took the rudder.

Gerak stepped over and grabbed the weights.

"Cast the net," the captain ordered.

Gerak watched the net follow the weights as it ran out over the railing to make sure there were no snags. The captain checked the line of the net floats behind them. He checked the sea ahead of them.

"Stand by to come about to starboard."

Gerak ran to the mast and released the ropes from the bulldog. He held them with one foot against the mast. They traveled straight a bit more.

Gerak adjusted the ropes to keep the wind in the sail as they turned. Gerak hopped on one foot around the mast as the captain pulled the rudder. The captain watched the line of the net and checked the sea. They came about and made a complete circle with the net.

"Drop the sail."

Gerak released the rope, and the sail slid down the mast. He caught the slack and folded the sail on itself to prevent it from going over the side and dragging in the water. He threw ropes around it near each end to keep it neat. With that done, he hurried to the stern, and they hauled in the net, removing the fish as they did. The captain looked down at their catch when they finished. He slapped Gerak on the back.

"Not a bad first haul. It's bigger than I've been getting for a full day's run lately."

"Now, we need to keep them fresh until we get them to the market, Captain."

"Well, the sun is up. All we can do throw them in the well and cover them with canvas."

"I have something better, Captain," Gerak said and flourished his wand."

"What is that stick for?"

"Actually, it is a wand. Watch this. Frala frio," he cast the spell, and a stream of frost spewed from its tip. He chilled the pile of fish until they were covered with a blanket of frost.

The Captain reached down and felt it. "That is amazing!"

"Now we cover them with the canvas," Gerak announced.

"What else can you do?" he asked as he covered the fish.

"There are lots of things. I can lift objects with a mere spell and a flick of my wand."

"Can you put a curse on Molean's boat?"

"Master Zarlaam only teaches us good magic, not curses."

"Well, that is good."

"But there is evil magic out there."

"Follow the words of your teacher. He would know what is right."

"How can I fight evil magic if I do not know it?"

"Your mother and I taught you the ways of right and wrong. I'm sure that it will apply in magic also. Let's set sail in hunt for more fish."

Late in the afternoon, they caught another haul. Gerak chilled them as well. They sat back against the stern and watched the sunset.

A whale blew hard close to the boat, and the spray drifted across it.

"Have you ever wondered exactly how big those things are, Captain?"

"No more than I can see as they swim past, I know they are big enough."

Gerak whipped out his wand. "Levetar water beast." He flicked his wand back and forth. Slowly the whale rose entirely from the sea. It was over seventy feet in length and taller than their mast. Its belly was a light gray in color, and its upper body was charcoal.

They both gasped at his massive size.

The whaled cried in protest. Gerak lowered it gently back in the water.

"I hope you haven't made him angry."

It swam away. Gerak watched to make sure it didn't return to do them damage. He sat embarrassed for not thinking about the whale's possible reaction to such treatment.

The next morning, their first catch was twice the size of what they had. Gerak chilled them with his spell, and they set sail home.

Molean was standing on the wharf when they tied up. He looked at the pile of the fish in disgust.

"Half your catch will be rotting," He declared to them.

"That is for the scale master to decide," Captain Kalthazar said.

They loaded their haul onto crates on dollies and pushed them to the scales. The portly scale master examined every fish.

"My, these are cold. And fresh! When did you catch them?"

"This morning. Luckiest haul I ever had. I thought my nets would burst open from the load. But I have a good First Mate to help me," Kalthazar bragged and threw an arm around his son's shoulders.

The man paid him a good price for their fish. To Gerak's surprise, his father gave him half the money for the catch.

"You'll need this for your books and things."

Gerak slipped the coins in his pocket.

"Now, come with me."

Gerak followed him through the streets of the city to a small tavern. A large boar was painted on the wall over the door. "Boar's Tavern" was painted below that. Gerak knew of the Boar's Tavern but had never been inside.

His father walked in, found a table against the back wall and sat facing the room. Gerak joined him. A middle-aged, hefty barmaid came walking over. She wore her blouse cut low in the front showing her ample cleavage.

"Hello, Captain. Did you have a good catch today?"

"Fair. Meet my son and First Mate, Gerak."

"Hello, Gerak. He certainly looks like you." she reached over and squeezed Gerak's bicep. "Oh, and strong too. You raise them handsome, Gerak."

His father smiled. "We will have bowls of your beef stew and ales, Sheila."

"Coming right up, Captain," she said as she rubbed his arm a couple times before she left.

"Why do you come here?"

"Molean is not welcome here at the Boar's Inn and Tavern. Plus, I started a fight with him in the Crow's Nest and am not welcome there. Besides, the food here is good."

"She seems to have taken a liking to you."

"Aye."

Sheila returned with their food.

"The Captain tells me you are studying to become a gentleman."

"Yes, ma'am. I am learning many things," Gerak responded with a wink at his father.

They ate without a word and sat back to relax as they sipped their ales. Gerak was surprised as he watched his father barely touched the ale beside his bowl. When he was finished, the man leaned back in his chair to relax and would take an occasional sip of the brew.

"Son, I have a need to tell you something."

Gerak looked in his father's eyes. He saw a softness he had rarely seen before.

"Your mother was the most wonderful woman in the world, and I have missed her greatly. But it's been several years since she passed away. She will always be in my heart and memories."

"She will always be in mine too, Captain."

"Well, just so you understand the way things are. Life must go on. I have mourned her departure long enough. I've been seeing Miss Sheila a bit since you were away."

"Oh," Gerak said, not knowing what else to say. He didn't quite understand at first what his father was meaning. When Sheila came over to take their bowls, his father reached up, grasped her by the back of the neck, pulled her to him, and kissed her. Gerak suddenly felt his father was betraying his mother's memory.

That evening they retired to rooms upstairs in the tavern, and Gerak heard Sheila join his father in his room. They never discussed the issue further, but Gerak's feeling of resentment towards his father for betraying his mother crawled through his skin and wound its way around his heart. Over the next month, they fished and hauled in hardy catches. His father had plenty of money reserved for his educational fees.

One evening, Gerak and his father strolled along the wharf towards the inn when a lass called at his father from her balcony room. "Hey, Captain, how about you and the young fellow joining me for a fun time." She leaned over the rail and to show her busty cleavage. Gerak blushed and looked away.

"What's the matter, son? You still haven't had the pleasures of a woman yet?"

"Well, no, sir."

"Clementine," he called up to her.

"Yes, Captain?" she cooed sweetly at him.

He tossed a gold coin up to her and followed it with another. "I'm sending my boy up to you. Send me back a man in the morning."

"I certainly shall, Captain." She turned away and disappeared into her room.

"Here is your coin for some drinking. You go on up, and she will treat you nice for the whole night."

Gerak watched his father walk away, then joined the lady in her room. He spent several nights with her over his summer stay. He had to wait for his turn with her a time or two. He thought about relationships between men and women, and his resentment toward his father and Sheila softened.

One morning in late August, Gerak sat holding the tiller as his father lounged on top of the nets after a very successful haul.

"Captain, I need to leave tomorrow to head back."

"This is a mite early, is it not?"

"Yes, sir, but I need to seek out a man about a magic book I heard he has for sell."

"Why must you seek him out?"

"Well, I know not exactly where he is. I have to go to a place I saw him last year."

"Did he not tell you where he lived then?"

"No, I didn't talk to him directly. I just heard he has a book for sale. "

The next morning, the captain gave Gerak a pouch of coins and shook his hand goodbye.

"You need to be careful riding about these roads alone. Especially going places you have never been before."

"I have more than just sword fighting skills to protect me, Captain." His grin was more of a smirk. Gerak rode off without looking back.

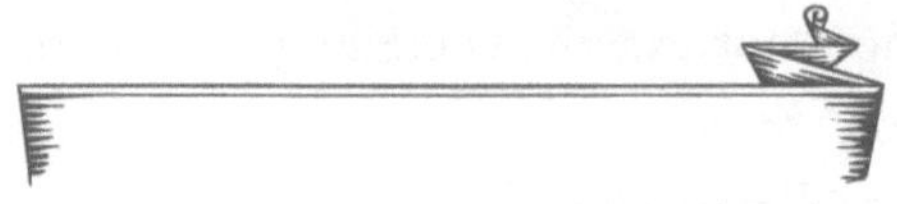

CHAPTER FORTY-FIVE

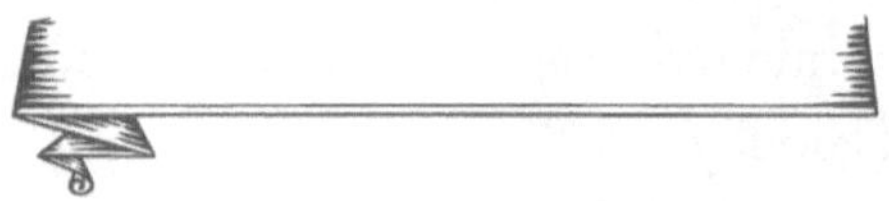

After several days of travel and checking every village, Gerak stepped into another small village tavern and stood just to the side of the door in the dim light as he surveyed the room with his hood hiding most of his face. He tried to disguise his build by making his clothes hang loosely on his frame as he surveyed the occupants. Most of the patrons were local villagers having a pint of ale before calling their day to an end. Some were travelers with questionable appearances. Those few sat with a hand on the hilt of their daggers or swords. He moved his left hand to rest his own dagger next to the hilt of his sword. He stopped and gazed at one figure in particular. He smiled and moved to a table near the local town folk as they eyed him nervously. He dropped his backpack against the wall as he sat facing the room. A young woman came over to him.

"Welcome to the Wheat Mill Tavern, sir. What would be your pleasure today?"

"Food and two drinks. How fresh is your stew?" His soft words caused her to lean closer to hear him.

"The stew was made fresh this afternoon. What would you prefer to drink, sir?"

"Do you know the name of the man with all the papers on the table?"

She spoke without looking up. "All I know him by is Kieffer, sir."

"I will have a mug of ale. But first, deliver a drink of his preference to Mister Kieffer." He placed silver coins in her hand.

She lost her friendly smile. "Yes, sir." She went behind the bar and drew a draft of ale and filled a bowl with stew. She grabbed a bottle and walked across the tavern to Kieffer's table as he squinted in the faint light at his writings.

Gerak watched as they exchanged words, and she motioned towards him. The man slid his glass across the table. She poured him two fingers of the drink and watched as he consumed it quickly. He held the glass out for a refill. She looked at him a moment but poured him another.

"Invite the man over, and let's see if he wants to buy another."

Gerak had laid back his hood as she approached with his stew and ale. She looked at him with one eyebrow raised, as she probably realized he was not much more than fifteen.

"The gentleman has extended you an invitation to his table to buy him another drink."

Gerak grabbed his backpack and ale. "Bring a fresh bottle of his rotgut and my food."

He walked across the tavern and sat opposite from the old man. They exchanged stares silently. The old man's face was thin and wrinkled with age. He wore an ugly scar across his right cheek that was perhaps evidence of a duel in his younger days. The lad glanced at the book and smiled.

"You are a difficult man to get to meet, Mr. Kieffer. I've traveled through several villages to find you."

"Well, there are a few places around that I'm not welcome to visit. Who are you to be looking for me?"

"Bershome Paxtare."

The bar maid arrived with a bottle and Gerak's food. He gave her another coin and took the bottle. He poured Kieffer half a glass full. The man lifted it in a slight toast and drank until it was empty. He held it out for a refill. Gerak half-filled the glass and corked the bottle. Kieffer watched him set the bottle across the table away from his reach. He sipped the whiskey slowly as Gerak gave attention to his stew.

"Why do you seek my company, lad?"

Gerak chewed and swallowed before answering. "I heard your name once. In the company of a gentleman named, Zarlaam."

"That couldn't have been a nice line of conversation."

Gerak leaned closer and dropped his voice to a whisper. "Actually, I only heard two things. I heard your name and that you had a book of magic for sale. Do you still have the book?"

Kieffer squinted at the lad. "Are you an apprentice of the old master's?"

He stopped with a spoonful before his mouth. "That is not your business to know."

"He would not take a liking to such a book in your possession."

"What he likes or dislikes is not your concern. Besides, he has to discover I have it first."

"You walk a fine line of disobedience against your uncle, don't you, lad?"

Gerak questioned himself for a moment if using that name to hide his identity was the best move. "He hasn't told me that I could not have your book. In fact, he is not aware I know about you at all." He ate more.

"Books are very expensive, lad. Particularly one of that type."

"I'd also be interested in any new parchments of the craft you may have as well."

"I have a few, but they and the book aren't here. We will need to travel to my place to fetch them."

"How far is it?" He waved an empty spoon in the air.

"That depends on how you look at it, lad. If I had a horse, half a day's ride."

Kalthazar sat back and scowled at the old man. "What would you be considering a reasonable price for your book?"

"We can discuss that after you see it." He stroked his beard and smiled.

"How many chapters would you say are in the book?" He fluctuated his voice on the word chapters instead of using the word spells in public. He didn't want anyone in the tavern to overhear what he wanted from Kieffer.

"Quite a few, sonny," he said as he leaned in and reached for the bottle.

Gerak grabbed the bottle, trapping the old man's hand beneath his and held the bottle firmly to the table. The old man grimaced at the strength of the squeeze on his hand. "I'm not a dumb kid to be trifled with old man. I asked the price."

The old man smiled crookedly. "Ten crowns, lad."

"It would cost five to hire you a horse. Half of one for this bottle. That will leave you four and a half for your book. That is not counting what I deduct for however many chapters I already have in my own book that are the same in yours."

"You'll not have very many of them, lad. However, I can throw in some parchments of interest to balance things more to your liking. But it is too late in the day for traveling. These roads are filled with dangerous cutthroats about in the night, and the air gets a touch too chilly for my aging bones."

Gerak released his grip on the man's hand, and Kieffer poured himself a full glass of whiskey. He corked the bottle and set it beside the glass. He gave his full attention to the amber liquid as he sipped it.

"I'll see you in the morning, Mr. Kieffer. Whatever arrangements you have for the night are your business.

"I'll be right here, lad," he said and took another sip.

Gerak strolled to the bar. A stocky, middle-aged man wiped a glass with a dingy, white cloth.

"How was your supper? Care for another ale, lad?"

"The stew was fine. I need a room, please."

"Certainly. I have one private room left. Or you can have a bed in a common room for half the price."

"Private, please. I also need to hire a horse for two days."

"I don't I hire out my horse, sir. Where would you be traveling?"

Gerak looked in disgust across the bar at Kieffer nursing his glass.

"Would you know where that old man lives?"

"He lives out in the woods just off the main road to Wexbey. I'd say it is about half a day's ride.

"Would you know of a wagon or transport going that way tomorrow?"

"Matter of fact, I do. My daughter will be going to fetch me some supplies. You could purchase a ride if you like."

"But, the wagon will already be making the trip."

"Aye, and the load would be less of a strain on the old mare without extra weight."

Gerak smiled at the justification of his fee. "What time is she scheduled to leave?"

"First light."

Gerak put a coin on the bar. "I have my own horse. I want a ride for that old man. Also, I'll have another bottle of his gut rot. I'll take it to my room tonight."

"I know it is none of me business, lad. But old Kieffer is shady company for a young gentleman such as yourself to be associating with."

He took the bottle with a stern look at the barkeeper. "Yes, sir. Thank you for advising me. But I agree with you. It is none of your business, and you would be wise to forget ever seeing my face."

The man's eyes danced between Kieffer and Gerak before looking down at the mug in his hand. He shrugged, set the mug on the shelf behind him, then slid a key across the bar to Gerak and went about straightening up for the evening.

Gerak took the key, went to his room, and bedded down for the night.

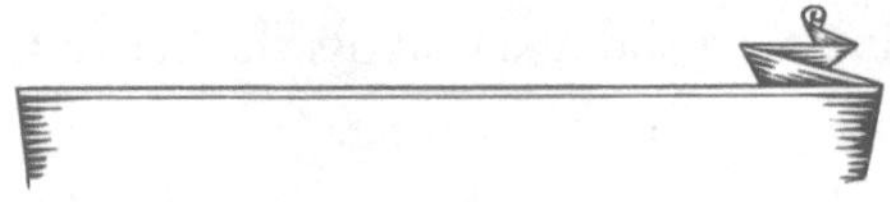

CHAPTER FORTY-SIX

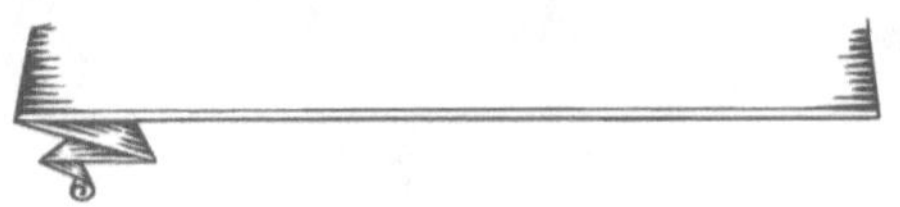

The next morning Gerak came downstairs and saw Kieffer sleeping at the table with his hand grasping the empty bottle.

"Well, we will be leaving as soon as you get him loaded in the back, sir," the barmaid said.

"Would you grab his bag, please?" Gerak took the bottle from Kieffer's hand and hoisted him upon his shoulder to carry him out to the wagon.

"My, you are a strong fellow," she said as she walked behind him.

He deposited the drunkard in the back of the wagon without a word. "Allow me to assist you up, my Lady." He offered her his hand. She took it and climbed on to the wagon. He mounted his horse.

"Thank you ever so kindly, sir. I told Father you were a gentleman."

"Why would you need to say that?"

"He told me to make you mind your manners. But I see you need no reminding. By the way, my name is Sausy."

"Thank you, Sausy. Do you know about where his house is?"

"Yes, but he will most likely be waking up about midday as it is, and that will put us close about that time.

He rode along beside her wagon, and they conversed to make the trip seem to go more quickly.

The wagon hit a large bump, bounced, and landed with a thud and rattling of the empty bottles in the crates she hauled.

"What that heck?" Kieffer bolted upright in the back of the wagon. He looked about him in a confused state. They looked back at him.

"I managed to secure you a ride and save you some expense, Mr. Kieffer."

He grabbed his leather satchel and scrounged through it. Satisfied nothing was missing, he set it down and pulled out a silver flask. He opened the flask, held it to his mouth, and sucked on it hungrily. Frowning, he held the flask upside down and shook it. When it surrendered none of his coveted liquor, he stuffed it into his bag in disgust. A growl rumbled for his throat. "Tell me, lad, have you a bottle? I need a little hair of the dog. If you know my meaning."

Gerak reached into his saddlebag, pulled a bottle out, and handed it to the man. Kieffer pulled the cork with his teeth, spat it into his hand, and sucked on the bottle with visible relish.

"You will need to make that last. Unless you have plenty stored at your home."

The old man lowered the bottle slowly and corked it as he gave Gerak a hateful stare. "You are too young to appreciate the spirit of the brew, lad."

"I'm old enough to have seen the evils of it. You are just like my old man."

"Had a temper, did he?"

"Especially after he had a bottle in him."

"Well, lad, I'm a peaceable sort. The spirit mellows me out."

They rode in silence with Kieffer stealing snorts from the bottle from time to time. Sausy stopped the wagon by a stack of stones knee-high and announced their arrival. "Here is your trail, sir." She pointed at a faint path beside the stones.

"What? You aren't going to carry me the entire way? You are cheating this lad on his money."

"It is only a few hundred feet as you have told me before, and I doubt the trail is wide enough for my wagon."

Kieffer took his time gathering himself and climbing off the wagon to amble down a trail.

"Huh, without so much as a goodbye. Watch yourself, Gerak. I have seen his nasty side a time or two. But he was never bad enough to have Father ban him from our tavern."

"I'll keep that in mind. You have a good day, Miss Sausy."

"Goodbye."

Gerak turned his horse and followed the old man. The trail was hardly more than a footpath among the trees. Here and there, he noted a tree limb had been broken and hung down from protruding into the trail. He easily caught up to Kieffer without trouble and stayed behind him to avoid being forced into conversation. The man was quite content to talk to himself and the bottle that he carried.

The thatched shack he lived in looked as old as the man himself. It sat in a clearing with what once was a small garden now overgrown by weeds. A sawhorse sat near the door with a log on it awaiting cutting for firewood. A broken saw frame was leaning against the horse. Across the clearing was an open thatched roof shed. Kalthazar dismounted and loosened the cinch on his saddle. The horse took a deep breath in gratitude.

With a grunt, Kieffer plopped down on a bench outside his hut. He looked at Gerak with a sneer.

"May I see your book?"

"That is the problem with you young ones these days, no patience. Give me a moment to catch my breath. That is a long walk for an aging man."

"If you would allow me to fetch it, you could tell me where it is."

"No, I'll get it." He stood up with a grunt and stomped into the hut.

Gerak heard him rummaging around and finally then returned with the book. It held about fifty pages between leather bindings. Gerak held out his hand for it.

Kieffer held it close to his chest. "Fifteen crowns first."

"Last night, you were asking ten. Besides, I am entitled to examine what I am considering for such an outrageous price."

"These are very powerful spells. They are worth twice that."

"You were declined your asking for five crowns."

"You were eaves-dropping in the tavern?"

"I'm a light sleeper. Your arguing awoke me. Also, the walls are thin."

"Well, I was having financial difficulties and was desperate."

"I don't see how your lifestyle has prospered since to make negotiations in your favor."

"You are a cruel lad to take advantage of a man when he is financially impoverished."

"You are a fool to think I am one and you can take advantage of me and my money."

"You need to learn manners and respect for your elders."

Gerak put his fists on his hips. "My learning needs are not your concern. My patience grows thin. I'll see the book, now."

"Just be warned, Master Zarlaam would not be happy to learn that you have it."

"I would not be happy if he learns about it either. So make sure such knowledge does not come from you. I'll be examining the book while you gather up the scrolls you mentioned." Gerak held out his hand.

He held out the book in disgust and turned to sulk in his hut. Gerak flipped through the book with a smile of satisfaction. He walked over to a tree and sat against it as he examined the spells.

When he finished, he looked up to see the old man sitting on the bench in front of the hut. Several rolls of parchment rested on the floor beside him. He laid the book down and went over to the hut. "What are the scrolls about?"

"What did you think about the book?"

"I haven't decided yet. How many scrolls are there?"

"Seven."

Gerak picked them up and tucked the scrolls under his arm. He pulled out his pouch and dumped some coins in his hand.

Kieffer sat up straight and held out his hand. He licked his lips as Gerak counted out the coins. He stopped at nine and returned the remainder in his hand to the pouch.

"That is not what I asked for."

Gerak turned away. "Your bottle last night and today, plus your ride, make the difference. Now, if you have any more next summer, I'll be coming by."

"Bring more coins next time, lad. My next scrolls will not be cheap."

"Don't try to sell me something I already have, either." Gerak put his new possessions in his saddlebags and tightened the cinch.

"How about a ride back into town, lad?"

"I'm not going that way," he said, mounted his horse, and left without a farewell. He turned north on the road and nudged his horse to a canter because he was eager to return to the Hall of Knowledge and learn more magic and show Zarlaam and Bershome. He had many miles ahead to figure out how to have fun with his new magic.